Good Eggs

Rebecca Hardiman

ALLEN&UNWIN

First published in the United States in 2021 by Atria Books,
an imprint of Simon & Schuster, Inc., New York.

Published in hardback and trade paperback in Great Britain in 2021 by
Allen & Unwin, an imprint of Atlantic Books Ltd.

10 9 8 7 6 5 4 3 2 1

A CIP catalogue record for this book is available from the British Library.

Hardback ISBN: 978 1 83895 274 7
Trade paperback ISBN: 978 1 83895 275 4
E-book ISBN: 978 1 83895 276 1

Printed in Great Britain by Bell and Bain Ltd, Glasgow

Allen & Unwin, an imprint of Atlantic Books Ltd
Ormond House, 26–27 Boswell Street
London WC1N 3JZ

www.allenandunwin.com/uk

Good Eggs

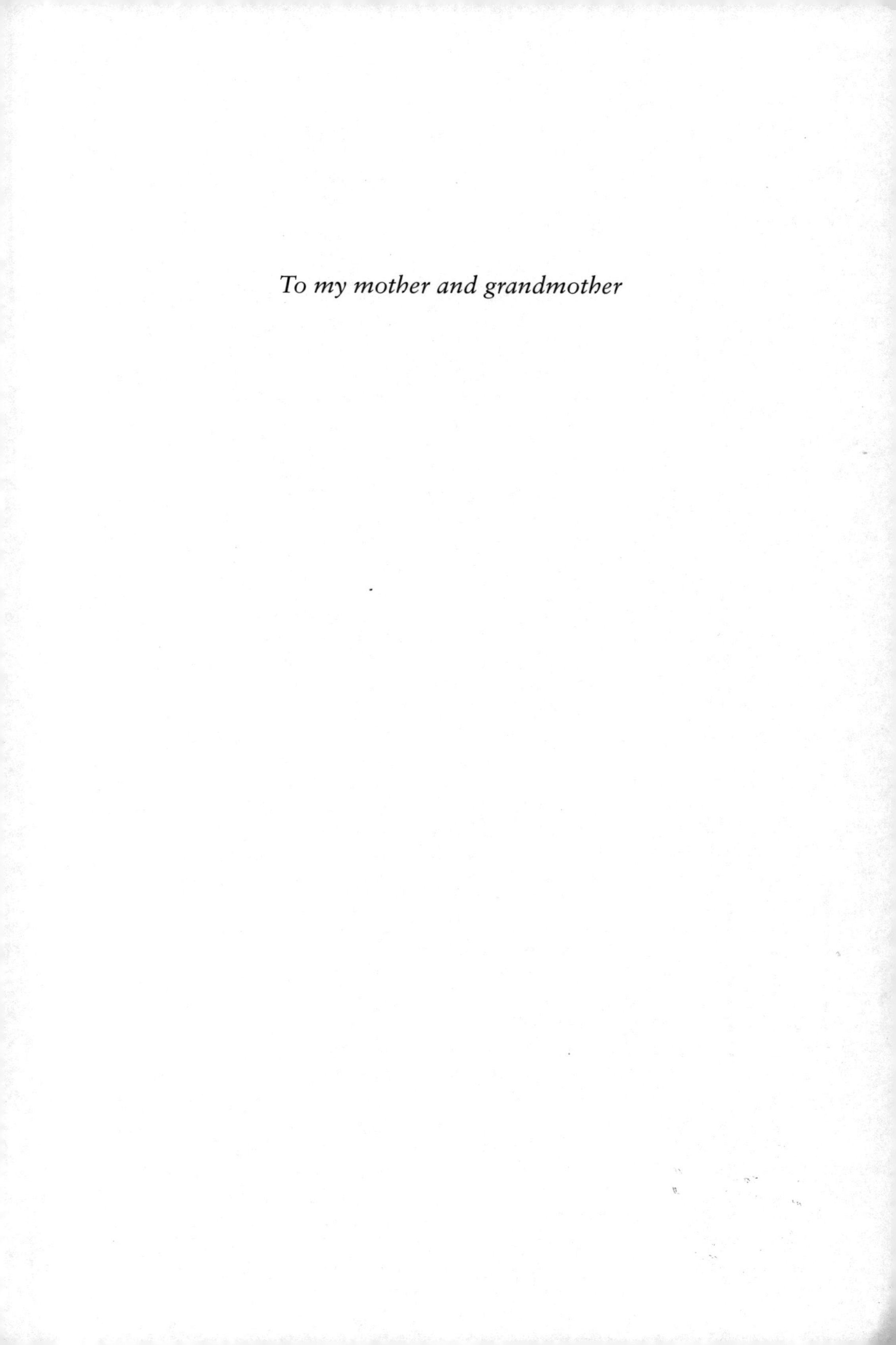

To my mother and grandmother

1.

Millie

Three-quarters of the way to the newsagent's, a trek she will come to deeply regret, Millie Gogarty realizes she's been barrelling along in second gear, oblivious to the guttural grinding from the bowels of her Renault. She shifts. Her mind, it's true, is altogether on other things: the bits and bobs for tea with Kevin, a new paperback, perhaps, for the Big Trip, her defunct telly. During a rerun of *The Golden Girls* last night, the ladies had just been mistaken for mature prostitutes when the screen went blank (silly, the Americans – overdone, but never dull). After bashing the TV – a few sturdy blows optimistically delivered to both sides in the hope of a second coming – she'd retreated to her dead Peter's old sick room where she's taken to sleeping ever since a befuddling lamp explosion had permanently spooked her from the second floor. Here, Millie had fumbled among ancient woollen blankets for her battery-operated radio and eventually settled down, the trusty Philips wedged snugly between a naked pillow and her good ear, humanity streaming forth. Her unease slowly dispelled, not unlike the effect of a five-o'clock sherry when the wind of the sea howls round her house post-apocalyptically. Even the grimmer broadcasts – recession, corruption, lashing rain – can have an oddly cheering effect: somewhere, things are happening to some people.

Now a BMW jolts into her peripheral vision, swerves sharply away – has she meandered? – and the driver honks brutally at Millie, who gives a merry wave in return. When she stops at a traffic light, the two cars now parallel, Millie winds down her window and indicates for her fellow driver to do likewise. His sleek sheet of glass descends presidentially.

'Sorry!' she calls out. 'I've had a frozen shoulder ever since the accident!' Though her injury and her dodgy driving bear no connection, Millie feels some explanation is due. She flaps her right elbow, chicken-wing style, into the chilled air. 'It still gets quite sore.' Millie offers the man, his face a confused fog, a trio of friendly, muffled toots of the horn and motors on past.

Before heading to the shop, Millie had phoned her son – technically her stepson, though she shuns all things technical and, more to the point, he's been her boy and she his mum since his age was still measured in mere months. Millie began by relaying the tale of the unholy television debacle.

'Blanche had checked the girls into a hookers' hotel without realizing,' Millie explained, 'and the police –'

'I'm just bringing the kids to school, Mum.'

'Would you ever come down and take a look? I can't bear to have no telly.'

'Did you check the batteries?'

'It doesn't run on batteries. It's a television.'

'The *remote* batteries.'

'Aha,' says Millie. 'Well now, how would I –?'

'Let me ring you in two ticks.'

'Or you can take a look when you come for supper?'

'Sorry?'

'Remember? It'll be your last chance, you know. I leave Saturday.'

'Fully aware.'

'I may never come back.'

'Now you're just teasing me.'

'And bring one of the children. Bring all of the children! I've got lamb chops and roasties.'

She had, in fact, neither. A quick inspection of the cabinet, during which she held the phone aloft, blanking briefly that her son was on the line, yielded neither olive oil nor spuds. A glimpse in the fridge – the usual sour blast and blinding pop of light – revealed exactly one half-pint of milk, gone off, three or four limp sprigs of broccoli, and a single cracked egg.

'Or maybe I'm the cracked egg,' she muttered as she brought the receiver to her ear.

'That,' her son said, 'has never been in question.'

Once inside Donnelly's, Millie tips her faux-fur leopard-print fedora to one and all. Millie Gogarty knows many souls in Dún Laoghaire and villages beyond – Dalkey, Killiney – and it's her self-imposed mission to stop and have a chat with anyone whenever, wherever possible: along the windy East Pier, in the shopping centre car park, standing in the bank queue (she would have no qualms about taking her coffee, used to be complimentary after all, in the Bank of Ireland's waiting area), or indeed right in this very shop.

She sidles up to Michael Donnelly, Jr, the owner's teenage, pockmarked son who slouches behind the counter weekdays after school.

'Did you know in three days' time Jessica Walsh and myself will be in New York for the Christmas? My great-great-great-grandnephew' – she has slipped in an extra great or two, as is her wont – 'used to live in Ohio, but we're not going there. Sure, there's nothing there! I visited him once … oh, I don't know when, it's not important.' She crosses her arms, settles in. 'Christmas morning and not a soul in the street. Kevin and I – he'd just gone eighteen – we took a walk, mountains of snow everywhere, and there we were standing in the middle of the street calling out, "Hello? America? Is anyone there?"'

'That so, Mrs Gogarty?' Michael says with a not entirely dismissive smile. He turns to the next customer, Brendan Doyle, whom Millie knows, of course, though Brendan appears to be deeply engrossed in his scuffed loafers.

She beams at them both, trailing away towards the tiny stationery section, a shelf or two of dusty greeting cards whose existence would only be registered by her generation. The young no longer put pen to paper. They text message. Her own grandchildren are forever clicking away at their mobiles with a frenzied quality Millie envies; she can't remember the last time communication of any kind felt so urgent.

She selects a card embossed with a foil floral bouquet – 'It's Your Special Day, Daughter!' – and reads the cloying message within. Once in hand, the itch to swipe the thing, the very last thing under the sun that Millie Gogarty, daughterless, needs, gains powerful momentum, until she knows that she must, and will, take it.

She checks the till. Michael is ringing up Brendan's bars of chocolate. The last time he'd crossed her path was in the chemist's – he'd been buying a tube of bum cream, the thought of which now makes her giddy. Her pits dampen as she prods open the cracked folds of her handbag, pushes its chaotic contents – obsolete punt coins, balls of hardened tissue, irrelevant scribbles – to the depths so that it gapes open, a mouth begging to be fed. Her stomach whoops and soars. Her heart, whose sole purpose for days upon days has been the usual, boring biological one, now thumps savagely. With a wild, jerky motion she will later attribute to her downfall, she plunges the card into her bag.

Millie breathes. Feigning utter casualness, she plucks another card, this one featuring a plump infant and an elephant. She smothers a laugh. *Perhaps Kevin's right: perhaps I've finally gone mad!* She steals another glance at Michael, who meets her gaze, nodding imperceptibly, and so she chuckles, as if the words inside particularly strike her fancy. Millie has sensed a calling to the stage all her life and she holds out a secret hope that she might still be discovered. Indeed, for a moment, Millie Gogarty marvels at her own audacity, pulse pounding yet looking for all of Dún Laoghaire as calm as you like. Her mind turns to supper – one of the grandchildren could turn up – and so she boldly heads towards a display of crisps and nicks a packet of cheese and onion Tayto and a Hula Hoops.

Flooded with good cheer and relief, she fairly leaps back into her car, the spoils of the morning safely tucked beside her. She's situating her left foot on the clutch, right foot poised to gun the engine and soar off back to her home, Margate, when she hears a timid knock on her window.

It's Junior from the shop, not a smile on him. A panicky shot of darkness seizes her. Millie reluctantly draws down her window.

'I hate to do this, Mrs Gogarty, but I have to ask you to come back in.'

'Did I leave something behind?'

He glances at her bag. 'You've a few things in there I think you haven't paid for.'

There follows a pause, long and telling.

'Sorry?' she says, shifting into reverse.

'I'm talking about that.' He jabs a fat, filthy finger at her handbag. The boy – barely sixteen, she reckons, the twins' age, probably in fifth year – yo-yos his eyes from the steering wheel to the bag, back to the wheel. 'My dad said I was to phone the guards if it happened again.'

Phone the guards!

Millie assembles her most authentic aw-shucks grin, hoping to emit the picture of a hapless, harmless granny. But her body betrays her: her face boils; pricks of perspiration collect at her hairline. This is the sorry tale of all the oldies, the body incongruent with the still sharp mind – tumours sprouting, bones snapping with a mere slip on ice, a heart just giving up one day, like her Peter's. Millie's own heart now knocks so violently, for the second time today, that she has the image of it exploding from her chest and flapping, birdlike, away.

Junior's still staring at her. She puts the back of her hand up to her brow, like a fainting lady from an earlier century; she can't bear to be seen. Then a single, horrid thought filters through: if the police become involved, Kevin will find out.

Kevin cannot find out.

He's already sniffing around, probably trying to build a case, with a stagey, lethal gentleness that terrifies her, to stick his poor mum into some godforsaken home for withered old vegetables. Millie Gogarty has no plans to move in with a bunch of wrinklies drooling in a corner. Her dear friend Gretel Sheehy was abandoned in Williams House, not five kilometres down the road. Gretel, needless to say, didn't make it out.

Now a second, equally ghastly thought: what if her grandchildren, the Fitzgeralds a few doors down, or all of south Dublin gets wind of her thievery? The potential for shame is so sweeping that Millie rejects the idea outright, stuffs it back into her mental lockbox where, wisely or not, she's crammed plenty of other unpleasantries over the years.

Wildly, she considers feigning an ailment – a stroke, perhaps? It, or something like it, has worked in the past, but she can't, in her muddled thinking, remember when she last trotted out such a deception and vaguely suspects that it was here in Dún Laoghaire.

'I'm really sorry,' Michael says. He's actually not, despite the acne, a bad-looking lad. 'The thing is, I've already phoned the police.'

2.

Kevin

Kevin Gogarty gets the call over pints at The Brass Bell, one of the city centre's oldest pubs, known for showcasing promising comedians on its tiny makeshift stage in the upstairs room. Kevin had had his shot at the mic years and years ago, when he'd had the notion of becoming a stand-up comedian. He'd bombed badly with a running gag about blow jobs and priests that he later felt had been ahead of its time. Still, he loves the mahogany carvings and brass beer pulls, the shabby Victoriana of the place, and it's where he and Mick, his former colleague and best mate, meet on the rare occasion when he can get out on the lash.

Leading up to Christmas week, the pub is mad packed with drinkers – everyone across the land is on the piss. It takes Kevin a full minute, plenty of sorrys and hands landing briefly on strangers' backs, to nudge through the throngs and arrive at the bar, where he sighs happily: he's out of the house with Mick, who's sure to regale him with plenty of suss about the old magazine.

The barmen are on the hustle as ever, pulling pints of ale and stout and cider three, four across, taking orders from customers all down the long bar. It's miraculous they never fuck it up, adding up your total, making fast change, no till required, mixing up Bacardi and Coke, Southern Comfort and Red, Irish coffee, whatever you like. If barmen ran the country, Kevin thinks, the economy would doubtless not be in the shitter.

Just outside, he can see, despite the cold, tiny huddles of smokers commiserating, blowing out their luxurious cancer plumes. No more smoking indoors any more – who would ever have thought? He feels like an ould fella, but can't help marvelling at how much Ireland has changed. Used to be this place was smoke-fogged and jammed like this at lunchtime any day of the week. No one has the dosh any longer, given the brutal, embarrassing slaying of the so-called Celtic Tiger. In the few months he's been carpooling children in his whopping seven-seater, negotiating homework, refereeing sibling rows, cooking up plates of fish and chips and peas, the world seems to have shifted, the air seems to have leaked from the recently buoyant Dublin economy. The days of dossing, of not taking any of it too seriously, are up.

When Kevin's mobile first rings – unknown caller – he rejects it and then spots and salutes Mick from afar. He hears music competing with the din – ah, Zeppelin. 'Over the Hills and Far Away.' A Guinness in each hand, Kevin weaves his way expertly, cautiously, back to the bit of table Mick's eked out for them, not coincidentally, Kevin is certain, beside two very beautiful, very young women, early twenties if that, a glass and mini-bottle of Chablis before each.

'Mind if we squeeze in here?' Kevin says.

The hotter one – wide, clever eyes; breasts that have clearly not been suckled upon, by babies anyway; blinding Yank teeth

– regards and dismisses him in the same millisecond. Kevin absorbs her indifference with a wince.

'Done with work,' says Mick. 'For the year anyway.'

'Ya fucker.' The two men exchange a lengthy handshake and Kevin's feeling so generous of spirit – the tree is up, the kitchen stocked with food and drink, Grace'll be about for a few days anyway, maybe he'll even get laid, a Christmas miracle! – he throws his arms around Mick.

'Listen, I might have a lead for you,' says Mick.

'Not sure I'm hireable.'

'Fuck off. You know your man Royston Clive?'

'You're joking. Isn't he meant to be a notorious prick?'

'Yes, but that notorious prick's launching something here. He's looking for someone to run the place. And they're funded out the arse.'

Kevin's mobile rings a second time: it's the same unfamiliar number. A worm of worry begins to grind its way through the anxiety-prone soil of his mind. It could be Grace phoning from the road; it could be Mum with some wretched request. Or it could be Sr Margaret reporting Aideen's excessive tardiness or that she's skived off another class. Or it could be Aideen's run off again or hitchhiked or maybe some sick fucker has his beloved daughter tied up in an abandoned garden shed, a rag wet with chloroform shoved down her gob, ringing him for a ransom …

With his little rebel Aideen, it could be any bloody thing.

Kevin tries to refocus on Mick who's onto a deliciously salacious tale of a late-night tryst on the publisher's desk in the offices of his old haunt. This is of particular interest to Kevin as it concerns his old boss, John Byrne, pompous, know-it-all, shiny-faced gobshite that he is. Kevin desperately wants to enjoy this story, wants to deep dive into this dirty little affair with its sordid little details.

'Now, you may or may not recall,' Mick lowers his voice, 'but our esteemed publisher is into role play and I don't fucking mean Shakespeare.' Mick leers. 'You'll not believe his favourite character of all. No joke now: a naughty schoolboy in dire need of a proper arse-spanking.' Mick guffaws, flashing greying fangs.

Kevin makes the appropriate responses, the convincing shifting facial gestures, but his mind pulls back to the unfamiliar number just as it flashes up a third time.

'Give us a sec, Mick,' he says. Then, into the phone: 'Kevin Gogarty.'

Despite being only recently unemployed – Kevin has taken to trotting out, in an exaggerated Texan accent, that he is a 'temporary stay-at-home dad' – he hasn't stopped answering the phone as if it may be the printer or the creative director or a sales rep on the line.

'Mr Gogarty? This is Sergeant Brian O'Connor in Dún Laoghaire Police Station.'

Kevin stiffens. 'Yes? Is Aideen OK?'

'Aideen? Sorry? No, I'm sorry having to bother you, but actually we've got your mum here. Could we ask you to come in and collect her? She's in a bit of a state.'

'What?' Kevin plugs a thumb into his free ear. 'Is she alright? What's happened?'

The hot girls, upon hearing the urgent pitch in Kevin's voice, immediately stop speaking and look over, but they're only a background blur to him now.

'Did she have a fall?'

'Oh no, she's fine,' says O'Connor. 'Didn't mean to alarm you. No, she's in grand shape, physically speaking. It's just – we've had a bit of an incident. She was found with stolen goods in her handbag, I'm afraid.'

Kevin allows for a long moment of silence to ensue during which he experiences a familiar emotional arc that begins at anger, crescendoes into hot rage, and peters out, finally, into a sad little trickle of self-pity. He thanks the policeman, rings off and stares at Mick, who, blissfully single, needs only to worry about where to order his next pint and which footballer will make the gossip page. Mick has no family, no brood of children. Kevin has four children! He is still, eighteen years later, reeling from the shock of four. Two boys and two girls to lie awake and worry over at three in the morning, to look after and cook for, to mould and shape into good and honourable souls. To say nothing of his pilfering mother who is, again, in need of rescue. He drains his drink, gets up.

'Sorry, Mick. I've got to go.'

'Nothing serious?'

'Oh no, strictly your run-of-the-mill shite,' Kevin says bitterly. 'My mother just got picked up for shoplifting. She's in with the guards driving them all, no doubt, to the brink of mass suicide. Jim Jones, was it? He had nothing on Millie Gogarty.'

3.

Aideen

Three kilometres south of Dún Laoghaire, in the small, pretty seaside village of Dalkey, Aideen Gogarty sits at her father's laptop tapping the word 'pine' into the search box on thesaurus.com. She is penning a poem to Clean-Cut, the Irish pop singing sensation who croons mostly remixed mid-'70s and early '80s soft-rock hits. Clean-Cut, who is, in fact, dishevelled and bewhiskered, sports a wild, moppish bleached blond 'do and is as tall as an American basketballer, in stark and amusing contrast to his four tidy and diminutive backup singers. After considering each synonym on offer – ache, agonize, brood, carry a torch, covet, crave, desire, dream, fret, grieve, hanker, languish for, lust after, mope, mourn, sigh, spoil for, thirst for, want, wish, yearn, yen for – Aideen rejects the lot as embarrassing and a bit crap.

She scans the bookshelf and the piles of paper inundating Dad's desk in search of his thesaurus from university, which was his father's before him, preferential to Aideen on the grounds that it's old school and therefore authentic. Aideen yearns – hankers? – to be authentic.

As she spots the ragged *Roget's* cover, she happens upon a photograph of a beaming, freckled schoolgirl in a brown uniform, a scarlet notebook clutched in her arms. It looks to be the cover of some sort of academic brochure. A cringeworthy photo – what eejit would willingly pose for their school's poxy PR? – but, curious, Aideen studies the other pictures splayed across the glossy foldout: there's a gaggle of girls bearing cricket bats on a pristine pitch, arms thrust upward in victory; a 'Residential Room' featuring fuchsia try-hard cushions; and, the most commanding image of all, a wrought-iron sign on a grassy knoll that reads MILLBURN SCHOOL FOR GIRLS. The slogan beneath, HONOUR, LEADERSHIP & ACADEMIC EXCELLENCE, is not the one Aideen's heard regarding the place: 'Noses up, knickers down.'

As she folds over the final page, Aideen is surprised to see, stapled in the top right-hand corner of an otherwise blank application form, a photograph of herself, one tiny yet hideous spot quite visible on the bridge of her nose.

Aideen tries to process what is so obvious and yet unbelievable. But all she comes up with is, *Huh*? She mentally combs through recent family aggro, trying to find a precedent for such a radical and covert move. Yes, she's 'acted out' lately – deliberately cracking her sister's mirror (no regrets there), dipping into Mum's handbag once too often, getting in a touch of trouble at school. And, then, her marks are a bit shit.

Still. Is the fact that the application form has not been filled out a good sign?

But the photo.

She hears a yell and through the window spies her younger brother, Ciaran, monkeying across the bars on his play set in the back garden. Behind him, dull clouds hover sharply against a dingy Dublin sky. Ugh, and there's her twin sister, Nuala (codename Nemesis). Nemesis meanders towards the front of the house. She is scanning the horizon, no doubt, for boys, flipping her deep black, overgrown mermaid's mane first left, then right, then left again, as if her hair is crossing the road, as if she's a California chick from a Katy Perry video when she's actually a vacuous phony from boring, provincial Dalkey.

Aideen checks the laptop's internet history over the last week and, with sinking heart and a sudden desire to take to her bed, she sees quite plainly that Dad's been visiting the Millburn website as often as three and four times a day.

Fuck.

She begins to hunt round his shelves and drawers, for what, she's not exactly certain, confirmation, evidence, one way or the other – *please, let it be the other* – that she isn't totally and irreversibly doomed. Millburn is a *boarding* school, probably filled with haughty, confident girls who will hate her. She hears the back door slam. Quickly, Aideen slides the brochure beneath its original mess just as Nemesis and one of her newer, nicer tagalongs, Gavin Mooney, appear in the doorway.

Her sister's beauty is a painful fact of Aideen's life, or maybe *the* painful fact, especially poignant because of their twinhood. It feels to Aideen as if the girls are compared, directly or indirectly, nearly every day of their lives, and though no one has ever overtly stated it, Aideen knows she's the brain, not the beauty. A modelling scout once stopped Nemesis in Stephen's Green, forked over his business card and winked at her and said she ought to get her headshots done, that she was 'a vision' (of utter bitchery) and he had a studio in town where they could shoot. Nemesis had Sellotaped the card to her dressing mirror and gushed about it to the point of vomit-inducing boredom (hence, the mirror's righteous destruction). Boys ring her *every day*. No male has ever phoned Aideen Gogarty, a fact about which she feels an undue degree of shame and sorrow. She is desperate that no one be privy to this, ever.

And then there's Mum and Dad, nauseating on the topic of Nemesis. Our Nuala's so sporty, she's the top acrobat at school! Our Nuala's so talented, she got the lead in the school play! Our Nuala's so kind, she made this painting of our perfect family and it's all so lovely!

There once was a girl who seemed sweet
An actor, gymnast, athlete
With dark stunning hair
That made all the boys stare
She's fooled the world, thus I retreat.

'I need the computer,' Nuala announces in her entitled way, bouncing impatiently on tiptoes.

'Hiya,' Gavin mumbles. He wears a navy tracksuit and white-on-white Puma high-tops.

'You could say hello to Gavin.'

But Aideen is distracted by the gothic Millburn School lettering displayed blatantly on her father's computer screen. Determined that her twin, of all people, not know about this – *boarding school!* – she ignores Nuala and steps backward to block the screen.

'Ooh, what's the big secret?' Nemesis sniffs evilly.

'Hi, Gavin.'

'Whatever,' says Nemesis. 'I need the computer.'

'I'm using it,' says Aideen.

'I need it.'

'Fuck off.'

Nemesis slits her eyes at Aideen, but since a male is present, she merely huffs off, Gavin trotting after her, like all of them. Aideen decides to snoop further, later, when everyone's asleep. This, in the wee hours, is when she gleans any real information about the goings-on in the Gogarty household. Mum and Dad talk a big game about openness and honesty and all that bollocks, but then they go and hide anything of interest or value. She once found a pregnancy test in her mother's loo – negative, she eventually understood after studying the box and then the stick. Which probably explained why Mum had seemed so blue in the days that followed. Unbelievable to Aideen that her mum would want more kids when she's always at work!

Then there was the letter addressed to Dad, which Aideen spied in ripped shards at the top of the bin: 'We're sorry to inform you that the position for which you applied ...'

Aideen heads to the kitchen, warms up the lasagne per her father's tiresome instructions – he's an over-explainer and a worrier. She piles more logs onto the dwindling fire, pokes at it, still shell-shocked. It's true that the Gogarty household has been strained, especially since her mother's tourism consultancy firm landed some big new client and Dad lost his job in magazines. Nowadays he's often to be found moping about with huge, needy eyes, inserting himself into every bloody moment. It's equally true that, though her parents bang on about how clever and observant she is, that she has 'emotional intelligence' (which means ...?), Aideen knows she constantly disappoints them. She makes 'bad choices', which is parent-speak for not the choices they would make. Fine, OK, but to ship her off like an outcast to live with a bunch of strangers?

'Aideen! Is this the site you were looking for?' Nemesis calls out from the study, sing-song mockery in her voice, and, as Aideen enters, a sadistic, shitty little grin on her face. These are precisely the moments Aideen most misses Gerard, her older brother who left in September to take up a psychology course at University College Cork, and who, unlike her parents, actually listens.

Gavin, head down, eyes averted, begins to retreat backward from the room. Aideen approaches the computer screen and sees that it's filled with photos of magnified medical blobs. It's a webpage of spots: crusty lesions, bulbous, bursting whiteheads. Nemesis throws her head back in a witch's cackle and zooms in on a black-and-white retro advertisement of a distressed, spotty 1950s teen above a dialogue bubble that says, 'Doctor, will these pimples scar my face?'

Nuala is right: Aideen is not attractive enough, she never will be, which is truly tragic because, above all else, she secretly covets being coveted. Clean-Cut is lovely to her at HMV record shop signings and backstage VIP fan zones and even when he tweets her directly, which he's done twice, but that's more about her being a loyal fan, someone who's worshipped the singer and his short crew since they were nobodies from Rathfarnham. What boy, what *real* boy, would ever choose Aideen Gogarty, especially in the shadow of her twin's radiance? Even her horrible family doesn't want her. Some ugly island of fury, or maybe injustice, or maybe just everyday sibling envy, loosens in Aideen, rekindling a dormant spark of self-loathing that's been festering for months.

Which may or may not justify what happens next. She snatches the first weapon at hand – the fire poker she'd unintentionally left stuck between two now blazing logs in the hearth, as it happens. It is a glowing, sizzling neon hot rod; it is a tool to brand cattle with or some grotesque instrument of CIA torture.

It would do perfectly.

Aideen launches at her sister. Both scream. Nemesis runs and Aideen gives chase and they race round the first floor, as they used to, happily, in earlier years. Though Nuala is six minutes older, Aideen was the unquestionable leader of their childhood larks. She made most executive decisions: Scrabble over Monopoly, bunk-bed rotations (back when they shared a room), who would hide and who would seek. Nuala shadowed Aideen for years until, gradually, inexplicably, she didn't. Now they slam with violence through the grand, high-ceilinged rooms, Aideen emitting bloodcurdling roars to petrify the horrible troll whose simultaneous yells are much girlier. At some point, Gavin pursues them and yells at them to stop and then gives up.

Of course, Aideen has no intention of actually burning flesh; she's just trying to terrify the silly bitch. She'll later try to explain this, though no one will listen. No one ever does. The sisters end up duking it out where it started, fireside, in a silence punctuated by the odd grunt. Hair is yanked, skin slapped, pinches exchanged. When Gavin finally reaches them and ends it, Aideen is straddling her sister, whose wispy, slender arms are pinned down by each of Aideen's bony knees, the poker towering high, trembling and still trailing a thin whisper of smoke above them.

4.

Millie

From her perch on a metal chair in a shoddy, windowless chamber that reeks of cigarettes – oh, for a smoke! – Millie spies her handsome son breezing into the Garda station. He doffs his overcoat, revealing a smart grey jumper and a pair of cuffless woollen trousers. Lean and trim still, Kevin is a man to notice, increasingly distinguished with age. The thick wedge of hair helps, only patchily grey and barely receding. His face, shadowed lightly in stubble, is kind and expressive, a face that Millie would almost call bookish with its strong jaw and brow, and wiry Yeatsian eyeglasses. Given his range of comedic tendencies – a single arched eyebrow to self-efface, frequent squinting in faux scepticism, a throwing up of his massive hands to capitulate – he can easily enchant most rooms: a working man's pub down the country, a posh soirée, a recent party at the house where Millie was later told (she'd been mysteriously omitted from the guest list) he was carrying on like a celebrity DJ, pushing chairs and tables asunder to fashion an impromptu dance floor.

But will his charm do the trick at Dún Laoghaire Garda Station?

At the moment, he huddles, former footballer that he is, listening intently to Sergeant O'Connor, the man who'd brought her in. She's often wondered whether Kevin's athletic prowess – running, tennis, squash – isn't a direct result of seeing Peter in recovery all those years, as if Kevin grew up bent on avoiding his father's fate. Now he nods frequently and then seems to interrupt with a lengthy speech, and nods again, arms crossed. All her life, it occurs to Millie, men have convened with other men, making decisions on her behalf. What, she wonders, given this particular situation, might the Golden Girls do?

Finally they're moving, a single menacing unit, a dark little cloud of doom, towards Millie Gogarty, who has the dizzying sensation that everything is topsy-turvy, that he's the adult and she the naughty child. Has he come to scold or threaten or yell? Or to take pity on his mother and her eccentric ways, to forgive and forget?

'Are you right there, Mrs Gogarty?' says O'Connor, once he and a younger officer and her son have scraped their chairs towards her. It's been ages since a group of men acknowledged, let alone flanked, her, and a lifelong inclination towards the opposite sex nudges her spirits slightly upward. She smiles shyly at them, begins to see that she can rise to this occasion. After all, she conquered Peter's strokes, three of them; she taught him how to speak again. She suffered through his death and, long before that, the death of Baby Maureen. Surely this is but a blip.

Kevin's sitting not a foot from her, aloof and stern, unwilling to meet her eyes.

'Can I get you anything?' says O'Connor. 'Coffee, tea?'

Millie declines, then nods her head to show she's steadfast, prepared.

'The problem we have here is that this isn't the first time you've taken a few bits from Mr Donnelly's shop, isn't that right? You see, he was willing to let it go the once or twice, but now you're laughing at him – you see my meaning?'

'Gentlemen,' says Millie bravely, though there is a detectable quiver in her voice. 'I believe this is all a bit of a misunderstanding. You see, I was in the shop and my good friend Kara O'Shea, do you know her? She's the mother of Henry and Dara O'Shea, wonderful sailors, the pair of them, crossed the channel in a boat no bigger than a bathtub, now when was that? No, I don't suppose –'

'Sorry,' Kevin brays, suddenly on his feet. 'May I have a word with my mother privately, please? Just briefly?'

The room is barely cleared before he whirls around, glaring, and quite definitively, she sees, prone to neither mercy nor amnesia.

'They want to charge you with shoplifting, Mum,' he hisses, 'so the old-lady ding-dong act is *not* going to fly here.' An explosive speck of spit soars towards Millie, who instinctively dodges it, watches as it lands on a metal stool that has probably hosted the rumps of hundreds of the town's most hardened criminals.

Millie wonders if the coppers have gone off to one of those two-way mirror rooms she's seen on *Law & Order* to watch the drama unfold. There is, she notes, a boxy window on the wall facing her. She assumes a calm manner, smiles up at her boy who, after all and despite everything, she loves mightily.

'I would give my eyeteeth,' says Kevin, 'to understand exactly why you're smiling right now.'

'This can all be sorted. I've been going to Donnelly's for years. I'm a loyal customer.'

'Loyal customer!' Kevin's jaw gapes, his eyes two fierce slits, like eyes a pre-schooler would gouge with a plastic knife into a play-dough face. 'I'm seriously beginning to wonder if you are *compos mentis*.'

Millie's skin prickles. This is just the sort of technical jargon that would be rattling around the brain of someone who's researching how to make it look as if his mother isn't the full shilling and ought to be put into a home.

'Here, just take it all back! I don't even eat Hula Hoops!' she cries, upending her bag onto the floor and setting free an astonishing shower of contents. Later, she marvels at her own stupidity since, if the men are indeed bearing witness, she's just handed them a smoking gun. Out stream the stolen crisps and the birthday card and, with a decided thunk, a single browning banana. Millie snatches this up; in all the excitement of the day, she's forgotten lunch.

'Tell me, please, that you're not going to eat that.'

'I'm famished.'

'Look, do you have a notion of a bloody clue how much trouble you're in? You do realize, don't you, that if you're charged, this could make the papers?'

'Ha!' she bellows. 'For feckin' a packet of Tayto?'

'For feckin' every week in the same feckin' shop! I warned you the last time.' He gets up, paces the room in tiny tight circles, panther-like. He is working himself up to, or down from, rage – she can't tell which. 'They've got a list of every item you've ever pinched.'

'What are you talking about?'

'Donnelly had CCTV installed a month ago,' Kevin says.

Millie scrambles to her feet. 'Please, Kevin! Please! I can't go to jail! Oh no. Oh no. Oh no.' Dizzy, she buttresses her palms against the rickety table, which squeaks goofily with every application of pressure. She might indeed collapse, no put-on this time. As a girl she'd pocketed a peppermint or a pencil now and again, but stopped when her father, always solemn, had threatened to report her to the manager who'd surely drag her off to Mountjoy Prison. But these days, she seems to have so little control over her slippery fingers, this terrific itch to take.

Now Millie hears footfalls – a cadre of them – and has a sudden hope that the officers behind the glass have been moved by her, this well-intentioned woman who's quick with a smile, after all, leaning against a table in an interrogation room begging for mercy. But the steps pass and fade.

'Hang on now. Calm yourself.' Kevin steps back, guides her into her chair and sits himself down. 'No one's going to jail yet. Let's not overdo it.' He begins to reach a hand out to her but stops mid-air. Kevin's affection feels so often aborted. 'Look, they want to make a point, they want to show you the seriousness of this. You'll have to face the charges.'

'Publicly?'

'We can have it handled quietly but I can't promise it won't get around.'

Millie buries her face into her hands, once one of her better features, now twin claws road-mapped in thick, wormy veins. Dainty, her Peter called them, ladylike.

Her son sighs, knocks on the table gently with his right fist, then rubs his pate to and fro, his most obvious gesture of high stress. 'They're willing to come to an agreement ... but there are some conditions.'

'Anything.'

'You'll have to admit to the wrongdoing, apologize to Donnelly. And show in good faith that you're trying to overcome your problem.'

'Yes, yes, I can do that.'

'You've got to stop this. You understand, Mum? This. Must. Stop.'

Millie lets her head fall, with enormous relief, into her hands. 'What would I do without you?'

'There's one more thing.' He coughs. 'We're going to have to set up a home aide to come into Margate.'

'A what?'

'Someone who pops in, a companion –'

'Into the house?'

'No, into the horse stable. Yes, into the house. Jesus. The alternative is to face the charges in court. And since they have actual footage of you tucking Donnelly's knick-knacks into your bag, I don't much like your chances.'

'I don't like the sound of that, Kevin. A stranger in my own home?'

'Just a few times a week. Twenty hours.'

'Twenty hours!'

'It's a three-month probation period, starting right away, as soon as we can find someone – Mick's sister does some sort of recruiting, she might be able to help on that front. If you fulfil your end, the charges will quietly go away.'

'I don't suppose that's negotiable?'

'That *is* the negotiation, Mum. You've committed a crime. You have no leverage here.'

'I don't mind the apology bit, that's fair enough. But the companion ...'

'Better than the alternative.'

Millie bends to collect her spoils and slowly lines them up on the table, one after the other, a menagerie of ridiculous items she neither wants nor needs. If anything, she considers herself anti-materialistic. There's only a handful of possessions on this earth she gives a toss about – the long-ago photo of Kevin that Peter had first shown her, the missalette from Baby Maureen's funeral, Peter's engagement ring – an heirloom emerald-cut emerald flanked by diamonds and worth a pretty penny, as a matter of fact.

'Shall I have a word with Sergeant O'Connor then?' says Kevin.

'Alright,' she says, 'yes, OK. We can get that all sorted when I'm back from America.'

'No, Mum,' Kevin says, looking away. 'I'm afraid America will have to be postponed.'

5.
Kevin

The only creatures to greet Kevin as he pushes open his massive front door and sweeps into the cluttered front hall – mucky shoes, an abandoned bowl of Corn Flakes, *fuck's sake*! – are Grace's two tabbies, Beckett and Cat, neither of whom much like him. They meow and brush competitively, incessantly, against Kevin's trousers. He sighs: more living things need him, and so soon. Aideen has failed to feed the cats. Aideen has also failed to answer her mobile, which he's tried three times prior to ensconcing his miraculously mute mother back in Margate, only to get Aideen's rude voicemail: 'It's me. You know what to do.' *Beep*. On the third call, Kevin had said, 'And *you* know what to do.' He got zero satisfaction from tapping the 'end' button on his mobile violently. *You can't even slam down a phone any more*. He envisions his daughter upstairs sulking right now, obliviously plugged into her laptop, that talentless silly-boy drivel blasting her fragile eardrums.

Kevin bends to pet Beckett and the cat nips his hand. He swats at the little brute as it scampers away, then calls out,

'Aideen, Nuala, Ciaran!' His ceilings are at least fourteen feet tall and every room is cavernous. In order to be heard at the Gogartys', you must scream. He has, it occurs to him, the very thing he always vowed not to have: a household of screamers.

Kevin contemplates, with mounting tension, all that he must do in the coming hours – update Grace on Mum's latest dip into petty larceny, though she's in Dubai, which means it's probably next Wednesday there; ring up Mick for a line on finding a caretaker; wrap the growing mountain of over-the-top Christmas presents amid the current family goat-fuck; and get some greens down his children's gullets. One of the only exceptions to Grace's generally relaxed parenting philosophy is an insistence on the children's high and varied vegetable consumption. Which is fair enough. Born and raised in England, Grace was the loving, scholarly eldest of five children living with their indefatigable single mother (dad fucked off to a married-but-separated bankruptcy lawyer in the next estate). Theirs was a junk-food household in which crisps stood in for carrots and the thought of eating meat prepared in any way other than fried was scandalous (even the bread was fried). Watching years of her mum in the kitchen and then out of it, juggling a patchwork of low-wage jobs, fuelled Grace's drive; a career, she saw, was paramount.

The first time Kevin met his future mother-in-law, in fact, she was trying to press a plate of chips and sausage on him. It was late for Grace's mum, but not for Kevin and Grace, just in after a few pints at her local in Surrey. They were on break from college in England where they'd met and had hours of night to go. Grace had come up behind her mum in the kitchen and wrapped her arms around her and *remained like that.* As if familial affection wasn't a quick peck or a clap on the back or an almost embarrassing thing to be got through. It was as natural as breathing and something to linger on. They were all like that, the whole lot of them. Grace told her mum not to mind Kevin one bit because her boyfriend – that was the first time she'd said it – was more than capable of making his own bloody food. 'Am I?' he'd said, pulling a panicked face. His mother-in-law had laughed – she was an easy laugher, like her daughter. What an excellent quality, he'd thought, a direct and effortless access to joy. Later, Grace had whisked her brothers and sisters off to bed and brought him into the lounge and shut the door and put on a film – *Weekend at Bernie's* – though they never got past the first scene. It became code. You want to watch *Weekend at Bernie's*?

Now Kevin lumbers into the kitchen and pours a generous glass of Malbec into the last clean receptacle available: a plastic dinosaur sippy cup still somehow in rotation. Gradually he becomes aware of a dim, faraway noise, a thudding, like a plank of wood being knocked repeatedly. Kevin heads towards the back of the house where the pounding grows louder. It's Nuala standing outside thrashing her fists against the back door. As he unlocks it, he starts in with 'I told you lot to stop –'

'Daddy!' she screams, lunging into his arms. She's frigid; her nose is alcoholic-red and streaming. She simultaneously cries and talks; she is a mess of blubbering wet.

'Slow down, pet, hang on,' he says, patting her back and ushering her into the house. 'Take it easy.' How many women, he wonders, must he comfort in one day?

But then, here's his Nuala, the most cheerful and confident of his crew, clinging to him just as she used to, like they all used to. So he holds her. She feels insubstantial, so light, in his arms. He forgets how young and innocent, how tiny and unworldly, how vulnerable his children are, and then he thinks: what kind of a total gobshite forgets this? Her shampoo smells disturbingly of manufactured coconut and he wonders about its toxicity. He kisses Nuala's head once and then again.

'Oh my God, I was outside forever,' she squeaks between gulps of air. Kevin brings her through to the kitchen, gets out the cocoa and the sugar and puts milk on the boil.

'Poor darling,' he says. 'How did you ever manage to lock yourself out?'

'Aideen did it!'

Kevin slaps the countertop with his palm. Which hurts.

'And she came at me with the fire poker,' says Nuala. 'She actually tried to burn me.'

'Bloody hell! You shouldn't have to …' He squeezes her shoulder. 'Where's Ciaran?'

'Neighbours'.'

He exhales. 'And where is Aideen now?'

'I don't know,' she says, 'and I don't care.'

The need to avenge his victimized daughter – nearly burnt and then put out of the house in arctic weather! – coupled with the need to hunt down her assailant, to project blame for this chaos onto his clever, complicated, perpetually miserable teen, is so powerful it practically fells him on his ass. He vaults up the staircase taking two, three, steps at a time with his lean runner's legs and bounds towards her door, strictly verboten to all Gogartys without a ridiculous series of knocks and gentle requests for permission to enter.

Tonight, he charges in. The room is an accurate representation of his daughter's age or state of mind or both. Other than a shrine to Clean-Cut in pristine condition, disorder reigns. Cluttering the floor: a stick of deodorant fuzzy with carpet fibres, various inside-out denims and socks, a Dunnes Stores shopping bag from which spills a handful of bras acquired during a recent mother–daughter shopping venture, which, as so many recent outings tend to do, had run afoul. Beside Aideen's bed sits a mug of cold tea, a milky skin stretched taut across it, and a plate of this morning's toast crusts – Aideen, in her growing hermitry, has taken to eating meals in her room.

Kevin checks every other room in the house, each inspection more frantic than the last so that, in his hurry, he stubs his thick bullet of a toe hard on the iron frame of Gerard's bed and gives himself over to a loud, satisfying 'Goddammit!' He bounds down to the basement – sometimes Aideen hides out down there on a mouldy beanbag chair reading in the crawl space where they keep the luggage and where he's asked her a hundred times not to be. But there's no sign of her.

He returns to the kitchen, breathing heavily now, and snaps up his mobile. He tries Grace's phone and then Gerard's – Aideen sometimes confides in her older brother – but no answer. Kevin worries about Gerard – his general lack of ambition given the cutthroat state of the world, especially when there are so many pubs to frequent – but he's eighteen and Kevin mercifully no longer *needs* to keep track of him.

He can reach no one.

Kevin delivers Nuala, fully recovered, a mug of cocoa. Pacing, he gulps his wine, lays out the facts of his shite day: he's had to collect his mother from the police station; the whereabouts of his wayward daughter are unknown (at least he hasn't totally banjaxed things up, he thinks grimly, at least the other three are safe, alive); his wife, as usual, can provide neither advice nor support – she is pontificating from a podium or courting international clients at a hush-hush private club or eating fried samosas in a desert tent.

As he peels open the last tin of cat food, his mobile rings.

'Did something happen up there?' It's Mum.

'What do you mean?'

'Aideen's here but she won't say a word.'

'Aideen's at your house?'

'I'm only delighted to have her. Any chance you could come down and have a look at the TV? We could use a bit of distraction. What's the film about the American prostitute with the teeth who goes shopping? What's it called, Aideen?'

'Can she stay with you tonight?'

'She won't want to, Kevin.'

'Tell her she has no choice. She caused a whole kerfuffle down here and I need to clear the air.'

'*Pretty Woman*, yes, that's it. Brilliant girl.'

Kevin puts down the phone and heads directly to his desk, where he finds the application for Millburn School.

6.
Millie

After Kevin dropped her home, Millie had retrieved the bottle of sherry normally reserved for special occasions (though special is clearly not the apt adjective here – 'ghastly', say, or 'horrific' may be better descriptors). Into the kitchen went Millie to fetch a glass when she spotted the red answering-machine light aglow and listened, with a shudder, to its single, dreadful message.

'You wouldn't per chance have that spare travel pillow you mentioned that I could bring aboard? Don't bother yourself at all, but if you put your finger on it, that'd be grand.'

Jolly Jessica. Millie had forgotten about JJ, the driving force behind their New York City trip, who, half a year ago, had triumphantly written 'Big Apple' in red biro on the 20 December box of her Famous Irish Writers kitchen calendar below a moody portrait of Brian Friel. What a mockery of their months spent poring over hop-on-hop-off bus tour pamphlets and Broadway listings with the travel agent in town, two silly old biddies telling each other over coffee and cribbage how ludicrous it was, then having the courage to make it possible – only to have it, in fact, become impossible once more! It was enough to reduce Millie's already depleted spirits to despair, full stop.

Imagine regaling JJ with the sordid details of her shoplifting spree, the shameful arrest, the interrogation room! It had been difficult enough attempting to stay low in the back of the police car. *Thank Christ she'd worn her fedora.* JJ's opinion of her would irreversibly plummet. Jessica Walsh is a woman who regularly delivers nosegays to the ailing at Our Lady's Hospice in Harold's Cross, who's always giving Millie artsy homemade trifles – velvet pouches with 'M.G.' stitched onto them, picture frames crafted from shells she collects along Sandymount Strand. If you were the sort to drop a ha'penny on the pavement, Jessica would be the sort, despite her girth and tendency towards asthma, to lumber after you with it. That's Jessica, a good egg. Which left Millie no choice. She'd have to lie. She began concocting some muckety-muck about Doctor Such and Such insisting that air travel is unsafe, given X tablets he's just prescribed for Y condition, and that they'd have to hold off until she'd adjusted to them – say March, when her probation period would be over.

At the sound of the bell, Millie had been astonished to find her granddaughter on the doorstep, an unprecedented visit from the child, of Kevin's four, whom she knows least.

The girl's teeth clattered with the cold, no jacket on, mute as a lump of charcoal. Like her brothers, Aideen's a brunette, her hair wavy and caramel-streaked in a certain light, and her smile, when employed, quite fetching. It's true that her knees tend to jut out a wee bit, causing her feet to appear not unlike two flippers, wide and cumbersome; but this too, of course, shall pass. Aideen strikes

Millie as an outrageously self-conscious teen, too shy or unwilling to sustain friendly eye contact in a prolonged way. Poor duck.

In the first hour, the girl hardly utters two words.

In the second, Millie suggests, as though it's just occurred to her, that she spend the night.

Aideen, catatonic, is perched in the window seat that faces Millie's beloved Irish Sea. The girl nods, or maybe it's more of an inadvertent jerk of the head.

'Hungry at all?'

Another jerk.

As Millie weighs the decadence of adding more briquettes to the dying fire, Aideen stands up. 'Should I sleep in Dad's old room?'

'Oh, it's only early. Sure you won't have toast?'

Aideen's not a big eater; if anything, she's always been on the slightly sickly side, or maybe runty's the word. When the girls were born, Aideen, a pound lighter than her twin, was yanked out of Grace with uncooperative lungs and goopy, glued-shut eyes, two tiny pink fists clenched at her ears. More than once Millie's wondered whether those fists aren't still a bit clenched.

'Tell me what's happened,' Millie says. 'I won't judge you. Go on, love. You'll feel better.'

Aideen's face becomes something of a battlefield upon which she struggles to maintain composure against the threat of imminent emotional surrender. She sniffs and blinks. The muscles at her mouth bravely wrestle a trembling frown. 'Can I move in with you?'

Millie resists her first impulse, which is to leap into the air with a whoop. Here's a bedroom, she would like to say, there's a towel, a blanket we'll find! And though soap, say, or toothpaste or milk might be in short supply, we'll make do. *I don't need a caretaker*, Millie thinks, *I can be the caretaker.*

But as touching, as tempting, as the simple proposal is, Millie knows the idea is lunacy. Kevin deems her a batty incomp at best; he'd sooner abandon his daughter in certain unlit, graffiti-laden corners of lower Sheriff Street in the wee hours as allow Aideen to move into Margate.

'What's happened? Did you have a row with your sister?'

'I hate her.'

'Oh now, that's –'

'You have no idea what she's like. She's a total bitch.'

'Aideen.'

'You said you wouldn't judge.' Aideen glares across the room at Millie. 'Do you know about Millburn?'

'Sorry?'

'The boarding school?'

'Millburn School?'

Aideen sags back onto her seat, openly crying now. She is beside herself. Millie can remember with great clarity first laying eyes on her gorgeous granddaughters in the maternity wing at the Rotunda. Millie, always on the broody side as Peter liked to tease, had reached across to the bassinet and picked up little Aideen, straitjacketed in cotton and unbearably light. It was astonishing, like holding a swaddled bundle of air.

Millie had kissed the infant on her translucent skin and rocked her, pacing the gloomy, dim hospital corridors, talking incessantly, of course, describing each patient who passed and the stout floor nurse with the ample bosom and cross eyes who glanced at Millie in a bossy, disapproving way that made her feel young and giddy. And why shouldn't she have felt giddy? Here was something life rarely offered up: a chance to start fresh with a human being, the daughter of your son, before you've gone and fecked things up.

'What about Millburn School?' says Millie.

'They're sending me there!' Aideen cries. 'They're sending me away.'

'What?'

Aideen wipes her face. 'Did you know about it?'

'Me?' Millie balks. 'Sure, your father tells me nothing. When did this all happen?'

'I don't know. I'm not even supposed to know about it. I just found the, like, papers.'

'But why?'

'Because they hate me.'

'Nonsense. Nobody hates you. It's probably because of your Leaving Cert next year. They want you to buckle down.'

'Bollocks.'

'Let me ask you something, Aideen. Where did you find those papers?'

'Dad's desk.'

'You didn't see any for a nursing home there, by any chance, did you?'

Aideen says nothing.

'No snaps of gaga pensioners in wheelchairs? A granny pushing a walker, something of that nature?'

'I like that word, gaga.'

Millie sighs. 'I reckon he wants to ship me off as well. Maybe we're in the same boat.'

'I don't think so, Gran.'

'There's a lot you don't know,' Millie says darkly, and then: 'I've got it. We'll run off somewhere – the pair of us. We'll stow away in one of those big ships in the harbour but we won't know where we're going. We'll come out from some dark cupboard after two weeks' time, blinking into the sunlight, and we'll be in Africa and we'll go on safari.'

'Look who sounds gaga now,' Aideen says and, for the first time all evening, allows for the feeblest of smiles. Millie thinks, *Pretty duck*.

7.

Kevin

With care, Kevin chooses Dobbins as the most suitable venue for tonight's tricky dinner during which he and Grace (home at last, in the flesh!) hope to broach the specifics about Mum's new companion, a topic that, since her arrest and true to form, she has steadfastly refused to engage with. Whether she's made mental preparations to welcome a companion into her home, he couldn't say. In fact, other than an unhealthy consumption of back-to-back episodes of the liberated ladies of Miami (he'd replaced the remote batteries), Mum's focus seems primarily bent on pestering the Fitzgeralds down the road to return a crate that she'd pressed upon them years ago.

Lit primarily by tiny white votives in glass jars, Dobbins is formal and hushed and discreet. The hope is that Mum, known for ditching her family at restaurants and sidling up, uninvited, to other parties at other tables for an evening she finds more interesting, will be intimidated enough to resist her urge to roam.

They settle, give their order. Kevin notices Mum, quickly tipsy, begin to eye-stalk potential ambush targets. Their waiter, middle-aged and haughty despite a goofily crooked, sparse moustache, delivers a margarita glass of prawn cocktail to the table just beside them, where a strikingly incongruent couple sits – the woman is stunning, olive skinned with wild, kinky hair; her companion is an overgrown, pleasant-faced ginger gorilla of a man.

'Oh, that looks gorgeous,' Mum says ostensibly to her own family, but Kevin knows better. 'I must say I do like a good prawn cocktail, don't I, Kev?' Mum raises her voice and glances over at the couple. 'Of course, you really have to go to Ballybough for the prawns, that's the first thing.'

Quietly Kevin says, 'Let's skip the second thing.'

'The second thing is the cocktail sauce, of course. Needs a soupçon' – Mum smiles coyly as she does whenever employing her schoolgirl French – 'of horseradish.' Then, directly to the woman, she says, 'If you don't mind my asking, are you Indian or Pakistani?'

'Mum, have you been tippling again?' Kevin says with a wink at the couple. 'Let's leave them to it, shall we?'

'Not at all,' says the man.

'I'm from Trinidad.'

The man smiles kindly at Mum. 'Did you order the prawns as well?'

'Who, me?' says Mum. 'I wouldn't dream of it – too many prawns!' To Kevin, she says, 'What did I order?'

This is part of the drill: his mother always pretends not to know what she ordered and then, when the dish arrives, she feigns great shock, as if she's never set eyes upon a bowl of Dublin Bay mussels or a rocket salad, let alone ordered it.

'Smoked salmon, was it?' Mum says.

'I have no idea,' says Kevin.

'Or soup?' she says. 'Whatever it is, I just hope it's small. In America you should see – oh, you wouldn't believe the size of the plates you get there! That's the problem with the States, the plates!' She laughs.

'Why don't we let these –?'

'But the people! The jolliest people you've ever laid eyes upon. Oh, I do love Americans. 'Course they're all fat as a house, but lovely and kind-hearted. Have you been?'

Before the woman can respond, Mum knocks back the dregs of her wine and says, 'Can I just say, if you don't mind, but I'm very curious about mixed-race couples. Your skin is more mulatto, I suppose you'd call it? Actually,' she leans in conspiratorially, 'if you want to know the truth, I prefer coloured people to whites.' She beams. 'Always have.'

Even Kevin, who can usually eke out a quip in the face of most embarrassing situations, who prides himself on his ability to smooth over the various mortifying social gaffes of his doddering mother, is struck dumb.

After a beat, the redhead says, 'That makes two of us,' and begins to laugh, and then they all chuckle.

But that was never going to last.

As his mother tucks into her starter – soup, as she bloody well knew – Kevin, bracing himself, says, 'We've found a companion for you, Mum. Or, rather, Mick's sister has. A woman called Sylvia Phenning. I haven't met her yet but apparently she's very nice. Willing to tidy up and she does a bit of cooking as well. She's American, actually.'

'An American?'

'Yes, from Florida somewhere.'

'Oh, I couldn't have an American.'

'You just finished saying how much you love them.'

'Well, in America, yes.'

'But here in Ireland you don't?' Kevin can't help smiling.

'In my own country?' She shakes her head as if the notion is plainly idiotic.

Kevin and Grace exchange the scantest of looks – no one besides his wife gets any of this. The rest of the world sees only quirky charm. Briefly fortified, he turns again to his mother. 'The best part is she's available to start right away. You know yourself, finding someone just before Christmas – we got very lucky.'

'Did we?'

'I think it's a good plan,' Kevin says. Mum's clearly lonely rattling around Margate on her own – a bit of company's just the thing – and a second set of eyes keeping watch can only be beneficial. There are, after all, only so many times Kevin can gallop in when she burns her hand on the cooker and tells no one despite the risk of infection, or dismisses a bruising fall on the stairs, or accosts the gardener's son in her nightie, inviting him in after dark to join her for a brandy and a biscuit.

Kevin says, 'We may want to consider, further down the line I'm talking, other scenarios, given various health issues –'

'Health issues?' says Millie. 'I'm in fine fettle.' She looks over at the couple for support, but, her audience lost, she turns back to her own family and taps her frozen shoulder. 'This alone will not be my undoing.'

'Of course not,' Grace says. She looks particularly lovely tonight – soft grey cowl-neck dress, dark hair in a chic layered bob. 'How's the shoulder, Millie? Are you still doing your stretches?'

Kevin marvels, always, at his wife's ability to not react to the type of shit that would cause his own brain to rupture. She is a skilled disarmer. She's able – with demanding clients and unreasonable children alike – to grasp volatile situations in hyperspeed and neutralize high emotion in a way that magically makes all feel heard, including him.

Then again, it's not *her* mother; nuclear family can be uniquely nuclear.

Grace says, 'I just worry that the house is a lot of work, even for someone with your energy. No one could be expected to keep it up.'

'I keep it up just fine,' Mum snaps.

Kevin exhales heavily. 'We're talking generally, just something to think about. Something could happen to you, say, when Sylvia isn't there. Remember your fall last winter?'

'That was June!'

'It was *not* June. There was ice on the road.'

'I had on my sunhat.'

'That does not preclude ice.'

'Pass the butter, will you, love?' Mum says.

Grace reaches for Kevin's arm and squeezes, but he can't interpret whether the message is *Cool it, you moron*, or *Steady on*. 'And then,' says Kevin, 'there's also the question of driving. There've been at least two accidents in the past year alone. That I know of.'

'You yourself were in a crash not so long ago, Kevin – amn't I right?'

'We are *not* talking about me.'

'Well, why not? Why shouldn't we talk about you?'

Except for the couple beside them, who now pointedly avoid eye contact, other diners begin to glance over, one or two openly rubbernecking, bloodhounds on the trail of some meaty family strife. Kevin rolls out an all-star grin and with a nod of his mug across the room manages to silently order another bottle.

The Gogartys work their way through their main course as a wary, uncharacteristic détente descends. Kevin chews but doesn't taste his meal, and he's soon itching to motion for the bill. But the waiter ignores him and wheels over a glass cart of dazzling desserts, meticulous in their tiny chocolate smears and pointillist drops of syrup. He indicates towards each dish, sharing its name and a fussy explanation: pineapple with ginger and crème fraîche, hazelnut soufflé, Mont Blanc croquant.

'Sounds like a pen,' Mum interrupts. 'Or a toasted cheese sandwich.' She giggles. 'Or a toasted cheese pen.'

'And this,' he continues, frowning at her editorializing, 'is a traditional plum pudding with –'

Mum's hand darts out and she snatches the plate. 'This one, yes.'

'Oh, madam, these are for display only. Our pastry chef will be happy to prepare a fresh one for you.' He takes hold of the saucer but Mum won't let go. For a suspended, punchy moment, the two tug-of-war over the pudding. Kevin, despite himself, feels hysterical laughter building in his gut.

'No, Millie,' says Grace gently. 'That one's lacquered – that one's inedible.' She tries to pry her mother-in-law's hands from the plate, but Mum refuses to release it.

'Oh, just let her eat it,' says Kevin under his breath, with the realization that the evening's been a perfect failure – she will never agree to even consider a nursing home, she will never give up her car keys, she will only drive him mad all his days. 'With any luck, it's poisonous.'

8.

Millie

Dawn on Christmas morning finds Millie digging through her dining room drawers, cobbling together re-gifts to bring to Kevin's. For himself and Grace, she finds a set of coasters each with sketches of Sydney tourist sites. Aideen might be tickled by a packet of seaweed (used for preparing sushi, or so she was told). For Ciaran, the little one, she has a cap with matching gloves – there's a dribble of sauce on one thumb, but nothing a spot of soap wouldn't remove. She'll give Nuala nail varnish (her hairdresser's always pressing bottles of them into her hands) and for Gerard, home for the break, a Chinese cookery book – though, now that she thinks of it, is there a kitchen in his bedsit?

She spends the rest of the morning watching the road and the telly and the clock, and the road and the telly and the clock. She waits to ring JJ when she knows her friend will be at mass and she can leave a 'Happy Christmas!' on her answering machine. The day after her arrest, Millie had phoned JJ with her medical myth. Jessica had listened and then, with false cheer, said, 'Sure, we'll get there yet, Millie' before ringing off. Millie had then phoned the travel agency and postponed her journey, which had cost her vast quantities of pounds and pence, to be sure. Now that it's out of her reach, the trip has taken on even weightier import: she fantasizes often of herself and Jessica descending a tour coach at Times Square and roaming the bustling streets. Maybe she would have found some flashy neon corner of Broadway and set out her hat and crooned Irish ballads – 'Danny Boy' or 'The Fields of Athenry' – the Yanks eat that sort of thing up. Maybe she would have enjoyed corndogs with ketchup for dinner, purchased a massive refrigerator and reinvented herself, never come home.

At half past one, when she can no longer stand the silence and chill of the house on what's supposed to be a day of warmth, Millie drives the few minutes to her son's home and knocks, a pre-emptive strike. In one of the many complicated struggles between herself and her son, she never fails to turn up a touch early and he never fails to invite her a good hour or so after he actually wants her.

'Happy Christmas,' he says and then he grins. 'I thought we'd agreed on three o'clock?'

'Had we? Happy Christmas, love!' she sings.

'Come in, come in. You've brought gifts.' He takes some of the parcels, wrapped in the *Indo* sports section, and bends to kiss her cheek.

'Oh, those are nothings.'

'Indeed.'

Kevin ushers Millie into the sitting room where she promptly gasps: the sheer abundance of ripped-open presents, paper everywhere, ribbons, bows, stuffed animals and new trainers and bottles of perfume and jumpers and small jewellery boxes and balled-up gift wrap, like the IRA's been and gone.

'I know,' says Kevin. 'I was just about to –'

'Holy Mary, Mother of God! So many presents! And kids in Africa with not even a bowl of rice.'

'Can we not, just this once?'

Millie, miffed at being censored, places the rest of her trifles beneath the massive evergreen. The room mysteriously empties and she finds herself alone, growing peckish and a touch resentful. She doesn't care for the way her son has dismissively plonked her into one of two overstuffed, inexplicably white armchairs, as if she's a dithering geriatric. She mulls the self-regard, the absurd decadence, of white upholstery in a family home.

'Happy Christmas, Millie!' Grace says, clad in a goofy Santa hat and heading towards her with a crystal flute of champagne, nearly friendlier, thinks Millie, than her own son. Kevin joins them and the three adults toast, but without the buzz of the children nearby, Millie has the sense of being in enemy territory.

Presently, she hears shouts and then the youthful thuds of footsteps tramping downstairs. Bit of life. Gerard and Nuala and then little Ciaran appear beneath the dining-room archway. They greet Millie with gorgeous hugs. Gerard is the image of her Peter – long-faced, soulful-eyed – and she adores him for it. All the Gogarty children are beautiful, in fact, kind and bright and confident. Well done, Millie wants to tell Kevin and Grace.

Nuala begins playing wobbly waitress on her new rollerblades, skating in jagged movements between kitchen and dining room, delivering an endless number of placemats, cutlery, dishes. At one point, she smacks into a doorway, upsets a glass of milk in her hand, and laughs. Millie, who always prefers mistakes to mastery, enjoys the sight of it.

She glances through the front window and studies young families and couples, old men in caps strolling along the road, the sky a smoked grey, but with a hint of sun. Everywhere her fellow Dubliners are calling in to each other's homes – this is her favourite bit, like when she was a girl – to wish each other a Happy Christmas and share a drink and a bit of fun, bit of craic, and greet whoever's come home from the States or London or Australia or wherever they emigrated to, so dire was, and is now once again, the Irish job market.

The eldest, Gerard, unbidden, situates his grandmother at the head of the table, serving her wine, pushing her chair in, chatting about his courses and Cork, channelling the adult behaviour modelled before him his whole life but which he seems to have only just awoken to today. Millie forgets herself and actually bats her eyelashes at him, so unprecedented is all this fuss. She takes a long look at her grandchildren – she is old, she can do as she pleases – and a powerful current seizes her, followed by a familiar jolt of panic: this moment, like them all, is already passing. And gone.

Where, she wonders, is Aideen?

Finally, when Millie is sure to pass out from hunger pangs, Grace calls up the stairs for the girl and Millie notes a vexed look, some message transmitted, between Kevin and his wife. They pull the Christmas crackers Grace's mum sends every year from England and unfold their paper crowns and don them and take turns reading aloud the silly jokes within. Plates are passed and filled – ham, roast potatoes, Brussels sprouts, green beans, gravy, Yorkshire puddings – when Aideen finally slinks in like some scowling scullery maid, practically crawling in on all fours so clearly does she not wish to be acknowledged. Indeed, her presence seems to unleash a palpable whiff of doom onto this otherwise festive table with its elegant tinsel icicles dangling from each corner, lit ivory tapers jammed into gleaming candlesticks.

'A happy, happy Christmas to you, Aideen!' Millie cries, standing to embrace her. She hasn't seen the girl since their sleepover. Aideen tries to slip by, but an undeterred Millie clamps both hands on her granddaughter's shoulders and lands a damp kiss on Aideen's ear and whispers, 'Any news?'

Aideen shakes her head and pats Millie awkwardly on the back as if consoling a stranger who's just become unaccountably overwrought. She wiggles out of Millie's embrace, but Millie's not offended, familial affection being anathema at this age. No one speaks as Aideen, seated, spreads her napkin into her lap and studies with a blank, inscrutable adolescent gaze the feast laid out before her.

'Well, this looks only stunning,' says Millie, already losing track of how much booze she's consumed.

The children's well-groomed table manners quickly abandon them as they dig into their grub and compete to dominate the conversation. Kevin leans quietly towards his dour teenaged hatemonger and squeezes her arm, hunting for a smile. Aideen ignores him.

Towards the end of the meal, Kevin rises, clinking the tines of his fork against his flute, which has the adverse effect of making the entire clan talk louder.

'Speech!' Ciaran yells, smacking the table. 'Speech, speech!' He grins at his father. Everyone adores Ciaran – with his gapped teeth and chirpy voice – in a way that makes Millie slightly cool towards him, her natural affinity bent always towards the historical underdogs of the world.

'Happy Christmas, everyone!' Kevin says. 'Lovely to all be together and to have Gran here, and thrilled to have Gerard home.' He nods to his older son. 'I for one should like to thank you all for your most thoughtful gifts, not least of all the pair of hairy navy slippers that have already kept me snug against the icy tundra of our bathroom tiles. And to you, darling.' He looks at Grace, but stops short of sharing the details of her present, which irks Millie.

'I feel very lucky – this is the eighteenth Christmas, I believe, in this house,' Kevin continues when Millie suddenly lets loose a rogue, undeniable burp. In her dotage, she is prone to, and has no control over, eruptions of air escaping her from various orifices, precisely at the most disadvantageous moments. The belch – comically lengthy, almost like a teenage boy's showing off in front of the lads – cuts a shocked silence in the room. Then all four children – yes, even Aideen – erupt into howls of laughter.

'Gran!' they shrill with delight. 'How could you?'

Kevin, in the role of long-suffering father to this rowdy crew, lifts his glass even higher into the air and says, 'Well, Mum, you've stolen my thunder again. I think that about says it all. Cheers, everyone! Happy Christmas!'

'Sorry, love!' Millie says, pleased to be the cause, however inadvertent, of this moment of lightness. In point of fact, she feels positively buoyant. She is not thinking about her arrest or

Jolly Jessica's daughter's apartment in Brooklyn, where she was supposed to be having her Christmas dinner, or the imminent arrival of a perfect stranger in Margate.

Now a second impressive belch rings out, longer, louder, ruder. The culprit, Ciaran, snickers and emits a series of mini-burps.

'Ciaran!' says Nuala. 'How rude!'

'Leave him alone,' says Aideen. 'He's only messing.'

'And who put you in charge?'

'Guys ...' says Gerard. 'Come on.'

'You are not cute,' fires off Aideen. 'And your personality is a zero.'

'Aideen,' says Kevin. 'Enough.'

'Dear Diary,' says Nuala, miming with an imaginary pen. 'Today I am a sad, sad girl. Boo hoo!'

'Enough!' Kevin says.

'I'm not feeling well,' says Aideen, and she's up on those flipper feet, plate in hand, slapping towards the staircase.

'Please sit down, darling,' says Grace in a tone that makes Aideen acquiesce though she stomps back to her chair. 'It's Christmas. We're eating together as a family.'

Aideen snorts. 'This family's shit.'

The shift in mood, with these words, feels dangerous, irreversible.

'Aideen!' says Kevin.

'When were you going to give me and the family my happy news?'

'Such a drama queen,' Nuala mutters.

'Acting like everything is fine,' says Aideen. 'Well, it's not fine. And I'm not going.'

Kevin pales.

'Going where?' says Gerard.

'Aideen, why don't we –?' Kevin says.

'When were you going to tell me, Dad – like, the night before? Like, sleep tight. Oh, and by the way, this is your last night at home.'

'Tell you what?' says Nuala, gleefully revelling in this little slice of schadenfreude.

'This is not the time or the place,' Grace says. 'Take a deep breath and we'll –'

'No!'

'We'll discuss this with you, Aideen, we will,' says Kevin. 'We just didn't want to bring it up before Christmas, love. We don't want to spoil the Christmas.'

'Well done, Dad,' says Aideen, adopting her father's deepest sarcasm and adding a hefty dose of undisguised teenaged wrath as she slams, finally, out of the room, 'it's not spoiled at all.'

9.
Aideen

Had her father not put a hockey stick atop her suitcase, Aideen may not have retaliated so aggressively. But the stick is a particularly maddening reveal of his vast disappointment in her very person, since he knows full well that she'll never use it, and yet, with an undying hopefulness in all the potential she can't seem to fulfil he silently urges her to pack it, as if the school will change her.

Aideen removes a carton of eggs from the fridge and steals upstairs. She is done with the crying and the begging and the arguing that have marked an impressive meltdown which has, over Christmas and into the New Year, drained all emotional energy reserves from the Gogarty residence. She has seen its ineffectiveness; she has retreated to her usual and only base of power – silence. Her eyes, when she accidentally met them in the mirror after a splash of water on her face at dawn, are terrifically swollen. She spent the night awake, every minute of it, brooding and sending messages to Sharon, her best friend, who moved to Glasgow last year. She tweets to Clean-Cut, and his reply, *Ur our best fan sending xoxoxos,* has been read a mind-blowing number of times. It's the closest thing to a love note she's ever received. Last night, Mum and Dad had cruelly snored away, not a lick of compassion for her anguish, blissful in the knowledge that their Aideen would soon be dumped off at boarding school.

During their countless arguments and Aideen's attempts at negotiation in the days leading to this one, Mum had said, ad nauseam, that Millburn wasn't just about recent strife in the house and Aideen's choices, but that she might very well enjoy making her own way in a different school than her twin. More important, her Leaving Cert studies were upon her and it was time to get serious about school. Plus, the boarding part was just Monday through Friday; she'd be home every weekend.

Aideen understands this explanation for what it is: parental bollocks.

Initially she had refused to pack – why should she assist in her own demise? – but envisioning the crap Mum and Dad would wrongly choose (hello, hockey stick), she eventually relented and unhappily gathered up her essentials beneath the pitying gaze of Ciaran and even Nuala. Upon Sharon's advice, she'd headed to the liquor cabinet at two in the morning and lifted a bottle of spirits – vodka, she was advised, for its odourlessness – and six of Dad's warm cans of lager. Aideen has no desire to drink alcohol – she dislikes the taste of it – but Sharon suggested it might help endear her to the girls at Millburn. She tucked the booze deep into the bowels of her duffel beneath a pile of navy school uniforms.

Before she left for work, Mum had stood in the doorway to Aideen's bedroom. This was the goodbye Aideen had imagined the most and, though she had resolved to remain wooden, she soon found herself sobbing.

'Oh, my love,' Mum had said into her hair, which was crushing. 'Don't cry. You'll be home Friday.'

'Please, Mum, don't make me go. Please.'

'You're going to be fine,' Mum had said. 'Better than fine.' Mum had released her then, hands on Aideen's shoulders, smiling. Smiling!

In Irish History class, Dr Scanlon's been teaching them about the dead Irish heroes, Patrick Pearse and Eamon de Valera and that whole lot, the leaders for independence and self-determination, the righteous warriors, the rebels. Like them, Aideen will transform her powerlessness into revolution. She enters her parents' bedroom and, without pause, fires a single brown egg at their beloved painting, *Gretel and Hansel*, a mess of primary colours, neither Hansel nor Gretel remotely discernible unless you count two crusty faceless blobs in the upper corner, a present given to them by their art collector friend and showcased, since their wedding day, above their bed.

The first egg splats between two streaks of teal paint with a satisfying crack. The second glops down slowly, the weight of the yolk dragging down the gummy egg-white, toppling on itself until it lands unceremoniously on the bed's tufted grey headboard. She launches another and another and another and another – one for every Gogarty! – and then tosses the carton in the middle of the duvet.

Aideen stands back and takes measure of her destruction. It's not exactly radical. It's not exactly Michael Collins with guns blaring holding off the British soldiers at the GPO. More damage needs to be inflicted. Aideen removes the biggest, sharpest knife from the kitchen drawer and returns to the eggy painting and stabs it straight down the middle, from stem to stern, like a surgeon splitting open her patient's insides. The gash is so long, there's no chance the wound can heal. *There now*, she thinks, *it's totally fucked, like me.*

10.
Kevin

The school's image – and fee – is pure Dublin 4, which is to say posh and clubby, but the grounds themselves are dubious. Once you pass a grand set of ornate gates and tool up a theatrical, windy drive, Millburn School is a set of low and flat and square, beige, grim, rain-stained buildings strewn about in random clusters across a quilt of fields. It's as if a blindfolded pilot had hovered in the sky dropping matchboxes across patchy lawns of dying grass and then, growing bored, gave up and headed on home. It's artless and so, to Kevin's mind, mildly offensive. If you're going to make something, keep beauty in mind.

The relentless drizzle doesn't help. Unbelievably, Aideen has only grunted perfunctory yeses and nos throughout the drive to Millburn where the school, along with a Spar, two churches and the Cock-a-Doodle, an eighteenth-century farmers' pub, constitute the immediate area's sole business establishments. Even when Clean-Cut's remix of 'I'm Not in Love' had come on the radio and Kevin had cranked up the volume for his daughter's benefit, she didn't flinch. *Fair fucks*, he conceded: when he was her age, he had nowhere near such self-possession.

All along, Kevin's instinct has been to mitigate Aideen drama as just another stage, even if they've been stuck in it for some months now – narky attitude, sulky mien, self-isolation. When talking to Mick, he jokingly refers to it as The Troubles. Kevin, an only child, sympathizes with the twin thing – the competition, the compelled sharing, the inevitable comparisons drawn, especially with two such different girls.

He takes comfort in recalling the other children's difficult periods, frustrating while you're in them but always fleeting, and only recognized as such in hindsight: Gerard's shit-kicking any kid who tried taking a toy off him, Nuala's refusal to eat anything but yogurt, Ciaran sucking on his dummy well beyond toddlerhood – it wasn't so long ago that they'd be putting on the kettle to warm up the grubby yoke so it was squishy and wet, just as their son liked it.

As he steers towards visitor parking, Kevin tries to quell a building anticipation – absurd and meaningless and wrong, he knows – to once again feast his eyes upon the school administrator, Ms Rose Byrd, whom he'd met when he'd come to register Aideen. Ms Byrd is a young blonde goddess, simultaneously athletic and voluptuous, in possession of perfect mini-globe breasts leveraged against an unlikely prim cream-coloured blouse, the juxtaposition of which had driven him wild and had made him behave in a quite possibly embarrassing manner. At that brief, initial meeting in her cramped office, Kevin thought he'd been rakish, blasé, cracking wise about his own youthful school days, namedropping a playwright he'd been only slightly chummy with, though her blank look made it clear she had no idea who he was talking about. Kevin later thought plenty about that blank stare and came to view his quippy flirting as obvious, lecherous, decidedly middle-aged.

Now he kills the motor and turns to his daughter. 'You know the boring tale of how Gran sent me to dairy-farm camp in Tipperary two hundred years ago?'

He stops when she responds with a deliberately wounding sigh. He had hoped she might take comfort, for once, in one of his only boyhood tales appropriate for adolescent ears, especially since so many thematic parallels exist: banishment, homesickness, despair. The truth is he had hated every sodding minute of that camp: tugging on cows' teats in the black dawn, cutting bog until egg-like blisters swelled up on his suburban hands, kipping on a cot in a barn with a smelly woollen army surplus blanket, two hours of mind-numbing Irish study a night, and the locals who blackballed the Dublin kids as city-slick gobshites. What's his point? Exactly why is he subjecting his daughter to a similarly miserable fate? Has he crossed over to the dark side of adulthood, which, before becoming a father, he'd made a solemn vow never to do? Decades later, doesn't his own somewhat rebellious youth remain the backbone of a freethinking nonconformist character? Hadn't he, after all, led a school boycott of Coke because of its support of apartheid? Hadn't he formed a band, The Right Wailing Willies, in his parents' garage? True, they'd only rehearsed a handful of times since two of them had no instruments and one was tossed out on the grounds that he secretly owned several Bee Gees albums. Still, it had all been in the spirit of bucking the system.

Now look at him: at fifty-three, he's driving his semi-problematic teenager to one of Dublin's most elite girls schools, paid for with the dregs of their savings account, because she's a bit ... what? Unhappy? Frustrated? Challenging? Look at his mediocre, not even real, problems, these tiny bourgeois anguishes he's accumulated. What is he *doing*?

'My point is,' says Kevin, 'you're exceedingly tough and outrageously capable.'

All morning, he's been trying to thwart a panicky sense that he must seize this landmark moment, one she'll always remember; he has only two years left to infuse her with character and love, redemption, affection, *parenting*. He reaches across through the artificial blast of heat to take his daughter's hand, an act which his own father, or mother, for that matter, never could, or would, have done. Mum's affection seems to have only come on with old age, and when he draws from his hazy impressions of his father before he'd taken ill, he thinks of the man as a distant, unknowable giant.

Kevin squeezes Aideen's fingers and says, 'I love you very much.'

Aideen slaps his hand away and opens the car door.

A bell rings and figures in blue skirts and jumpers with matching ties appear from every corner of the campus, as if they'd been waiting all along to spring from hidden spots. They haul heavy knapsacks, zigzagging among buildings in tight clusters, and Aideen, as if already resigned to the place, removes herself from the car and dutifully files in. Kevin drops her bags inside the residential building and rushes in to catch up with her.

As they approach the main office, he clears his throat, wipes moist palms down the front of his shirt, which, he notes, has a crust of fuck-knows on it, and thinks, *Don't be a tit.* He is acting the maggot, he knows. He is a married man. But, as it turns out, Ms Byrd's office is empty. He feels briefly devastated and then appalled at the intensity of his disappointment. This was to be, he sees, the highlight of his day, his week. After driving back to Dalkey, he has job sites to navigate, dry-cleaning to collect, and then lunch and various rounds of pick-ups and drop-offs and snacks and homework and hockey and soon enough dinner and his cycle, this humdrum rut of his, this *life*, continues.

Kevin pokes his head into the office beyond Ms Byrd's, which is the headmistress's giant chamber, with the idea to call out a cheery hello, but there is no sign of Ms Murphy, the eccentric hunchback who's led the school since the mid-century with a no-nonsense ethos, a fearsome figure in black robes with legs a razor has surely never traversed. Apparently, she's infamous for regaling her students with disturbing survival sagas, offering up bizarre survivalist tips, like using wax paper to wipe your bum if the bog roll's finished or turning your knickers inside out to get a second, sensible wear out of them. The thought of Ms Murphy's skivvies is too much to bear so early in the morning, so Kevin trudges on, his daughter still ahead of him, beaming out to all in her path fear and thinly disguised self-loathing in equal measure.

They quickly find the entire school gathered in the assembly hall listening, or not, to a heavy milkmaid of a woman reading off a string of dull announcements to a sea of blue. He spots Ms Byrd, who is mostly obscured behind a row of matronly staffers. Bad luck. An organ starts up accompanied by a frail, anaemic version of 'How Great Thou Art'. Only the old and the very young actually sing; the others lip-synch or stand sullenly in their class queues, gazing dreamily about the room and thinking of what? Boys? Their periods? The meaning of life? Fuck all, if Kevin knows. And what of his own daughter, who is probably terrified? He looks down each row but she's already blended in or skived off; she's nowhere to be seen, and so, he realizes with a pang, he can't even say good luck, goodbye.

11.
Millie

Millie, beside a modest fire in her grubby hearth, four fingers wedged like birds' wings beneath each armpit, gazes through the oversized picture window at her sopping garden. She can never regard the unlikely pair of palm trees that sway in the ceaseless Dublin winds without also imagining, farther down her beloved coast, the bustling harbour with its handsome sailboats and ships, the red-capped lighthouse, the craggy shoreline. Perhaps one of these days she'll walk the East Pier and treat herself to a 99 from Teddy's, the ancient ice-cream stand that still serves, as in her girlhood, its signature whipped ice-cream cone, a Flake bar stabbed into its side.

Now Kevin steps into the frame. When he sees Millie seeing him, he tugs an imaginary tie from above his head as if he's being choked by it. Beside him a tall, striking blonde keeps stride despite towering knee-length leather boots. She is rolling a suitcase behind her, which pierces Millie with fear. Is the woman *moving in*?

Of all the scenarios that troubled her fitful sleep last night, the one that Millie's home aide will be a prude come to hold her old-lady hand and tsk about the untidy kitchen and make Millie feel a guest in her own home worries her the most. Millie dislikes, in a Pavlovian way, goody-goodies, busybodies, librarians, primary-school teachers of a certain age, social workers and nuns (though she can tolerate a not overly preachy priest, the type who mightn't say no to a few fingers of whiskey now and again).

'Morning.' Kevin enters the house alone, which is curious, closes the door behind him, and delivers a perfunctory kiss onto her wrinkled cheek.

Millie takes his arm. 'I've got one perfect egg in my fridge and if you play your cards right I might even boil it for you.'

'Sylvia Phenning is here – she's just outside waiting to meet you.'

'Today?'

'Yes, well, I tried to ring but your phone appears not to be working.'

'Someone put it somewhere funny.'

'Have you checked inside the toilet?' He grins.

'That was a fluke.'

'Look, she's really very, very nice. You're going to love her.'

'Love someone bossing me around?'

'Not at all. You're the boss. But listen, you *are* planning to behave, right?' Kevin stoops slightly so that he can look directly at her. 'Right?'

Millie shrugs and thinks, *We'll see.*

Sylvia Phenning turns out to be young, wide of eyes, pale of skin, with impossibly perfect, large horse teeth and lips painted a tarty frosted coral.

'It's so nice to meet you!' she sing-songs. Half an arm's worth of golden bangles jingle and clatter as she extends a formal handshake to Millie. During it, Millie feels a tight, covert squeeze, as if Sylvia recognizes Millie's reticence, but that it's all going to work out.

'You brought your luggage?'

Sylvia taps her suitcase. 'Oh, this? Oh, I'm on my way to a friend's for the weekend.'

There's one crisis averted.

'You're American?' says Millie.

'How can you tell?' Sylvia replies and then over-laughs, which Millie perceives to be a very American thing: excessive laughter at one's own not-funny joke.

'Sylvia's from Florida,' Kevin announces as if this is a thing of great wonder.

'Miami?' says Millie, thinking of Blanche and Dorothy.

'No, it's a place called Clearwater. Not far from Tampa.'

'Oh, but it must be dreadfully hot in Florida! I couldn't bear that heat,' says Millie.

If Sylvia is offended, she doesn't show it. In fact, she smiles and stage-whispers conspiratorially, 'I know what you mean. You *always* need sunscreen.'

Sylvia seems to intuit the layout of Margate and moves in the direction of the sitting room, where she takes in the piles of rubbishy clutter, the shabby neglect, and goes immediately to the front window, oohing and aahing about the sea.

Millie hangs back. 'Just need to spend a penny.'

'Huh?'

She leaves the room wondering how much translation will be required.

On her way back, Millie catches sight of a luggage tag dangling from Sylvia's case and, curious, steps closer. It's a chestnut-coloured leather yoke, a beautiful piece. She peels back the cover flap: encased in the tag is a small lined slip of paper on which letters and numbers are written in a loopy script but, with no reading glasses in reach, Millie's too blind to make out the inky scratch.

She does not meditate on her next act, though she's momentarily choked by that very thought: how many decisions in her life have been made without terribly much deliberation? Ah well, she shan't deliberate on *that*. Her fingers hastily loosen the belted tag from the bag. Realizing she's without pockets, Millie slides the thing into her sizable décolletage, like a bawdy madam securing a tip for one of her girls. She smooths out her blouse and checks herself in the hall mirror. Who, for the love of Peter and Paul and all that's good and holy, is going to notice Millie Gogarty's bosom anyway, ample yet woefully obsolete? The young think you don't mind becoming postsexual, but the fact is, Millie knows, you do. Of course you do.

'This view is to die for!' says Sylvia when Millie returns. 'I think I could just look out here all day long. I love Ireland. I'm an Ireland-ophile.' She smiles. 'Is there a word for that?'

'Actually, it's Hibernophile,' says Kevin. 'Though I don't think I've ever heard anyone use it. Mum, did you want to tell Sylvia about your day-to-day schedule and all that good stuff?'

Kevin promptly vanishes to the back of the house, leaving Millie no choice but to point to the couch drawn up to the fire, the lone defence, except for a tartan blanket, which is in certain and dire need of a wash, against the room's chill.

'He likes to order me around,' says Millie.

'Aww! That's kind of sweet,' Sylvia drawls. 'He must really love you.' She warms her hands at the fire and says, 'Kevin mentioned maybe we should mix it up a little, schedule-wise? Like, I could do two mornings and two evenings? I could start at nine and give you breakfast?'

'That's too early. I'll still be in bed.'

'How about ten?'

'That's a bit late.'

'Oh, OK, well, we can figure out a good time – what about, what do you like to eat for breakfast?'

'I'm too old for breakfast.'

Sylvia gazes at Millie as if looking at a piteous animal lying injured in the gutter. 'Can I ask you something?' Though Millie does not respond, Sylvia continues. 'I'm kind of getting the sense that this isn't really your choice, is it? To have me come in and help around?' She leans forward and drops her voice, as if they are in cahoots. 'I totally get it, believe me. I'm sure I'd feel the exact same way. But you should know: I'm all about honesty, OK? You just tell me what you want me to do, I'll do as much or as little as you want. I'll let you kind of lead the way, OK? Does that sound alright?'

Millie, somewhat placated, nods. Sylvia does not seem outrageously offensive, nor judgemental, nor unkind. 'I suppose I should've offered you a cup of coffee.'

'I would love a cup of coffee,' Sylvia says. 'Why don't I come with you and you can kind of show me around?'

Seeing the kitchen from her guest's perspective, Millie, for the first time in yonks, becomes sharply aware of every surface covered, as it is, by another dirtier one: here, a dish crusted with bits of mutton and mash, there a mug with a stiffened tea-bag. Does the American think it wretched? Even the bowls and plates shelved in a closed cupboard, upon closer inspection, are as in need of a wash as any piled up in the sink or the long-defunct dishwasher. The stench is sour, the bulbs blown, the carpet mysteriously damp, always. On the cooker, where only one of four rings functions, an ancient saucepan sits filled with ancient burnt milk. It is to this pan that Millie heads, picking up the nearby wrench that she uses to leverage on the last working burner.

Sylvia doesn't blink. 'What a big space,' she says. 'You should see the kitchen where we're staying. It's teensy.'

'You're married?'

Sylvia barks in laughter, revealing a surprising flash of silver fillings on nearly every one of her chompers, like a fleet of board-game battleships. 'Oh God, no! Been there done that. No, no, I live with my sister's son, my nephew.'

'Oh? How old is he?'

'Seventeen.'

'Is he? Well, as a matter of fact, I have two beautiful granddaughters who happen to be sixteen years of age.'

'Twins? You're kidding. We should introduce them. He doesn't really know anyone here.'

Millie finds herself humming as she hustles to the jar of instant coffee and then back to the stove, in constant motion, bustling from kitchen to nook and back as if stopping might make Sylvia vanish. She listens as Kevin clomps back down the hall. He sidles into the kitchen doorway, winks at Sylvia, and actually grabs his mother as if in a waltz and dips her. Millie, game, gives a jaunty little kick with her left foot.

Later, alone in her Peter's room, Millie sheds her cardigan and blouse and brassiere, and Sylvia's luggage tag, which she'd long forgotten, falls to the floor.

12.

Aideen

Fifth year, Aideen's, occupies three rectangular dormitories on the second floor of Fair House or 'Fair', the residential building overseen by Miss Bleekland, a remarkably tall, stern, plain-faced automaton invariably dressed in a blouse and long checked skirt that does not fully mask an artificial leg, the mysterious cause of which provides endless fodder for gossip. She conveys disapproval not in tone, which rarely alters, but in cadence, a robotic, pronounced rising and falling of each sentence. Frequently spotted popping mints despite her exhaustive reiteration of the no food, no gum, no sweets rule, Bleekland never smiles, never even hints at mirth.

Each Fair House dormitory accommodates eight teens suffering from various degrees of homesickness, stress, exhaustion, eating disorder, constipation, or general discontent. Many boarders, it turns out, aren't Irish. By the end of Aideen's draining initial day, she'd hardly spoken to any girl in her dormitory, but counted at least four Spaniards, one Norwegian, and a couple of Asian and white girls from Zimbabwe and South Africa whose parents are ambassadors or business moguls or whatever it is that rich foreigners do, she thinks, that requires dumping their children in this soulless institution.

Neither of her meagre stowing areas – a drawer and a cupboard – is lockable, so Aideen's first task is to stash her contraband, which she's already regretting having brought. First off, she could get caught. Second, though she has in her possession enough alcohol to get herself and half the dorm langered, she has never actually drunk more than half a flute of champagne, and that was at Mum's recent birthday bash, so it hardly counts. In fact, she had disliked feeling so quickly disoriented, so out of her skin. One of the many things she respects about Clean-Cut is that after his California tour he returned home and declared himself 'straight edge' – no alcohol, no smoking, no drugs – though he then got massive abuse in the press about it. Straight edge in Ireland? *You must be fucking joking!* Anyway, the idea of her bringing out a bottle of vodka to the girls in her dorm would require the kind of confidence she does not currently possess.

At lights-out one evening, Aideen waits until all are asleep and then slips down the hall and tosses the vodka bottle into the enormous rubbish bin that sits at the end of the vast bathroom. The clunk of its landing is shockingly loud. A younger student whom she doesn't know shuffles sleepily past her and glances at Aideen, beer cans in her clutches. Aideen waits till the girl's gone and eases the rest of her loot gently into the rubbish.

Given the flimsy vinyl curtains that leave sizable gaps on either side of the stalls, Aideen has showered at Millburn less frequently and far more quickly than she normally would. This is another problem. There is not enough privacy in the bathroom, nor in her poky bed area. The only way to change your clothes – and there's no chance Aideen's going to risk revealing her woeful flat-chestedness to a pack of far more developed she-wolves – is to do so in the toilets. Aideen's been the recipient of not a few odd looks, and not much friendliness, as a result. All the Millburn girls have been together for years; no one's too interested in befriending the new girl who probably has BO, definitely has the odd spot (when it comes to girls choosing friends, looks matter more than anything), and, Aideen is aware, is an outsider.

Even after a week, she hasn't grown used to the ear-splitting series of bells that eject the Fair girls violently from slumber. They're all sleepy-eyed, half-dressed, yawning. With pale streaks of dawn slashing through the windows, the lot of them shuffle down to the dining hall with its hovering stink of fried sausage. The offerings, identical to yesterday's, include triangles of rubbery grilled bread beneath a glowing heat lamp, pitchers of 'juice' (diluted MiWadi) and a mess of fried eggs, gummy, like the toast, and gross.

'Total crap,' comes from a voice behind her.

Aideen, clutching her plastic tray, inches up in the queue and hears, from the same voice, louder now, 'My fucking beagle couldn't keep this down.'

Aideen turns to discover that the owner of this voice is, as she'd suspected, Brigid Crowe, a very pretty, racy, somewhat intimidating fifth year who sleeps two beds away from her. Brigid leads the post-lights-out confabs, boldly declaring herself to be a non-virgin and someone who's dabbled in hash. She is the same girl who Bleekland gave a terrifying earful to for her hammy snoring during prep, three torturous, silent hours of study that take place nightly in this same dining hall – one table per girl to deter talking, though a sophisticated network of note-passing appears in full force. Other than trying to fall asleep in a roomful of strangers honking, snoring, howling, babbling, crying and masturbating, prep is probably her most vulnerable time, when Aideen must squeeze tight her eyes and try to resist thoughts of what Mum and Dad and Ciaran and even Nemesis are up to.

Brigid, who's made it known she can get fake IDs for weekend clubbing at a tenner a pop, twirls a long swatch of blonde hair streaked fuchsia with four fake nails, the thumb having presumably fallen off.

'Yeah,' is the best Aideen can do, with a shy smile. 'I've been mostly just sticking to tea.'

'I'm dying for a smoke,' says Brigid. 'Want to go out after breakfast?'

Notwithstanding the fact that she doesn't smoke and hates the stink of it, Aideen nods, since this is the first invitation that's been issued to her.

'Hockey pitch?' Brigid grins naughtily, revealing a pair of deep, cheeky dimples. 'Sixth years go out there.' She studies Aideen brazenly. 'What's your name again?'

As Aideen grapples with the idea of openly smoking cigarettes in broad daylight on a pitch that can be seen from any school window, including the headmistress's, a younger girl timidly approaches them and explains that Aideen's wanted in Miss Bleekland's office.

'Oh, fuck,' says Brigid with sympathy and what Aideen hopes is a hint of admiration. 'Sounds like you're in the shit.'

'Aideen.'

'Sorry?'

'My name is Aideen.'

13.

Millie

Millie hears Sylvia letting herself into the house at nine o'clock, as she has done all week, with a key Kevin furnished – she is exceedingly punctual, efficient, proactive. By half past nine she's gently knocking on Peter's door with a tray, after which begins the glacially paced ritual of Millie getting dressed. Often, midway through, in her bra and raggedy knickers, Millie will sit on the bed and consider aloud the weather, the state of her socks, the state of world peace. Sylvia never rushes her. She is angelically patient.

Later in the morning, if the weather's decent, they'll stroll along the local roads and Millie will chat to each neighbour in turn, eager to introduce her new American friend, 'Sylvie' or, yesterday, just 'Sil'. Together they greet dogs, toddlers in prams accompanied by impossibly youthful mums or slightly frosty or confused foreign au pairs, the occasional stranger, and, more often than not, the O'Learys, a pair of kind bohemian sisters who never married, on their own daily constitutional.

One cold, wet afternoon during their second week together, the women are making their way to the promenade. Millie holds forth on a wide range of topics – the necessity of adding flaked almonds to the top of a chocolate cake, how Aideen's getting on at her new school, JJ's estranged son who only rings when he needs money, rheumatism, Millie's cup size. Throughout these soliloquies, Sylvia listens with a focus and earnestness, a genuine interest, which makes Millie feel practically smitten.

At a dip in the road, the American takes Millie's arm to steady her. Ahead, Millie hears, but can't yet see, the roar of a double-decker making its speedy way down the narrow, bendy, pavement-less stretch of road.

'To the wall!' Millie yells. 'The driver's a madman.'

The women, laughing at their self-imposed emergency, scramble to the edge of the road and flatten themselves dramatically against the ancient stone buttress. Millie catches sight of the sea, choppy and beautifully brutal. As the massive bus hurtles past them, she turns to see a blur of the driver waving to her and she salutes him in turn.

'You saved my life!' Sylvia laughs. 'Come on, we should head back anyway. I have a surprise for you.'

The surprise isn't at all what Millie had expected. It's not a plant or a tin of Rice Krispies treats, which Sylvia had brought on the first day. It isn't a thing at all. Sylvia takes Millie into the kitchen and opens the press beside the sink.

'Ta-da!'

Her cabinet is unrecognizable. Its bottom shelf has been scrubbed clean and lined with some sort of blue absorbent mat and every teacup and saucer and mug that Millie owns is not only sparkling clean, but all together, of a whole, and placed tidily one beside the next. On the shelf above, a perfectly neat stack of clean salad plates sits next to an equally neat stack of clean dinner plates atop a sheet of the same blue padding. Order, overwhelming and logical and stunning order, has been imposed.

With a sort of flourish, Sylvia reveals the next press. This, apparently, is where the drinking glasses are to be kept, and the next, which heretofore contained incongruous items, now houses her baking accoutrements though more beautifully. Flour and sugar are no longer in their paper packets; Sylvia's poured each into tall glass jars sealed with cork lids, like something out of a home design magazine. Next, the spices, and the pasta and rice, and the tinned goods, and so on.

Sylvia has disembowelled her kitchen.

Millie stands in the centre of the room, quite agape, tugged by fierce and contradictory emotions. Sylvia had no right to go poking into her things with neither permission nor warning and effect so radical a change. Exactly who did she think she was? She's just an employee, after all, paid under the table and only here a week or two. Furthermore, what did this unsolicited makeover say about Sylvia's judgement of Millie herself? That her kitchen was a tip? That she's a bit of a disaster? This line of thinking – that maybe Sylvia doesn't understand her, after all, or maybe Sylvia pities her – engenders in her a disproportionate sadness.

At the same time, Millie is experiencing a surge of gratitude. The woman had clearly spent hours on this project for the sole purpose of pleasing Millie, even if she hasn't fully succeeded.

Sylvia means well. And it's undeniable that her presses and all of her drawers – for the drawers, too, have been revamped – are far more functional and, yes, even superior.

'When did you do this?' she finally says.

'Oh no! You don't like it?'

'It's not that ...'

'I've been doing it little by little. I finished this morning while you were resting.'

Millie steps towards the first cupboard and stares in astonishment at a set of cups and saucers hand-painted with delicate pale roses climbing sage vines. 'Where did you ever unearth these?'

'Oh, those.' Sylvia smiles. 'Those were in one of the upstairs bedrooms, stuffed under the bed. I thought it was garbage at first because they were in a plastic, like, shopping bag.'

'I haven't laid eyes on that set for years.'

'It's so pretty! Let's use them for our tea.'

'I couldn't use those for every day.'

'Why not? Why not have your tea in the nicest cups you own? You deserve it.'

'Do I?'

'No one deserves it more.' Sylvia studies Millie, looks befuddled or cross, and fires off, as she tends to do, a sort of confrontational truth. 'You short-change yourself too much. You know that?'

These words move Millie, stirring in her an eagerness to undo her initial ungracious reaction. 'This must have taken you ages. It really does look smashing.' In fact, it does. She just might even thank Kevin for bringing this absolute dote into her home.

'Do you really like it?' says Sylvia. 'I love doing stuff like this. I was gonna do some of your other rooms too, if you don't mind?'

'I don't know why on earth I'd put those under a bed. What was I at?'

Sylvia picks up one of the delicate tea-cups and puts it on the tray. 'They look antique.'

'Like me.'

'Stop!' Sylvia chuckles. 'Really, though, you have so many nice pieces.' She flips on the kettle and points towards the French mantel clock on Millie's windowsill. 'Like this. My mom had a clock just like this. I bet it's worth something.'

'*That?* A thief wouldn't take it. It's always at least ten minutes behind.'

'But you could get it fixed. I could bring it in for you next time I'm going to town? You never know what kind of fortune you might be sitting on. You know that show, *Antiques Roadshow*? I'm not sure if it's on over here? But, like, every week, people bring in stuff from their houses, just like this clock or whatever, or a lamp or a vase they find in their basement, and they have, like, experts who tell you how much it's worth. Sometimes someone will have a painting they think is incredibly valuable from the 1800s or whatever, and it turns out to be a fake and worth nothing.'

'Ha!' says Millie. 'That would be me.'

Sylvia natters away as she brings the tea things over to the table and the two of them take their seats.

'But then someone else will bring in a chandelier they always thought was total junk,' she's saying, 'or, one time, this woman found earrings in her mom's jewellery box and they turned out to be worth, like, fifty thousand dollars.'

'Well now, that I have. My engagement ring. It's a family heirloom. I never wear it, mind you. I lost it the first day I ever had it, did you know that?'

Millie launches into a highly detailed, if inaccurate, saga. Peter and herself were picnicking outside a pub in Ballsbridge or maybe a field in Killester or another part of the city, perhaps, and she'd dropped the emerald ring in the grass and the two lovers combed the banks of the river until they gave up. But wouldn't you know, a kindly lady named Mrs Olive Keogh found it in a bin or maybe on the pavement outside a shop or on a café table beneath the sugar bowl. She'd posted a sign that read LOST RING and Peter, returning one last time to look the next day, spotted the poster and reclaimed the ring. And then Millie had invited Mrs Keogh to afternoon tea – scones, salmon sandwiches, the works – at the Shelbourne.

'Wow,' Sylvia says, 'thank God he found it. But I don't get it – like, why don't you ever wear the ring?'

'My fingers swell up, you see.'

'Oh yeah. Well, I hope you keep it in a safety deposit box or something.'

'Is that what they do in Florida?'

'Well, yeah, if it's worth a lot. You said it was valuable?'

'Very, but no, I wouldn't trust bankers. Too cute. I've got it here in Margate,' says Millie.

'But what if someone were to rob your house?'

'Don't worry: it's locked away, snug as a bug in a rug.' When there'd been a string of burglaries on the road years back, Peter had brought home a safe for their valuables. Her ring, tucked safely into one of Jolly Jessica's velvety monogrammed pouches, was one of the only possessions she'd ever bothered securing. 'And the key is hidden as well.'

'Oh, that's good, that's smart,' Sylvia says, adding a teaspoon of sugar into Millie's cup and stirring, without her even having to ask.

14.

Kevin

The tray on which Kevin has placed a pot of tea with a sugar bowl and milk jug and a poached egg and buttered toast and two paracetamol jitters with each footstep up the staircase of this beloved house that they'd wisely purchased long ago, before the market lost its mind. He nudges the door open with the toe of his runner, still damp from his soggy jog earlier this morning, and approaches the mess of the bed where lies, somewhere, his wife.

'I've got the cure to what ails you,' he says, setting the tray beside her.

'Nothing will cure this,' she says and then a swatch of her dark hair peeks up from the depths and she reveals herself: eyes gunked with slept-in mascara or kohl eyeliner, shadowed pools beneath them the colour of a cadaver pulled from the sea. Still hot, though.

'Good God, woman, what *did* you get up to last night?'

Kevin means this to sound jaunty, but a hint of resentment or jealousy or something dark has perhaps leached in.

'You're too good,' Grace says. She sits up against the headboard, the faint stain of egg yolk still evident, inducing in Kevin a mini-rage still. They'd fought over how best to handle Aideen's extreme act of vandalism, waffling between trying to understand her pain and wishing to punish her harshly. The matter was left unresolved, where it may likely stay – for the moment, anyway.

'Never let me out again,' she says, dragging the duvet up to her neck and rubbing her temples in quick, tight circles. Kevin mock-fusses over her, punching up pillows, and then pretends to get into an actual fight with one. He jams all the cushions behind her and then takes her head into his hands and massages it, like he used to. She moans in gratitude.

'Oh ... that's brilliant. No, please! More! I'm dying.'

'What time did you get in?' he asks, though he knows full well that she had stumbled through the front door well after two and had gorged on some sort of drunken snack – a toasted cheese and tomato sandwich, by the looks of it – before falling onto their bed, fully clothed, and immediately and violently snoring.

'No clue. One?' She brings a trembling cup and saucer to her lips. 'Oh, shit.' She jerks up, sloshing tea. 'Shit. I forgot. Someone from Millburn phoned the office late yesterday but I never got the chance to ring back.'

'What with a drinks party and all ...' He smiles to show he's joking and then he winces. Wasn't there a time – oh, yes, nearly two decades ago, that ridiculously carefree period before they started breeding – when he'd never had to signify a joke? He would just crack wise. Nowadays, he feels the need to raise an eyebrow, shrug a shoulder, anything to explain, or offset, or soften the blow of edge lest his words be misconstrued by those he loves.

'I'm on it,' he says. 'Her Majesty is requesting all sorts of toiletries. Hair gel or lubricant.'

'Don't even,' Grace says. She gulps down the tablets with the dregs of her tea and then chops her egg up with the side of a fork. 'This is lovely.'

He can hardly believe that this lie flew. Aideen, aggressively unprissy, has not requested toiletries, would never do such a thing. The truth is that, in short order, his daughter has managed to get into trouble, though Bleekland, being the sort of sadistic schoolmarm who gleefully relishes witnessing the parental reception of bad news first-hand, had refused to reveal any information over the phone despite his pressing. She had just asked him, firmly, to meet with her first thing. Kevin has a strong notion to douse this little ember himself, without his wife's knowledge. A fresh installation of mayhem so quickly following the wreckage of their painting will inevitably lead to further stress. At least, this is how he inwardly justifies his lack of forthrightness; of course, other motives are at play.

'Whatever it is, can it wait until Friday?' says Grace. 'Are you alright? You look knackered.'

'Fine. Actually, I'm heading over there today. I've got to go into town anyway.'

'Oh?'

'Mick has a line on a job,' he says. 'It's a long shot. Some digital nonsense I'm not qualified for.'

'Would you not take a course?'

Kevin resists snapping at this, since this is not the first time she's proffered such simplistic advice.

'Nice to have a prospect, anyway,' she says, 'but, you know, it could take a bit.'

'It's already been a bit.'

'Not to worry. Listen,' Grace says, 'don't count me in for dinner. I'm going to be late tonight.'

'Again?' He can't help it.

'No choice,' she says, frowning. 'Believe me, I'd much rather be here.'

'Would you?'

'You're not serious?' She half-smiles, curious or befuddled, and heads off to the shower.

After pressing his best trousers, Kevin spends a good ten minutes trying to locate his sole belt, a sad worn and woven thing he eventually finds dangling from Ciaran's bed railings decapitating a teddy bear. Christ, is nothing of his his? In the loo, he rejects a splash of Hollister Jake, given him by his kids for some birthday, sealed still, as being too obvious. Oh, he really is the village idiot. He is a man in his middling years – a married man, a relatively contented married man, yes? – foolishly sprucing up for a woman at least a quarter-century his junior who may also be married and who probably has not registered his existence. To say nothing of the odds that he will even come across Rose Byrd today. His appointment with Bleekland is in Fair House, and Ms Byrd's office is in the school building. Not that this proximity has stopped his brain all morning from attempting to concoct some plausible excuse to stop by the main office and drink her in: the speck of dark mole in the north-east corner of her upper lip, the generous curve of hips beneath her pencil skirt, the wet eyes with a hint of naughty.

As luck would have it – or the sheer force of subliminal will – Kevin spies Rose Byrd while sitting outside Bleekland's office contemplating the trio of telephones attached to the wall in front of him. The object of his lust strides unwittingly towards him, her eyes scanning a substantial pile of file folders she's clutching, cheeks flushed rouge from her brief steps out of doors between campus buildings. She's sporting a pair of sexy black cat-shaped eyeglasses he's not seen before and a blue wrap dress that covers and yet reveals her, and which he immediately imagines unfurling from her in slo-mo. She is clad, like every woman in Dublin, in dark leather boots to the knee, hers adorned with thick silver grommets and zippers that run from ankle to mid-calf. He would like to unzip them. He would like to peel them from her legs and work on whatever's beneath. Tights? Suspenders? Bare skin?

'Mr Gogarty,' she says, skidding to a halt.

When she smiles at him with those lips, the colour races to his cheeks and the blood to his groin. He is fourteen years of age. Though he longs to transmit a suave sense of detachment, Kevin, instead, gawks dumbly at Rose Byrd. It's like he's ingested a pill or a tab of E; there's something about her that hits his bloodstream – he feels *good*.

'Ms Byrd, how are you keeping?' He's unsure as to etiquette – a nod feels too cold. A kiss? Good God, no, not a kiss. A small wave? Too awkward, for she's upon him now. He opts for a handshake.

'Oh,' she says. 'You're frigid!' and tosses off a husky laugh.

She, however, is not: her hand is warm, it's hot, and this, his first skin-to-skin contact with Rose Byrd, Millburn School Office Administrator, is pure sex voltage, or potentially mind-blowing sex voltage, and it surges through him in a dizzying flash.

'How is Aideen getting along?' she asks.

Behind Rose, Kevin suddenly spots that old battle-axe Bleekland limping her way through her absurdly large, self-important lair towards them. In seconds, he will have missed his chance.

'Grand,' he says, ushering Rose Byrd forward as if to speak in confidence. 'Listen, I'm wondering whether it might be possible to have a word with you after I'm through here?' He widens his eyes comically, as if the thought of his meeting with Bleekland is all terror. 'Just an administrative thing ...'

'Oh?' Her lovely head tilts, flummoxed, towards his. A musky, expensive whiff engulfs Kevin, puts him in mind of Brown Thomas and the sales staff there who spend their days spritzing women as they breeze through on their lunch hours in search of seductive props. Ms Byrd says nothing more, continues to hold her face at an angle, earnest and curious, forcing him to forge ahead with his nonsense cover story.

'I wanted to see about setting up pocket money, some account for Aideen for after school. She says the girls go up to the Spar and buy sweets.' Then, because her gaze unnerves Kevin and her presence obliterates the filter he might otherwise pass his words through, he adds recklessly, 'Though I suspect that's not all they buy.'

Whatever the shite does he mean? And more to the point, what must the lovely Ms B *imagine* he means? What strange or illicit thing can one even purchase at Spar after all?

'Oh, you mean cigarettes?' She nods knowingly – she is cool, he sees, on top of all the rest, she is smooth – and he's afloat once again. Did her cells, he wonders, surge from that handshake too? 'But actually that would be Miss Bleekland's turf,' she says. 'She takes care of all Fair House matters. And here she is now.'

'Right,' he stammers and his mind feels like a mess of scrambled eggs as he tries, the old bag's hand now poised on the door handle with her face flat and unreadable as a piece of particle board, to come up with some other legitimate reason to cast eyes on Rose Byrd again, and soon. It must be soon.

'Actually, I meant to ask,' she says, righting an earring back that has presumably loosened and turning to him a final time, 'did you receive the orientation packet? I thought I'd posted it, but then I noticed this morning there was one lying on my desk, and since Aideen is our only new student this term I thought maybe I'd forgotten?'

'I'll come by and nab it on my way out,' he says, suppressing the urge to pump his fist in victory.

'Oh, no need. I'll send one of the girls over with it, no worries.'

'Mr Gogarty,' says Bleekland, no trace of humanity on her sour set of features. 'Please come in.'

'I'll pop round after this,' says Kevin. 'Want to say hello to Aideen anyway.'

'The children are in class now, Mr Gogarty,' Bleekland scolds. 'They are not permitted to have visitors until school hours are over.'

Kevin could brain the old witch. But then Rose Byrd, with a trace of mischief, shocks him into a state of bliss. 'I'll have the materials at the main office if you want to swing by when you're through here?' She's smiling and, when Bleekland turns, she sticks her tongue out and winks at him. *Winks. At him.*

Kevin Gogarty fairly dances into Bleekland's office. 'Ready when you are,' he says.

Behind the closed door, Bleekland delivers, in bizarrely staccato blasts of information, the following narrative: his daughter purloined from his own home supply copious amounts of alcohol, including a quite decent bottle of vodka, which he can't believe he hadn't noticed missing. Kevin's first thought: this is the type of prank, frankly, that he himself had pulled in his own adolescence, though he'd usually had the good sense not to get caught. The astonishing part? The drink was discovered, Bleekland explains, *because Aideen was trying to get rid of it. Another student witnessed her throwing it, undrunk, out!* Aideen, thinks Kevin, is surely the most curious of all his brood.

'We have a no-tolerance rule regarding alcohol in Fair House, as I'm sure you can appreciate. When this rule is broken, when a girl' – here Bleekland's voice becomes agitated – 'brings alcohol into the residential building, it is a very serious matter.'

'Mrs Bleekland –'

'Miss.'

'Beg your pardon. Miss Bleekland, the truth is, Aideen's a good girl, she really is, she's a very caring person, but she's been having a hard time lately. She's a twin and there's been some ... disagreeing, and her brother left home recently – he's away at college and she misses him. And her best friend moved to Scotland last year. Look, I reckon this whole episode was just a sort of symbolic rebellion, you see. She didn't want to come to boarding school. She has a hard time fitting in. She probably thought it would help her in that capacity, make her seem cool. Terrible judgement, yes.'

Bleekland's face does not shift in any way. 'It's possible that Millburn isn't the right school for Aideen, Mr Gogarty. You probably don't know that the only friendship she's struck up is with the single-most troubled girl in fifth year, a girl who is rarely allowed home.'

Kevin, not remotely surprised, says, 'I'm really surprised. Look, I have to say, I think she just needs to settle in. I think she'll do splendidly here, given the chance.'

'Whether she was acting out of rebellion, as you say, or because she had every intention of drinking an entire bottle of vodka and a number of cans of lager' – here again the rising perturbation – 'for which the school would be held liable, you see, the rules are the rules.'

'I understand, I do, of course,' Kevin says, thinking, *Fuck, they're going to expel her.* 'But would you consider the fact that she was throwing it away? Obviously she came to her senses, regretted what she'd done, and decided, in the end – a bit late, I'll give you that – but decided nonetheless to do the right thing, which was to not drink it, and to not share it with the other girls, to not do the wrong thing.' He has an image of Aideen climbing out of his car the first day they'd pulled up here, probably scared shitless, but still brave, resilient. 'Please let that be what you judge, and not her initial mistake. She'll do better, I promise.'

15.
Millie

Donnelly's is no longer a viable destination for the bits and pieces, which leaves Millie no choice but to head to the dreaded supermarket, a goliath for the modern hard-core food shopper. Erected in the pompous early noughts, the shop looms crass and superior just off a busy roundabout, its armies of carts gleaming and symmetrical beside the grand set of automatic double doors, its smug self-pay car park encased in a translucent pod.

'Paying for parking in my own village,' she harrumphs to Sylvia. Millie hasn't bought a week's worth of groceries in months – nay, years. As she once happily explained to a supermarket employee after gawking at the price of a pound of salmon (pulled from the harbour!) she's offended by the shop, and if she's being honest (which, in truth, she often is *not*), Millie is philosophically opposed to such a grand show of decadence as toting home a great gaggle of plastic bags filled with more food and drink than is necessary. Millie Gogarty is a survivor, a citizen of the Republic of Ireland whose mother clutched her brown ration books doled out in wartime with the triumphant sense of rising to the occasion; she is a great believer in *making do*. She makes do, on a weekly basis, with a pint of milk, a sliced pan, rashers and butter and tea, a jar of jam, and the odd egg.

'Look out!'

Millie snaps back from her reverie to find her trusty Renault is smashing with an almighty volume into a concrete wall that runs the periphery of the car park. With a loud crush of metal, she and Sylvia scream in unison. The car, in its momentum, bounces backward into the direct path of a passing motorcyclist.

'Watch out!' yells Sylvia. 'Stop the car!'

Sylvia yanks the handbrake, which immediately halts them. The biker swerves away, nearly loses his balance, and then rights himself just in time to flip Millie off.

'Fucking eejit!' he screams loud enough for shoppers returning their empty trollies nearby to hear. 'Get off the bleedin' road!'

'Oh my God,' says Sylvia. 'Are you OK?'

Even for a woman like Millie, who craves diversions of almost any kind, this is a lot. Adrenaline courses through her like she might explode with it, and her left hand feels welded to the gear stick. She releases her fingers, one by one, from their mighty grip. The good news is there's no pain in her body – toes, limbs, fingers, all check.

'Mrs Gogarty?'

Millie rips the keys from the ignition as if they're to blame. 'I'm OK,' she says. 'Are you OK?'

This is her third minor accident of late (though she plans to share that particular data with no one) and each has given her a case of momentary madness, a jittery out-of-body experience that her physical being is unravelling.

'That was … oh my God,' says Sylvia. 'We should check for damages.'

Millie gets shakily out of her Renault and the two women stand at the front of it, bearing witness. The bumper is bent to bits and the front left light is decimated. Shards of translucent plastic are splayed across the tarmac and black angry scuffs like graffiti markings are scrawled on the wall in front of them.

'You sure you're alright?' the American says.

Millie nods, but her mind's already jumping forward to consequences. She's trying to think lucidly about priorities here; she mustn't muck this up. 'Listen,' she says. 'Kevin can't find out about this. I'm in enough trouble already.'

'It's not that big of a deal,' says Sylvia. 'Just some minor damage. At least no one was hurt.'

'But he'll use this against me. He keeps threatening to take the car keys off me.'

A delivery truck backs into the loading dock with its insistent reversing beeps while shoppers push laden trollies towards people carriers, the world around them carrying on.

Sylvia says, 'Why don't we – maybe we should get some coffee somewhere? What about that nice café we went to last week?'

'Any innocent person could drive into something, you see? Jolly Jessica has had her share of dents and bumps. Even Kevin has.'

'Of course. I really wouldn't sweat it.'

'Please.' She stares at Sylvia. 'You've got to promise me you won't tell him.'

'The thing is, I give a, like, report each week to him, you know, what's happening, where we go, what you're eating, and whatnot.'

Millie sniffs. This is the first she's heard of a report. Things on paper always lead to trouble. 'I'd like to see those,' she says.

'Oh no, it's not – it's just a phone call, I mean. Like a five-minute phone call.'

For the first time, Millie turns with suspicious eyes to Sylvia. Is the woman spying on her, reporting all sorts of gossip to the very person who should be privy to none of it?

'Kevin just wants to make sure you're OK.'

'He most certainly does not,' says Millie. 'I think Kevin's trying to put me in a nursing home, you see. He thinks I shouldn't be living alone and this'll just give him more ammunition.'

'OK, hold on,' Sylvia says. 'Let me just think for a minute.' In the quiet that follows, Millie's panic does not dissipate. 'OK, let's just say for a sec that I don't tell Kevin.'

'Yes, yes!'

Sylvia looks pained. 'If he found out, I'd be fired.'

'He won't. He'll never find out.'

'I don't know …'

'I could pay you extra.'

Sylvia jerks her head in surprise. 'What? No. I couldn't – I would never do that.'

'Oh but no,' says Millie. 'Even if you don't tell him – he'll still find out, won't he? He'll see the car's not in the drive. It'll take days to repair.'

'It's not that much damage. It won't take days.'

'This is Ireland,' says Millie. 'Everything takes days.'

'What if we –? No, no.'

'What?'

'Oh my gosh.' Sylvia frowns. Even frowning she's quite attractive. 'Well, I was just thinking ... what if we tell Kevin it was me? That I was the one driving?'

It takes Millie a moment to fully absorb the kindness, the loyalty, the selflessness, of this offer. 'You would do that?'

'I'm not gonna say I'm totally comfortable with –'

'That's a brilliant idea.'

'You think? It might work? But it would have to be our secret.'

'Cross my heart.' Millie puts a hand on her sternum.

Sylvia says, 'I mean, you shouldn't be in a nursing home. That's crazy. And if Kevin finding out about a little car crash will help his case, then why should we do that?'

Millie throws her arms around Sylvia, considers delivering a giant, grateful kiss onto the woman's neck, but decides against it. Into her shoulder, she says, 'What did I do to deserve you?'

Sylvia, mid-hug, says, 'Don't be silly.' Then she takes Millie by the shoulders and says, very directly, 'You're awesome. You are an awesome person. Never forget that. But top secret, right?'

'If I breathe a word, you have my permission to take me into the town square and stone me.'

'Town square!' Sylvia laughs.

'Come for dinner on Friday? You and your nephew.'

'Oh, that's not necessary.'

'I insist!'

Millie can phone up the mechanic later to come and collect the car. For now, she links her arm in Sylvia's and heads into the supermarket, a dinner menu – roast beef, mash, green beans – already presenting itself.

16.
Kevin

Kevin's job interview is at Starjar.com, an Irish offshoot of a British celebrity entertainment and media fiefdom. The offices take up the second floor of a bank gone under just off Grafton Street. Kevin sits in the swanky waiting area rubbing his not yet blatantly middle-aged head. Clammy-palmed, funky-breathed (tooth decay having been reduced to lowest-level priority in the general scheme of things), he's been waiting nearly an hour. This job – *deputy* banana – let's just say he can see it now: a singular staff (literally), crippling non-family-man hours, a shoestring budget, pick-ups and write-arounds, the writers being unpaid interns exchanging free labour for a by-line. Which means hack jobs, which means rewrites, which means more work, which means utter shite.

Still. It's the only editorial position Mick knows of in the entire country and Kevin is singularly qualified for it. He's worked for celebrity magazines, here and abroad, his entire career. He knows every bit of the industry – from writing arresting headlines to finessing colourful interviews with reluctant stars to choosing the of-the-moment cover subjects who will most register on newsstands. Kevin must demonstrate this all today; he must wow Starjar despite his aversion to self-pitching, the whole endeavour being embarrassingly obvious and about as attractive to him as spending the morning sitting on a damp cardboard box begging for coins in a city alley.

No one here, save one builder milling about with a drawn stubbled face, which brings a comradely surge of comfort to Kevin, looks older than twenty-two. Hipsters in coloured drainpipe jeans and grey infinity scarves and dense, square librarian glasses drift in and out in a blasé fashion, as if the world were theirs. Or maybe it's the same hipster entering and exiting.

Presiding over the front desk is one such fashionista – black net shirt over a black lace bra, bare full lips, two thin silver discs sliced through a coffee-stained tongue – who occasionally rests soulless eyes upon Kevin as he fakes his way through a stack of glossy design 'zines, tapping his 'good' (gangrene onset) shoes against a hand-tufted, wavy-patterned designer rug that is doubtless the equivalent of a year's worth of car payments.

The hopeful jubilation Kevin had experienced at dawn – donning his suit (*beyond* obsolete, he winces), fixing himself a cappuccino – has waned considerably during his sixty minutes in this room with its absurd plastic-moulded, ass-numbing chairs and blank canvases in identical blond-wood frames hung in neat, symmetrical rows. Finally, the desk girl removes her ridiculous telephonic headgear and rises, summoning him with a bored two-finger wave. Nearby, a drill or floor sander or machinery of some sort whirrs at great volume. The whole place seems under construction, in stark contrast to, say, Kevin, who currently feels as if he's deconstructing, or at least on a slow-mo daily unravelling.

He squeezes the handles of his portfolio, reassured by its presence and heft. All weekend, between carpools and cooking, absent Grace (in the West of Ireland for a team retreat), he'd culled twenty years of clips down to a handful of high-gloss sleeves and sandwiched them between two pieces of soft, worn black Florentine leather. Vetting the portfolio was the first creative work he'd done in ages (unless indulging in silly extramarital fantasies counts).

Kevin had never actively sought a career in celebrity journalism; he'd meandered into it. After university, he knew exactly the things that did not interest him – banking, law, medicine, sales – but he hadn't a bog about what did. When he and Grace moved to London just after college, Kevin had tried his hand at stand-up again. He soon realized he lacked the perseverance, the hunger, required, but he did like writing the bits. He liked writing. Grace would head out to work – she was already climbing the ranks at British Airways then – and he'd sit in their sunny flat in Clapham South with a carafe of French-pressed coffee and twenty Marlboros and write sentences and then go back and rewrite them, again and again, trying to make them better until they weren't hideous, until they were alright actually, and the carafe beside him was empty. Writing presented problems he felt he could solve.

Grace was Kevin's first, and only, reader. She was outrageously supportive, as he was of her meteoric rise in BA's marketing and promotions department. They wouldn't put it thus, but they were a team. She urged him to submit to literary magazines (he didn't) and to attend author readings around the city (he did). During summer weekends, they'd buy meat samosas and a bottle of rosé from the shops and arrange their borrowed deckchairs on the common and talk until it grew dark. Grace would read aloud from *Time Out* and they'd choose an affordable outing or two for the following week – a spin through the National Portrait Gallery (free) followed by coffee in the ancient crypt at St Martin-in-the-Fields just across the way, or a Brixton poetry slam (two quid) or fringe plays that took them all over the city. The last show he remembered seeing, *The Shadow of a Gunman* for a fiver in a Kilburn community centre, made him homesick.

Meanwhile, a friend of theirs from university was moving to Australia and offered Kevin his job, the oxymoronic position of fact-checker at one of the most vilified tabloids at the time. He'd gone on to spend years at various gossipy magazines, endlessly begging, cajoling, hair-pulling, brainstorming, and indulging in carefree, heavy after-hours drinking. He'd enjoyed the work, and the camaraderie of it, immensely, and while it wasn't creative writing exactly, it was writing – and he was getting paid. Some nearly twenty years later, his career had ended in sixteen head-spinning high-wire months at the top of an Irish masthead when, due to budget cuts, he'd been summarily laid off.

Despite the ubiquitous presence of industrial-sized bin bags sagging and spilling forth like entrails and a definitive air of unsettledness about the place, the boss's nameplate has already been hung outside his frosted-glass door in large font: ROYSTON CLIVE, PUBLISHER. According to the kind of catty details one might find in one of Kevin's now-defunct publications, *Tattle Tales*, Clive is a colourful and brilliant, if insufferable, queen from the London exurbs with hundreds of thousands of Twitter followers and a famously decadent double town house in Mayfair. Apparently if you swipe at a screen on the wall, the sofa heats up your bum.

Kevin sighs, envisions his grandchildren plugging in their easy chairs or charging their cushions. All this crap has already seeped poisonously into too many corners of his own household, eradicating key signs of his times. The thermometer to check whether the turkey's done, the pump he uses to fill the bike tyres. Even their wine opener requires batteries and lights up as the cork ascends, like a UFO lifting off the earth. Why every minor irritation and inconvenience must be conquered, mapped out in some Silicon Valley office among a precocious group of twenty-year-old hypereducated, overly indulged, grossly entitled techies, a prototype created, a market interrogated, capital raised, a product 'rolled out', is beyond his fathoming. Where is the challenge, the spontaneity, of solving simple problems with common sense? Chilly arse? Get a blanket, put a briquette on the fire. Better still: go to bed, be thankful you're alive to feel the cold.

The door swings open and out steps a petite bearded, round-nosed man-child who calls to mind a twenty-something Papa Smurf.

'Kevin? Did I keep you? So sorry. Royston Clive. Come in, please.' Clive smiles but in it Kevin reads an unmistakable whiff of insecurity. 'Sit down, please. Has that little minx already fled? Oh, Gemma!'

The girl, Gemma, returns.

'Hold all my calls. Unless it's Ted, in which case tell him to kindly go and fuck himself with a rusty stick.'

Clive cracks up while Kevin, trying to mask his instant revulsion, settles into a black leather Eames knock-off, or possibly an original. Kevin is not a tall man, yet here he feels like a giant in a dwarf's lair. Royston plops himself into a rolly chair behind a massive alpha desk and swivels towards a slick silver laptop and begins typing. With no eye contact, he says, 'So, Kevin Gogarty, what makes you tick?'

'Sorry?'

'An American – a rather famous filmmaker, actually, you'd know his name – once asked me that at a dinner party in some Hollywood Hills mansion. Can you imagine? I said, "Dinner companions who don't ask dull questions." Would you care for coffee? Gemma!'

Gemma reappears, leaning against the doorjamb like a moody adolescent undecided whether to bother sticking around for the grown-ups' convo, which has proved, thus far, to be a total yawn.

'Two coffees, pronto. And bring some of those jam-biscuit thingies. Even though I really shouldn't. But I've got Davey today at five, don't I?'

Gemma frowns and slinks off. Clive leverages himself against the edge of his desk and pushes off from it, whirling past a corporate gift basket bursting with the sort of impersonal, inedible crap – dried-fruit cookies, honey-coated pistachios – that would only be unsealed and consumed in an apocalyptic scenario.

The bearded pip-squeak arrests his chair, peels open a square of Nicorette, and says, 'So tell me this: what makes a great magazine? In ten words or less.'

'I'm Irish.' Kevin summons up a winning smile. 'I can't possibly describe anything in ten words or less.'

'Give it a whirl.'

As if you could nutshell an entire industry in a top-ten list. Typical clueless vexing youthful little tit. Lacking any sense of nuance or modesty, thinking he knows everything and if he doesn't, then it's hardly worth knowing. What is it with this global proclivity – he vaguely feels America or the UK is to blame – to simplify and wrap up or water down instead of recognizing the complicated and inherent fucked-upness of life?

'Let's see,' Kevin says. 'Stunning photography. Revealing interviews ... top celebrities ... access to the big names, of course, the ability to pitch –'

'Oops! You're out of words.'

Kevin would like to reach across the desk and pummel Royston Clive's cocky mug with his ridiculous Father Christmas facial hair – sparse in some bits, more Galway fishmonger than publishing guru. He takes in the kid's three-hundred-quid shirt and his glittering ferret eyes and knows he's just the kind of tight arsehole who'd throw his credit card at a bartender and loudly announce drinks on him, and then spend the rest of the night reminding all within earshot of his largesse.

'I'm joking. But you did skip one,' Clive says.

'Did I?'

'Eyeballs.'

'Sorry?'

'How many people are seeing the ads.'

'Oh, but that's not really my –' Kevin struggles to remove the superciliousness from his voice. 'That would fall more under your area of expertise, wouldn't it? Church and state and all that.'

'No,' Clive replies with a wicked glint and begins fiddling with his phone. He seems unable to sit still. Maybe he's on something. This generation is always on something. 'Not here it doesn't.' He taps the screen of his mobile and screams, 'Are you handpicking the fucking beans?' and taps again, grinning at Kevin for approval. 'Without the ads, what's going to support your media content?'

Media content! Would you ever fuck off? The little pissant winks at Kevin and removes the gum, now a hardened cement-coloured blob, like putty, and sticks it directly onto the beautiful teak grain of his mid-century desk where, Kevin now notices, others have been abandoned. It's a war-torn landscape of discarded Nicorette mines.

Hands locked behind his head, Royston Clive spends the next ten minutes holding forth on the 'ingredients' of a successful celebrity news blog 'cocktail'. He follows this up with his own immodest saga of success, most of it utter bollocks, shamelessly interweaving erstwhile celebrities – one of the Spice Girls, the Duchess – into every tall tale. As in, 'Fergie once arrived to a photo shoot with a royal wrangler and twenty others in her entourage demanding piping hot Moroccan mint tea and fresh mangoes. In fucking Fulham!'

Kevin hopes he appears thoughtful and engaged, but wonders how desperate he really is. Could he actually arrive here every morning and work for such an absolute dickhead? Gemma returns with a pot of tea and cups and saucers and a plate of Jammie Dodgers.

'I said coffee!' Clive roars and smacks his desk.

'Oh,' says Gemma.

'You're fired, you lesbian!' he screams and laughs.

Gemma rolls her eyes and leaves.

'OK, seriously, I'll tell you, though, here's the thing.' Clive picks up an emery board and begins sanding down a thumbnail covered in transparent glitter varnish. 'I'm not concerned remotely with your taste.' Clive's phone buzzes. 'It's Andrew from that reality show. You know the one with the hot unibrow? You should see his ass.'

Kevin ekes out a faint chuckle as Clive pushes away his phone. 'Look, I know your work, I'm familiar. I'm a fan.'

'That's kind of you to say,' says Kevin, reaching for his portfolio and cursing himself for leaving out the black-and-white studio shot of a shirtless and well-oiled David Beckham on a Harley gazing moodily off-camera. That alone, he sees now, would have landed him the job. 'I brought along some samples—'

'My problem,' says Clive, tossing the nail file aside and pouring tea into his own cup, 'is your lack of digital experience.'

'Right, well, yes, I did want to address that. The bulk of my career has been in print, that's true. But at *Tattle Tales*, as you know, we had a companion website that did really very well, a launch that I headed up.'

'Two thousand unique visitors per week. Put it this way: chlamydia.com probably gets more eyeballs.'

Kevin fake laughs at this lunatic, though there is truth to his words. Kevin had resisted the digital stuff from the start, nearly lost his job over a bitter dispute in which he was supposed to do lots more work online for the same money.

'There's a big difference between print and online,' Clive waxes on. 'I'm not talking about breaking a story a month or every two weeks. I'm talking about breaking stories *all day long*. It's a completely different beast. And, really, you know way more about print media than I do. I've never even worked in print,' he says, as if print is a huge pile of dog shite tracked into a just-installed lounge carpet. 'But obviously it's much slower. You have, what? Three weeks, a month to develop a story. You're not *breaking news*. I mean, news is cheap now – it's fucking free! I put a story on the site that some fading singer's breast implants have dropped out of her housecoat or Hollywood's most hetero movie star is actually getting rim jobs from his poolboy in Beverly Hills. That's old, that's everywhere, in twenty minutes. You want to talk viral? Just look at the Jamie Grosnance mess.'

Jamie who? Kevin nods knowingly, though unease flutters in his gut. The truth is he's receded somewhat from the celebrity news cycle in the past month or two.

'May I?' Kevin says, reaching towards the teapot.

Clive chuckles evilly. 'I mean, I'm the last to judge illicit activity, you know, a bit of blow or whatever, but that night was off the charts. And the text messages? You can't make that shit up.'

Ought he to fake his way through and then go home and bone up on pop culture – twenty minutes' chat with Nuala or Aideen ought to cover it – or cop to being out of the loop, which would almost certainly tank his prospects? Kevin smiles. 'Better than fiction.'

'OK, so you're the editor, the Grosnance story comes in, you have to put it up live in sixty seconds. What's your headline?'

Kevin's mind races even as he tries to project calm. Is Jamie Grosnance a film star, a reality TV show star, a YouTube star, a pop star? Gun to his head, he'd guess music but it's too risky to guess. He decides to go general so as to avoid making a consummate arse of himself. 'Maybe a play on the drugs … something like "Jamie's blown it again".'

Clive looks with mild derision at his interviewee. 'It wasn't coke, though. It was crystal meth.'

'Ah, right,' Kevin mumbles. 'How about …' He's blanking. '"Bad boy on a bender."'

Given he's had milliseconds to produce it, Kevin feels this isn't half-bad, but Clive looks decidedly underwhelmed. He picks up his phone and begins typing and says, 'Listen, I appreciate you coming in, but I don't think this is the right fit.'

That's it? He's ruined his chance because of one uninspired, off-the-cuff headline? 'I'm sure I could come up with something better.'

'You're fine.' Clive stands up, yet he seems barely taller than when seated.

Kevin unfurls his runner's legs, gets to his feet. 'Fair enough,' he says. 'You wouldn't mind, would you, if I took one for the road?' He reaches for the final Jammie Dodger.

Clive regards him with a mixture of curiosity and pity. 'Go for it.'

Kevin stuffs the biscuit into his mouth. Clive is already screaming for Gemma. As Kevin nods a goodbye from the door, his interviewer grins and says, 'Nothing personal, mate, but I need someone who's up on all this shit. Jamie Grosnance is not a bad boy. She's not even a boy.'

17.
Millie

Friday at dusk, before her guests arrive, Millie finds herself crouching in her garage on the hunt for her secret stash of smokes. Who she hides them from, or why she bothers, she hardly knows. Millie hasn't broached the topic of smoking with Sylvia – being American, Sylvia is presumably puritanical regarding carcinogenics. Millie keeps her vice from Kevin too, given all the tedious abuse he's hurled upon her after he himself quit, and then again following her tumour scare two years ago (an unsightly lump the size of a walnut jutting from her chin, biggish but benign).

Millie eyeballs the rickety stepladder, which she employs to root out gunk from gutters every decade or so – not going to part with two hundred bob for *that* – and climbs gingerly to the top step and feels blindly along a high, cluttered shelf. She can't remember where she put her ciggies, or anything. Once, she found a packet with a gold lighter in her oven. What a mind she has to put twenty Dunhills in the cooker!

She gropes about for the light switch, which, when toggled, casts a murky illumination on piles of junk everywhere: tins of motor oil long solidified, skeletons of bike-frames from decades past splayed rudely on the ground. Would any of the Fitzgerald kids down the road have a ride on these? The fact that the chains spill off them, that the saddles sit on two rusty stumps – this does not deter her. Then again, Millie's a bit miffed with their builders pounding and drilling day and night, all to install some vile, ostentatious extension. Still, she might call up to Laura Fitzgerald and make the offer of the spare bikes – the woman does, after all, make a lovely ham and butter sandwich.

Millie ignores the SMOKERS DIE YOUNGER warning emblazoned in bold lettering along the packet's side – she's old, she smokes, she's not dead – and is soon exhaling when she hears footsteps and voices at her front door. Her dinner guests are early. Millie has only a murky grasp of Sylvia's history. She knows the girl had recently arrived in Ireland, her nephew in tow, to work as a roadie with her then-boyfriend, a drummer from Irishtown who turned out to be moody and difficult. When the band split up, Sylvia and the boy, Sean, stayed on, having little to go home to. Since then, she's been taking up odd jobs, trying to save money, get herself sorted. Sylvia has mentioned this Sean, the son of her sister who died tragically young. He's on the quiet side, apparently, helpful and artistic but insular, maybe lonely or homesick. Millie – with a brainwave – invited Aideen to come along.

Sean turns out to be short, with soft features, an abbreviated brow, penetrating liquidy eyes and an olive pallor that bears no resemblance to his aunt's paler complexion. She's certain Aideen will like him. With his hair like a mess of thick weeds, he's not unlike that scraggly Irish lad Aideen adores, carefully chosen by some cynical music mogul to embody everything hopeful and heartbreaking about youth. Sean wears a checked shirt, two buttons missing down the middle, and dark low-slung jeans from which the neon elastic of his undershorts peeks out.

When Millie squints into his face, she sees some lost thing in it. He nods and says a polite hello, but keeps his eyes trained shyly on the hall carpet. Sylvia has brought wine, and as she opens it, Millie prepares a glass of squash for the boy, diluting the orange syrup with carbonated water from her old-school siphon, a treat she keeps on hand for the grandchildren.

'Aren't you very good to come all the way out here,' she says. 'Your mum told me you're not in school?'

'My aunt,' he corrects gently. 'Yeah, I'm working towards my GED. It's, like, a high-school diploma. I'm almost done.'

'Sean's a big reader,' says Sylvia. 'He's always reading, like, serious books.'

'I'm not a citizen,' he says. 'I guess it's, like, impossible to enrol here?'

'Is it now?' says Millie. 'Well, you don't need to be learning Irish history and the Irish language, anyway. How is any of that useful? Tell me something. A secret.'

Sean ponders this and says, 'I'm an atheist?'

Millie claps her hands. 'I'm an atheist as well. Another!'

He smiles. 'OK. I hate when people talk baby-talk to their dogs.'

'I hate dogs!'

'No.' He laughs. 'You can't hate dogs.'

'You're right. Sure, they're harmless.'

'They're so devoted. They just want to hang out.'

'What about your favourite place in Dublin? If I know anything in all the world – and I hardly know a thing!' She giggles. 'I do know my Dublin.' In truth, she has been getting rather lost in her Dublin of late – so many new housing developments and shopping centres and office parks, so many once-optimistic cranes, all now frozen mid-air across the city's skyline, like a herd of long-necked dinosaurs mid-graze, just before the asteroid hit.

Sean motions to the view through the picture window, specks of lights forming a twinkling horseshoe across to the north side and all the way to Howth. 'I'd say right here is pretty nice.'

Millie's positively beaming. 'I grew up just down the road, in Killiney, you see. Have you been there? I'll show you a photograph.' Millie roots around the shelves and shows Sean a framed picture of a house that isn't, in fact, the house she grew up in – that was torn down ages ago to make way for apartments – but it's close enough; it *feels* like her home.

'Sylvia told me you're a musician,' Millie says. 'Is that right?'

'Well, that's kind of my –'

'My granddaughter's due here any minute. She loves pop music. Well, sure, I suppose you all do. Throw on a few of those briquettes, Sean – there's a good lad – the fire's dying.'

Sean carefully, methodically, arranges three briquettes into an erect triangle, fills the gaps with wedges of reeking firelighters and gets a quick blaze going. He stops when Aideen slips quietly into the room. She greets the Americans and gives Millie a limp embrace, waving off her excessive kisses.

'She's as pretty as you said, Mrs Gogarty,' says Sylvia. 'Isn't she, Sean?'

Sean, colouring, says, 'Yes, ma'am,' and they all laugh. He tongs the rogue embers that have sparked onto the hearth and returns them to the fire and then, with the little broom, brushes the dirt and ashes onto the shovel and deposits it all back into the fireplace. With nothing more to do, he sits in the only unoccupied spot, beside Aideen. When he stretches, his arms reach up through the air and Millie spots a flash of flat, swarthy stomach and a trail of dark hair crawling scandalously towards his navel.

'I'm so glad you're here,' Millie says to her granddaughter. 'Because, guess what? Sean likes music.'

'Oh my God,' Aideen says.

'What's so bad about that?' says Millie, delighted. She looks at Sean. 'Did you know your aunt has promised to put me in her suitcase one day and take me as a stowaway to America? Look at this, three guests in one day! Proof of what I always say: it's feast or famine round here – isn't that right, Sil? I've had no one here all week –'

'Well,' Sylvia says, 'Kevin came by –'

'And today I have you and Sean and now Aideen,' she says, already feeling the wine's effect. 'Tell me something sexy.'

'Gran!'

Millie looks Aideen up and down: somehow the girl, who appears to be deeply blushing, has gotten even skinnier since she started at Millburn. 'Tell us what that new school of yours is like.'

'Crap,' says Aideen.

'Is it really?'

Aideen nods.

'How's the food?'

'Crap.'

'I'll need to have that crap broken down a bit,' Millie says and Sean laughs. She is beginning to quite like Sean. 'What do they give you for tea, I wonder?'

'Sausage rolls. Which are vile. Or beans on toast.'

'But who doesn't love beans on toast?'

'Not these beans,' says Aideen. 'Not this toast.'

'Poor Duckie. Well, you're here now, and that's all that matters.'

'So you, like, live at your school?' This is the first question Sean has addressed directly to Aideen. 'Like in a big dorm room?'

'Yeah,' says Aideen. 'Just during the week, though. I come home, like, at the weekend.'

'I'm picturing an army barracks.'

'More like a lunatic asylum.'

He grins. 'Really?'

'Well, like, this one girl – she's homesick every night. It's really sad. She doesn't want anyone to know so she, like, cries into her pillow. I feel bad for her. And another one – her parents are always sending her money and expensive presents and things but they never visit. She only goes home at Christmas and the summer. She's been there since she was six.'

'I'm practically a pauper,' Millie says. 'Oh, that reminds me – did any cheques come in, did you see, Sylvia? I usually get my dividends this time of year.'

'Yes, a couple did. I deposited them Wednesday, I think it was. Shoot, did I forget to give you the receipt?'

'Oh, I have no idea. I'm sure you did. Never mind. These things are a terrible nuisance, aren't they, Sean? Young people don't need to be talking about money.'

Sean shakes his head politely and then turns to Aideen, smiling. 'So you like music too?'

18.

Aideen

Aideen, buoyant, flies down Gran's road on her bike alongside the blackened Irish Sea and the black road whose lights are intermittent at best and generally shit. Brutal gusts of wind sting her face and ears and fingers but she doesn't much dwell on it, or care. She owns the fucking road! Once she turns onto a more private lane, she shrieks, laughs maniacally, and kicks her feet up from the pedals, a pure downhill glide, Clean-Cut's take on 'I'd Really Love to See You Tonight' blasting in her ears. *But there's a warm wind blowin' the stars around / And I'd really love to see you tonight.* She tries to work out Sean's age. Seventeen? Eighteen? Does it matter? He has rock-star hair. He wears a leather jacket. Has he had sex? Aideen's grasp on the fundamentals of sex are murky at best, though Brigid's always offering up various bossy, unsettling particulars during the midnight chats at Fair: pinch a condom at the tip, have a towel nearby, expect pain.

Ahead, Aideen sees an old man walking his dog and she calls out an uncharacteristic 'Hiya!' and coasts past man and beast and lets the scene that just occurred in Gran's living room seep luxuriously into her mind, something she will do relentlessly over the next week, both alone and aloud with Brigid back at Millburn: relive, deconstruct, repeat.

When Sylvia and Millie had left to get the dinner on, Aideen, dead nervous, had immediately moved to the fireplace and begun shifting the briquettes.

'Your grandma's a trip,' Sean had said.

'That a good thing?'

'Oh yeah, definitely. She's really funny, don't you think? "Sean likes music!"'

'That's the worst Irish accent I've ever heard.'

He had laughed and tried again: 'I'd love to get a jar down the pub.'

'Stop!' Aideen had clapped a hand to each ear in mock protest. 'That is truly awful.'

He was smiling at her. 'So what music *do* you like?'

'Oh, I love Clean-Cut,' Aideen said. 'He's my favourite. I've seen him, like, four times.'

'Clean-Cut?' Sean shrank back and raised both palms straight up before his face, as if warding off an infectious disease. 'Is that the really tall dude with the beard who sings, like, all covers?'

If anyone else in Aideen's orbit reacted thus – and some have – she'd have stinging words for them. But Sean seemed to be teasing her, sweetly, and of course there was no question of her responding with even a hint of hostility.

'He writes his own songs too,' she'd said, looking up into his face. It was almost painful, certainly not possible, to straight-on gaze at this boy with his soulful eyes and his beautiful head of hair, which was thicker and glossier than her own. 'He's actually amazing, really down-to-earth, you know, nice to his fans.'

'Oh, really? That's cool. But so that's it? Clean-Cut all day, twenty-four-seven? No other music?'

Aideen suddenly wished this weren't so. 'What about you?'

'I like lots of different stuff, all kinds. Right now I'm really into old music. Sonic Youth, Nirvana. Fugazi. I could make you a playlist if you want?'

Aideen felt that this conversation – her first like this ever – amped up her entire existence, as if she'd been unwittingly plugged into just one earbud all along and now, talking to this boy, the second one just exploded on. When he'd gone to locate his mobile, she'd frantically wiped the oily residue that had accumulated on the slope of her nose and forked her hands through her hair. Hearing Sean come back towards her, she glanced her sweaty hands down the front of her jeans, though they felt immediately clammy again. More than anything, she feared he might want to shake her hand or touch her fingers, even inadvertently, or who knows, and come away with a damp hand and regret ever having met her. More than anything, she wanted him to like her.

'I'll send you some links.' This was happening. 'If you don't like them, then, well ...' He shook his shaggy head. 'We can't be friends.'

She laughed. Were they *friends*? She'd only just met this guy an hour ago.

There once was a boy with green eyes
Pop boy bands he truly despised
He'll make me a list
Will I ever be kissed?
He looks at me, I'm paralyzed.

Phone in hand and without looking up – thank Christ, because she would have passed out, her face felt so aflame – Sean had said, 'What's your number? And your email?'

Now Aideen emits another liberating shout into the sky. She pedals mightily, can't get home fast enough. She's bursting to send Brigid a text message.

Once she reaches home, Aideen tries but fails to slip by the tenacious parental net.

'Aideen?' Dad calls from the sitting room. 'Can I've a word?'

'I'm really tired.'

'Won't take a moment.'

Sighing, she nudges the door open with her high-top, stands uncommitted in the doorway. 'Sorry I'm late.'

'You know you're grounded.'

'From Gran's?' She rolls her eyes.

'No, not from Gran's, obviously. But don't think you're roaming free this weekend.'

'I know, but I didn't drink any of it. I was throwing it out.'

'Look, let's just – just come in and sit down a minute. I've barely heard a peep about school. How's it all going?'

She hears a ding from her phone, alerting her to a new message. 'Fine. I mean, I hate it, but ...'

'How's your grandmother?'

'Good.'

'Oh? Tell me.'

Aideen slings a hand on her hip. 'Good, fine. She was talking with the helper most of the time.'

'Sylvia?'

'Yes.'

'Do they seem to get on?'

'Yes.'

'Does your gran like her?'

'Yes.'

In a robot voice, he says, 'Yes. Yes. Yes. Please disconnect my wires.'

'Dad, I'm tired.' Her phone dings a second time. She pulls it from her back pocket, types in her PIN – lest Nemesis try to pry – and sees an unfamiliar number and the following heart-stopping message: 'Sent some tunes. Dare u to dislike them.'

'I think it's going to work out with Sylvia,' Dad's saying, clueless that her life has just irrevocably transformed. Adults never know what the fuck's going on. 'Your gran seems to have come round to her pretty quickly, thank God.' He chuckles. 'Though apparently she's not used to driving over here.'

The message, having arrived so fast, indicates so much. Aideen's desperate to get upstairs. But even she, master emotion-masker, can't suppress a coy smile, which her father scrutinizes curiously.

'What's *that* about?'

'Nothing.' She lunges out into the hall before he can detect further joy, sings out 'Goodnight!' and tears up the stairs and even grunts a hello at her twin in passing.

19.
Kevin

Kevin stinks. Earlier, he'd splashed across his neck and torso, spectacularly it now occurs to him, his new Euro-trash bottle of cologne, which, if the advert's to be believed, promises to transform him from a smelly wanker to a carefree gent just coming in off the green. With any luck it'll mask the noxious evidence of his anxiety, since it's bitterly frigid today yet his pits feel a touch swampy. Not exactly ideal for one's first toe-dip into potential infidelity. And Kevin means this to be ideal.

In one hour's time, provided this bank queue ever bloody well moves, he will be seated opposite Rose Byrd in Land of the Young, a hip little gastropub located on a crooked, narrow, obscure road north of the river, a place he's selected for this, their initial clandestine meeting. Kevin takes a small measure of dorky joy in the symbolism of his restaurant choice since, as a boy, he'd been fascinated with the mythical story of Oisín and Niamh wherein Niamh brings the naïf to the Tír na nÓg, the underworld where youth, beauty, and pleasure rule. Rose can certainly provide the beauty and youth; he's happy to supply the pleasure.

Bada-fucking-boom. Ever since this flirtation has begun, he's become quite adolescent. Nothing nearly as intense as his and Grace's courtship, mind you, which had begun in the college library of all places – not the pub or the disco or at a drinks party. Kevin was shelving books part-time and Grace consistently sat at a window table, swotting long before exams had rolled around, a pair of John Lennon specs inching cutely down the bridge of her nose. Her beauty – dark, glittering eyes, a light spray of freckles across strong cheekbones, inky hair, much longer then – sneaked up on him. He began to look out for her, have a peek at what she was reading (history textbooks, invariably). He tried to chat her up. Not a chance! He liked that, the challenge she posed. One day, he waited until she stepped away and then he slipped a poem onto her book. It was not a love poem; it was a poem about heartbreak by a bitter British alcoholic poet, which Kevin had spent a long time choosing. Underneath it he wrote, 'If you don't come for a drink with me, I'll end up like this.'

He taps his debit card against his wallet, checks his mobile. How only one cashier is available at Monday lunchtime, the fact that Kevin's precious minutes are being usurped, is too irritating to ponder since he can't afford, emotionally, to blow his stack right now. He certainly won't use his card at the pub. Ever since he was made redundant, Grace has taken to more faithfully eyeballing the bills, increasingly convinced they may be a hair's breadth from ruin, one cheque between Dalkey and destitution which, however inaccurate, is not impossible.

Kevin has the irrational sense that if he is even a minute late, Rose will vanish, a thought he cannot bear, having wrestled with his surprisingly strong temptation versus his heretofore adequate moral standing and long-held sense of his own occasionally dodgy but fundamentally good honour code. Kevin has, for example, forbidden himself to order wine today. A glass of luncheon Muscadet will lead to another and a third and would strip him of any scraps of restraint or judgement he might by then be clutching onto, the raft of his murky moral fortitude. He knows himself enough to know that if he got The Look from Rosie B. and was even slightly inebriated, he'd find them a bed or a backseat or a wall or the rough bark of a giant oak in Stephen's Green if needs be.

The biggest surprise in this dirty cerebral dabble of his has been his natural bent towards deception. Turns out he's quite a good sneak, which was never a skill he needed to hone much, even in his school days (Mum being necessarily focused on her husband's long decline into illness). Kevin deliberately arranged this afternoon's tête-à-tête, for example, when he knew his wife would be in Limerick for a day-long meeting followed by a dinner with the president of that city's preeminent university. The fact that she hasn't sensed some withholding on Kevin's part, some furtiveness, underscores a growing belief that she is not tuned in, that she's lost that lovin' feeling. After all, they've been together so long, know the meaning behind each put-upon sigh or off-pitch word – any are a cinch, too easy, too predictable, to decode. They barely need to speak. A single raised eyebrow suggests, haughtily, 'Bollocks.' The translation of a bodily shift towards the bedside lamp: 'Fuck off. I no longer find you appealing.'

Maybe it's just simpler, more tranquil, to coexist in parallel, to embrace the path of least resistance? Grace arrives home, boots kicked off, bag dumped on the hall floor, asks about the children on a perfunctory need-to-know basis. If no one is injured, if there's no blood, no corpse, then she feels no need to know. The trials of his day, which, from want of adult company, rot away in him through the long morning and afternoon until early evening when he's bursting to relay to her the bitty details, go largely untold. She remains, or acts, oblivious. Grace, it would appear, feels no need to unburden herself with the minutia of her stressful day. She eats, if she hasn't already, from a plate he's kept warm in the oven, and pours a hefty glass, wrecked from long hours of meetings, barely the energy left to unpeel her stockings and slump in front of bad television.

But he knows all of this; what he doesn't know about are Rose's evenings. He imagines, for no particular reason, her tossing clams with garlic and linguini in an earthy flat with cluttered, bohemian shelves, playing Satie or sitting, eyes closed, at her childhood piano, her short silken robe fluttering open ...

He wouldn't be running late if it weren't for Ciaran having just rung from school in need of his trainers for PE. He loves no one more than his children, yet their capacity to unwittingly destroy a possibility of fun or escape in his life, from a catnap to a singles match to a possible tryst, slays him in a way he finds decidedly unfunny. As Kevin glances to compare the accuracy of his Timex with the digital wall clock, emitting a soft 'bloody hell', he sees that the current customer at the cashier's window is his mother's helper, Sylvia Whatsit.

Sylvia's pushing a slip beneath the glass partition and saying, repeatedly, 'withdrawal', as if she is in Croatia or Portugal and not among English speakers. Eventually, the cashier counts out a pile of banknotes and Sylvia begins walking in pink-tinted croc-skin boots in his direction.

Kevin, not wishing to make small-talk, panics, as if she'll intuit from his face where he's headed. He shifts his body slightly away and studies his mobile with a pang of guilt. He ought to say hello, of course, and inquire after his mother. So much for his honour code. Any soul who tolerates Millie Gogarty day in, day out deserves to be greeted at the least. But the idea of being one step closer to his cash and, therefore, his rendezvous, pulls his thoughts back to Rose Byrd. He relives the moment she'd scribbled her number nonchalantly onto Aideen's orientation packet and said, in a decidedly non-administrative tone, that he should contact her directly with any question, 'any question at all.'

He opens a few of the screenshots he'd taken of their brief, heady text message exchange, a conversation he's wisely deleted from his history, and which is now, at any rate, burned onto his animal brain.

Fancy lunch?

Who's this?

Ouch.

Gotcha! Hi Kevin.

Kevin's gone off to throw himself into the sea. Try back later.

What sort of lunch?

The platonic sort. The sort where you tell me about your ghastly childhood and your deferred dreams and I don't tell you what I want to.

That doesn't sound platonic.

'Kevin?' It's Sylvia, standing in front of him, waving. 'Hey there.'

Kevin arranges a look of mild surprise on his features. 'Sylvia. How are you keeping? Is my mother here?' thinking, *Christ I hope not, I don't have time for a granny stick-up at the bank or a faux stroke on the promenade.*

'She's home. I just had to run some quick errands.'

'Oh, great. All going well then? Is the car fixed?'

'Yep, though I'm not sure I should be driving it.' She laughs.

Kevin chuckles politely as the queue finally begins to shift and he steps forward. 'Better you than my mother. Trust me.'

Today, with the kinetic bonanza of the post-Christmas sales – as if the country en masse hasn't given and received enough crap these past weeks – town is teeming. Kevin reaches into his jacket pocket for a mint or a piece of chewing gum as he nears a destination at which fresh breath has never been more of an imperative, but his hands instead fall upon a smooth, hard rectangle and he realizes it's his lost iPod, found again. Grace had given it to him last year, after thoughtfully loading it up with his classic rock favourites. It was the sort of gift that could cause a man to remember that the person across from him is *his* person.

He could still return to the car park and climb into his seven-seater. He could drive home. He could pick up steaks and a decent bottle of wine and build a fire and shoo away the children and they could have one of their long chats of yore, planning the future – a holiday in Thailand, say, or buying a run-down cottage in the country and fixing it up. He could drive home to his wife.

Instead, Kevin inserts the buds deep into each ear and holds down the power button and, amazingly, it boots up. Not since roaring around town in his Docs and his motorbike jacket and his clunky Walkman has Kevin felt the surprising bolt of joy that portable, blasting rock music offers, unwitting passers-by clueless that you're pounding down the road, star of your own private film with your own private soundtrack. It's like a swift, satisfying karate chop of mojo. He circles past Creedence and Clapton and The Doors, whom he actually despises (Grace wrongly believed he was a fan and he hadn't the heart to delete it), and cues up the most badass song he can think of: Zeppelin's 'The Ocean'.

Instantly, the music's thrashing, pushing to the corners of his mind, at least for now, the fact that he's on the brink of something creepy and terrifically damaging to the ones he most loves. The lyrics speak directly to this moment upon him. *Got no time to pack my bags, my foot's outside the door / I got a date, I can't be late ...* Kevin stops himself from screaming and head-banging along with Robert Plant and settles, instead, for more sedate, middle-aged, half-hearted lip-synching.

He realizes, just as the bridge winds down and the song crescendos again into beautiful noise, that this might actually be one of his life's rare perfect moments. He slows down, stretching out the delicious anticipation of his small miracle. *A gorgeous woman is waiting for him.* He practically glides down Talbot Street. He remembers once when he and his gang of schoolmates found a substantial stash of Heineken atop a rubbish bin at the end of this very road. Some underage crew just like them had probably been spotted by the coppers and dumped the loot with plans to return later. What a boon! He remembers the lads and himself taking the piss mercilessly out of each other later on the top floor of the last bus, heading merrily home on a night's worth of free gargle.

Land of the Young is one of Dublin's first all-organic, nouveau farm-to-table eateries. The menus are mini-blackboards framed in twine tethered to a chunk of chalk; baskets runneth over with polished Granny Smiths no one will ever bite into and someone has carefully pyramided scores of limes in gleaming white-lacquered mod bowls.

Rose Byrd sits at the restaurant's most discreet table, situated in an alcove towards the back. Kevin can't help wondering whether this is deliberate. In what he fears is an obvious attempt to belie the heart hammering beneath his Oxford, he waves and heads confidently over.

'Hello, hello, hello. You found the place OK?'

Rose, in pale silky yellow, stands. She wears a flowy top that masks her tiny waist and skinny, ink-blue denims not unlike those his daughters sport on weekends – seriously, what is he *doing* here? – tucked into dark, expensive-looking platform anklets. Thin hoops of gold perch at each ear.

Rose Byrd meets Kevin Gogarty's eyes, but if there is a message there, he cannot decipher it. Her lips part into a smile and Kevin likes to think, but isn't sure, that the bottom one is slightly aquiver. He takes her hand and holds and squeezes it, since it feels too raw and soon to go anywhere near her with his lips.

'Hi,' she says. 'Oh yes, I know this place. But from what I hear they've no money to renew their lease. Closes end of the month.'

This information makes Kevin feel a village fool. He hasn't chosen the *in* place after all. He breathes and can only hope she won't judge him. The truth of this scene occurs in a single clear flash that he soon disregards: he is a married man desperate to prove to a much younger woman who is also his daughter's school secretary how cool or interesting he once was.

Kevin flags down a waiter and Rose suggests champagne. Despite his vow of sobriety, he orders a bottle, which costs roughly one-eighteenth of his former monthly paycheque.

'So …' he says, settling onto a transparent chair that immediately wedges his shorts straight up his arse. Kevin wants to hear her opinions on every single thing, from her political views to how she takes her tea. He is ravenous to learn her.

The waiter retreats after doling out their bubbly and Kevin says, 'To you,' and they clink glasses and he drains his in one greedy gulp. Once they place their order, Rose leans forward, lays her delicate chin onto two delicate fists, elbows spread on the table, and says, 'I'm assuming you wanted to discuss Aideen's progress? At school?'

She looks so earnest that Kevin stops breathing, overcome by mortification. He has misread her words somehow, wrongly translating friendliness as flirtation. Rose Byrd poker-faces him for a painful second longer, then throws her head back in demonic laughter, a great roaring chortle that he did not envision her capable of. This goes on for some time until she wipes her eyes with her napkin, recovering, and then pats his forearm reassuringly.

'Your face!' she finally says. 'Priceless!'

Kevin, having been stripped of all pretence and feeling barer and more afraid and excited than he has in some time, can wait no longer. What he wants is so transparent, and her joke, though a touch mean, has boosted his confidence, banished his fear of rejection. He reaches towards Rose and takes her chin into his hands. She is no longer laughing, though there is some sort of smile, almost daring, in its place. She tilts her head slightly leftward and he greets her as he wanted to in the first place. Their kiss – in the daytime, in a proper restaurant where no other diners are eating the face off each other – lasts several long, lusty seconds until they naturally break away, pausing to look with disbelief at each other.

'That was a mistake,' he finds himself saying. 'I'm married.'

'Ssssshhh,' she says. 'I know.'

20.
Millie

The cheese soufflés are golden and rising, and Millie's put a bottle of Chablis to cool in the freezer. Sylvia, who's spent the day organizing the second floor – it's gas how determined she is – has accepted a second invite for dinner chez Gogarty.

Prior to Sylvia's arrival, Millie seldom consumed what would properly be considered a meal. She might peel a banana and hover beside the fan heater, which, on the coldest mornings, she drags laboriously from room to room by its cord like a stubborn dog on a lead. Or she'll lean against the kitchen counter to save dirtying a dish and wolf down buttered toast, assuming there's butter, or fix a bowl of Corn Flakes, assuming there's milk. This is dinner. Despite years of Peter's high praise for her Sunday roasts and shepherd's pies and pork chops, Millie abandoned the kitchen after his death, having developed a sharp disdain for cooking, especially for one. At eighty-three, she is aware of some masochistic tendencies but draws the line at self-imposed reminders of her already conspicuous solitude.

But with Sylvia on the scene, Millie feels the call of cookery once more. She's growing fonder of the woman by the day – nay, the hour – charmed, even, by some of her companion's odder quirks: Sylvia's incessant application of Vaseline to her lips, forever warding off some imaginary onslaught of chap; the yellow Splenda packets she powders into her tea and coffee like arsenic; her undiminishing sense of marvel that the Irish keep their butter on a dish in the press; her bottomless curiosity – those overt questions about everything from nose-hair clippers to locksmiths to Irish law; her inability to pour milk without first sniffing at it with deep suspicion; her amusement at any advert featuring a Dublin accent; and, above all, her naive, matter-of-fact, entitled, refreshing and decidedly un-Irish way of making everything under the sun seem within reach and perfectly possible, as if goals and dreams are legitimate and attainable, and problems exist not to complain about or sweep under the carpet, but to solve with directness and efficiency and good, practical common sense.

Right now, for instance, Sylvia is whisking a concoction of sugar, bleach, and tepid water in a basin to reinvigorate a jarful of listing peonies she'd gifted Millie days before.

A tea towel in each hand, Millie carries the piping hot ramekins to the kitchen table. 'Come sit and eat before these bloody things collapse.'

'This is my first soufflé ever,' says Sylvia, guiding Millie into her chair before settling into her own.

They're dipping spoons into their dishes when Sylvia picks up her ringing phone. 'Oh, excuse me. I have to take this.' She steps into the hall. 'Yes, this is her.'

Rare is the moment Millie feels irritated with her companion, but this interruption does put her nose slightly out of joint; soufflés are infamously persnickety after all. She's considering whether to make a fuss or not (probably not, Sylvia being generally too kind to give out to) when she hears her aide's voice from the next room exclaim, 'Oh my God!'

Whether in shock or excitement, it's impossible to say, but Millie is certain big news has been relayed. She gets up, winces at the scraping sound her chair emits, and inches towards the door, snatching the salt and pepper for cover.

'Are you sure?' Sylvia's saying. 'Oh my God. OK, hang on, can you hold one sec and I'll get a pen.'

Millie dives back to her place just as Sylvia returns, miming frantic need of a writing instrument. Her face reads ... what? High emotion? Joy? Fear? She grabs the pencil Millie hands her, mouths 'thank you', and hustles back into the hallway, half-closing the door, whereupon Millie takes up her stance once again.

'When would that be?' Though Sylvia's dropped her voice, Millie can just make out the words. 'What are we talking about, like, in terms of cost? ... Oh, God, really? I don't know what to say ... OK, yes. So I'll call you as soon as ... Thank you *so* much.'

When Sylvia returns, Millie is seated once more, casually blowing on her piping dinner.

'Everything OK?'

'Yeah. Sorry about that.'

'That sounded important?'

Sylvia opens her mouth, poised to speak. Though Millie feels certain she will explain or emote in some way, Sylvia seems to think better of it. Instead, she shakes her head.

'Yes, fine, fine,' she says but Millie knows she's lying. 'I'm sorry about that. Let's dig in.'

21.

Aideen

At breakfast, the eggs, undercooked and yet crunchy, are revolting enough that Brigid, quitting the queue in disgust, announces she's officially on hunger strike (which will quietly terminate when the kitchen ladies roll out the custard at lunch). Aideen sits before a bowl of soggy cereal carefully crafting a morning text message to Sean when Elena Antonia, a brilliant, thick-lashed Barcelona beauty, dashes in late, as always. Elena's a character – she's always cursing and singing Neil Diamond songs in a remarkable alto and poking fun at her 'frigid' Irish roommates.

'What shit are they serving up today?' she says.

'The usual,' Aideen says. 'Brigid's going on strike.'

'You are good friends with her?'

Aideen nods. 'Why?'

'Nothing.'

'What?'

'I don't know if you know but Brigid was friends with a girl last year here, a really nice girl, and she left school. And it was Brigid's fault.'

Aideen scans the room, sees Brigid striding towards them. She plops next to Aideen as Elena drifts away. 'You text him?'

Aideen has been the recipient of quite a few messages from Sean Gilmore, most of which are brief and straightforward, but Aideen's decided that not every crush has to be pure poetry. Not every boy tosses off lyrics like Clean-Cut who, currently on an Eastern Asian tour seems to have forgotten his die-hard Dublin fans, with zero tweets to or about them since leaving Ireland. Which is *rubbish*.

Sean's first message – 'Did u listen? What u think?' – might appear fairly forthright, but to Aideen and Brigid, who discussed it at length, the fact that it was sent in the morning (9:18) had sparked a fascinating debate over the course of two smoke breaks (for Brigid – Aideen prudishly waves away Brigid's repeated offers). Does the time of day imply urgency? Is she his first thought upon waking, as he is hers?

In any case, none heretofore could have prepared Aideen for today's message:

R you ever allowed to have visitors or do they shoot all males on sight?

Aideen and Brigid look at each other and squeal, a noise Aideen has never before emitted. Gobsmacked, one of her favourite words – she is *gobsmacked*. She stares at her phone in a giddy daze and envisions Sean roaring up the winding drive to the school on a motorbike (does he even drive?), tossing a lit butt across the car park (does he even smoke?), and now he's holding her round the waist (she doesn't know what she's wearing in this fantasy; she only knows it's decidedly *not* her school jumper). He swoops her away from all of this because he cannot bear another moment without her.

As the final bell screeches, the Millburn girls, wet-haired and puffy-faced, shuffle through the atrium, folders and text-books and pencils in hand, a long and dull and endless school day ahead. Miss Bleekland, clutching her mints and a note-book, ready to record any perceived violation of the school rules, no doubt, drags herself into the dining hall to eyeball the slowpokes.

Quickly Aideen types:

No males allowed unless related. Long-lost cousin? ☺

'Perfect,' says Brigid.

'Aideen Gogarty,' says Bleekland, a harsh tremor rising in her voice. 'The third bell has rung.'

Brigid shoos Aideen's hands from the phone. Even with her friend's goofy, gammy glasses and blobs of white greasy Sudocrem dotting her face, Brigid still looks somehow diabolical.

I could sign out today with my friend at 4 and then meet u
at the river across from the school where we always go

She raises a questioning eyebrow at Aideen, who hesitates and then nods her assent. Brigid taps 'send'.

'Aideen Gogarty! Brigid Crowe! I would not want to revoke your sign-out privileges this afternoon.'

'No, Miss Bleekland,' says Aideen. A *ding* sounds almost immediately.

'Coming now,' says Brigid and then adds, in a whisper, 'you stupid fucking cunt.'

Aideen sees that another message has arrived and it requires no parsing:

OK then see you at 4.

From half past three until teatime, fifth- and sixth-year Fair girls who wish to leave campus are required to sign their names in a great leather tome. This ledger, splayed like Dad's *Oxford English Dictionary* on a pair of wooden wings, sits outside of Miss Bleekland's power base, that glass-walled watchtower of an office where she's always on the lookout for opportunities to apply her well-honed lack of humanity to some unwitting victim. Aideen despises Miss Bleekland's ferocity: she's as hawk-eyed with monitoring the book as she is with each charge and each tiny shift in Fair House, from an open window to a perpetually flushing toilet, keeping abreast of who's in and who's out, who's going where with whom, who's homesick, who's retching in the toilets.

Today, as the two friends sign out, Brigid flips off Bleekland behind her back and, pooling their money – €10.54 – the girls leave through the gate and down the path to the Spar. Freedom! For an hour and a half anyway. In the shop, Brigid winks at the old man manning the till and purchases ten Marlboro, considered, she often remarks, the most upmarket brand of smokes in the country. The girls cross the road and head to the strictly forbidden area near the river. 'River' is a misnomer in this particular part of the city – it's more of a trickle – but the girls had accidentally discovered a forgotten, largely torn-up pathway above the water hidden by thick, unwieldy foliage beneath a graffiti-laden bridge under which they can sit in privacy and gab.

Once they're settled, Brigid says, 'Did I tell you I'm supposed to meet Connor at The Peak Saturday night? Did I not show you a pic of him?' She scrolls through her phone. 'He's a total ride.'

Ugly boys are just boys, according to Brigid, but cute ones are a 'ride', a 'bang', or, the ultimate, a 'screw', and every screw under the age of twenty in Dublin, apparently, is vying to get into Brigid Crowe's knickers. To hear her friend tell it, boys up and down the southside are forever hitting on Brigid, snatching at her bum on buses, or bumping up against her tits on a packed Dart in a way Aideen can tell she loves. And then there are Brigid's drinking boasts, a veritable shopping list of alcoholic consumption: in under three hours last Friday night, she claims to have consumed four Southern Comfort and reds, three pints of Carlsberg, and one shot of something, and she was 'absolutely gee-eyed by then'.

'Aideen?'

It's Sean. How he found them so easily, and so quickly, Aideen can't figure, but here he is. He wears a buttery beige suede-like jacket and a blue shirt with a stiff collar over a white ribbed undershirt. He dresses so unlike Irish boys. Aideen spies dark, wiry sprigs of hair flattened at his collarbone. He bullseyes a killer grin directly at her. He's a ride, a bang, and a screw.

'Hi – oh, shit.' He laughs. 'Cover your eyes a sec.'

But Aideen doesn't. She continues gazing at Sean, who cups

his hands together and shouts at a figure, a dark-haired man, middle-aged, on the opposite side of the river.

'Hey!'

Across the water, they see the man open a long dark coat to reveal a remarkably unattractive, doughy, pale, pasty torso. He is naked. The flasher's too far away to pinpoint any specifics, which of course is what he would like them to do, but Aideen does take in a dark squab of pubic hair.

'Oh my God!' she says, in a shocked, babyish way that she's mortified by.

Brigid screams out, 'Copper bush!' and Sean and Brigid break their shite laughing.

The man quickly belts his coat closed and hikes up the rocky riverbank, scrambling and stumbling through weeds and mounds of dirt, darting between the trees.

'And don't come back until you grow a bigger willy!' yells Brigid, which causes Sean to practically piss himself. Why has she brought Brigid? Brigid is witty and wild and worldly. Aideen is a dull doll, practically inanimate.

'Now I see why you guys hang out down here,' says Sean.

Brigid laughs and introduces herself and says, 'It's too cold to be a perv today.'

Sean has another chuckle at that. If Aideen were to leap from the bank into the river and float down it calling 'Help!' they probably wouldn't notice.

'I love your jacket,' says Brigid.

Aideen studies her friend's dimples, deep and suddenly ugly, like two baby belly-buttons, two innies, squashed on her impish face.

'Do you go into Bruxelles ever?' Brigid asks. 'I feel like I've seen you there.'

'No,' he says, 'I don't have a fake ID.'

'Oh, I can get you in there. I know the bartender, Jonathan. He's always giving me free drinks. The last time I was in there he gave me two pints of Guinness.'

'Cool,' says Sean.

'I'll be in there this weekend. I could get you in?'

Aideen has been so stupid. Of course he prefers Brigid. Brigid is cool. She gets fake IDs. She drinks in pubs. She gives blowjobs.

Sean looks steadily at Aideen. 'Will you be there?'

She could write a sonnet on the colour of his eyes alone, which are green and sorrowful. 'I don't really go to pubs,' says Aideen.

'Where do you go?' He's smiling. 'Other than Clean-Cut shows?'

'Should we sit down?' says Brigid.

Sean positions himself beside Aideen so that their knees graze. She wants him never to move.

'So,' he says, 'what did ya think of the music? Too loud?' He looks crestfallen. 'Too fast? Too noisy?'

'Maybe a bit much.'

'OK. A bit much isn't the worst thing. Did you like *any* of it? Come on!'

'I liked some of the lyrics, like that song "Pepper",' says Aideen. 'That's kind of poetic.'

'I don't think anyone has ever said that about The Butthole Surfers ever.' He's watching her with a curious expression. 'What about The Ramones? Did you like them?'

'Oh, they're brilliant, I love The Ramones,' says Brigid, exhaling a jet of smoke expertly from the right side of her annoying mouth. 'So how is it you don't have to go to school?' She's tossing her butt and already lighting another. Showing off.

'We've been moving around a little,' he says. 'I'm working on, like, credits towards a diploma.'

'Lucky bastard. Your mum's your teacher?'

'Nah. My aunt. She kind of oversees it.'

'Where's your mum then?' says Brigid.

'She died,' Sean says.

'Oh, sorry, that's awful,' says Brigid. 'Was she sick?'

'Brigid!' says Aideen.

'Just asking.' Brigid shrugs. 'Jesus.'

'No, that's OK,' Sean says. He shifts slightly, his knees abandoning hers. 'No, she actually OD'd.'

'Oh fuck,' says Brigid.

'You don't have to, like, say anything about it,' Aideen says.

'That's OK,' he says. 'No one's asked me about it in a really long time.'

'How old was she?' Brigid says.

'Thirty-six.'

'Shit,' says Brigid.

'Yeah.'

Aideen and Brigid exchange a look.

'Was it just you two?' says Brigid.

Now Sean's eyes close. He nods.

For a girl who secretly believes she's good with words, Aideen cannot think of a single one to express what she would like to. There isn't one. Summoning her courage, she reaches across and pats Sean's shoulder. Awkward, a bit of cringey. But then Sean grabs onto her hand. Even though Brigid is sitting with them, beginning to bang on about some debs blowout in town and how someone is supposedly bringing good hash, it's as if she isn't there at all.

22.
Kevin

Towelling off, Kevin studies the slick coffin-shaped hotel tub and in his mind puts Rose Byrd into it. There she is, basking amidst suds in a bikini, tropically patterned, an island conch coyly covering each breast. Why tropical? He has no clue; it's always thus, in the same way that Grace's fantasies, when she used to divulge them to their mutual hilarity, invariably starred a hulking hotel porter with a country accent in a woollen cap.

But back to Rose, who's untying her scant top, which, despite the ridged shells, does not clack to the floor, but merely floats away. Kevin, too, would like to merely float away. She begins to soap her breasts, simultaneously starting with tantalizing circles around the soft, broad outlines and speeding up as her fingers near each vortex. She's moaning when his mobile begins to bleat from its spot on the slate tiles (within reach, in case his would-be mistress or, indeed, wife should call). MOTHER flashes up. And again. And again.

Kevin rejects the third call from her today. Maybe now she'll actually leave a message, though she's suspicious of voicemail as a rule, the mad old bird. And when she does bother to say anything, it's enough to give him a sore head. 'Kevin, I've lost my reading glasses and my mind, oh, and the clicker and where are my car keys? I need to get to the salon and drive everyone there stark ravers.' Or, 'Kevin, would you ever pick up a spot of milk for me? And I suspect the gardener's gone off with another crate of my fruit because the trees are looking rather bare.'

He dresses and then stretches out on the impeccable bed with its grand views, watches as his fellow Dubliners cross the Liffey over the Ha'penny Bridge with an enviable sense of purpose. What, pray tell, is *his* purpose? To shag his daughter's school secretary in a hotel frequented by rich foreigners?

Rose is nearly an hour late. He turns on the TV – every channel pure shite – and downs two bottles of minibar beer in rapid succession, checking his phone incessantly. He drafts and deletes and drafts a message to her, which he finally sends: *Here*. As in, coolly, he hopes, *I'm here, will you be too?* When no response is forthcoming, he analyzes whether she got held up or if she's a no-show, considers his next move, rejects a second text message on the grounds that it would appear either self-emasculating (is that a thing?) or stalker-y. Can he not see this for what it is? A chance to opt out, to drag his selfish, potentially family-wrecking arse out of this pompous hotel, which, to add more fuel to the fire that is his current reign at the top of the shitlist, is incurring yet more debt, unbeknownst to his family.

And then, a knock.

Kevin notes, with some satisfaction, that the raps gain in

volume and number: Rose Byrd wants in. He goes to the door, eyes her through the peephole in distorted close-up. And yet pretty still. *My God*, he thinks.

Kevin cracks the door a hair. 'Can I help you?'

'Hiya, sorry!' Rose giggles and shifts her face to fill the space between them. 'Oh no, have you been here long?'

'I was just leaving.'

'Oh no, you weren't.'

She leverages a foot inside the door and pushes past him, spilling into the room, footing wobbly, eyes glazed, laden with a large canvas bag from which looms a bottle of something. Her sense of balance deserts her and she turns and pitches forward again, blasting a wave of hot, beery fumes at his face, and then rights herself.

Kevin barely knows Rose Byrd sober, let alone trolleyed.

'Nice room,' she says. Before he can respond, her mouth is on his. It's a surprisingly unaggressive kiss, given her boozy entrance, and it's this sense of her withholding that soothes his bruised feelings, as if she's trying to show him that she's got more and better tricks up her sleeve. He relaxes, kisses her back. Kevin is standing in a hotel room getting off with a woman who is not his wife – a moment both natural and totally alien. Soon, he begins to free her blouse from its vice-like clutch beneath very tight, very skinny jeans, and his hands are climbing the velvet length of her back.

Moments later, Rose releases him with a gasp. Kevin opens his eyes and she flashes him a sort of smug smile and then burps, not demurely, and squeezes together her legs.

'Dying for a piss.'

She weaves towards the toilet, leaving the bathroom door open so that he's privy to the sound of a fierce, gushing stream of urine. *Sexy.*

'Check out this fucking bath!' she yells. 'Are there jets in here?' He hears water – has she turned on the taps?

Kevin ought to snap up his wallet and walk directly through the door, leave this soused woman-child to pass out alone on the stiffly made bed, go home before irreversible damage occurs, dismiss this all as an embarrassing mid-life episode, the turning point when he saved his marriage.

Rose clomps back into the room, fumbling with the midsection buttons on her blouse. Kevin glimpses a tantalizing flash of magenta lace. He is so weak.

'Look,' he says, 'are you alright?'

'Bloddy bloddy blah.' She kicks off two tan suede ankle boots adorned with complicated steel hardware; the second one clips Kevin's shin painfully. 'Oh, wait! I brought champagne!' she announces. 'Where'd I put my bag?'

'Rose.' He's speaking in the firm, paternal tone reserved for his children's bygone meltdowns, when they were near to foaming at the mouth, invariably brought on by exhaustion or hunger. 'Look, maybe we should do this another time. You're a bit pissed.'

'No, I'm not,' she cries, spraying the air.

'I'd hate for you to wake up tomorrow morning and have no recollection of how ridiculously virile I was.'

'I like virile.'

He's nearly wincing with the pain of giving this up. 'And despite the fact that I find you …' Kevin pauses, embarrassed.

He's been texting this woman saucy one-liners for the past two weeks, but here in the flesh he feels far too chicken to verbalize anything of substance to her. 'I find you deeply attractive.' He swallows and thinks: wallet, door, home. 'I find myself thinking about you. Frequently.' He stands up. 'That said, I think we'd better call it a night.'

'Fuck that.' Rose swoops in on him. His little speech seems to have had the opposite effect: it's made her keener. Weak and vile man! Despite his inner protestations, he can't resist what is happening. It all seems already to be in motion. A gorgeous creature is pushing him onto a sleek king-sized bed, very non-marital, very Hollywood, and she's quickly astride him. After some doing, she manages to remove her blouse, and then, strip-show style, lassoes it round her pointer finger high in the air, rotating it a good four or five loops before finally launching it across the room where it whacks a standing lampshade. They both crack up.

'Are you sure this is what –?'

'Ssssh,' she says, attempting to rest a finger on his lips, but it jabs his left nostril instead. 'Too much yackety-yack.'

She motions for him to put his head back down on the pillow. Rose Byrd is reaching for Kevin's belt, *Kevin's* belt.

'Chill,' she says, 'relax, you.' And so he does. He chills. Now she starts to tug down his trousers, but with difficulty, so Kevin helps by wiggling out of them. Pantless and prone, he experiences the miracle that is Rose lowering his boxers.

She is poised to take him in her hot, clammy, drunken clutches. She bends towards him so that her lovely face hovers just above his crotch, which has Kevin ready to fire away. He tries to calm himself, closes his eyes, empties his mind.

Suddenly, she jolts away with a muffled 'Agh!', a genuine yelp of horror, as if she's just seen a swarm of maggots wiggling through the dregs of a stinking bin of rubbish.

'What?' He lifts his head. 'What is it?'

'Oh my God.' She jerks, sitting back on her haunches.

Flooded with a barrage of nasty possibilities, the prime one being, *Will this woman vomit on my penis?*, Kevin sits up. 'Are you going to be sick?'

'Fucking hell!' She peers down at his pelvis and tosses off a reckless laugh. 'Oh my God! Did you know you've got grey pubes?'

She throws her head back into peals of girlish giggling, every last one a cruel cackle to haunt him all his days. Speechless, he snatches at the bedsheet and prudishly covers his apparently decrepit bits.

'No, no, don't be like that,' she slurs, yanking the sheet from his body. 'I'm sorry ... No, no, no, lie back, lie back. It's kind of cute. I don't mind.' She tries to climb atop him once more.

Kevin, unable to meet her eyes, able only to feel utterly ridiculous, looks away. A digital clock on the bedside reads 9:48. He has time still, plenty of it – two hours before the child-minder will start hounding him. His gaze shifts to the wiry magenta bra which Rose had ripped off, only a few hot moments ago, in lusty haste. Beneath the spotlight of the bedside lamp, a tag reads 'Dunnes Stores'.

Where his daughters get these things. And his wife.

Kevin tries to call up the details of Aideen and Grace's recent Dunnes debacle. Grace had inadvertently embarrassed Aideen in the changing room, something to do with a shop assistant.

He remembers that Grace had come home upset, that an outing meant for fun had soured.

'Shit,' he says and extricates himself from the warm tangle of Rose Byrd under the bedclothes. 'I've got to go.'

23.
Aideen

Though rampant, secrets are strongly discouraged by Fair House staff, and so suspicion and a good old-fashioned aversion to privacy filters through every slice of life here. The girls, for example, can't lock possessions in their cupboards or drawers despite the fact that some of the sixth years are eighteen years of age and could (and do) enter a public house and get arseways legally. Should one misplace one's mobile and need to ring home and complain bitterly about being here again, as Aideen tends to do on a Sunday an hour or so after getting dropped off and forced to say goodbye to her parents and siblings, this weekly mournful orphan ritual must be done with clumps of similarly whingy boarders eavesdropping in the queue behind her. Case in point: at this very moment, in the second-floor bathroom of Fair House, Aideen sits, though it's going on two in the morning, beneath lights that are burning, ostensibly for those in need of a toilet or drink of water, but, really, Aideen knows, to ensure all is illuminated.

But, Janey Mac, the secret half-hour she's just spent! Certainly no one could tell that Big Things have transpired from the look of her. Her body betrays no evidence of her first deep-dive into romantic fumblings other than a flushed, slightly stinging face. But her heart? A different story altogether.

Aideen perches, feet tucked beneath her, on a toilet in the third of five stalls, staring at the cheap translucent paper they're meant to wipe their bums with. She mentally rehearses her story a final time and pushes down on the flush lever. Almost immediately she hears the expected Pavlovian footsteps, like a football hooligan instantly parched at the pop and slow fizz of a cracked-open can of Carlsberg. Aideen unlatches the stall door and, sure enough, there's Bleekland, sporting a surprisingly plush aquamarine robe knotted fiercely at the front with a matching belt, a veritable hockey ref in starting position, legs spread mannishly, feet rooted to the bleached floor tiles, a sour scowl marching across her pinched grey mug.

'Where have you been?'

Even considering the potential trouble she's in, Aideen finds it difficult to take Bleekland seriously once her eyes fix upon the woman's yellow flokati duck slippers, furry-billed, with black-and-white plastic eyeballs that stare crossways at the floor. She resists a powerful gurgle of laughter.

'Sorry?' says Aideen, widening her eyes and then scrunching her nose up as if to say, *How bewildering!*

'We've been looking for you,' hisses the old shrew. 'Where have you been?'

'I didn't realize ...' Aideen allows this perplexed fragment to trail away, as if she's just receiving the intel, as if she hasn't heard Bleekland dragging her poxy log-leg round the second floor, opening and closing every dormitory door, a soldier rooting out enemy barracks. 'I've been here sitting on the toilet.' She coughs and then, with a downward gaze, goes in for the kill. 'I've got my period.'

Bleekland blanches. Like most of the Fair House girls, Aideen knows very well that any vaginal reference, however oblique, is guaranteed to put off the craggy septuagenarian who possibly has never herself acknowledged being in possession of a sexual organ.

'I checked this room,' says Bleekland, bitter irritation clear in the rise and fall of her words. But Aideen detects relief: Bleekland had actually thought she'd disappeared. Just at this moment, Nurse Flynn scampers in, heading directly towards them opposite the tidy row of identical sinks where six girls at a time brush and scrub and rinse daily. Flynn's unable to suppress an evil little grin that spills across her wan pancake face. She is the dum to Bleekland's Tweedledee. On boring prep nights when Aideen's finished her schoolwork and read through her secret stash of pop music zines, Flynn sometimes serves as a handy muse.

There once was a sadist from Bray
Who hounded the Fair girls all day
Phony caring career
Put you out on your ear
Nurse Flynn clearly never got play!

'There you are!' The second-in-command, clad, predictably, in dishwater-hued, gender-neutral pyjamas, narrows amphibian eyes at Aideen. 'Where have you been? We nearly phoned the guards.'

'I've found her, Nurse Flynn. Thank you. You may go back to bed.'

'But where did you –?'

'I'm sorry to have woken you,' says Bleekland unapologetically. 'Goodnight.'

Would they really have called the police? Aideen exhales quietly, the heat of accusation momentarily cooled from her, and relives the moment – twenty minutes ago yet already taking on a surreal, legendary status – when Sean had said, 'You're really pretty.' Though she may well get expelled, especially following just after the vodka and beer incident, Aideen's mouth threatens to turn upward into a massive shit-eating grin.

'I'm sorry,' she says. 'I felt really sick but I didn't want to wake you.'

'You should have.'

'I had no tablets so I looked –'

'What kind of tablets?'

'Just Anadin.'

'There are *no* tablets allowed of any kind in Fair House!'

'I had a really heavy flow and terrible cramping ... So I came back in here –'

'Go to bed at once,' Bleekland barks, eyeballing her sceptically, not nearly as convinced as Aideen would like.

'I'm sorry,' Aideen says again, in a meek voice, with an obsequious hangdog shrug.

'Next time you don't feel well,' Bleekland says, glaring at her before Aideen shuffles down the hallway, one hand cradling her tummy, milking it, 'come to my room. Students do *not* self-medicate. Students do *not* ramble through the corridors after lights-out.'

What had woken Bleekland up in the first place? She couldn't possibly have heard Sean and herself in the storage cupboard or Aideen's life would have just become an absolute shit-storm. Bleekland must've happened to snort awake and did a check and spotted Aideen's empty bed. She curses her own stupidity. In her excitement and haste, she'd forgotten to plant a pillow beneath her duvet.

Aideen slips back into bed, and after sifting through the various probabilities and scenarios, becomes satisfied she's in the clear. How, she wonders, can a few moments be so life-altering? She's now a girl who, like only two or three of her dormmates willing to admit it, has been felt up. Is she now a girl with a *boyfriend*?

Over a series of days-long, flirtatious, momentum-building text messages, Sean and Aideen had hashed out the particulars: time (midnight), what to do if he was caught inside the building with her (say he was her cousin), what to do if he was caught on the green (act deranged and flee). As always, Aideen felt freer, smarter, and funnier in writing than in person. Typing, she could quip cleverly in a way that didn't come naturally in conversation; with premeditation, she was herself.

They'd planned the visit, dubbed Operation Midnight, down to him chucking pebbles at her window, without considering that it was a pebble-less campus. Sean was forced, in the end, to hurl his heavy silver key ring that says 'Billabong' on it. Alas, midnight came and went with no ping on glass. Aideen had lain rigid, straining to hear anything, but all was still. Later, after she'd nodded off into a wet puddle of spit on her pillowcase, a clank awoke her, but it sounded more distant than it should have, and Aideen groggily realized Sean was targeting her dormmate Caroline's window. Caroline was a highly strung girl given to gaspy asthmatic outbursts and hypochondria, especially on PE days, but she was also the soundest sleeper in 2A; Aideen was in the clear.

With thundering heart – a night-time visit surely raises the bar of Sean's expectations – Aideen had stood on her bed and looked down. She waved shyly at Sean Gilmore in his shitkickers, shivering in leather, cupping his hands together and blowing into them. She pointed to the double doors. Aideen whisked stealthily through the corridors and down two staircases in her flimsy nightclothes. She'd chosen a plain T-shirt and stripy pyjama bottoms and then debated about whether to wear a bra. She didn't need one, of course, she never really did, but he might think her a slapper without one. Then again, would he deem it strange for a girl to have a bra on at bedtime? And would he even find out? (In the end, she'd opted for one, preferring him to think her quirky over slutty.)

Aideen had skulked into Bleekland's office, felt a wisp of fear like gas churn in her gut, snatched down the front-door key on its 'Honour, Leadership & Academic Excellence' ring. If Brigid could see her now! Before her stood the hottest ride she'd ever personally known (Clean-Cut notwithstanding) who'd come across town in the middle of the night to see *her*!

'Hi,' he'd said.

It was a powerful moment. Aideen Gogarty couldn't have written a haiku, a limerick, a free-verse poem, a text message, a tweet, anything that could more closely capture beauty than the fact of that single word and this boy standing before her with his loose, manic hair, a faded hipster Black Betty T-shirt beneath the jacket, a pale scar, like one of her brother's white fishing grubs, planted along his thick brow, all of it. This would have been enough, and yet there was more.

'Next time should we pull a Rapunzel?'

He was already referring to next time! And so boldly she took his freezing hand in hers. Sean raised her fingers to his lips and kissed her hand gallantly. Honestly, was this really happening to Aideen Gogarty right here in the entry of Millburn School's residential house? And then he was kissing her. She'd never had her mouth explored by any person other than her doughy, sceptical dentist who seemed never to believe that she'd flossed. At first, Sean's little eel of a tongue barged into her mouth, darted to and fro as if lost, not a thing like the hundreds of screen kisses she'd seen and studied, where it all begins on the outside and works its way in. No, Sean's tongue was trying to get somewhere, Sean's tongue was in a hurry, and she stood with her mouth awkwardly agape, unsure of how exactly to reciprocate. She felt foolish and ungainly, worried her tongue would land on the wrong target, and at first it did: the dry corner where his lips met, then wetly, clumsily, the double-barrelled groove of skin below his nose.

'We can't stay here,' she said and led the way through the common room, ashamed of its childish decor and mortifying list of house rules handwritten on a dry-erase board. They entered a large storage cupboard where Miss Packer, the kindly cleaning lady who always smiled at Aideen and said 'Ah, God love you', housed her mops and brooms and dusters. There was a gap between the shelving large enough for them to sit side by side on the floor, backs against the wall – not comfortable, exactly, but it would do.

They kissed again. His tongue calmed some, more of a ramble, an exploratory roam. This was somehow exactly as she'd imagined and yet nothing at all as she'd imagined. She found herself responding, gradually gaining confidence. Before long, they were heavy-breathing. Aideen struggled valiantly to process all that was happening and to reject the image, which seemed to be on an endless mental loop, of Bleekland or even sweet, pudgy Packer bursting in on them. She began to worry about where she'd put the front-door key – was it still in the door or had she slipped it into her pocket? Without allowing herself to over-ponder – she was terrified he'd be uninterested or, worse, disappointed – she stopped and placed Sean's hands on her breasts over her top. And then she thought, *There are two ice packs on my tits* and giggled. He removed his hands immediately.

'I'm sorry,' she said.

'No, I'm sorry,' he said.

They sat. She had a wild notion that maybe she should just reach over and press her hand into his crotch. She was curious how it would feel: like a squashy carnival sausage? Or a skinny wooden stick you find strewn on the strand when the tide is low, one you might toss for a dog to fetch? In the dark, she could only see the outline of him. She felt his hand land gently on her hair.

'I saw your grandma today. We brought her lunch.'

'Grandma!' she echoed mockingly and felt delirious. 'That's, like, so American.'

'Poor old Millie Gogarty, you know? I feel sorry for her, all alone in that house.'

'I know, me too. She can really drive everyone completely mental, though,'

'She kind of reminds me of my mom. Like before. Like with all the crazy shit she busts out with, you know? My mom was kinda like that.'

'You must miss her.'

He didn't reply and then Aideen said, 'Gran is a head case but she means well. One time I really needed money to get tickets for Clean-Cut –'

'Not that plonker again!'

'Look at you with the Irish verbiage.'

'You are forbidden to utter his name in my presence.'

God, how she fancied him.

That's when he had told her she was pretty.

'But you can't even see me.'

'I have your face in my brain,' he said and they laughed.

He ran his hand along her bare arm; she shuddered. Then they heard a door closing from the floor above. Aideen immediately ripped away from Sean and jumped to her feet. 'You have to go.'

She grabbed his hand, tiptoed from the closet all the way to the exit door where, out in the open, they were most vulnerable. Jesus, she *had* left the key in the door. Aideen unlocked it frantically and pushed him out of the building – she laughs at the thought of it now. But before he left, as if he couldn't resist, he kissed her a final time, even as she smacked him off and shoved him out. She ran to Bleekland's office to replace the keys, hands shakily trying to find the hook, and, before climbing the stairs, turned to watch him already all the way across the broad, uninspired lawn, running off into the moonless night.

24.

Kevin

Purely by happenstance, while at the garage getting a bulb replaced on his own car, Kevin learns that it had been Mum, not Sylvia, behind the wheel when her Renault had gotten smashed up. Taking Kevin's cash, the mechanic says, 'Hate to say it but she's becoming one of my best customers.'

Kevin thanks the man cheerily, but he's deeply livid. Not only is his mother a danger on the road, but the accomplice she's roped in for subterfuge is the very person who's supposed to be keeping her safe, not lying to his bloody face. He zooms out of the garage, pulls to the side of the road, and finds Sylvia's number on his phone.

'Your services,' he says coldly upon her 'hello', 'are no longer required.'

'What?'

'I'm sacking you.'

'I don't understand.'

'As of today.'

'But was something – is there a specific thing that –?'

'Yes, there is. You lied to me. You said you were driving the day she crashed but it wasn't you, was it?'

'Oh, that.' She sounds unfazed. 'I'm sorry. That *was* my fault, but she was really worried about your reaction. She was totally freaking out. She thought you would take the car keys from her.'

'Goodbye, Sylvia.'

'But wait –' she says and so he does; he waits for the inevitable heartfelt apology, the grovelling – not that he intends to act upon it. 'What about my money? I'm still owed for three shifts this week.'

He hangs up and turns in to the supermarket. Grace is home early today so he's planned an above-average meal; he badly needs to assuage the guilt that has begun to consume him. He needs to right his wrong.

Kevin's holding a clutch of scrawny carrots in the produce aisle, determined to never contact Rose Byrd again, when someone smashes violently into his trolley.

It's Mum.

'Am I invited?' she says, eyeing his packets of minced meat.

'To the parents' hockey dinner? Not your bag, Mum.'

'What's that sourpuss for? Can I entice you to tea today? Sylvia has the day off.'

'No, but I do need to talk to you.'

'Oh?'

'Not here.'

'Why not here?'

'Because I don't want to get into a big thing standing in the middle of the supermarket.'

'I didn't know we were getting into a big thing.'

'Look, I'll meet you at the coffee stand in ten minutes, good?'

He waits twenty minutes for her. She's probably pocketing apricots or blabbing at the poor butcher about the appalling state of his cuts. Finally, when his mother joins him, Kevin says, 'I've let Sylvia go.'

They are seated on tall backless stools at a tiny bar table with paper cups of bitter coffee, pools of shopping bags heaped at their feet.

'I've had to fire her, Mum. Don't look at me like that.'

'Why on earth ...?'

'I had no choice.'

'But she was just at the house yesterday.'

'Yes, well, that was her last day, I'm afraid.'

'I have no idea what you're talking about. I'm ringing her right when I get home.'

'Let me – just sit down. Let me explain.'

'She's due tomorrow.'

'No, she isn't. She's no longer coming.'

'You can't just do that!'

'I thought you didn't even want a caretaker?'

'How would you know what I want?'

'Look, just calm down. Jesus, good thing I didn't mention this near the pineapples.'

Mum doesn't laugh.

'You've been keeping something from me.'

'I don't know what you're on about,' she says.

'You crashed the car again, didn't you?'

Maddeningly, she shrugs. 'You don't mean that little bump here, at the car park? Ah sure, Kevin, come on now, that's just –'

'That was the third one in half a year. It's just not safe.'

'What does that have to do with Sylvia?'

'Sylvia lied to me. She's supposed to tell me what's going –'

'Spy on me!'

Kevin sighs. 'No, of course not. I'm the contact person and she's supposed to let me know when an incident like this happens.'

Mum snorts. 'Incident!'

'I realize you have no respect for the concept of responsibility whatsoever, but the fact is that she was totally irresponsible for not telling me the truth. It's unacceptable. I can't trust her.'

'Well, I trust her and that's what matters. And it's my fault anyway because I told her not to mention it – I didn't want to worry you. This is all a fuss over nothing. She's still got the job.'

'She has not.'

'She has.'

He shakes his head. 'Look, I'm sorry but it's done. Anyway, it's done.'

Further domestic drama greets him on the home front, this one mundane and death related: Ciaran's fish, Pika and Chu, present as quite dead, two stiff floaters in one aquarium. Given the appalling state of the tank, over which a film of dark charcoal fuzz has grown ominously across the rocks and fake fauna and rusted treasure ship, Kevin can't say he's terribly surprised.

He mentally scrolls through various openings and riffs and, deciding to wing it, calls out, 'Ciaran, love, come here, will you?'

Ciaran, his most obedient child, bunny-hops into the room in red tracksuit bottoms and a T-shirt that reads TAG YOUR IT, whose grammatical error never fails to irk his father. Does nobody approve a T-shirt before it's shipped from China? Or is it deliberately misspelled to thwart the mainstream? Cool, the universe seems at great pains to repeatedly point out to Kevin, has bypassed him.

'I have some news.' Like all of the Gogarty kids but not their parents (Grace's imaginary tryst with the milkman, which is an old joke between them, notwithstanding), Ciaran is blue eyed, his lashes bovine. 'Pika and Chu have died.'

Ciaran cries so instantly it's astonishing, as if Kevin pushed a button on him marked 'grief'. His narrow shoulders slump, the tears streaming.

'I'm sorry,' says Kevin and he is. He holds his little boy closely, a hard lump, to his surprise, rising up in his own throat. He gulps. He feels rattled, off his game.

Kevin had promised himself he wouldn't ring or text message Rose Byrd again, and he hasn't and he is not going to be *that guy*, it's nonsense, the whole thing, and over now, it was a few measly kisses (albeit stirring, erotic, filled with longing and possibility). Still, kisses that should never have happened, and there are worse and farther lines to cross and he won't be crossing them. (Yet in two hours, he will feel crushed, gutted, when she writes, *Can we meet up? I'll be nice, promise*, and he forces himself to ignore and delete, ignore and delete.)

Kevin strokes Ciaran's back, murmurs soothing words. As the son of a woman who pooh-poohed anguish – 'You'll be grand!' Millie used to say to any sign of emotional upset with a pat on the bum and off you go – he tries to make it a point not to rush the heavy stuff.

'You know,' he says, 'I think Pika and Chu were quite a happy pair, far as I can tell. Delirious, I should think, if not exactly bright. I mean, they were always swimming in circles, forgetting that they'd just swum in circles and then – hey, hold the phone! I've got an idea! Let's swim in circles.'

'Daddy!' Ciaran scolds, smiling and crying.

'Feckin' eejits! No, but the truth is, they always got to be together. That's a good thing, to have a fellow fish. And then you would come in and brighten their whole world just by tapping some smelly flakes of food into their tank. They had a grand old time of it,' he says and then adds, 'deadly.' He winces, but his son doesn't seem to notice his gaffe.

Ciaran lifts his head from Kevin's chest and says, 'You think so?'

'I do.'

'They're never going to be alive again.'

'Well,' Kevin pauses, 'they'll be together in heaven.' He says this uncomfortably since he hasn't believed in heaven or religion or God or any of it for years, yet he finds that fatherhood compels him to perpetuate these myths.

'Hi, Mum,' says Ciaran.

Kevin hadn't even heard Grace come in, but here is his wife, striding towards them, coat still on.

'What's happened?' she says, going immediately to Ciaran.

Kevin rolls his eyes towards the fish tank to communicate the double carcass situation.

'Oh no. Oh, I'm sorry. Poor darling.'

The boy climbs into his mother's arms and she rocks him slowly. Kevin finds this tableau powerfully moving. He has a strong urge to blurt everything out – she has always been his primary confidante; so little in his life seems real until he shares it with her. If only he could talk to Grace about Rose!

Ciaran sits up. 'Can we bury them in the garden?'

'I think it's better to have a water burial,' says Kevin. 'We can whoosh them out to sea where they started. How 'bout Mum says a few words?'

'No, you should,' Ciaran says.

'You're right,' says Grace, but Kevin sees the briefest cloud pass over her features.

'No,' says Kevin, feeling such a tenderness for his wife now, his unwitting victim. 'Mum gives speeches all the time. Trust me, no better woman for the job.'

The Gogartys have lost track of how many guppies they've flushed down the loo over the years. Yet, as unceremonious a ritual as it appears, the children are inevitably moved. Standing at the toilet, Ciaran proves to be no exception. But he's a resilient kid – all Kevin's gang are, really – and by teatime, he's tapping away on the laptop, all vestiges of melancholia vanished.

'Any word from Starjar?' Grace asks Kevin later as they climb into bed.

He did not practise full disclosure in his retelling of his clusterfuck of a job interview. He omitted key details, including his request for an extra bikky on his way out, the singular embarrassing moment that has haunted him since. 'Nothing yet.'

'Well, if they don't hire you, then they're just thick,' she says, extinguishing her light. He lies, scrolling through his phone, his back deliberately walled between them. She ignores this, cuddles up behind him. She finds his thigh beneath the covers and runs her fingers along it and he freezes. He doesn't – he can't – reciprocate. He can't do this. With a platonic squeeze of his shoulder, she eventually gives up and shifts back to her own side.

25.
Millie

Despite the fact that the central heating at Margate, cranked up of late at skyrocketing cost to impress Sylvia and Co., is currently clanking away at high volume, the house remains mercilessly cold. Millie turns the oven to its highest mark and leaves it open – at least one room will be warm for Sylvia's hastily planned visit.

After she rings the doorbell, which she never does, Sylvia silently hands over her key. 'This is all my fault,' she says.

'It isn't. It's mine.'

'I should've told Kevin the truth.'

'Not at all. I begged you not to,' says Millie.

'How did he even find out? I thought we were in the clear.'

'His friend's mother's brother works in the garage.' Millie sighs. 'That's Dublin for you.'

Sylvia says, 'I just wanted to say goodbye and thank you. I'm really gonna miss working with you. You're the coolest boss I've ever had.'

'Kevin has no say in this. I'm going to clear it all up. Come and sit down.'

To Millie's horror, Sylvia's eyes fill. Millie has never seen her companion succumbing to negative emotion; her range heretofore has only encompassed all manner of high spirits, from jolly cheer to breathy gratitude.

'What did Kevin say? Was he monstrous?'

'No, no, he was fine. It's not that.' The American makes a sort of choking noise.

'Sil?'

Millie notes a striking oversized turquoise bangle that encircles Sylvia's slender wrist. She's curious about her caretaker's gypsy jewellery, especially a ring that serves to fuse together her second and third fingers like a bridge, as if they're webbed.

'Did I ever tell you that's what my mother used to call me?' says Sylvia.

'Are you crying?'

'No.' She sits perfectly still. 'Yes.'

Millie takes a breath and says, 'Is this about the medical thing?'

'What?'

'I couldn't help overhearing – are you sick? Sil? You can tell me.'

Sylvia shakes her head no.

Millie exhales. 'Thank God. I felt sure – it sounded like you were talking to a doctor the other night ... during dinner?'

'I'm sorry. This is, like, totally unprofessional.' She wipes her sorrowful eyes with the back of her hand, flashing a tiny grey heart tattoo that she'd had done in San Juan or San Quentin, some bloody San. Sylvia sweeps the fluttering sleeves of her cotton tunic across her face. 'I'm good. I'm fine.'

'Maybe I can help?'

Sylvia locks briefly into Millie's gaze and then looks away. 'I don't think so.'

'You can tell me, whatever it is?'

She looks up at the ceiling, her hands balled into tight fists, which she actually shakes, and, in anguish, screams. 'Aaaagh!'

'What's happened? You're scaring me.'

Sylvia's face collapses into her hands. 'That call you overheard? That wasn't about me.'

'Sorry?'

'I'm not sick,' she says. 'Sean is.'

'Jesus, Mary, and Joseph,' says Millie, stunned and quite unprepared for such a revelation. 'You can't possibly mean your nephew, the healthiest-looking lad ever to be seen? But how could it be?'

'I know, I know. It's hard to believe, but it's true.' Sylvia wipes her face, but tears continue to leak down it.

'Sick how?'

'He has a rare autoimmune disease. He's had it for years and he's been OK because it's usually, like, dormant, but he's had a few flare-ups over here.'

'What's it called?'

'It's his liver. Bad cells basically devour the good ones. The Irish doctors don't have a clue.' She stops. 'Sorry, no offence. You know I don't mean it, but ... it's just so different over here. Like last week, he needed blood work, but since it was a bank holiday weekend, there was no technician there until Tuesday.'

'Some of our hospitals are only a fright. Where is he, which hospital? Beaumont?'

Sylvia balks. 'He's been in and out of every one of them.'

'Poor girl,' says Millie. 'Why didn't you tell me all this before?'

Sylvia removes a mini-packet of tissues from her bag and blows her nose. 'I didn't want to burden you.'

Millie, with an eye to redemption in general, has a strong, uncharacteristic urge to solve this. She shakes her head back and forth, strokes the woman's hand, and idly wonders if this is how to comfort someone. She can hardly remember – it's been so long since her solace was required. 'There's nothing they can do? There must be something.'

'That's just it. There is,' says Sylvia. 'That phone call ... Apparently there's some new treatment, it's experimental. Stem cell.'

'Oh, that's something!'

'Well, yes, but it's – the whole situation's impossible!' Sylvia throws her hands up. 'It's not even here, it's in New York. Anyway, come on, I'll stop being morbid. I'll make us tea.'

'Feck the tea. Why is it impossible if there's a treatment?'

'He'd – we'd – have to go to New York,' Sylvia says. 'There's a hospital there, Columbia Presbyterian,' says Sylvia. 'They specialize in treating this.'

'That's good news, right?'

'It would be if we could afford it. Well, the surgery – the worst part about it is – the hospital says they'll do it for free because it's some kind of cutting-edge thing – he'd be like their guinea pig – but we'd still need to get the aeroplane tickets and the hotel and the meals and all of that. It would cost thousands and thousands. I've been racking my brain for weeks now trying to figure out how to get us there. But it's hopeless.'

*

After Sylvia leaves, Millie yanks up her aluminium garage door and quickly wrenches it back down, plunging herself into blackness. Her breath plumes into the tiny shed as she looks for a tool to address the frigid house situation, calling in a repairman being anathema, at least before she herself has tinkered with the radiators.

Seeing as she's here, Millie decides to perch on her little step stool and fire up a celebratory smoke. The cigarette tastes at once chemical and repulsive, but she smokes through this, sucks in another drag, and another, and begins to relax, letting her mind circle pleasantly back to the moment when she handed Sylvia – coerced her into, more like – a cheque. Sylvia's relief and gratitude were infectious; Millie was near tears herself. Thirty thousand euros are her pennies for a rainy day. Sylvia has turned out to be her rainy day. The American had rejected it again and again, firming Millie's resolve that Sylvia, and Sean, deserved it. It was what ought to be done. In the end, Sylvia would only accept the cheque as a loan. She'd even penned an IOU on the spot, at Millie's kitchen table, and both had signed it.

Millie looks through the garage window, smokes, thinks of Sean waking up a healthy boy in hospital, and then the eccentric anorexic, Maureen McMahon around the corner, who, in a few hours, will be pushing her toddler's pram right past Margate. How the devil she'd gotten pregnant with two hockey sticks for legs and a handful of raisins for her daily breakfast (Millie has heard on good account) is an enigma. Still, the two of them are a delicious daily jolt of youth on this otherwise elderly stretch of road with its shrivelled-up fruit and veg. A few doors down, the O'Leary sisters, Finola and Mary, are a pile of withered aubergines. Noel Crowning, the creepy bachelor solicitor who lives in one of the new bungalows, with his dry lips and dripping nose, is a limp, dirty spud. And what about Millie Gogarty? She considers. 'A date,' she announces to the garage. 'Shrivelled, but with meat left on it still.'

When she returns to the house and first smells smoke, Millie brings her reeking fingers confusedly to her nose and then sets about prying valves open and shut in the sitting and dining rooms, until she reaches the kitchen.

Inside, she is greeted by a hazy veil of smoke that clouds her vision. The oven is an inferno, flames at least two feet high, smoke ballooning wildly from its mouth, so much of it, and the stench of hot grease overwhelming. No alarm has warned her yet that her kitchen is, quite clearly, on fire.

Millie cries out and backs away, shuts the door and stands for a horrified, paralyzing second. Not enough time to call for help; if she doesn't put it out now, the whole room – the house even – could go up. She runs to the hot press, snatches a pile of towels and hurtles herself back into the kitchen, trying to cover the flames. But the towels do nothing; it's as if she threw a teaspoon of water at a bonfire. *Water.* She turns to the sink, dodging flames and beginning to cough.

Frantically, Millie soaks the rest of the pile under the tap. She hears sizzling as she whacks the drenched towels at the oven and the cabinets around it, which are starting to catch. It's working, it looks as if it's working. Millie steps closer towards the oven, so that the right-hand sleeve of her polyester robe instantly ignites. So focused is she, Millie doesn't even notice this turn of events until the burning reaches her skin.

26.

Aideen

Aideen scrolls past Clean-Cut's newest single, an original, 'Baby Baby Baby Baby Baby', and selects The Cramps from Sean's latest tunes. Her ear tends to reject most of his choices – harsh, kinetic, furious – but she pays attention to the lyrics. After carefully applying Brigid's mascara, she packs her things for the weekend in a borrowed duffel. She'll win no cool points with Sean if she's carrying the flash bag her mother had gifted her, all gold links and quilted stitching, big as a pizza pie. Mum had meant well, but it was galaxies off Aideen's current style radar.

For the other boarders in Fair House, this hour, just past four o'clock on a Friday, is the singular weekly high point, set giddily free, as they are, from their day-to-grinding-day institutionalized existence. Her roommates Abigail and Faye, often to be found bickering about the luxuriance of a certain mare's mane or the length of its tail, are the last of this room to have left to catch their train bound for Kildare, where they groom their Irish cobs or jump over ditches and fences on their show ponies. These small clashes are, in fact, rather funny and, though Brigid finds them dull, Aideen is growing to quite like both girls.

Without notice, the dormitory door blasts open, slamming against the mint-hued breeze-block wall.

'Fucking wanker!'

It's Brigid, crying furiously and stomping towards her in maroon Docs recently acquired in Temple Bar and dark opaque tights thick as a hotel tablecloth. Aideen knows Brigid's moods – her friend arrives at fury and good humour at breakneck speeds – but weepy like this, girly upset with evidence of pain quite plain on her face, this is new.

'What's happened?'

Brigid throws her rucksack onto her bed – the two girls now sleep next to each other after Aideen, sensitive, by experience, to the potential of hurt feelings, had delicately negotiated a swap. Now Brigid removes a half-smoked fag, stinking and flaccid, from her jeans pocket. 'I go to sign out, right? Bag's all packed. And that bitch comes in –'

'Bleekland?'

Brigid nods and sticks the smoke between her lips and fumbles with agitated fingers inside her jacket for a light. She moves towards the large window crank.

'Are you insane?'

'I don't care,' Brigid says, but then crosses the room and braces a full laundry hamper against the door.

'You'll be expelled!'

'That's the idea.'

'Seriously?'

Brigid lights up, blows a series of perfect 'O's into the chill air, though most of the smoke clouds right back into the room. 'So I'm signing out and she puts her finger where I'm writing and says to stop. And I'm like, what the fuck? It turns out – can you believe this?' With her denim shirtsleeve, Brigid roughly wipes fresh, furious tears away. 'So my dad's phoned up and told them I'm not allowed to leave. I'm grounded.'

'What?'

'That's what I said. I said, "No, I have permission to go this weekend. It's been three weeks." I mean – I'm supposed to meet Brian tonight at The Tiny Trickle. I *have* to go.'

Aideen has yet to meet Brian, Brigid's new nineteen-year-old pizza deliverer/drug-dealer boyfriend, but she's been raving about how hilarious it is to get high with him, how you laugh about obvious shit until you nearly piss yourself, and then, three minutes later, you don't have the foggiest idea about what was so funny. This had all sounded, to Aideen, a bit daft.

'Put that out, OK?' Aideen watches a long tube of wobbly ash dangle worryingly over the windowsill from the crooked tip of her friend's Silk Cut Purple.

'So my dad, *such a fucking wanker*, he told the school that I can't come home till Easter!'

The ash drops and scatters. Aideen approaches, blows it away, thinks of her own father, who is beyond annoying half the time but never cruel. 'But why?'

'Probably so he can bring all his models home to screw.' Brigid's photographer father – dark and chiselled and worldly, a jaunty cap covering squinting eyes, from the one picture Aideen's seen – and her mother separated when she was a baby, and he has full, if dubious, custody.

'And he doesn't even have the balls to tell me himself; this is coming from *that sadistic piece of shit*.'

'Can't you call him?'

'He's already on a plane to LA for some big event. And anyway, he's not going to change his mind. He never changes his mind.'

Aideen can think of nothing helpful to say.

Brigid spies Aideen's duffel. 'You're meeting him now?'

Aware that her imminent joy will further upset Brigid, Aideen nods sombrely.

'Well then go. You'll miss your bus.'

Town is crackling. Against darkening skies and the omnipresent threat of rain, shopfronts and windows are lit up. Aideen stops, listens to the rhythmic clicking of heels on ancient pavement, peals of laughter, bursts of chatter, roars of buses, car brakes, hawkers peddling fruit and brollies and knock-off Coach wallets. She pulls out her knit gloves from AllSaints, bulky and rocker-chic, Gerard's Christmas gift to her, and passes pubs whose windows already sweat with the late afternoon crowds gathering inside, end-of-the-working-week celebrations gaining momentum. When a door to one of these opens, she hears a snatch of Mum's favourite band, The Waterboys. *I wandered out in the world for years / While you just stayed in your room*. Dublin revelry is underway. Ladies and gents, please!

Now a sizable hen party moves en masse towards Aideen. The bride-to-be, in a white hoodie, THIS BITCH IS GETTING HITCHED spelled in rhinestones studded across it, is being smacked on the head with a quite large and pearly pink inflatable penis. Her mates, a loud group of twenty-something bottle-blonde British babes, already blotto, make their way merrily through the streets, taunting solo men in their path in false posh accents: 'You, kind sir! Won't you take off your trousers, sir!'

Aideen steps onto Grafton Street, whose pulse is visceral and contagious. Whenever she's in town, Aideen ditches her torpid Millburn gait and picks up the pace. Mum used to bring her here on a Saturday, just the two of them, for a film and a burger and chips after. It's so unlike Dalkey where no location – not even the remotest cliff, the loneliest dirt path in the middle of fucking nowhere – is safe from discovery. She once came upon her postman eating his lunch beneath a private cluster of conifers in Dillon's Park, gazing out at the craggy, wild beauty of Dalkey Island. 'Hiya, Aideen,' he'd said, surprised that she stood gawping at him. 'Care for a crisp?'

When she reaches Bewley's, she leans, breezily, she hopes, against its shopfront window, inhaling rich blasts of arabica with every swinging open of the grand glass-encased doors. She watches her fellow citizens pass, meet up, say hello, go inside. She tries to look bored.

At 4:40, Aideen allows herself to look furtively up towards Stephen's Green and down towards Trinity. The place is, as always, a madhouse, and she wonders if she ought to go in and get them a table. But the plan – confirmed this morning – is to meet in this very spot.

At 4:48, she distracts herself by studying a nearby couple. They're young – eighteen, maybe – and as soon as the guy approaches, he snogs his girlfriend. A long snog in the sober daylight. Aideen watches as he hands her a small shopping bag and she peers in and squeals.

At 4:59, she sends Sean a text message. *You still coming?*

At 5:55, Aideen leaves the café and allows herself to be dolefully swept up by the throngs. She makes her way to the Dart station, where she buys a ticket and a packet of Monster Munch and then, going back to the newsagent's, ten Marlboro and a box of matches. She doesn't even know why. Mostly because fuck it. She smokes two cigarettes as she waits and then boards the train bound for Dalkey.

27.

Kevin

With care, Kevin situates his mother, her right arm bandaged and cradled in a gauzy sling, in the passenger seat of his obscene seven-seater, yet another wanton display of the Gogartys' culpability in global overpopulation, as his mother has so often and with superior glee reminded him. But not today. Today, as mother and son coast down the wet roads of Dublin en route to Rossdale Home, she is furiously mute.

'It's just until the burn heals,' Kevin had said in various verbal brews all through the preparing and packing – 'stopgap', 'a couple of weeks', 'a temporary measure'. The previous evening, the two had spent long, dismal hours in the grimmest emergency ward he'd ever encountered, crawling as it was with scarlet-faced alcoholics, bruised, bloody, reeling, mumbling to imaginary foes, and one tiny middle-aged woman, her swollen left eye the colour of a smeared sunset, weeping into her hands.

Mrs Gogarty must have her wound dressed daily, the on-call doctor had explained; she was to rest and be minded. Kevin had been deeply shaken to discover his mother rocking on the carpet of her blackened kitchen, clutching her scalded arm and coughing. It was as close to death as he'd ever allowed himself to think of her. In his terror, and without premeditation, he'd held her very carefully, his poor mum, so as not to brush her injury, and brought a glass of water to her lips and then guided her into his car.

'You'll be back in Margate in no time,' he says to her now, finessing the lever which, in theory, activates the windscreen wipers. But they move too erratically and slowly to sweep the fierce rain clear and the road blurs. 'Spying on the neighbours and losing your keys.'

Silence.

'Did we remember your toilet bag?'

Silence.

'Reading glasses?'

Kevin spots his old schoolmate Tommy O'Dwyer blowing on a cup of takeaway coffee, pulled up alongside the kerb outside the chippie, yakking away on his mobile. Kevin waves, then returns to his calamity.

'You'll be well looked after at Rossdale,' he says. Which is true. From what he's gathered, Rossdale, staffed by experienced and caring professionals, is a reputable home (so long as you disregard that unfortunate tabloid tale some years back when a pregnant nurse's assistant and a randy diabetic codger with hairy ears were discovered humping in the front pew of the home's makeshift chapel). Her wound will be tended to, pain meds doled out, meals cooked. And frankly, it's not the worst way to introduce what might become a necessary eventuality.

'Why can't I just stay at yours? You wouldn't even need to be home.'

Since the fire, his mother's eyes seem to have sunk impossibly deeper into the bottomless, shadowy crags of her once patrician face. Now they're like two slick, dark pebbles sinking helplessly into quicksand.

'All the kids coming and going would be lovely. Just set me up with a glass of water and a crust of bread and I'll be grand.'

A crust of bread!

He sighs. 'It's not that simple.'

'You complicate everything.'

'Be that as it may, you have a quite serious second-degree burn, Mum. What if you're hungry and no one's home? What happens when you need to use the toilet? How will you bathe?'

In the next lane, a city bus lumbers loudly along, its entire side covered in an ad depicting a mum and dad and a freckled son and daughter sitting in wide-eyed thrall of a Jaffa Cake below the words 'Jaffa Time!' Kevin speeds up with the idea to overtake it, but the road ahead bends and offers no visibility. He releases his foot from the pedal and watches as the happy clan moves mockingly forward, poised forever in anticipation.

Kevin feels bad. His mother seems to him more fragile now, more vulnerable, and, he knows, lonely. On the other hand, she's a thief, (an arsonist?), a misanthropic malcontent, an exaggerator of mammoth proportions, a driver of sane sons to vivid fantasies of matricide. He breathes. To their right is the ocean. With the tide out, the strand is expansive, promising. Yellow kinky tumbles of seaweed are tossed everywhere, as if the sea swallowed them and, on second thought, vomited the whole lot back up. To their left, Kevin and Millie whizz by what used to be prime waterfront real estate, the odd pub, a hair salon that

Mum frequented until an ugly row about being overcharged three quid for a conditioning balm that was applied without her consent. From the tip of the lighthouse at the East Pier to Bray Head, Kevin could practically map out the southside with the sites of humiliations, scenes, rescue missions.

He brings the car to a halt in front of a fairly large, nondescript detached residence with a wheelchair ramp that extends from a pair of double doors to the pavement. The Gogartys, one smiling politely, the other scowling, are ushered into Rossdale Home by a chubby twenty-something in a plush scarlet tracksuit. The place is redolent not of foul odours, as one might expect, but of Sunday dinners, lamb stew and garlicky potatoes, maybe, though his mother would never concede this, or anything.

The common lounge appears respectable if a touch shabby. Most of the odd-bod fittings and furniture had been purchased in an earlier decade, to be sure, but it's been taken care of properly enough, in the old way – all the mahogany bits gleam and vaguely emit a pine-esque church varnish scent, there are no visible tears in the upholstery, no dark puke patches or unsavoury secretions on the carpet. A peculiar collection of seats – a chintz sofa, some upholstered rockers – is lined up in the dead centre of the room, as if a child's game of musical chairs is about to begin. On one of the rockers, a thinning cushion bears the needlepointed words, IT IS WHAT IT IS. Across the Victorian mantelpiece above a blazing gas fire, someone's taped up dozens of Christmas cards: baby Jesus in his manger, a choir of angels in the sky, carollers proclaiming the good news, religious claptrap Kevin knows will drive his mother spare.

'You must be the Gogarty family?'

Sheila Slattery, the director of Rossdale, whose arse Kevin's been cyberkissing the past twelve hours, is just the sort of over-friendly, over-breathy woman his mother usually adores – a younger Jolly Jessica.

'Mrs Slattery,' says Kevin, removing his cap, a sartorial legacy of his father's, who was prone, in his day, to don one on formal calls. 'I'd like to introduce my mother, Mrs Gogarty. We're very grateful for the last spot, Mrs Slattery.'

'Speak for yourself,' says Mum.

Mrs Slattery beams at them as if Mum hasn't just been hostile, revealing a wide gap in her front chompers like a loo window whose dark shade has been pulled down for privacy. It's a flaw so obvious and winning, Kevin suspects it alone could endear her to his mother.

'Right then. The paperwork looks to be all in order. Let me show you to your room first, Mrs Gogarty – does that sound good?'

They take a lift to the third floor and proceed down an orderly hallway.

'Here we are,' says Mrs Slattery. 'This is you.'

Kevin and Mrs Slattery and Mum stand at the threshold of a small peach-coloured chamber split down the middle by a cloth curtain suspended on hooks dangling from a half-moon of metal. On the right side is an empty twin-sized hospital bed, a modest chest of drawers, a bed-stand with a reading light, and a bible.

'Won't be needing that,' says Mum, nudging the book perhaps harder than intended, perhaps not, sending it skittering to the tile flooring.

'Mum!' Kevin picks up the book and replaces it on the bedside table.

'No worries at all,' says Mrs Slattery, though Kevin can see that the aggressive bible push has surprised her, made her re-evaluate his mother as decidedly uncharming – an inevitable evaluation, perhaps, but one he was hoping to put off at least until he'd made it back to the car. He's terrified they will change their minds. 'We've made a mistake!' they'll say. 'Take her away at once!'

'There's someone I'd like you to meet,' says Mrs Slattery. She pulls the curtain back. There lies, much to Kevin and his mother's surprise, a tiny, shrunken, slumbering, possibly comatose, almost entirely bald woman well into her ninth decade. Someone's tucked the poor soul up snugly beneath a fading ivory counterpane. Nestled, she puts Kevin in mind of a girl's doll from another century.

'This is Mrs Jameson,' says Mrs Slattery. 'Your new roommate.'

28.

Millie

As she does now and then – typically in the mornings – over the next week, Mrs Jameson turns a set of vacant milky eyes, like half-cooked egg whites, onto her gawking, impatient roommate.

'Good morning!' trills Millie one day. 'Or should I say good afternoon? I think you've been asleep since Tuesday. I said to one of the staff, "Is my roommate by any chance in hibernation? Is ursine the word for 'bear'? Or lupine?" I've never seen such sleep.' Millie pauses to gain breath and hover with deep curiosity above this blank of a woman who may, in this moment, be entertained or vexed or, indeed, filling up her catheter.

If one were to categorize Rossdale's residents into types of business models, say, Mrs Jameson would be a sole trader. No one from the world has thought to send her a postcard; her phone hasn't rung; she's had no visitors. She is alone. Of course, Millie doesn't exactly consider herself a conglomerate. She hasn't been inundated with Gogarty TLC. She is barely speaking to Kevin, which makes his harried visits – as if he has scores of errands to run despite being currently jobless – brutal.

He spends most of the time asking the aides to do up the shades or wipe down the bed tray, or he chats up the one or two young nurses (some of whom look worse off, or at least fatter, than Millie). He regales them with tales of his brief employment years ago as a hapless, haemophobic volunteer in a local clinic. They laugh.

Yesterday, Kevin had swooped in with a lavish 'Good afternoon' and an extravagant kiss on his mother's frazzled head, entirely dismissing her admittedly childish behaviour. She harrumphed – can't do much with *that* – and, with pursed lips and a scowl, jutted her chin towards the peach wall and remained stubbornly thus. All of which required immense will power. She was fairly bursting to complain about the custard, which is stone cold and the colour of earwax, and to tell him that the rhubarb is flavourless, the rooms tropical, the doctors supercilious, the nurses patronizing, the aides indifferent, the nights eternal, the pills choke-worthy, the proximity to death unbearable. She said none of these things, and experienced a hot lump clawing its way down her throat when he closed out his visit with a second spectacular kiss.

'I'm really enjoying our chats,' he'd said with a wink.

'If I were you, Mrs Jameson,' Millie continues now, 'the first thing I'd do is check my handbag.'

Mrs Jameson levels a watery, disconcerting gaze at, or sort of at, Millie.

'Not to alarm you – Kevin, my son, you see, now *he's* an alarmist. He worries about his knees – he's an athlete, you see. Wonderful tennis player. Very graceful. And then, oh, Gerard's exams! That's his eldest. Will he fail? Will he meet a nice girl?'

Millie throws up exasperated hands to punctuate her monologue. She decides, having studied the woman's soft folds of skin and collapsed neck and hand-stitched eyelet cover, that back when Mrs Jameson was not bedridden, before whatever befell her, she was a generous woman with a creative streak and a wicked sense of fun, a good egg.

'Didn't I wake up and see that naughty nurse – and I don't mean "naughty nurse"' – Millie giggles: she has begun to appreciate the liberating benefits of a mute roommate – 'rooting around amongst your belongings, both hands digging in there, well-manicured, too, I can tell you.' Millie mimes a person snooping through someone's bag.

Mrs Jameson yawns. 'That's true.'

'Sorry?' says Millie.

Mrs Jameson clucks twice, and smiles.

'I wasn't even sure you could – and here I am talkin' the face off ya. You have no idea all that's been going through my mind while you lay sleeping. I've come up with your entire life story, in case you're interested?'

'That's true.'

'Sorry?'

'That's true.'

Mrs Jameson smacks lips like onion skin together and runs her tongue along her upper gums and then her eyes flutter and close just as Millie's bedside phone rings.

'Hello?'

'Mrs Gogarty?'

'Speaking!'

'Guess who?'

'Sil? Is that you?' Millie covers the mouthpiece and to her roommate announces, 'It's my American friend. I must tell you.'

'Mrs Gogarty? Are you there?'

'I'm speechless! How did you track me down? Did Kevin tell you I was here?'

'Well, I couldn't just neglect my favourite Irishwoman, now, could I?'

'Oh, he's put me in this place. Did they tell you?'

'I called your house a bunch but it just rang and rang. And so I called Kevin's house and his daughter answered and told me there'd been some kind of fire?'

'Oh, we mustn't talk long. This is a transatlantic call. Just let me hear you breathe.'

'What?'

'That's gorgeous.'

'What happened?' says Sylvia. 'There was a fire?'

'Oh, it was horrendous. I nearly died. Did you not hear? And Kevin came in and found me in the kitchen. But never mind that. Tell me, how is our patient? When is the surgery?'

'It happened a few days ago.'

'That was fast.'

'And he's recovering now. So far so good.'

To Mrs Jameson, Millie says, 'The surgery was a whopping success!'

'The doctors say it's going to be a long recovery, longer than we thought. You should see him – all tied up to machines and eating Jell-O. He's such a trouper.'

'I'm just thrilled to hear that,' cries Millie. 'For you both. Just chuffed.'

'All thanks to you.'

'Oh now ...'

'It's such a relief, I can't tell you. But what about you? How long do you have to stay in there?'

'Between yourself and myself and Mrs Jameson, I don't think I'll last long here.'

'Mrs Jameson?'

'I miss our chats, Sil. I really do.'

'Oh, me too,' says Sylvia. 'I hope you get home soon. You think in a few weeks?'

'Well, the kitchen – you wouldn't know where you were, black as night.'

'Oh my goodness.'

'Here's what I want you to do: book your ticket right back home and come and help me escape. Take me to the land of the free!'

Sylvia snorts and says, 'Wouldn't that be great? Oh, shoot, I have to go. The doctors are calling me in for an update.'

'Ring me again, won't you, when you've got a bit more time?'

'Of course.'

'Or give me a number where I can reach you?'

'Oh sure.' Sylvia rattles off a whole slew of digits, which Millie takes down on a scrap of paper.

'When are you coming back to Dublin?' says Millie, but they must've got disconnected because the line's gone suddenly dead.

29.

Kevin

Kevin pays a maddening ten quid to ensure his vehicle's not stolen during dinner and shuffles towards Mulberry Garden to celebrate his twentieth wedding anniversary. Back when he was gainfully employed and things felt rather less disjointed on the home front, he and Grace had discussed marking this landmark with a romantic trip – a bank holiday getaway in Corsica or an extravagant fortnight in Argentina. They'd take tango lessons; they'd spent long lusty afternoons on their private hammock. They'd pass out in blissful siestas in a Recoleta boutique hotel room, a wicker fan rotating coolly overhead.

But they've no money for such frolics and she's grown tired of sleeping with him, whether in a Buenos Aires hammock (even possible?) or not. All mention of their dream trip faded. For a time, Grace envisioned a party in the house, a blowout with a signature cocktail, proper invites, the children mock-roasting them in a rehearsed skit (Kevin tends to find these pony shows twee, but they love performing them and so he holds his tongue). That trickled down to a soirée with just their intimate circle – less work, more fun, and cheaper. And *that* diluted to this: the two of them meeting for a meal in Donnybrook.

Grace is late. Kevin sips his G&T and checks his phone. Yesterday, he'd deleted Rose Byrd's contact information, an act whose irrevocability makes him feel at times slightly heartsick, at other times, like right now, grateful and relieved, his fate decided.

He sees his wife arrive and check in with the host. A man at a nearby table regards her, which pleases him. Kevin swallows and slides his mobile inside his jacket pocket and examines his fellow well-heeled diners, preferable to examining himself, but introspection crawls through his mind anyway. Even if a suitable job in his dying industry became suddenly available, honestly, would he want it? He's had every conceivable experience in the magazine world; he's slain those dragons. What he needs, he knows, is something different, something to unstick him. Whatever, or whomever, he engages lately seems to turn to shit. To wit: Mum despises Rossdale and will never cease dogging his days with complaints. Aideen, let's face it, continues to view her own family as a brood of odious arseholes worthy primarily of contempt, which she is singularly equipped to dole out. But mostly what he doesn't care to ponder as Grace wends her way towards him is what twenty years with her means or doesn't mean or ought to mean. He does not want to reflect on whether they're confusing love with loyalty at this point, or that the children who have been the glue are devolving into its antidote, or, and this is too cynical, he knows, that the two of them are held together by a deeply rooted laziness, an abhorrence to having to dismantle their cluttered, complicated household and divvy up all the useless and embarrassing suburban crap they've accumulated lo these many years. Laptops, emery boards, kettles – these cannot possibly be the mortar of a marriage.

Now his wife of two decades stands before him – she stifles a yawn, which he finds darkly hilarious on their big celebratory night – and Kevin, anxious and overheated, removes his jacket as he rises to greet her.

Once their meals arrive, Grace admires the decor and says, 'I want to book in that new place, the organic one – what's it called?'

'Hmmm?'

'I thought you'd been there? The chef's from Cork ...'

'Pass the wine, will you?'

Grace refills Kevin's glass and nudges at a pale cake of potato gratin. 'It's driving me mad ...' she says.

'Oh, the restaurant? The one where Mick and I had dinner a while back.'

'Mick?'

'Yes, Mick.'

'You don't go to restaurants with Mick.'

'Mick does require nourishment other than stout from time to time.'

'Let me try a bite of your sole.'

'I sold it long ago, darling.' He tries to smile but it feels more grimace than grin, more drug-addled clown than good-natured husband.

Grace reaches across the table to stab a wedge of his fish. 'How were the kids today?'

'Pugilistic comes to mind,' he says.

'Nuala and Ciaran? Oh, this is lovely.' She chews, always has, in a way he finds somewhat grotesque, like she's working a mouthful of heavy, wet sand, a grain of which will inevitably lodge in one of her incisors, though she won't notice or bother to remove it until bedtime. It's sometimes difficult for him to recall just how intimidating her beauty once was.

'There was a big row, mostly Ciaran's doing.'

'Oh?' He can see she is put off by this topic. She does not care to hear disparaging information about her offspring. This inevitably causes in Kevin a palpable need to play up all tales of their bad behaviour, to prove to Grace, he supposes, what it is he's been doing all day, how hard he sometimes works to keep the peace.

'He found out about Gavin and teased her mercilessly. He was really quite a devil. Cute little devil, though.'

But Grace has stopped listening, her fork frozen mid-air like a professor's pointer, and her confused expression raises an alarm in Kevin. 'Found out what?' she says. 'What about Gavin?'

'Oh, nothing. It's silly. Just that they're apparently a thing now, you know. Officially. He gave her a necklace, quite sweet actually.' He picks up his glass. 'Did I not tell you?'

'No, you didn't. And more to the point, *she* didn't tell me.'

'I'm sure she will.'

Grace resumes her chewing. 'Well, to be fair, I got in late last night so she didn't really have the chance.' Grace turns wistful. 'First real boyfriend! He seems quite nice, though, doesn't he? When did all this happen?'

Kevin considers lying. But he realizes there's no point: Nuala wouldn't lie along with him. His children, three out of four of them anyway, are do-gooders, far more scrupulous, perhaps, than their father.

'I don't know. Around the time Aideen started at Millburn.'

Grace sets her utensils down, first the fork, then the knife, and puts her head into her hands.

'Darling,' he says. 'Please don't be upset. She's ...'

'She's what?'

'She's very private and –'

'She is not *private*,' says Grace. 'I'm her mother. She's not private with her mother.'

'I don't think you should take this personally.'

'Of course I take it personally!'

'She'll tell you in her own time.'

'Don't patronize me, Kevin. And, anyway, why didn't *you* mention it?'

'It's not a big thing. I don't know. It really didn't occur to me.'

'Didn't occur to you? A milestone –'

'Don't let's get histrionic.'

'Don't tell me what to get.'

'How is this my fault?'

'I didn't say it was your fault.'

'It sure feels like my fault.'

'Maybe our communication has broken down even worse than I thought.'

'She's got a boyfriend!' Kevin's volume is higher than he'd intended. His wife shushes him with a fierce jab of finger to lips and a face that's bloodthirsty. Well, he won't be quiet now: he feels a mighty truth surging to the fore – the gun's been fired, the horses are stamping in their stalls – and he has the goods to hurt her. The impulse to unburden himself and fumble towards some direction of truth is too exhilarating to ignore. 'There's a lot that goes on you don't know about,' he says. 'You've barely been home.'

'That's not true.'

'It is true.'

'Well, if it is true, it's because I have a job.'

'You also have a family.'

'Oh, please.'

Grace is glaring daggers at him. He hears the soft chimes of a text-message alert. Could it be from Rose?

Grace takes up her wine and, squinting as if she doesn't recognize him, says, 'You can't even see it.'

Kevin knows she's on the cusp of deploying something dangerous here and he ought to deny her this small satisfaction. But he can't help himself: he's always craved her insight – thoughtful and considered, wise, bent towards optimism – regarding just about every topic, especially himself. How many times have her co-workers, her underlings, even her bosses, come into her office over the years and shut the door to disclose some agony or problem or anxiety and left the better for it?

'See what?'

She looks coldly at him. 'That you've been wallowing in a pool – no, not a pool, an ocean – of self-pity since the day you lost your job. That you're filtering every single thing, everything, the kids, your mother, me, everything, through the most toxic lens. You're not even yourself. You're a misery guts.'

He wants to cry foul, to argue the point, to reciprocate, to wound her back, to tell her she's the miserable one. He's just fine, he needs only understanding, support. He wants to scream. He wants to punch something. To hit the table. To drink a whiskey. To get away.

Grace's mouth is slightly open; her teeth have purpled from the wine.

'Well, then, here's to our marriage,' he says viciously, holding up his glass in a faux toast. The chimes on his mobile ring again.

'Look, Kevin, I'm just trying –'

'Excuse me.' He gets up, tosses his napkin onto the table, frantic to be gone.

'We're in the middle of a conversation.'

'Oh, is that what this is? Feels more like an ambush.'

'Will you sit down and let's talk? Please.'

'Don't worry,' he says. 'It'll give you time to reload.'

Kevin huffs off towards the men's bathroom, fucking furious that his wife can still, all these years later, deliver precise pinpoints of pain (and truth?) at high-voltage levels. He enters a gleaming white cave of a room where nothing is discernible: no fixture, no tap for the water, no proper sink, only a porcelain trough, no towels or hand dryer visible. He feels disoriented. Where stall doors might normally stand hangs, instead, a massive sheet of frosted glass the width of a kitchen counter but without knobs or pulls. He pushes with both hands into various spaces along it. As he turns away in disgust, his shoulder brushes up against the wall, and a sleek invisible door magically opens with a whoosh, revealing a toilet, which, Kevin is pleased to see, looks exactly as a toilet should.

He plonks himself down upon the commode and reaches for his phone just as he remembers that he'd removed it from his back pocket and placed it in his jacket. Which is hanging on the back of his chair and which could very well be bleating incessantly this moment not thirty inches from his wife.

Kevin bashes his way out of the absurd bathroom and quells a sickening sense of doom, a rising hysteria. His adrenaline is jacking so high he could probably reach the table, a room away, in one Herculean leap. He can't see Grace. Has she left? That would be fine, that would be workable, he could figure it out, he could apologize for this absurd fight about his daughter's first boyfriend. *How was that so important only two minutes ago?* But no: she's bent over her phone, sitting exactly where he'd left her.

'Houdini couldn't find the jacks in here.'

He eases back into his seat, hand immediately checking for the reassuring bulk in his jacket. But the mobile's not there. He slips his fingers into each side pocket, empty, both, and then looks at Grace, bearing such sorrow it's as if her face is a crumpled bit of linen, and he realizes she's holding *his* phone.

But there's nothing to see on his phone, nothing incriminating. He'd wiped all of Rose's text messages from it a while back. He'd wiped her contact information. Yet Grace won't look at him. She swipes his screen and there's a photo of Gerard and Kevin hamming it up in the kitchen, and she swipes again and there's another photo of Gerard and Kevin in the kitchen, taken a second later. She's not flicking through his text messages; she's flicking through his camera.

The screenshots.

His wife is reading the early exchange – raunchy, incomplete, an insider's incomprehensible exchange – of this once-burgeoning thing, this nothing thing that's already over.

'Grace,' he says.

For a time, she refuses to even look at him, but when she does, her eyes are murderous.

'Grace.'

Now she's standing up, reaching for her metallic clutch.

'Wait!' Kevin scrambles up out of his chair. 'Wait. Hang on. Let me explain.'

Now she's taking up the shawl from her seat.

Their marriage, like any, has had its share of conflict – money stresses, differences in child-rearing philosophies, a terrifying cancer scare (the lump was benign), arguments about the uneven distribution of labour, and hundreds of other mundane, irritating quotidian differences long since worked through and laughed at even. One late night in London in the early days, they'd had a big row and he'd stomped theatrically out of bed in his jocks, shoved on tracksuit bottoms and slammed out of the flat. They'd howled around the place later, when he returned to discover he'd stormed out in *her* trackies.

But until this moment, celebrating their twentieth wedding anniversary, none of their cross words have ever felt so perilous, or permanent.

Now she's walking out the door.

30.

Aideen

Even the wholesome square of gingham on Nuala's Dorothy costume, one of fiction's most notable goody-goodies, manages to look sexy on her sister. An hour ago, there'd been a row over the ruby slippers Nuala attempted to get away with as part of her stage debut – two-inch platform stilettos that screamed 'floozy' and that Dad unconditionally forbade.

'I'm putting my foot down,' he'd said with a nerdy chuckle. All had stared at him with steely contempt.

When the Gogartys arrive Friday evening at the school auditorium where *The Wizard of Oz* is set to begin, Mum sits at one end while Dad, at the other, positions Aideen beside Gran, who's been signed out of Rossdale for the evening and, frankly, has been a bit of a glommy burden so far. In less public circumstances, Aideen would tolerate her grandmother's blatant insecurity better. She gets being at sea, obviously. But a) she's in turmoil, and b) she's in the second row of her ex-school where a pack of mean girls barely acknowledge her – never really did – and though she wishes she didn't give a toss about what they think, the truth is it's not the height of cool to be seen shackled to one's octogenarian granny.

Soon enough, Dorothy's world collapses in a cheesy Kansas cyclone re-enactment. Even the dimmest audience member could spot the set of large, bony hands from backstage that visibly reach out and shake Uncle Henry and Aunt Em's shack. Which is funny. Aideen, laughing, points them out to Gran.

Gran laughs and whispers, 'I adore you.'

Aideen puts an arm around her. How insubstantial Gran's shoulder feels, just air and bone.

As they were leaving the house earlier, amidst the usual whining and moaning of the siblings (none but Nuala was looking forward to the night's slice of culture), Dad had hooked Aideen's arm into his.

'A quick word? Look, your gran's in a bad spot at the moment. She's feeling alienated and abandoned and with the burn – it's just not a good situation, as I know you can appreciate.' As he delivered this pile of utter shite, Aideen had watched Gran through the window, bent over the gravel drive, bashing something with the pointed tip of her golf umbrella. Satisfied, Gran moved on and stood beaming at a bush, or nothing. Or maybe everything? Maybe they're just missing what Gran's seeing.

'I just want to be sure she's looked after,' Dad said. 'Let's be extra kind.'

'Is that a joke? I bloody well know that, Dad. *I'm* the one who *is* kind to her.'

'Language.'

'Bloody hell.'

In public outings, the Gogartys tend to occupy an entire room or row or pew or lift. Mortifying. Like, who else's parents so *over-procreated*? OK, quite a few in Dalkey – in fact, just down the road, the Broughlins produced seven children, all twelve and under, including two sets of twins who are rarely spotted without soiled clothing and inappropriately light jackets in wintry weather. Still, the size of her family vexes Aideen; she knows Dad takes a huffy pride in his clan, like he has all these people he loves and who love him. Aideen wonders if this is why people have children: to guarantee a critical mass of love. She spots her mother, who seems quieter than usual, gazing openly at Nuala onstage, straining to absorb every note the girl trills, wet-eyed, tissue-clutching. By the time 'Over the Rainbow' starts up, Mum's practically keening.

Her twin is admittedly better than Aideen had expected. In fact, she's really good – easily the most natural actor onstage and hers is one of the only voices consistently on key. But the play itself is a yawn, and the America-ness of it reminds her of Sean and again and again what she did wrong that he would vanish without explanation.

At first, Aideen had been confused. Had he misplaced his phone? Had he gotten lost? Was he sick? She had text messaged him repeatedly: *Sean? U OK? Hello?* But all for naught. She'd spent the weekend waiting, but nothing. An incomprehensible silence, like a death. A full week after their non-meeting, she's come to realize that Sean is done with her, that, contrary to his initial blindness, he now sees her as ugly, dumb, boring, undeserving, flat-chested, big-footed, scabby-kneed, uncool. (Ironically, the only source of comfort to her has been his music. Turns out heartbreak and Nirvana jibe well.)

Afterwards, the lobby is a sea of munchkins, a study in blue ombré – tights, make-up, caps, trousers and pinafores, overalls. There's a buzzy post-show energy about the room that makes Aideen feel even more unmoored – too many people excited, or pretending to be. Every few minutes, the stage door opens and a student performer anxiously peers out, blinking, embarrassed, at the crowds and the mums who've come bearing cut flowers wrapped in paper and boxes of Cadbury Roses.

Gran wanders off.

When Nuala, the last actor, *of fucking course*, appears, raven-tressed and blushing, a mild, local applause sparks up and Dad calls out, 'Hip, hip!' and Ciaran answers, 'Hurray!' Mum runs to Nuala, like a film's ending when the lovers reunite after a touching and funny but still worrisome string of misunderstandings.

'Fabulous, darling!'

Aideen turns away, eyes sweeping the room slowly, and, after some scanning, spies Gran a good distance off. She's latched herself onto a pair of middle-aged parents, both plain, in eyeglasses and anoraks, looking vaguely alarmed as Gran points to her own bandaged arm. Then Gran's other hand sneaks onto the arm of an unknown nearby munchkin where it remains firmly in place.

The Gogartys are positioned in a receiving line so that Nuala is now bestowed with accolades from each family member individually, in full bridal-party fashion. When she reaches Aideen, Nuala leans forward, cleavage practically leaking from her white top, and whispers, 'I have to talk to you.'

'You're up the pole?'

'What?'

Aideen shrugs. 'Nothing.'

'But not here.' She leans in closer so that a cluster of silky locks lands between Aideen's lips, emitting a foul, stiff blast of hair spray. 'Come to my room tonight. Once everyone's asleep.'

'What?'

'It's important.'

Sometime after eleven that evening, the Gogarty seven-seater pulls up alongside Rossdale and Dad kills the motor. A single bulb burns above the front door, illuminating a brass knocker that gives the impression of this actually being a home. The road is stunningly quiet and dark, no streetlights, no cars, no noise. It occurs to Aideen that Gran must miss the sound of the sea.

'Right,' says Dad. 'Here we are.'

'I need to stop by Margate and get some papers,' Gran announces, sniffing.

Dad hops pointedly out of the car and heaves open the sliding backseat door. 'Count of three,' he says.

'I have to go over my will. Make some changes.' Is she *winking* at Aideen? It's hard to tell in the dark, but Gran's face does have that wild shit-stirring look.

'I'll ring you first thing in the morning,' Dad says now, reaching across Gran to unbuckle her seat belt.

'Ring?' She blocks his hand from the buckle. 'I haven't gotten a single phone call since I arrived.'

'That is patently untrue,' Dad says. He leans Gran's umbrella against the car and offers both hands to her. Gran ignores him, sighs, and sits back, as if fireside.

'In actual fact, I did get a phone call. From Sylvia.'

Aideen stirs.

'Who?' Irritation creeps into Dad's voice. 'Oh, her.'

'Sylvia rang?' says Aideen.

'From America, no less.'

'That's splendid,' says Dad. 'Can I assist you out of the car, Mum? Let's – give me your good hand there.'

Gran bristles. 'I want to go home.'

'And you will, just as soon as you're fully recovered,' says Dad.

'Sylvia's in America?' This, from Aideen, is asked as casually as she can muster.

'The surgery was a success.'

Aideen says, 'What surgery?'

'Mum, it's late and Ciaran needs to go to bed. Can we talk about this tomorrow? Please, just give me your good hand.'

Gran's face fogs. 'Wait now ... Did I not mention ...? I suppose I didn't.'

'She needed surgery?' says Aideen.

'Oh no, not Sylvia,' says Gran. 'She's right as rain. The most thorough American you can imagine.'

Dad sighs. 'I thought you just said she had surgery?'

'No, it was the boy she looks after, her nephew. Did you never meet him? From Florida.'

'What in the world are you talking about, Mum?'

'Sean, Sylvia's young charge,' Millie says, as if they are all brain-dead, 'has a life-threatening illness.'

'Who's Sean?' says Nuala.

Throughout these detonations, Aideen has barely dared breathe. She's struggling to absorb this data dump, grateful that the darkness can hide her shock and also that Sean never laid eyes on her sister.

'In actual fact,' Gran says, 'he was on his deathbed, if you must know. He called at the house a few times with her. I will say, he helped me tremendously. Extremely helpful.' She looks directly at Dad. 'Odd jobs I've been trying to get accomplished. He rewired the lamp in the kitchen.'

'What do you mean Sean's ... *sick*?' says Aideen. 'I don't think so, Gran.'

'Do you know him?' Mum asks.

Aideen mumbles a sort of affirmative.

'Oh, I don't remember what the disease was,' Gran says. She removes her hat, scratches with gusto the back of her scrubby head. 'Some terrible life-threatening thingamajig. Not cancer but something ... cancer's cousin. Sounds like a play. Did you ever hear the like? Anyway, they flew to America. The two of them did. Did I not tell you?'

Afterwards, in the safety of her room, Aideen pores over every bit of the discussion in the family car. Sean is sick, and therefore, therefore, *oh my God*. If he's sick, what disease has he? Will he die? Will he come back to Ireland? And why had he not said a word to her? It's both the worst and best news: her boyfriend may be battling for his life in some US hospital bed, but it also explains why he abandoned her so callously. He must have taken ill that day she'd waited outside Bewley's or he was silently suffering, trying to be gallant, uncomplaining, heroic.

Two soft knocks sound on the door and Aideen sees the bright, blemish-free face of her sister.

'What?'

'Sssh! You were supposed to come down.'

Nemesis quietly clicks the door shut and, with perfectly dainty grace that makes Aideen want to hurl her clear across the room, she steps over piles of discarded knickers on the floorboards and sits with a sigh on the bed. She is so pretty: the clear, light eyes, the full, arched brows, the etched cheeks, all of it.

'Mum and Dad had a huge row, like. Huge.'

'About what?'

'I don't know.'

'You don't know?'

'I'm not sure. It was really late. I was asleep, but the shouting woke me up.'

'When was this?'

'Their anniversary – was it Tuesday? Both of them were yelling – like, top of their lungs. Louder than you've ever heard. And then Daddy –' Aideen hates that Nemesis still sometimes calls them Mummy and Daddy. It's a deliberately infantile ploy for their attention, a direct roadmap to yet more coddling and nice little preening poodle pats. *Good puppy, Nuala, go fetch.* In fact, Aideen's been toying with the idea of transitioning from 'Mum' and 'Dad' to 'Grace' and 'Kevin'.

'Don't cry. Fuck's sake.'

Nuala jams together her lips, but they tremble nonetheless. Aideen sees something like bravery in this minute battle. She is moved enough to do the unspeakable: she places a hand on her sister's back – precedent-setting – which immediately results in Nuala's total capitulation. In this state, Nuala's suddenly not so gorgeous. Her nostrils flare; copious tears leak from red eyes, leaving a trail of fresh pale tracks down those sculpted cheeks. But instead of bringing her hands to cover her face, as Aideen would surely do, loath to exhibit anything like real emotion, Nuala turns with a helpless shrug to her sister and collapses into her. Aideen momentarily freezes and then gathers Nuala up in her arms, as she so often used to without awkwardness or hesitation. She feels for her twin.

'It's alright,' says Aideen. 'It's going to be all right.'

'No it's not.'

'Everybody fights. Especially married people.'

'Not like this. I think they're getting a divorce.'

'That's ridiculous! Nobody gets a divorce. Why are you saying that? Did they say that? Did that word come up at all?'

'No, but, I mean, they're barely speaking. And he's been sleeping in the basement ever since.'

'Would you ever fuck off!'

'I'm telling you.'

'Bollocks.'

'You don't know what's been going on around here. I'm telling you. He waits till we're all in bed and then he goes down. I found the sheets in a big ball in the cupboard. If you don't believe me, go see for yourself.' They sit in silence until Nuala says, 'I wish you lived here all the time.'

31.

Millie

Half of Rossdale doesn't make it to the hall for tea. A tray is brought directly to their rooms or they're force-fed through their nose or belly-button or big toenail for all Millie Gogarty knows, poor sods. Of the patients – 'clients', if you please – who do roll or shuffle or otherwise make their way in, most head afterwards to the TV lounge, though there's constant moaning that they can't hear the thing (the truth: it would deafen a veteran trombonist). Millie typically spends her evenings babbling at Mrs Jameson. She's grown quite fond of her roommate despite the lack of reciprocity the relationship poses. But some nights, like this one, the thought of sitting in that quiet already leaves her with a sense of hollowed-out despair.

She eyeballs the lingerers, decrepit but conscious, hoping to silently invite one or two to join her, but no one appears to notice. Right, then, Millie goes it alone somewhat shyly, a recently acquired paperback, *Mentor of Desire*, tucked beneath her uninjured arm. The other one, wrapped daily in layers of sterile gauze and cradled in its navy canvas hammock, is part of a growing collection of useless limbs and sore body parts: frozen shoulder, gammy knee, a duo of unsightly corns.

After settling herself into one of the less comfortable armchairs – the price of her dithering – Millie delves back into the unlikely romance between a sensual Chicago professor of puppetry and a smouldering South Dakota farmhand when she feels eyes upon her. It's Anna, a timid, arthritic spinster with whom previous attempts at conversation have failed. Anna stands now in a puddle of golden lamplight openly studying Millie's book jacket, which depicts a lusty shirtless boy in razored jeans towering behind a buxom woman in square specs, the two of them locked forever in a hysterical portrayal of eroticism.

Millie practically snorts. The young ones carry on as if they'd invented sex. No one could accuse *her* of being a prude. She and Peter once did the deed at lunchtime on a tartan rug in a wood. Lunchtime! In a wood! Still, it's troubling that, try as she might, she struggles to recall with any real specificity most of her life's sexual episodes – all in wedlock and so long ago.

'Would you mind reading aloud a bit, Millie?' Anna says. 'I'm only desperate for a story.'

Mind? Why, Millie is flattered the woman even knows her name! She invites Anna to sit beside her, mock-dusts the adjacent seat as if she's hosting a supper party, and dives into a scene when things between the unlikely couple at Bucolic Acres have just begun heating up.

After a few paragraphs, Millie's acquired a small but intent audience: one passably lucid-looking fellow with white tufts of nasal hair launching in half-moons from his nostrils, and two harmless biddies collectively known as the Mary S's (Mary

Sullivan and Mary Smith), who are rarely seen one without the other.

'Roberta knew she wanted Hank,' Millie reads. 'Hers was a type of desire she'd never experienced so acutely before. Her body thrilled and her heart leapt when she saw him wiping his glistening six-pack with a rag while taking a break from the hay-gathering, or tinkering with the chisel plough engine, or patting down Rusty, his giant gelding.'

'Ah, so it's his giant gelding she's after, is it?' says Anna.

Millie and the little crew share a good laugh at this unlikely heckle, a rare infusion of mischief in these rooms, and all seem to settle into their seats with further ease, smiles fading comfortably, more committed to the promise of the evening's entertainment. They are listening to her.

'Could you quiet down over there?' A woman, obscure in the gloom, calls out. 'I'm trying to watch TV.'

It's Elizabeth Colding, seated about as far from the television as the room will allow, her ragged face riddled with rosacea – an alky for sure – glowering in their direction. Colding is an unpopular former policewoman with a face like a raw, veined steak who always trails a curious stench of fish sauce.

Millie raises a single shit-stirring eyebrow at Anna; given that she has an audience, she can't help but feel a touch revolutionary. She carries on reading with no discernible change in volume.

'Roberta stretched her hand towards Hank's chiselled six-pack. He flashed her a deep look of surprise. Roberta felt the thick, manly hair there. She moved her well-manicured nails to his big shiny belt buckle –'

'Oh, shut it, will ya? I can't hear the news.'

'Have you considered,' replies Millie with a regal, affected frostiness, 'moving closer to the television?'

'This is the television room, not the library, ya numpty!'

'She's the numpty,' says the old man, to Millie's great satisfaction.

'– to rake her fingers gently through the auburn thatches of –'

'Rude!' says Colding. 'Stop that!'

Somewhere across the room a knee cracks once, twice. It's probably Colding's, since she's beginning to unseat her lanky, skeletal frame from the dark depths of a sofa. Elsewhere a patient surrenders to a loud yawn. Millie imagines this as a film scene, only in this tragi-comedy, the players are gnarled, absentminded, shrunken, stubborn amnesiacs with swollen feet, bad tickers, faulty hearing, brittle bones, aching muscles, foggy vision.

For an oldie, Colding, who's now approaching the group in a menacing fashion, is surprisingly nimble.

'The cheek,' Anna whispers.

'Selfish ol' wagon,' cries Colding, a finger wagging. 'I'll shut you up meself.'

Millie's next act feels more within the context of a garden-variety sibling squabble than an egregious or violent episode (which is how the staff will go on to characterize it). She raises *Mentor of Desire* and hurls it with her good arm in Colding's direction. Years on the bottle must have dulled Colding's senses because she doesn't even duck and Roberta and Hank bounce near her feet and land, soft-porn-side-up, on the floor tiles.

An elderly gent whom Millie has dubbed Conall the Clueless wanders in during the taut, silent moment that follows and says, 'Would anyone have any nail clippers?'

Colding begins yelling all sorts of rubbish – 'I want to file a patient 12A form' – and then she stops. Furious patches of colour bloom on her face. She points to the book splayed on the floor. 'Where are you after getting that?'

'My granddaughter.'

'You're lying! That went missing from my room yesterday. Nurse!'

In dash the Rossdale busybodies who commence their scowling and interrogating. Millie is led from the room with soothing murmurs, as if she's unhinged, as if she needs mollifying, and made to wait in Mrs Slattery's office where, in time, she's subjected to a tedious lecture about appropriate behaviour and a boning-up on the Rossdale rules. Mrs Slattery informs Millie that the option to spend evenings with other Rossdale residents in the lounge – distracting enough, certainly helpful in tackling the darkest portion of her days – is off the table for the time being. It's a mean punishment, simultaneously overkill and petty, and Millie gets to her feet upon hearing it.

'That's outrageous!'

'Mrs Gogarty, please. Sit down. You're fine there. Come, please, sit down. Let's discuss this calmly.'

'How long am I to be stuck alone in my room?'

'You're not stuck alone. There's Emma Jameson with you –'

'Are you having me on?'

'This is only a temporary restriction, just for a few evenings.'

'A few evenings might be all I have left.'

'You nearly hit a resident with a book,' says Mrs Slattery.

'A paperback.'

'It's getting late. Let's regroup tomorrow, shall we? Things will look better by then, with a good night's sleep, don't you think?' Mrs Slattery claps her hands together. 'Was there anything else now before we get you settled?'

'Yes,' says Millie. 'When am I going home?'

Mrs Slattery, white of hair, sound of mind, clever, but with trembling fingers that suggest early-onset Parkinson's, a woman who looks not far off full-time occupancy here herself, sighs and seems to size up Millie. 'I'm going to be perfectly frank with you. I admire your energy. Your spirit. I do. I think you're wonderful. You remind me of my auntie Margaret, who was – she was a tough bird. You're right to keep a fighting spirit. But at the same time, you have to face some realities. You can't bury your head in the sand, Mrs Gogarty. It won't serve you. The truth is ... as we age, we're inclined towards some ... physical challenges, injuries, sickness, you know, and that's the reality. That's why you're here, so we can help you get back on your feet.'

32.
Kevin

While his fellow countrymen are headed to mass or sleeping it off, Kevin stands on a Sunday morning before a front door whose lace curtains prohibit any peek within. His own home, ten minutes up the road, is presumably filled with his slumbering children, though who's to know since he's been booted from it – without ceremony, mercy, or tears. Grace essentially told him to fuck off. She hadn't wanted to be rash, she said; she'd thought about it for days, hoped she could come to terms with his betrayal. But there was a moment during *The Wizard of Oz* when she'd looked past their children down the row of seats and realized she wanted to punch him in the face. And that impulse hadn't lessened. Her tone? Steady, even, neutral, the tone one might adopt to notify the cashier that you'd like to make a small withdrawal. He, on the other hand, was all heart. Instant panic. He tried to explain, to reassure, to beg forgiveness.

'Nothing really happened! I promise you,' he'd sputtered. 'One or two kisses but we never – it was never consummated. I love you. Don't do this.'

This exchange – eerily calm on her side, hot on his – had taken place, at Grace's insistence, at the bottom of the garden so the kids wouldn't hear. Grace had finally betrayed emotion when he'd said 'consummated'. She had glared then, the word seeming to strike her as particularly egregious – she'd never had much patience for his use of obnoxious vocabulary in weighted moments, his flair for the showy when the plain would do just fine. Grace wouldn't let him speak after that – went so far as putting her hands on her ears, eyes shut, saying, 'No, no, no.' She listed a number of stipulations and practicalities for the present, something about the little car and the bankcard, but the only one he heard was that he was not to contact the children until she'd had some time to think.

'You're not serious? Who's going to take care of them?'

'I'll figure it out.'

'You're going to hire someone to bring them to school and cook their – that's ridiculous. I can keep sleeping downstairs until things – we figure it out. They need –'

'Just go,' she says. 'I can't bear to look at you.'

He found that he was not far off crying, something he hadn't done since his wedding day. And those were tears of joy. After they'd come down the aisle as husband and wife and their guests were still inside the church, his new bride had turned to him and said, 'We did it.'

'We did.'

'So, too late to back out?'

There was no other woman for him.

But that night in the garden, Grace, shivering in a thin cardigan, turned her back to him and trekked towards the house.

'But, Grace, you're punishing them for –'

'No.' She stopped and turned. 'I'm punishing you.'

The kids were asleep when he later crunched onto the drive with his hastily packed bag. But as he turned to look up at his house a final time, he noticed, at the upper bedroom window, his little love, Ciaran. He froze. Could his son intuit somehow that his father was en route to exile? But Ciaran had just waved merrily down at him, oblivious to the momentous conflict. Which had gutted him. Kevin forced a smile and returned the wave and moved on, thinking if he just kept moving maybe he could outrun his life.

Without any real thought, he found himself driving to his childhood home; it was empty, after all, and he sought solitude. It had been tricky getting his mother into Rossdale, but definitely the right call. She was safe, she was cared for. As he pulled into Margate, all depressing grey wet stone, he saw that the nearby neighbours' renovations were in full swing – two workers' vans and a digger were parked beside a massive hole, not a thing here remotely conducive to peace. Mum had nearly managed to blow up the kitchen, so in reality how habitable could the place be? He wouldn't be able to make a cuppa or nuke a frozen pizza and the wine stash was likely low to nil. There would be little serenity here. Before he even got his key into the front door, Kevin returned to his car.

Mick, ever supportive, had the audacity to laugh when Kevin rang looking for a place to crash. He explained that he'd been kicked out, yet hadn't actually done the dirt (the whole dirt, as it were).

'I cheated emotionally,' Kevin said, mortified as the emasculating words left his lips. Yet he knew his wife was not wrong.

'Jaysus.' Mick's voice was all disgust – for Kevin or Grace, it was impossible to say. 'Of course you can stay with me. It's grand, but I don't have the flat in town any more.'

'No?'

'Long story.'

'Well, where are you then?'

A pause. 'I'm actually back in Mum's place.'

Now it was Kevin's turn to erupt into raucous laughter. He was breaking his shite laughing; he was hysterical. 'And you're giving me shit?'

'Fuck off,' said Mick. 'See you in a few?'

33.

Aideen

Standing just outside Room 302, Aideen watches as her grandmother squats next to Mrs Jameson's open cupboard and stuffs two apples and a bottle of water into a pillowcase stamped 'Rossdale'.

'What are you *doing*?' says Aideen.

'Aideen! Come in but, quick, shut the door.'

Gran appears to be hiding the bag beneath a pile of her roommate's cardigans.

'Is that a knife?' says Aideen.

Gran looks down to see a tip of cutlery protruding from her sling. 'Well done. I've been looking for that.' She sticks the knife into the pillowcase. 'Would you care for some fruit?'

Gran gestures at an uneaten bowl of stewed prunes, like a petri dish of soggy mini-brains. Aideen scoffs.

'Listen, I'm only thrilled you're here,' says Gran. 'I need to ask you a favour.'

'Gran, remember Friday night in the car when you were talking about Sylvia? After Nuala's play? You said Sean was sick and Sylvia had taken him to America. Where did they go in America?'

'New York. A specialty hospital there.'

'But, like, where? Like, which hospital? What did Sylvia say exactly? When she phoned?'

'She was checking up on me. I think she misses me. We became very close, you see.'

'But what did she say about *Sean*?'

'Did you know Sean?'

'Of course I know him!' Aideen huffs in exasperation. 'I met him at your house, do you not remember?'

When Gran says, 'I didn't realize you'd become friendly with him,' Aideen drops her head and gives her the broad strokes about their budding romance and its abrupt, aborted ending.

'Don't tell anyone, promise? I don't think Mum and Dad would like it.'

Gran murmurs knowingly.

'But he's OK now, right? You said the hospital thing was, like, successful?'

'Oh yes,' says Gran. 'They'll be back in no time.'

Aideen sinks onto Millie's bed with a frustrated sigh, her brow creased. 'Why wouldn't he tell me he was sick?'

'I don't know, Aideen. Maybe he didn't want you to worry. Would you not try ringing Sylvia? I've got her number here somewhere.'

'Jesus, Gran,' Aideen says, brightening instantly. 'Why didn't you just say so?'

Gran may have a distinct memory of taking down Sylvia's number, but what Gran does not have is a distinct memory of where the fuck she put it. Ergo, Aideen commences, with her grandmother's permission, to ransack Room 302. She riffles through Gran's scant belongings, rummaging among institutional bedclothes and discovering various oddities, all in character – breadcrumbs, literally, a crusty hotel sleeping mask. Strangely enough, when she lifts up the mattress, Aideen spots a book of city bus maps.

Meanwhile, Gran peels back the dividing curtain and starts narrating, in real time, to the creepy old lump in the next bed.

'We're knee-deep into trying to find Sylvia's phone number. My Peter always said I was better at losing things than finding them. Aideen's determined, you see, because – can I tell Mrs Jameson the whole story or hadn't I better?'

Gran really is cracked.

Even here, the bureau reeks of Margate, that peculiar coal-burning, salty seaweed stench that's insinuated itself into every bit of clothing and odour-absorbing item Gran possesses, as if the ocean waves themselves lapped across her rooms for decades. Soon enough, Aideen reaches the final uninvestigated turf: a tiny plastic rubbish bin near the door. Here, too, she roots through Gran's rejected unsavouries: a richly waxy Q-Tip, a browning apple core, and then lets the bin slide dejectedly through her fingers.

'I think you must have thrown it out,' Aideen finally concedes.

'She'll ring again, not to worry. And I'll tell her you want to speak with Sean. But listen, before you go, come here to me. You don't have any cash on you, do you, love?'

Aideen shrugs, takes out her phone, and retrieves from its case a folded up fiver. 'That's all I have. It's yours.'

Gran starts looking soppy. 'You are an absolute –'

'It's fine. Just, please, Gran, can you think of anywhere else that number might be?'

'A gem. You know that? You are the most –'

'What do you need it for anyway?'

Gran drops her voice to a stage whisper. 'This is coming off tomorrow.' She wiggles her sling and then winces. 'You noticed my little stash?'

'You mean the knife?'

'Exactly, in case I need to defend myself.'

'With a butter knife?'

'As soon as I've got all my supplies together, I'm checking myself out of here. They've banned me from going into the lounge and I'm just sat in this room day after day and I'm fed up. And your dad won't tell me when he plans to bring me home. I think I need his signature or God knows and I suspect he's stuffed me in here for good.'

'He wouldn't do that.'

'In any case, you won't tell a soul, sure you won't?'

'I'm no snitch.' Aideen shakes her head solemnly but she's humouring Gran with what is clearly a crackpot escape plan that will never come to pass. 'I could probably get you more money but it wouldn't be till next weekend.'

'*The Pirate's Persuasion*,' Gran's mumbling. She goes over to a pile of paperbacks on her roommate's bedside table and picks up each one and fans its pages until a scrap of paper feathers its way to the floor. 'Et voilà!'

'You're kidding.'

Gran beams. 'Amn't I getting a bit soft in the head, Aideen? I'd forgotten about this. I've been reading aloud to Mrs Jameson. I have this idea that she may be taking in more than we think. You never know, do you? Doctors think they know everything.'

But Aideen's not listening; she's snatching up the paper. Ten digits have been dashed out in Gran's shaky hand and Aideen takes out her phone and immediately begins punching in the numbers.

'I dial but you talk, OK?' she says, terror encroaching. Yet she feels certain that an explanation, a relief from her sadness and this awful limbo, is seconds away. Clarity is at hand. Her first attempts fail – there are international codes to be dealt with. But on the third try, after a brief lull, a long American ringtone sounds. Gesturing to Gran and readying herself, Aideen listens to two of these until she hears a click. And then:

'The number you have reached is no longer in service. Please check your number and try your call again later.'

'That's strange,' says Gran.

'Shit,' says Aideen.

34.

Kevin

Kevin is still in the act of knocking when the door swings open to reveal Mick's mum, Maeve, a lit, extra-long lady's cigarette in one hand, remote control in the other, tsking and frowning, head shaking unhappily to and fro.

'Well, well, well.'

'Hello, Maeve.'

'Mick's inside.' She sprays a column of smoke from a pair of fleshy lips in his general direction and turns, leaving the door just ajar enough for Kevin to squeeze through. 'You're on the sofa.'

Which is exactly where Kevin spends the next few days. By night, himself and Mick eat greasy takeaway and sit by the gas fire drinking cans of lager and talking shite. Maeve rolls in and out, fog-like, through the cramped and cluttered rooms. She appears to have an unhealthy addiction to playing online hearts, huddled over her computer screen or mobile in all corners of the bungalow. Kevin wakes on the velveteen sofa with a sore lower back, and after enjoying a long and satisfying morning piss, goes straight back to it, clicking on the telly or his laptop and overtly staving off any thought of – or plan for – the future. He tries to ring Gerard, but his son seems always to be out. He misses the nights coming up to Gerard's Leaving – quizzing his son on World War II, Sean O'Casey, the importance of tourism to the Irish economy. As for the others, Kevin had decided not to contact them, out of respect for Grace, but he finds himself pining for their company. He quits browsing the job websites. He starts playing hearts online.

Each morning, when his friend heads out for work, Kevin feels terribly low, a foundling left behind on enemy turf. It reminds him of a time when he'd been under the weather as a schoolboy and his mother had had some important plan and so dropped him at a friend's house for the day. He'd woken up later on the woman's sofa to discover with a poignant hit of shame that he'd vomited tiny piles of sick into craters all over his blanket. He'd experienced an almost physical yearning for his mum then, to be home.

At Mick's mum's place, Kevin spends an inordinate amount of time listening for Maeve's footsteps in order to avoid being alone with her. The house is small enough that he has quickly learned to decipher her whereabouts – the particular creak of her bedroom door as she frequently labours to and from the toilet, the irritable closing of the curtains after dinner, the shuffling into the kitchen for rasher sandwiches and tea.

On the fifth morning, just after Mick leaves for work, Kevin heads for the kettle, believing Maeve to have gone to the salon up the road where she's something of a legend, tinting and trimming the middle-aged set while trading in the valuable currency of local gossip. So he's surprised to find her sitting at the table without her laptop, no virtual hearts this morning, only a packet of Benson & Hedges and a box of matches and a filthy ashtray he can smell from the door.

'Oh, I thought you'd left,' he says. 'Cup of tea?'

'See that sink?' Maeve says, a stubby, nicotine-stained finger aimed towards a hoard of plates and cups. 'The washing-up liquid's just there. If you're planning on staying here another minute, you'd want to stop taking the piss.'

'Sorry, yes, of course. I've not been –'

'And you'll pitch in on the rent. Mick won't tell you that but I'm not shy. And I'm not an idiot. Let's start for now with one hundred fifty.'

Kevin mentally calculates the contents of his wallet – twenty-three quid, give or take.

'I think I know what's happened in your house, Kevin.'

'I don't think that's any –'

'Four kids and all,' she says coolly and sparks up another fag. 'You know, Mick's dad did the very same thing.'

'It's not the same thing.' Kevin knows the sordid tale – everyone does – though Mick's never broached the subject.

'Moved in with a young one when Mick was just sixteen months. I was pregnant with Deirdre at the time. They haven't seen their father in, oh, twelve years. That's not what you want, is it?'

'Of course that's not what I want. She's kicked *me* out.'

'If I were you, I'd do some soul-searching instead of sulking about licking my wounds.' She stares at him and then almost smiles. 'I'll take that tea now.'

35.
Millie

Millie's idea – to ditch this kip – is short on details, but the thought of it excites her and planning it has added shape and purpose to her dull days. She's been steadily contributing items to her stash, including a bottle of Imodium (in the unlikely event that the shits befall her en route), a couple of Ambien, and four pale-blue oblong pills (these lifted, in a moment of wanton recklessness, from the sloppily monitored meds cabinet). They're antidepressants or antianxiety tablets – it hardly matters which. She will either a) scrape together enough money for a taxi; b) figure out which bus routes she'd need (not exactly practical, though, since she'll have to leave under cover of dark and there are so few night buses; c) hitchhike (dodgy, but not to be unconditionally ruled out); or d) walk, the least pleasant scheme of all, Margate being some distance away, a trek that will require additional sustenance and water. Her load would be that much heavier.

'I have a pre-emptive confession to make,' Millie says, addressing the curtain between the two beds of Room 302. 'Are you a religious woman, I wonder? Of all the things in church I always hated, and there are plenty, there was nothing more terrifying than confession. Ridiculous, when you think of it, isn't it? Kneeling in a pitch-black box revealing all your sins to a man who acts as if he never sins. Maybe if it were a woman, maybe a female priest ...' She sighs. 'Ah, well. I'm skint at the moment, you see, and I believe you'd help me if you could. The minute I'm home, I'll send you a cheque.'

But when Millie draws back the curtain, Mrs Jameson's bed is empty. Alone, for the first time, in Room 302, she ponders the disconcerting implications: a family visit? Unprecedented. A medical issue? Possible. She hears a distant shuffled movement of feet beyond the door and, without further angst, approaches her roommate's standard-issue chest of drawers and finds, at the back corner of the middle one, an embroidered coin purse she'd already discovered yesterday but had chickened out of pillaging.

She takes the only cash within it – €45, which is enough – and pushes the call button.

It's been days since Aideen's most unsettling visit, a time fraught with doubts and the rejigging of narrative puzzle pieces. For one thing, Millie can't understand why Sylvia would be so difficult to track down. After trying the American number twice more, neither Gogarty could plausibly deny that one of two statements was true: Millie had written down the wrong digits, or Sylvia had given a false number.

It is all very strange. Or deeply rotten. Or innocent and explicable. Each time Millie turns over the suspicious bits – the sudden frenzied momentum of departure or the fact that Sean, the more she thinks of it, never *looked* sick, quite robust, if anything – she arrives at the character of Sylvia herself: attentive and good and giving, if mysterious, unknowable, but, sure, aren't we all? Who does Millie know and who, other than Kevin, say, and Peter in his grave, knows her?

Aideen had compiled a list of Manhattan hospitals – more than twenty on that narrow island, as it turns out. Not a single one currently has a patient by the name of Sean Gilmore. But then, Millie reasons, Americans are famously tight-fisted about information – it's not as if the hospital is going to give out, willy-nilly, the whereabouts or status of a private patient. Maybe in Ireland, depending on who you get on the other end, some chatty nurse who might know your neighbour's sister-in-law's cousin, but not in America. So it's possible that Sylvia's story sticks.

She pushes the call button a second, third, fourth time. *Is nobody coming?*

When the doubts resurface, a most awful nervous fluttering in her gut occurs, but Millie comforts herself with her trump card, in the form of that IOU somewhere in Margate. How many times has Millie's fate, or anyone's, hung upon a scrap of paper? Even if Sylvia had signed it in bad faith, which Millie can hardly believe, why, she has somewhere in her possession a document that she could legally put forth, if need be.

'There you are,' says Millie to the girl, Martha, who finally enters. 'Where is my roommate? Is she alright?'

Millie knows the answer by Martha's solemn face.

'I'm sorry to have to tell you, Mrs Gogarty, but Mrs Jameson died in the night,' the girl says, laying a wispy Christian hand on Millie's shoulder. 'You were fond of her, I know. Poor soul, but God love her. She's with him now, God bless. She's been suffering a long time, as you know.'

'Oh no,' says Millie, suddenly feeling as if she's been awake for days. She looks at Mrs Jameson's bed, the imprint of her friend still discernible upon it. Any poor sod could have been lying in that bed; tomorrow a new poor sod will be. These losses, she thinks, will be her undoing. Her next thought: *I'm after robbing a dead woman.*

Martha stands rubbing Millie's shoulder, which makes Millie want to thwack her.

'Did you know her when she was … better?' says Millie.

'Oh, I did, yes. She was here a long time.'

'Was she lovely? I have a feeling she was lovely, a sort of gentle, maternal type.'

'You must be joking!' Martha laughs. 'She thought she was the Queen of Sheba, always giving out to everyone about the "service", like we were her bleedin' maids. She used to be very wealthy, that's the word anyway, used to the finer things in life. I don't like to speak ill of the dead, I don't, but the truth is Mrs Jameson was a right pain in the hole.'

By the time Martha checks in on her later, Millie's made up her mind.

'Time to go down for supper, Mrs Gogarty,' she says. 'You ready?'

Millie's ready alright: she'll milk this place tomorrow for breakfast, lunch, and tea, but then she'll be on her bike. So to speak.

36.
Aideen

At breakfast – porridge, like a vat of wet concrete with floating currants that resemble gerbil turds – Brigid slams her tray down on their usual table in an isolated corner of the dining hall, the hem of her uniform drifting mid-shin and trailing a loose thread.

'The bitch,' she says.

Brigid's tray is, as ever, piled with food: four greasy plugs of sausage, two fried eggs, a bowl of dry Corn Flakes. Belying her skinniness, Brigid is a massive eater, and has even arranged a covert deal with Mrs Brown, the sweet oily-faced kitchen lady, to hold back extra desserts for herself and Aideen whenever rhubarb crumble's on the menu.

'What's happened?' says Aideen.

'She's watching us.' Brigid looks directly at a scowling Bleekland and boldly waves at her with a smarmy smile.

'Don't make it worse,' says Aideen.

'I don't give a shite.'

'What'd she say?'

'She was snooping around my bed again, found my ciggies. She's ringing Dad today.'

'Oh no.'

'She loves humiliating me.'

'Come on,' says Aideen. 'We've got double science.'

Fifth-year biology students are currently dissecting worms and frogs. Aideen, disinclined to delve voluntarily into a carcass, prefers the role of observer and note-taker – in life, too – while Brigid happily wields a disposable scalpel, prodding into the surprisingly bright yellow entrails of a flattened, splayed garden frog that did nothing to offend anyone, other than emitting a sharp waft of formaldehyde. Brigid tells Aideen that, though she's been barred from signing out, she's sneaking off to meet her pizza bloke after school and Aideen must provide cover.

'Right, so if that witch comes looking for me, what'll you say?' says Brigid.

'That you're in the shitter?'

'For two hours!'

The girls laugh but the thought of staving off the formidable Bleekland scares Aideen.

'Ladies, if you're bored, I'm happy to assign additional classwork,' says Mr Reilly from his desk at the front.

The girls return to the specimen, which strikes Aideen as woeful: to be slaughtered and have your carcass stretched on a glass slide and your bits poked around by a pack of grossed-out girls. When Mr Reilly steps into the hallway, Brigid reaches for a bottle of fish eyeballs and slips it into Aideen's bag.

'What are you doing?'

'I've just had the most brilliant idea.'

37.

Millie

If there's anything to be said for an involuntary stay in a nursing home, it's that one acquires the overrated virtue of patience. Millie and her fellow residents are good at waiting. They're waiting for a meal that never fails to resemble the previous one, in appearance or flavour; or for the humiliating help that's sometimes required in the toilet; or for pills and water; or for someone to pass the time with. Millie's final act of waiting here is upon her. Bandages removed, Aideen's borrowed rucksack at the ready, she's waiting for the lights throughout the third floor to click off, which they eventually do at half past ten. When all grows quiet, she picks up the bedside telephone.

'I'd like to book a taxi,' Millie whispers.

'Can't hear you, love.' Gruff voice, a real Dub, her favourite kind.

'I'd like to book a taxi, for three a.m. But can the fella meet me round the corner from here? He's not to ring the bell. Under any circumstances.'

'Is this a prank?'

'No, this is not a prank. I've got fifty euro.'

'Have you, now? Well, where is it you need to go?'

'Home, but I don't want the man ringing the doorbell, it'll wake everyone up.'

'So I gathered. What address are you to be collected at?'

'Rossdale Home. It's in –'

'I know the place. And where would you be going to?'

'I'll let the driver know.'

'I'm supposed to mark it down, for the order.'

'I'll tell him when he gets here.'

The man sighs. 'Right then, what's the name?'

'No name.'

'I see. So it's no name going nowhere at three?'

'That's it.'

'Am I to assume there's no number to go along with that?'

'And no coming to the door, please, don't forget to tell him.'

'Is this per chance Mrs Gogarty? Of Dún Laoghaire?'

Millie blanches. 'Who's this?'

'I thought I recognized the voice, Mrs Gogarty – howaya? It's John here, in Quick Taxis.'

'John?'

And then she knows him: John's the pudgy chap with the black beard who lives on JJ's road and never brings in his wheelie bins. 'John, hello.'

'Sounds like you're planning a top-secret mission there, Mrs Gogarty.'

'Not at all,' she says casually.

'Discretion all the way.'

'How's my friend Jessica?'

'She's grand, far as I know. Going over to her niece in Brooklyn next month, I believe.'

'Is she?' says Millie, thinking, *Good on ya*. She misses JJ – they'd have loads to gab about – yet she can't bring herself to phone. 'That's grand.'

'So I guess we'll see you soon.'

Nightshifts pare down from a handful to one nurse per floor, and tonight it's Agata, a pleasant Polish immigrant with half a shaved head and a single silver stud winking, beacon-like, from the tip of a strong nose which is currently hidden behind *Nasz Glos*, a paper she shares with the morning nurse from Warsaw.

'Still awake?' Agata says.

'I'm feeling a terrible chill tonight, Agata. Would you ever fix up a hot water bottle for me?'

'You have blanket?'

'I do, but I think I'm coming down with some awful something.'

'So sad news yesterday, yes? You are sad?'

'Determined.'

'Ah. OK.' Agata reluctantly folds her motherland news. 'I bring to you.'

'Lovely girl,' says Millie. 'Thank you.'

She refrains from kicking up her heels. A distracted Agata allows Millie to practically saunter down the third-floor hall, though Aideen's rucksack, with its odd assortment, is heavy upon the small of her back. With ease, Millie makes it to the stairwell – two flights down and Bob's your uncle. She descends the top floor, ninja-like, stopping every third stair or so to pause and stand flat against the wall, ears keenly alert, like some TV cop hunting down her perp. When she reaches the ground floor, she gathers up her courage to poke her head around the final corner, whereupon she spies a hairy bloke manning the central station, a sausagey bulk of a guy she's never seen before. Millie's noticed, on other occasions, a guard posted here, so she isn't surprised. What does surprise her is the high-tech security keypad embedded in the wall beside the door, red light blipping. How had she, a woman who might self-describe as fairly observant, never taken in this blasted contraption? With a need to reassess, she slips into the first bedroom she comes upon.

She finds herself in a dark single room, smaller than hers but otherwise laid out in the same institutional blueprint. In one corner, a soundless TV glows, throwing off snatches of light onto its occupant, a snoring blob beneath blankets. Millie stands near the door breathing. Is this ludicrous and futile? She must think. The security code would be posted or printed somewhere at the front desk, she supposes, in a drawer or, more likely, taped up next to the computer monitor. Agata's errand won't take much longer, though Millie's pleased she thought to switch on her loo light and close the door, in case the nurse is overly persistent. Chances are, the girl will probably just leave the bottle on her bed and get back to her reading.

Millie steps further into the room, closer to the lump, and gapes when she recognizes her old nemesis, Officer Elizabeth Colding, who in slumber looks gentle and sweet even as she lets loose the oblivious snores of a lifelong drunk. One of the woman's feet extends from the bed like a preemie swathed in covers from which peep two grotesque, gangrenous toes. Above her, ringing the wrought-iron bed (brought in from home, the surest indicator of Elizabeth Colding's dubious status as a lifer), dozens of stained-glass ornaments dangle – the kind of yokes you might find in a craft shop and bake in your oven, if you were the type of granny who did such things – in the shapes of puppies, stars, unicorns, hearts.

Ah, look at her.

Millie, moved despite her daunting task, steps towards the old lush, inadvertently causing a pair of glass angels to tremble against each other. A yellow kitten clanks against a gingerbread house, which taps, domino style, every other ornament down the line. Millie cries out, tries to still them with her hands. Elizabeth Colding stirs, but not enough to cause concern. Millie waits for a long moment until the room becomes still again.

She hears the yelp just as she's cleared the room, hand on the door. Millie spins around to see Officer Colding sitting up in bed like a mad Victorian ghost: face drained of colour, hair a chaotic clump of pipe cleaners, mouth a gaping 'O'. There's something in her wide-eyed zombie gaze that gives Millie goose-bumps, confusion and terror combined, a flash of things to come: reduced to a single room, alone and forgotten in a hospital bed, muttering gibberish, and written off long ago by every human being who's not paid to tend to her.

'Nurse!' Colding croaks.

'Sssh,' Millie hisses. 'You'll wake up the –'

'Nurse!'

'I'm not going to hurt you.'

'*Nurse!*'

'OK, yes, I took your book, I confess. But just as a loan. I had every intention of returning it. In fact, it's in my room and you can go up –'

'NURSE!'

Millie's out the door and back in the hall. She searches for someplace, anywhere, to hide. To the right is all corridor and doors; to the left, the front desk where she already hears the guard's creaking chair, en route directly towards her to investigate the mad Jane Eyre wailing. Millie might as well be stripped down to her skivvies, so exposed is she, no physical barrier between herself and himself, no cover to take. He will pounce, send her straight back upstairs where she will continue to do little but wait until she goes the way of Elizabeth Colding or, worse, Emma Jameson.

The only object that could possibly obstruct her is a giant dying fern sent, no doubt, by a relative in a faraway land to assuage guilt, and at some point stashed in a corner by a harried aide. There is nothing else around, and though her navy jacket is decidedly not green, she hopes it might help camouflage her.

From her hiding spot, Millie listens as the man moves one, two, three labouring steps in her direction, and through the stiffened branches, she sees he's got one ear cocked. The two of them, a foot apart at the most, share a long silence. Then, as these things happen, and reaffirming one of her long-held convictions (that one really has so little control over anything), an untimely, irredeemable, and not demure bout of gas escapes her cursed body. Before she can so much as excuse herself, the man is upon her, registering with amazement what he clearly perceives to be a mental patient farting in a potted plant.

'Well now,' he says.

Millie freezes.

He peers closer and says, 'Are you in need of ... of ... the ladies'?'

Part of her desperately wants to disabuse him of the mortifying assumption he must have made, that she's soiled herself, but the smarter part, the one appointed with the task of survival at all costs, knows she mustn't make a codswallop of this. She's come this far (well, two staircases and two corridors, but, symbolically, an odyssey). Nothing short of force can compel her back to Room 302.

Millie releases her held breath, folds her hands together prayer-like, and in as helpless a falsetto as she can summon, says, 'Papa?'

With kind eyes buried deep into late middle age, the guard says, 'What's that, love?'

Millie tries to shrink in upon herself so as to appear tiny and frightened. In what she later thinks of as her *pièce de résistance*, she lifts her face up towards him to strike a coy, girlish pose and says, 'Have you come about the ponies?'

'The ...?'

'In the stable?'

'Sorry?'

She flashes her battiest smile.

'Let's come out of there, bring you back to your room. Oh, you've got your coat on, have you?'

'*Nurse!*' comes screeching from Elizabeth's room. Millie should have smothered the old bag while she'd had the chance. Now she hears a flurry of commotion – maybe it's Agata on the third floor – a door shutting, footsteps sounding from above.

'Come on out from there and I'll get the nurse, help you back to your room.'

He reaches to assist her and Millie, with bold verve, deep-dives into the drama of her role, bristles and shakes his hand off her, as if her arm were on fire (at least *that* she can draw from real-life experience) with a pained squeal. The man steps back, mutters what sounds like 'Agata', and turns towards his desk, where he can have the nurse down here in under ten seconds.

Millie begins to cough modestly but, when he seems to ignore this and continues towards the intercom, she builds it all up to an almighty smoker's hack, as if her very guts will discharge themselves and land splattered on the floor between them.

'Water.' She points towards her throat. 'I just need a glass of water.'

He seems to weigh her request. If the timing were better, Millie would certainly not object to a lovely little palaver with this kind-hearted and not unattractive gentleman. But eyes on the prize, Amelia, as her Peter might have said.

'No problem.' He nods his head. 'Not a bother in the world. We'll get ya sorted with a glass of water, doesn't that sound grand?' Carefully, in an exaggerated show of civility, he extends, again, a gallant arm, which, since she's already chewing up the scenery, she accepts like a lady, as if he'll be escorting her to the grand ballroom for the next waltz.

He brings the intermittently coughing Millie Gogarty over to the lounge where, weeks ago, she and Kevin had waited for Mrs Slattery.

'I'll be right back. You sit tight.'

Millie grins at him like a half-wit and listens as he shuffles down to the kitchen. Then she dashes to the front desk, which is a mess of papers and file folders, a steaming mug of coffee, a telephone, tiny television, computer. Yellow Post-its are stuck like incongruent tiles across surfaces, but none seems to bear a series of numbers resembling any sort of code. She reefs open drawers, cabinets; she even climbs under the desk thinking someone might've taped up security codes beneath it, but no.

Now Millie hears movement from the kitchen. The man'll be back any moment. When her eyes fall a second time onto his coffee, she's struck by an idea: wicked and insane – or brilliant? She digs into Aideen's bag until she locates the pilfered pills. Removing the bottle of Ambien, Millie drops one pill in and watches it sizzle on the muddy surface. Footsteps approach. She adds two more and stirs the tiny dissolving burnt-orange magic beans with a biro.

Millie wonders, idly, whether she'll ever have use for her new-found knowledge: that three Ambiens reduce one sausage to a drooling heap in approximately twelve minutes. Behind the lounge door, she had listened as he returned to his desk, no doubt wondering where the madwoman had got to, and then eventually resettled into his chair. It was an excruciating limbo, but finally the guard drained the dregs of his laced coffee.

Now Millie must hurry. She beelines to the front door, sweeping by the guard whose broad salad plate of a forehead drifts languidly towards his shoulder. Might as well have ten jars in him, she thinks. She begins inputting any obvious combination of figures she can drum up: '1234', '1111', '007'. But the idiot flashing light continues to taunt her.

She races down the corridor as fast as her old-lady legs will take her, towards the back door, which leads to the garden, or the 'grounds'. She hasn't run in ages. Her lungs catch fire instantly, but she's curiously light of body. She's like a girl again, chasing down the soggy strand, hurling wet, reeking globs of rubbery seaweed at her brother, the two in fierce battle as always. But Millie skids to a halt at the back door where a second hideous light blinks mockingly at her.

To make matters worse, now comes the sound of knocking on the front door. The taxi. Hadn't she told your man not to knock? Readers on, she inspects the keypad. A second knock sounds. He'll wake the guard, or will he? From the desk, a phone begins bleating. Just as Millie's ready to give up and yank the bloody door open, come what may, she sees, at the bottom of the device, a microscopic red button marked 'disable'.

Millie presses this and the light instantly ceases to flash. She reaches for the door, turns the handle, and it gives way easily, freezing night air rushing at her as if she's slammed into a wall of ice. Millie makes her way slowly through the garden, stepping round shrubs though she inadvertently nails a flower bed. She keeps close to the building, away from the drive, and hovers at the corner of the house, scared to step away from it where she can be seen.

But she's managed to get herself out of the building, and this thought propels her forward, into the front garden, just in time to see her taxi reverse into the road. She lifts her arms high into the air and waves, but it quickly recedes.

Now it's very cold and very quiet. Millie doesn't know her next move, but she knows to move. She heads left through the garden of the neighbouring house and then the next one. It isn't until she reaches the corner of the road – four houses down – that the adrenaline begins to abate.

She has a painful stitch in her side, the rucksack already feels ten stone, her lift is gone, but never mind: the fact is, she's out.

Millie's plan, such as it is, begins to form when she comes upon the same home, 49 Glen Ground, for the *third* time, distinguishable from the other houses along the road only by the fact that one of its occupants has left a red bike helmet out to ruin in the garden. She is officially going round in circles, lost in a disorienting suburban maze of beige pebble-dashed housing, cul-de-sacs that present themselves without warning, and nondescript stone walls barricading strangers like her. Not a single car has passed Millie since her escape; nor is a light blazing in any window; all curtains and blinds appear drawn. They are in; Millie's out. And the truth is, she's winded, the stitch is worsening, and she can feel her slimy sock rubbing painfully against the left bony bit of her foot (to say nothing of her bunion), which means a blister is sprouting, which in turn means walking will not be a realistic option for much longer.

She has so little idea where she is; she needs to get off the streets and home. What, Millie wonders, if she were to knock on this door with the helmet and play the role of a harmless, lost lady in need of assistance? She could tell the kindly mum or dad within, who'll be sleepy yet open to civility and compassion, that she was returning home from the country

– Kildare, say, sounds rather posh – visiting her brother who runs a B&B – no, better make it a sister, she never got on with her brother and that hostility might bleed into her performance. She must've driven over a nail in the road because she's got a flat tyre. The car, she'll go on, is just down the road (yet too far to see from here) and could she possibly borrow their telephone for a taxi? At which point, the father, whom she now envisions as more likely to answer the door in the dead of night, who'll have patchy, disarming facial hair and a soft jowly face and a midlife paunch, will offer to drive her home to Dún Laoghaire. Along the way, he might ask where her own car is but she'll convince him not to worry, that she'll call a repair truck to tow it in the morning.

Millie peers more closely at the brass knocker, which is an Anna Livia replica, with that famously sorrowful face. The door itself is still decorated with a faux Christmas garland, which, it being mid-March, indicates to Millie a certain auspicious lapse in rules.

On the one hand, she knows this plan is vague, dangerous, ill-conceived, harebrained, cockeyed and likely doomed. On the other, what the feck else can she do? The guard at Rossdale may have woken up with the banging; Agata might have copped on to her absence. Perhaps the police have been called. With a certain swell of pride, she imagines the pandemonium. But this scenario, if it is, indeed, playing out, is problematic: they will ring Kevin and go immediately to Margate, beating her to the punch, and then force her back once more.

Millie reaches for the knocker and hears the muffled and distant but unmistakable sound of a car. The police? She instinctively ducks behind a hedge. *How many bleedin' bushes is she to find herself in tonight?* The car sounds about a road off and Millie wonders whether she ought to reveal herself and get a lift, or would she have a better shot at this house? As she weighs these options, she spies, among the rough roots, a torn, ageing chocolate-bar wrapper and then, stuck in the branches, a lone infant moccasin dangling from a ribbon. The slipper is lined with fraying beige fur and it's so tiny, it can't have fit any infant for long – a handful of weeks at most. She lets herself conjure up her long-ago baby. Maureen, in swaddling most of her few short months, never had need of slippers – or, for that matter, eyeglasses or tweezers or a sieve or a driving licence or a husband. And to think of all the shoes she herself has owned! Millie's throat tightens; a sharp pressure bears down on her chest. She has spent so many years stuffing such thoughts out and away, yet here they are, freshly devastating, as raw as something just slain, bloody and throbbing still.

Millie takes hold of the little object and turns it over and reads, stamped on its sole, 0–3 MOS. Maureen was a beautiful child, everyone said so, none more proudly, or often, than Peter. She and Peter and Kevin would stroll round the harbour after tea, Millie pushing the buggy, a huge metal yoke, all wheels, like a royal carriage, Kevin's little hand often taking proprietary hold of it. The baby was content on these walks, but happiest in her mother's arms. Oh boy, the ire that that miniature being could summon if Millie wasn't holding her was almighty! Hostile and glaring, like a stage actor who never phones it in, who chews it up, whether the scene calls for high drama or delicate subtlety, no matter. They laughed about it, herself and Peter. Called her Little Miss. She was what they talked about. And then she was what they never talked about.

One winter morning, Millie had warmed up Maureen's milk on the cooker as always, but when she reached the cot, Millie could feel the heat steaming off her baby without even touching her. Maureen was burning up. She cried out for Peter and picked the infant up and the child's limbs were lifeless, but the worst were her eyes, which gazed vacantly out at nothing. Millie had the ridiculous thought that if she just removed her swaddling, Maureen would cool off. But with just the nappy on, Maureen was the same. Two days later, Millie's infant took her final laboured breath in hospital, like the death rattle of an old, ailing patient.

After, Millie's mind was stuck on an endless, haunting loop. What if she had gone in straightaway without the bottle, what if they'd taken her into hospital earlier, what if Peter had driven faster, what if Millie had nursed her? And other, more painful questions: had Maureen sensed that she was loved, did she know it, or did she leave the earth not knowing it? Fingering the moccasin now, Millie tries to imagine what was on those miraculous feet, kidney-shaped and ridiculously tender, like two worn slips of soap, when they put her into the ground? She'll never know. She couldn't look, she couldn't look.

Now the car she'd heard moments ago is turning onto Glen Ground. Millie releases the moccasin and watches as its filthy ribbon coils back towards the branch. It's not the guards after all; it's a grey Morris Minor, the same car Peter once drove. A sign? Millie steps out onto the pavement and waves.

The car jerks over immediately, as if expecting her, and in the gloom the driver reaches across to the passenger door, unlocking and opening it in one movement, as if afraid she'll make a run for it.

'You shouldn't be hitchhiking, you know.'

She peers in: the driver is male, in his sixties, she supposes, eyes red-webbed with exhaustion or drink. He pats the passenger seat.

'I'm jokin', I'm jokin'. Get in out of the cold, sure, hop in.'

As he speaks, his eyes dart in what she concludes is an oddly furtive manner from the dashboard to the passenger seat and back, strange enough to give her pause.

'Plenty of dangerous types out and about,' he says. 'But you're safe with me, I can tell you. Capital "S". Where ya headed?'

Millie weighs the pros – no traffic at all, she could be in Margate inside of twelve minutes give or take – against the cons – abductor, freak, serial killer.

'Dún Laoghaire.'

38.

Aideen

Before the ambulance screams up the drive and Aideen's day takes a dark, irrevocable turn, talk on the north-east corner of the hockey pitch, where the smokers invariably converge at morning break, centres on the imminent mock exams. Sixth years, who will soon sit the real version, are, as a group, shitting themselves. In these fifteen minutes of freedom, some of them suck down as many as three cigarettes apiece, a pack of beautiful chain-smoking basket cases who seem to enjoy complaining bitterly about mind-numbing essays on Iago's treachery or Nordic fishing patterns or memorizing fifty pluperfect conjugations. Aideen and Brigid and the other fifth years gather in deference and sympathy around the older lot, registering their grievances and anxiety and coolness. Having the sweet luxury of time, they're not concerned yet. At sixteen or seventeen, a year from now is unfathomable; there's still spring and summer to navigate – coffees, dancing, shopping, music, beer, boys, trips. Possibilities abound.

Aideen, skulking mutely on the outer edges of this high-strung huddle, offers chewing gum to Brigid then takes a piece for herself. Brigid first, Aideen second. At some point and with no discernible origin, she's been wordlessly cast in the role of lady-in-waiting. She's the midwife, Brigid the goddess birthing their adventures and hijinks, gossip, their tales to tell. Aideen is grateful – flattered – to have been chosen, even as she smarts at the casual ease with which Brigid helms their friendship, the confident expectation that she's in charge. Like with the eyeballs. Even as Aideen had inwardly protested her role in the ridiculous scheme – to purloin Bleekland's Tic Tac container – purloin she did, an eager pup dropping a prize at her master's feet. Aideen's turning this uncomfortably over in her mind when an emergency vehicle, lights off but siren on, rips past them all on the pitch, through the car park, the courtyard, and yanks to a stop in front of the main school building.

'What the fuck?' somebody says.

'Maybe Ms Murphy finally croaked it.' This from Brigid. The others laugh. 'Ding-dong, the witch is dead.'

'You're evil,' says some lick-arse. Brigid also seeks approval, Aideen observes, but is better – masterful, even – at masking it.

From their faraway spot, strategically chosen to thwart getting busted, the girls watch in silence as two men emerge, one from each side of the vehicle. Moments pass and then the same two come back out of the school doors and rush towards Fair House. Now a third worker hops from the back of the truck, which puts Aideen in mind of a clown car. How many more will pile out?

On the horizon, they watch as Fiona Fallon, of all people, a girl who's never been on a hockey pitch without a hockey stick, kneepads, mouthguard, goalie mask, and the express objective to play hockey, suddenly begins galloping towards them with her awkward gait, the result of some horrific childhood hip injury that sets her apart from the others and that makes Aideen feel for the girl. Fiona waves her arms wildly – something is definitely wrong – and the conversation, which had begun to pick up again, goes silent as they await whatever news she will bring.

When Fiona's finally in close enough range that Aideen can see her face glistening with sweat, she bends over, panting.

'What is it?' one of the girls asks.

'Bleekland,' she gasps.

'What? What's happened?'

'She's collapsed. They're taking her to hospital.'

Upon hearing this, Aideen experiences a sort of tinnitus. All the words being said – and there are many, people talking excitedly at once in that way an emergency makes everything suddenly intimate and charged – all the exclamations and f-bombs and questions repeated dumbly, it's all gibberish to Aideen. She hears only a deafening ringing. She doesn't hear any of the girls, but she does see, when she finally gathers the courage to re-enter the moment and look up, her friend Brigid Crowe staring directly at her, the girl's face a perfect rendering of panic.

As the others stub out their butts and scatter back towards school in buzzing, titillated clumps, Brigid stares at Aideen with a silent command: *Stay.* The pitch emptied, they gawk wordlessly at each other until finally Brigid says, 'Who would've thought that would make you so sick?'

'Oh my God, Brigid.'

'She actually ate them? She didn't see they were bigger? Or, like, wet?'

'Oh my God.'

'Or that they smelled absolutely disgusting? Seriously?' Brigid gives a vicious laugh. 'She put a fish eyeball in her mouth and sucked on it?'

'Maybe she's just sick?' says Aideen. 'Like, maybe she had a stroke and this has nothing to do with that?'

'Don't be so fucking stupid. Of course it has.'

First Sean, then Dad out of the house, now this.

'Relax. Everyone was in the lab, so it could've been anyone who took it. And no one saw us in Bleekland's office, no one saw us. They can't prove a thing. We just have to keep our mouths shut.'

Aideen tries to make sense of the events that led to this moment, or rather, the moment last night when her friend had used tweezers to pinch three of the slimy, dead eyes floating in their foul-smelling jar and drop them into their house mother's mints. She remembers wondering who was the unlucky bastard at the factory with the job of removing these eyes from their sockets, to cut the nerves, detach.

'What if she dies?' Aideen whispers.

'From a fish eye?'

'Oh my God.'

'Will you stop fucking saying that? She's not dying. She'll be fine.'

'I wish I never came here,' says Aideen.

'And think about this. She might not even realize she ate anything, you know? She gets sick and goes to hospital. They might never, like, link it to the mints.'

'We need to tell them,' says Aideen.

'Are you out of your mind?'

'But what if –?'

'I'm not saying a word.' Brigid glares at her. 'And neither are you.'

'We can't just do nothing.'

'Relax. No one saw you do it.'

Aideen's body goes cold. 'No one saw *me* do it?'

'Us. You know what I mean.'

Aideen, disgusted with the pair of them, can't even look at her friend – her ex-friend – and, besides, she's too shaky to declare what it is she's about to do. Brigid will only try to stop her. She just walks away. The further she gets from the pitch, the faster she's moving, until she's legging it to Fair House, Brigid calling out pointlessly after her.

39.
Kevin

Kevin is subjected to a minor but unwelcome thwack of the *Irish Daily Star* on his shoulder.

'Oy. Sleeping Beauty.'

The incongruity of 'beauty' juxtaposed with Maeve's buffoonish face in his immediate field of vision – plastic eyeglasses that distort and enlarge, ridged smoker's lips traced in peach pencil – is jarring, and rips Kevin from a sensual dream which he aches to re-enter, but which immediately dissipates. Maeve, braless in a floral smock before him, is a morning-glory killer.

'Your phone's been blowing up.'

He sits up, scratches his head, wonders if the hairdresser's abode might be infested with lice. The irony. He's been feeling itchy. He's been feeling out of his skin in this cluttered, manky, foreign hovel, dependent for shelter on the salty mother of his oldest schoolmate. She's always encroaching into his morning ablutions. Yesterday, three long fake blonde hairs were wound deep within the bar of Ivory; another morning, he'd followed after her into the toilet and she'd forgotten to flush. The horror. Kevin, in his exile, feels increasingly unmoored without his children as day-to-day touchstones. He finds himself immersed in silly, rubbishy concerns. Are they flossing? Has Grace signed Ciaran up for the hockey tournament? Has a vegetable passed any Gogarty lips in the past week?

Maeve sniffs. 'You'd want a shower, love.'

'Cheers.'

'I'm just saying.' She sighs, pointing to a pile of empties he and Mick had fashioned into a pyramid on the coffee table the previous night. Mick had ended the evening talking a load of bollocks about some new condo development in Costa Rica he wants to invest in. Everything they discuss is a load of bollocks. 'You wouldn't want to show up at a school smelling like that.'

'School?'

Maeve presses his mobile into his hands: two missed calls from Rossdale Home, three from Millburn School.

'Millburn School for Girls. Good morning.'

'Rose, it's me.'

'Kevin.' Her voice drops. 'Oh my God.'

No doubt about it: he detects minor anguish. However dishonourable or whatever, Kevin experiences a miniscule ego hit: Rose Byrd misses him, this stunning creature half his age whom he'd left in a hotel bed half-naked and willing and willing and willing.

'Look, Rose, I'm sorry, but I thought you understood.'

'What?'

'If things were different,' he says gently. 'But I can't pursue this.'

'Oh my God. What is *wrong* with you?'

Kevin smarts, flushes defensively. Yet it's a fair question, one he's been trying to keep at bay all week. 'You've been ringing all morning?'

'I haven't! Do you have any idea what's been going on here? Have you talked to anyone here?'

'About what?'

'Edith.'

Maeve waddles into the room, ignoring, as is her way, the obvious fact that he's occupied.

'Kevin,' she says, 'would you ever pick up bread and butter?'

He waves her off and points to the phone.

'Chicken thighs, too, and a packet of rice.'

Into the phone Kevin says, 'Can you just hang on one sec?' To the mistress of the house he says, 'Yeah, sure, whatever you need. Just give me a second.'

As Maeve busybodies herself collecting the lager cans in a martyred fashion, the pyramid immediately collapses.

'I'll do that,' says Kevin irritably. 'Can I just ...?' He rolls his eyes at the phone. 'Just, it's a private call.'

'Oh, don't mind me, then. I'll just leave my own lounge, will I?' Kevin resists the urge to flip her double birds.

'Hello?' says Rose.

'Sorry. You were saying?'

'Edith's been taken to hospital.'

'Who is Edith?'

'Edith Bleekland. The head of Fair House?'

'What? What's happened?'

'She's been poisoned.'

'How spectacularly odd.'

'Kevin,' she says, 'they're saying it was Aideen.'

So that he can get this straight – no. He *can't* get this straight. It can't have been his daughter (an innocent child, well-meaning if narky) who caused Edith Bleekland to be lying in a hospital bed right now, fighting for her life – oh Jesus – after having had her stomach pumped. A tube has been inserted into the woman's mouth; warm liquids have been administered and removed.

Three times he tries Grace's mobile; three times, his calls are rejected. 'Then fuck you!' he screams into it. Though he's in the living room and Maeve's in the kitchen with a door closed between them, he can actually feel her stop gaming, stop smoking, stop breathing as she strains to glean what's happening. 'Fuck you too!' he yearns to scream. Defying Grace's request to stay away from the children, he slams out of the house, Maeve absurdly trailing him all the way to his car with her grocery list.

He has no memory of getting to the school. He just finds himself passing through its iron gates and he revs his way up to the main building. With the deepest sense of urgency he's possessed in years (his lusty fumblings and near-misses with Rose are already a distant, anaemic second – apples and oranges), Kevin strides into the school like a storybook giant cluelessly capable of crushing all in its path. Dead silence within – the girls must be in class. Is *his* girl in class? Since he received the incomprehensible news, he's been having trouble envisioning what Aideen is physically doing. He just can't process what he's been told.

Kevin knocks on his former would-be mistress's office door and she greets him with such professionalism he guesses, rightly, that the headmistress is afoot. Ms Murphy, stooped and drawn and shaped like an aubergine, steps from behind Rose and seems to glower at him, as if he's the one who set all this in motion. He *is* the one who sired the one, so, yes, perhaps this is on him, perhaps if he hadn't lustily chased after a ruthless boozehound, if he had stayed a good man, maybe he wouldn't be here. And where is his daughter right now? Has she been reefed out, held in some horrible little room like a common criminal? And where is his wife?

To her credit, Ms Murphy does not relish in relaying the gory details. She asks Rose to close the door on her way out, invites Kevin to sit, and then lays out the morning's awful events. Bleekland had been giving the first years their morning instructions, standing at the doors, notebook in hand, looking down (always looking *down*) at her charges. Mid-sentence, she appeared to swoon and, without notice, dropped the notebook and pitched over. Bleekland had attempted to straighten herself and then released a moan. She clutched her stomach and started retching, keeling over onto the ground. The girls screamed. One had the good sense to fetch an adult, and an ambulance was called.

'But she's – recovered?' Kevin says this with pitiful hope, like a child whose cat has just been crushed by a car in front of his eyes who then asks, 'Is kitty OK?'

'She's in Vincent's. The doctors performed gastric lavage – her stomach was pumped.'

Kevin pictures, for some reason, a doctor bearing down on

the handle of a stand pump designed to inflate a basketball, one foot holding down each end of the base, lifting up and pushing down.

'It must be done as soon as possible before the poison is ingested.'

Poison! Kevin winces. 'I don't ...'

'There's no antidote to formaldehyde, you see, so they have no choice. They have to do that. Luckily, the toxin was pumped out successfully.'

His chest, since he first spoke to Rose on the telephone, has felt dangerously compressed. Now his body loosens slightly, the tension ebbs, the muscles in his neck and arms slacken. *Successfully* is a beautiful word, his new favourite word. Then he thinks, *formaldehyde*? How would a sixteen-year-old have gotten her hands on formaldehyde? No, this can't be right. This is a mistake.

'Where's my daughter?'

'But there's a complication.'

'With Aideen?'

'No, Mr Gogarty, not with Aideen. With Miss Bleekland.' He sees, in her ability to make clear her immense revulsion with a simple combination of caustic tone and blistering stare, why she's such an effective headmistress: the woman is terrifying. 'There's a chance that during the gastric lavage, some particles might have entered the lungs. It's called aspiration pneumonia. It's treatable, but we don't know anything else at the moment.'

'What does that mean?'

Ms Murphy glares. 'It means we don't know anything else at the moment.'

Kevin drops his head. 'But how did this happen? I don't understand. How did Aideen – how do you know Aideen did this? She's not a cruel person. She's –'

'Mr Gogarty, we understand that your daughter and another student stole a number of fish eyeballs from the chemistry lab sometime in the last few days and got hold of Miss Bleekland's container of breath mints and, yes, I know it's difficult to believe. I've been here twenty-seven years and this is ...'

Kevin feels dreadfully ill.

'Miss Bleekland mistook the eyeballs for mints and ate them,' she continues. 'As clearly was the point. Please compose yourself, Mr Gogarty.'

'I don't understand. How do you know it was her?'

'She confessed it to Nurse Flynn. She thought it would help the medics.'

'Oh Jesus,' he says. 'I need to see Aideen.'

40.
Millie

Meanwhile in Dún Laoghaire, Millie stands in her back garden studying her windows. Weeks ago, she'd been evacuated from her sooty kitchen by her son, her scorched arm loosely wrapped in a kitchen towel (the wound has healed, though it's left, in its wake, a sizable scar, an inch or so of itchy pale-pink tissue that stretches across the width of her paltry arm like a sports watch). Now, the spare key missing, she finds she must breach Margate's perimeter in a similarly unconventional fashion, by climbing through Kevin's old bedroom window.

Millie tests an old crate with her foot and it doesn't give way. She lines it flush against the back wall and steps up on it and manages, with some effort, to achieve a toehold with her right foot in a sizable gap between crumbling bricks.

She really has let the place go.

It takes her three tries until she's able to swing her other leg up, quite scrappily, and heft herself to the window frame and slide the thing open. With her luck, she'll probably fall backward, smash her skull, and be found, concussed and amnesiac, and taken back to Rossdale, doomed to repeat this hellish cycle forever. Millie iron-grips the frame and climbs into the room, but she pitches forward and ends up splayed out on the carpet.

She has a worm's-eye view of Kevin's childhood walls covered in dog-eared paper – a sky-blue toile featuring the same pattern of faded sleigh-riding boys waving to one another from snowy drifts. Massive and intricate cobwebs have usurped the ceiling corners. She closes her eyes for a little rest and awakes, sometime later, shivering. Was the room always this chilly?

The house is silent. Millie goes into the sitting room and flicks on the lamp and hunts for the remote, a knee-jerk act that makes her feel more at home than nearly anything. She finds it beneath a sofa cushion, but when she clicks on the TV, she realizes there is no TV.

Her TV is gone.

Millie's first thought is that it's in the repair shop. But no, Kevin had fixed it. Which leads Millie to her final, inevitable conclusion: her TV's been stolen.

Ergo, her house has been robbed.

She casts her eye about the flawed, beloved chamber she knows better than any in the world with freshly suspicious eyes. Someone has definitely been here; things are *awry*. The CD player her son had gifted her long ago, a sleek, baffling device, has been ripped from its long-standing place on the bookshelf, leaving behind an impressively thick rectangle of dust. Her secretaire is open, the hinged desktop covered in a fantastic mess of papers and pamphlets, family photos, receipts, Christmas cards, lists. Some of this has rained down onto her knock-off Persian rug.

Millie gets down on hands and knees with mounting anxiety,

for she knows her desk is the most likely location of Sylvia's IOU. She comes across other official paperwork. Here is Peter's will – obsolete, but every few years, she rereads it; it's a sort of proof of his erstwhile love for her, his silent devotion. The longer Millie can't find that piece of paper, the more her memory of signing it dims, until she thinks, *Did I make it up?* But no: just before Sylvia had bid her a teary goodbye, before the fire, she and Sylvia had stood signing it in the kitchen.

En route, she nearly trips over a pile of post at the front door. She'd quite forgotten about all the mail she's missed. There's little of interest here, just a handful of bills and two envelopes from the Bank of Ireland. She seizes upon the first of these only to discover that her checking account is overdrawn by €200. Which can't be right. She has a good €3,000 in it. Millie rips open the second envelope – it's her monthly statement – and makes quick sense of the first: seventeen withdrawals, all in sums of between €40 and €80, taken in the previous two months, some twice a day, at different cashpoints in the village and beyond. The last withdrawal was made at Dublin Airport.

Millie cries out.

She can see Sylvia Phenning standing in the lounge with her thick sheet of hair and loud fingernails clicking on tabletops. She sees Sylvia – oh, treacherous traitor! – hovering tenderly nearby with a blanket and what, in retrospect, is so obviously mock concern, scorn even, snapping her smelly, sugary grape gum and asking slyly if Millie needs cash from the bank since Sylvia's on her way in to the shops anyway, it's no bother.

She has been the victim of an elaborate and devious con – not only seventeen unauthorized cash withdrawals, but a whopper of a loan in the name of a dying child! Kevin, it seems, has been right all along: Millie can't cope. She's an incomp. And a fool. An old incompetent fool.

A dozen vignettes starring herself and her 'friend' flood Millie's mind, each recast through this new, nefarious filter, allowing now for her companion's dark motives, the criminal designs spoiling every fond memory, as far back as the earliest days. No wonder Sylvia had been so willing, for instance, to protect Millie after the little accident at the supermarket, trying to get in with her charge, promising not to tell Kevin about the car.

The car.

Millie opens the front door, noting, as she passes through it, no sign of forced entry. Of course there isn't. Sylvia Phenning just waltzed in, didn't she, at any hour she pleased, with the key from beneath the fourth tile. She's no eejit. *Millie's* the eejit. She raises the garage door enough to crouch down and peek up. But the car is still here.

Then again, if Sylvia were scampering off to America, she wouldn't need a car. Still. Wicked, ghastly girl! How stupid is Millie Gogarty? Lapping it all up, the attention and the American treats and the cheap flattery, while the woman pranced around fetching tea and rubbing Millie's sore feet and bringing her little bouquets and pastries, probably paid for with her own money, always volunteering to take on the extra chore. Like the time Sylvia decided to reorganize all the cupboards. Probably to case the joint, discover more treasure.

Millie stops cold.

She rushes back to her desk, the fact of its disorder now stunningly obvious – Sylvia had probably ransacked it to retrieve that

IOU. In one of the secretaire's many cubbies, Millie finds the cassette tape entitled *50 Classics for Relaxation*. With decidedly unrelaxed hands, she opens it, and here's the key to Peter's safe, a tiny copper thing, like a doll's house key, just where she's kept it for years.

'Yes,' Millie murmurs, relieved there's one thing of import, her most valuable possession, Sylvia didn't get her grubby mitts on.

She brings it down to Peter's room, for she has a powerful need to hold her ring in her hands. Given her current financial situation, she'll probably need to bring it into town right away, have it appraised, though the idea of pawning her dead husband's ring, given at the start of their life together, causes her great distress.

Moments later, standing in Peter's closet, gawping at the empty spot beside her shoes, Millie cops on as to why Sylvia hadn't taken the key. She hadn't needed it: she's after running off with the whole bloody safe.

41.

Kevin

'Aideen?'

Kevin raps gently on the door, a rap that would, in words, translate to, *Let's have a gentle chat, love*, since his plan is to be a gentle and loving father and to gently and lovingly coax Aideen out of the storage cupboard. Others have tried and failed, including the headmistress standing curtly beside him, she whose patience with this morning's fiasco – a poisoned staff member prostrate in a hospital bed, a hysterical adolescent confession followed by mute self-exile – appears to be waning. To pile on the absurdity, Rose Byrd is also present, having clipped her way most arousingly across campus in patent leather pumps and a feathery white angora jumper, which, despite his having recklessly detonated his marriage, Kevin has the urge to pet.

His gambit is met with silence. He would like to rip the fucking door down and drag his ungovernable daughter from the storage cupboard and home to Dalkey to be thereafter grounded in perpetuity. But Kevin Gogarty plans to handle this in a calm and adult fashion; he will harness his connection with his daughter; he will be the one to lure her away from the mops and pails and disinfectants, whether by carrot or stick.

He clears his throat and delivers a second, equally restrained knock, but to no avail. He drops his voice and turns to the matronly head of school.

'I wonder if I might have more success speaking with Aideen if it's just the two of us?'

Kevin considers the irony of his choice of words, given the epic parental failure his current predicament so blatantly conveys. After glowering at him, the old matron turns and shuffles off, her sensible shoes whispering like hostages gasping to be rescued with every step.

'Mr Gogarty,' she says, as she's about to cross the threshold into the corridor, 'you realize this situation is untenable.'

'Absolutely.' He nods and smiles confidently, as if they've just met at a cocktail gathering and parted as new friends.

'I'll give you a few minutes, but then I'm going to have to take further measures.'

'Understood. Thank you.'

As the headmistress steps away, Kevin dares not so much as glance at her assistant, whose presence adds greatly to a sort of unpleasant, off-kilter buzz he's experiencing, as if he's downed a few flutes of daytime bubbly on an empty stomach.

'Ms Byrd,' says Murphy, beckoning the woman.

Kevin's not ready for Rose to be gone, not before he says something, though he's not quite sure exactly what. He needs to offer some gesture to signify that no harm's been done (untrue) and that all between them will, moving forth, be civil, if not cordial.

'Ms Byrd?' he says.

Rose turns to him with a face that's priceless: there is yearning, maybe, but also sorrow and solidarity and friendship, at least, the eyes squinting in kindness.

'Don't you tell a fucking soul about us,' she whispers. 'Or I swear to God I'll destroy you.'

Kevin recoils.

The squinting, he realizes, was probably more like a villainous narrowing of the eyes, the yearning more akin to hatred. Later, he will revisit this moment, freshly stunned, and wonder at the meaning, and the timing! Later still, about his gross lapse in judgement.

Rose steps away, the rapid-fire clicks of her heels comically punctuated by her boss's long-suffering footfalls. What a pair. Kevin turns from these terrifying women to his little girl and issues a more urgent succession of knocks on the door, six in all, hard enough that he can feel their vibrations.

'Aideen,' he hisses. 'Open up this door right now. Right this instant. This is absolutely – Jesus, this is – this is a very poor choice, Aideen!'

He tries to picture what she's doing in there. If she's crying, it's silently; if she's moving, it's stealthily. Maybe she's wiping the shelves with a rag and just taking the piss, enjoying the attention? Lord knows, between the shit-storm of home and having moved in with Maeve and Mick, he hasn't given her much lately.

'You're making this much worse on yourself with every single minute you stay in that room. If you don't come out, you're going to be in even hotter water and you're in enough already. Tell me what happened. Right now!'

Throughout this futile soliloquy, during which he feels the power between them decisively shift, Kevin's daughter remains mute. Christ, he used to be good at negotiating with the emotionally unpredictable. In the short time since he stopped producing glossies and persuading celebrity toadies to grant him access to their clients, *this* has sort of become his thing: the unsung parental mishmash of listening and redirecting, the ability to distract, to garner a laugh, tell a tale, provide support yet gently nudge, to feel his children's pain as he guides them to the right moral and practical choices, and generally, with crossed fingers, hope they don't turn out full-grown cretins.

'Look, I'm sure you didn't mean for any of this to happen because I know you wouldn't hurt anyone. This is just not something you would do. I mean, it's one thing if you and your sister have a go at each other, that's normal, but this is –'

The mobile in his pocket chimes. He pulls it out and 'Wife' lights up the screen. Oh, *now* she's available? *Now* she's interested? Never mind his torrent of calls, his being here on scene and she being, decidedly, there. He taps 'ignore'.

'I'm guessing this was your friend's idea? What's her name? Was she the one who put the –' He can't even. 'Or was it you? Look, if you don't tell me your side of this, then I'll have to ask her. I'll have to ring up her parents.' He sighs. 'You did the right thing telling them what Miss Bleekland ... digested. But you need to tell me what exactly happened, Aideen. You have to come out and face the music. And, look, I'll face it with you.'

He checks his watch, wonders if the headmistress has made it back to command central where she will soon summon the handyman to resolve this escalating problem.

'But one thing you can't do is stay in there forever. Firstly, you're going to have to use the toilet at some stage, right? And then you're going to get hungry. You're going to get thirsty. Tired. Your nails are going to need to get trimmed or you'll end up like that weird woman in the *Guinness Book*, you remember? Albanian, I think, with the curved nails, the world's longest nails, like, two metres long, hideous talons. You realize she can't do a thing with those? She can't shake someone's hand without slashing them to ribbons. She can't send a text message. The horror! In fact, all she can do is sit at her kitchen table and wait for the Guinness photo crew to arrive every year. Do you really want to be that woman?'

More silence. He knocks on the door.

'Right, then. Well.' *Think*, he commands himself. He wants simply to pierce her impenetrable soul – is that so much to ask? Kevin mines his own past for some knot of connection, some lowest common denominator to bridge them. He thinks back on his own teenage transgressions – underage drinking, smoking fags, sneaking out, sneaking in, sneaking girls out and in, unlicensed driving. None relatable in this context. He tries to call up some moment of desperation in his life. He remembers at one of his London stand-up gigs, he'd been riffing about men in pubs and then, hopping from the stool, he imitated an old man coming home from the market, hands fumbling in his front pockets. Feigning dismay, he'd said, 'Plums? I don't remember buying any plums.'

Look, it wasn't his greatest work, but the total silence seemed like overkill. He recalls staring out at the black room, the terror of that. With the spotlight glaring at him, Kevin could see only outlines of humans, a roomful of dark lumps. His impulse was to leg it offstage posthaste and he stood trying to decipher whether the exit was left or right when he heard, from somewhere towards the back, a ripple of familiar laughter. It was Grace. She was there. She didn't hate the plums.

'I'm here, Aideen, OK, can we not just talk this through?'

She snorts.

'Oh, we can't talk?' Kevin says. 'We're not friends now?'

'Friends! Please. You didn't want to talk when you sent me to this place.'

He hears a shifting, like she's switched positions.

'I never wanted to come here,' Aideen says with strong feeling. 'But you didn't want to hear that. You take Nuala's side every fight, every time, and you have no idea, you have no clue. You won't even listen.'

Nuala? What daft nonsense is this?

'You never listen.'

'That's not true.' Is that true? 'OK, maybe that's partially true. I've been –' He pauses to reflect and then says, 'Yes, you might be right. I'm sorry. And look, I know you may be stressed with what's happening with your mum and me. But that's temporary. That's not anything you need to worry about.'

From behind the door, Kevin hears a quiet sniffling and then a gasp of breathy release, like crying.

'Ah, Aideen.'

She emits a sort of choked sob. 'I didn't know that was gonna happen, Dad! It was just a joke, a stupid joke. I didn't even want to do it. I just got the mints from her bag. I didn't put the – I had no idea it would make her sick.'

'You didn't mean to hurt her,' he says, powerfully relieved.

'I didn't! Is she going to be OK?'

He sighs. 'I don't know. I hope so.'

His phone bleats. 'Wife' again.

He needs to tell Grace so much: 'Aideen has abetted in the poisoning of the housemother. I miss you. My new roommate is an elderly chain-smoking nag but, funnily enough, not such a bad egg, who follows me round her house launching disapproving missiles in your defence (she seems to think you're the bee's knees). Aideen's fuck-up was a terrible fuck-up, but her intentions weren't cruel. I wish you were here. I need your wisdom. You *are* the bee's knees.'

To the door, he says, 'Give me one second, Aideen.'

He accepts the call and whispers, 'Hello?' Kevin has the sense that if his daughter knows it's her mother on the line, some unspoken trust will have been violated.

'Hello? I can't hear you. Kevin?'

He moves through the room, past the table tennis and a backgammon set clearly interrupted mid-game, no one to ever know what the next move will be.

'I'm at the school,' he says quietly.

'What?'

He steps into the hall and says, 'I'm at the school.'

'Which school? I've just got off a three-hour panel and there are five missed calls from you!'

'I'm at the school,' he says a third time. 'Millburn. There's been an incident with the head of Fair –'

'Wait, hang on.'

He hears muffled, echoey chat from her end; his best guess is she's in a soul-deadening corporate hotel convention room with a bunch of yahoos.

'I'm just coming now,' she says and Kevin listens to an indecipherable back and forth. Then, into the phone, his wife says, 'Shit, they're calling me back in already. I have to go. Let me ring you in an hour? Aideen is OK, right?'

Kevin says nothing, but feels much. He hangs up, stuffs his mobile into his back pocket, and, head down, shuffles back into the common room only to find that what he's wanted so desperately has, indeed, happened: the storage-cupboard door's open. But when he steps towards the little room, his daughter isn't in it.

42.
Aideen

A bus into Westmoreland Street; a Dart from Pearse Street Station; the short walk from the village and, finally, Aideen is home where the still and empty rooms feel alien. What she wouldn't give for a humdrum morning of the recent past, to just pat Nemesis on the head and scream 'I'm off!' to no one in particular and bang closed the front door, a slice of buttered toast in one hand as she makes her way to school.

Immediately, she googles 'Dublin hospitals' and finds the closest one to Millburn. Adopting as formal a diction as she can muster, she rings through to the main desk. 'I wanted to check on a patient? Miss Bleekland?'

'Which ward?'

'Uh … emergency?'

Aideen is placed on hold for an interminable period during which she feels crucial minutes – when she should be planning and packing – pass.

Finally, a different woman comes on the line. 'This is Nicola. How may I help?'

'I wanted to check on Miss Bleekland? She was brought in this morning.'

'Who am I speaking with?'

'I'm her niece, Justine.'

'Justine ...?'

'Bleekland.'

'Ah, I see. We don't give out information on our patients over the phone, Miss Bleekland.' *Miss Bleekland!* She winces. 'If you come to the admissions hall here, you'll –'

'But I can't! I live far away. Please, it's really important. I just want to make sure she's OK. Please, can you just tell me?'

A pause, and then, 'She's your aunt, you said?'

'Yes.'

'Can I have the patient's Christian name?'

During the countless smoke-filled afternoons spent dallying down by the river, the midnight tête-à-têtes on adjacent bunks, the discussions over lunch tables and tea breaks, Aideen and Brigid and the other Fair girls have vilified – eviscerated, really – the head of Fair House with scathing nicknames, cruel limericks (Aideen), and ferocious imitations of exaggerated old-lady limping (Brigid). But it did not occur to Aideen (or, presumably, her ex-friend) to ever wonder about the woman's name, or, for that matter, any real-life detail, in terms of her being an actual human being, one whom Aideen is now responsible for having seriously injured. Or killed.

'I don't know!' she says wildly. 'Anne?'

'Who is this?'

'I call her Auntie Bleekland. Please, I'm very worried about her.'

'I'm sorry, I can't –'

'Is she going to die?' Aideen blurts this out with great anguish.

'I'm not at liberty –'

'Fuck!'

She crashes the phone into its cradle and lets herself slump down to the floor and gives in to an overwhelming surge of feeling, the undeniable fact that everything – *everything* – is totally fucked, and it's her doing.

'Please don't let her die,' she finds herself saying aloud, again and again, a pleading mantra. When her breathing calms, she gets up from the floor and wipes her face with her sleeve. She needs to move quickly. Where is she going exactly? She hasn't a whisper. Just away. She heads to the basement. Forbidding herself even a peripheral glance lest a madman lurks nearby, she finds her mother's rolly with its olive-hued shell and wheels it to the staircase, bumping it up to the main floor, debris and tiny clouds of dust coughing onto each step. Nuala and Ciaran will be home from school eventually and then, later, Mum – Mum will be livid. Worse: disappointed, ashamed. And poor Dad, for all she knows, may still be wandering around Millburn calling her name.

She scans each room for the most critical items a fugitive would need: phone, charger, earbuds, crisps. Of course, what she really needs is money, the one thing that eludes her. In Dad's office, she rifles through the desk but comes up with only a handful of coins, barely enough for a bus fare. Her grandmother might be a possibility if Gran hadn't recently, in fact, asked *her* for a loan. Anyway, Gran's at Rossdale. Which means Gran's house is empty. Aideen could go to Margate, at least for a bit, stop there and regroup, spend the night even, though it's a creepy prospect.

She slips the coins into her pocket and, sifting through the last drawer, happens upon a file which contains the family pile of passports: six slim burgundy volumes, hers with a scowling visage within that brings her back to the day they went to the camera shop for the photos, how she'd been uncooperative and mute, a right pain.

She shoves her passport into the suitcase. Maybe she'll go to America and track down Sean? This fantasy quickly gains traction; she has often imagined Sean and herself holding hands at his bedside. She could move to Florida and become an American student, attend a dramatic-arts school in a brick building where students spontaneously burst into song, where a teacher might notice her poetry, with wide hallways and thousands of lockers and gorgeous, horrible cheerleaders with pom-poms leaning in doorways, every one of them parting to let Sean and herself, deeply in love, pass through.

Of course, the fact that she's penniless and underage is prohibitive enough; even if she were to take such a bold step, Dad would only follow her over and drag her back. At the bottom of the pile, she finds her father's passport. He looks younger in the photo, his features sharper, the left corner of his mouth slightly raised, conveying a sort of silly self-consciousness.

A thought crystallizes. Dad couldn't follow her anywhere, were she to go anywhere, without a passport.

Dare she?

Rationalizing that it would be wrong and criminal to steal the thing, Aideen decides, instead, to place it somewhere out of the way, a little stalling technique, just in case. She can always put the passport back in its place, so. She turns to his crammed bookshelves and slips Dad's little book between the *Roget's* (still her favourite) and a badly worn copy of *Dubliners* and, to thwart potential eyewitnesses, takes the back roads to Dún Laoghaire.

43.
Millie

Sergeant O'Connor has grown a scrubby blanket of facial hair, like every second young fella in Dublin, since Millie last found herself sitting in this grotty interrogation room in Dún Laoghaire Garda Station. Same cheap chairs; same nicked-up slab table. But this time, the private room was at her request, in case Kevin should happen to pull up and witness his distraught mother through the window – an unlikely but not impossible scenario. Kevin will not be pleased when he discovers she's checked herself out of Rossdale and he'll think her a right fool once he's learned she's been duped, not by drugged-up teens or a band of gypsies, but by a scheming American with a sleek ponytail and a house key.

Maybe her being targeted by a swindler should not come as such a surprise. She's further on in years than many of her fellow Dubliners and she lives alone, with only the occasional visitor. Nearly all of her peers are long in the grave, a grim list to which she can now add Mrs Jameson's name. It's not that Millie is lonesome so much as desolate, parched. It's not that Margate is quiet, it's that, beyond witnessing from her window perch the tides drawing towards and away from her, the house shows so few signs of life. How easily she can remember her Peter coming through the door and tossing his hat to the hall table, or Kevin counting out push-ups in the garden, or her pals walking towards her up the drive laden with lemon cakes and gin for their weekly bridge game. Sylvia had made Margate feel something akin to that again, upping the bar of potential, as if good things might once more happen.

Millie hadn't realized just how the circumstances of her life made her vulnerable, nor that her need for company was so blatant, so exposed. This is her own bloody fault, the steep price for her naivety and foolishness, her embarrassing needs, her silly ego, her sense that if she didn't have a party trick, the party would end. She'd even voluntarily bragged to Sylvia about how well she'd hidden the key to her safe!

When Millie had rung the guards earlier, a woman on the other end had said she'd have to come in, reports must be made in person. Unable to locate her car keys, Millie had been reduced to 'borrowing' her neighbour's bike (every downstairs light was blazing, a solid indication that the Fitzgeralds were out of town, so no harm). She'd teetered her way on two wheels, wearing her floppy hat and a teal silken scarf, which she felt confident went some distance towards disguising her. She was pressingly aware that, at any turn in the road, the wind, which was fierce, might blow her right off and into the ancient wall dividing road from seafront, or she might crack her knee or pull a muscle or unwittingly hit a rock and find herself akimbo, flashing half the town an unprecedented glimpse of her faded knickers. The image kept her focused and on she pedalled, relieved when the station appeared on the horizon.

Such a mission might be viewed, by a less reckless soul, as high risk, given her Rossdale breakout only a few hours prior, and the very little time she now has to cement a plan before her son discovers she's on the lam (the ticking by of time, as ever, hounds and haunts her). But if Millie is to get to the bottom of all this without Kevin's knowledge – and she means to – Sergeant O'Connor looks to be her only lead.

He makes his slow, casual way over, bearing a takeaway coffee, which steams from its cardboard cup. O'Connor offers this to Millie, who shakes her head no – she hasn't time for such trivialities. He drags a chair to the table and sips from the cup himself. For some reason, it looks to Millie as if he's fighting a smile.

'Tell me, what brings you in today, Mrs Gogarty?'

'Absolutely appalling circumstances, the likes of which I've never known in all my years in Dublin, that's what brings me in.'

'Oh dear. I'm sorry to hear that. Why don't you tell me what's happened?'

He clasps his hands together and settles back into his seat as much as a person can settle into a folding metal chair.

'Do I have your word that what's said here stays here?'

'If that's what you'd like, yes, but –'

'I don't want anyone to know about this. My son has his own motives,' she adds. 'Let's just leave it at that.'

'I see.' O'Connor removes from a cleverly hidden shoulder pocket a small black notebook and clicks open a biro.

Millie gathers her thoughts, trying to organize a factual, linear narrative. If Millie is going to outsmart a con artist, for the love of Jesus, she's going to have to get smart herself.

'I would like to see the records from when I was ...' Her cheeks boil instantly. 'From when I was arrested.' Millie has never made aloud any reference to her petty-theft bust, never mind admitting the truth of it. But there, now, that's done. And isn't she still breathing?

'You weren't actually arrested.'

'That's right, we made our ... arrangement ... and the terms of that – the home help coming to me during the week, well, she turned out to be a very bad egg.'

'Home help?' His head tips softly to one side.

'Now, where he found her, I've no idea.'

'He?'

'My son. I'd venture to say under a rock. A slippery one.' She gives a bitter chuckle. 'Probably on the computer, through a service? I don't think I ever was told the details. He just showed up with her one day. And so that's why I'm here – I want to file an official gobbledygook for the robbery, of course, but I'd also like the contact information for Sylvia.'

'Robbery?'

'I think she got in with my spare key.'

'Who?'

'Sylvia Phenning, the woman Kevin hired to assist me. Does that name not ring a bell?'

'And you told Mrs Cantwell on the phone that she's an American citizen?' Millie nods. O'Connor scratches words into his notebook. 'Hang on, Mrs Gogarty. Let's backtrack just so

I'm clear. You're saying that when you were last here, some kind of deal was negotiated –'

'Yes, back in December, do you not remember?'

'I do, yes, but you're saying that instead of having charges brought against you – is that it? – you agreed to a home –'

'And I was forced to postpone my trip to New York. With Jolly Jessica.'

'Jolly ...?'

'But as it turns out, my home help was not very helpful. She robbed me. Well, not right away. At first she wined and dined me. Then she robbed me.'

'How do you mean wined and dined?'

'Well, she didn't ply me with Pinot Grigio,' says Millie with an exasperated laugh and wonders if he isn't a bit thick. 'I meant metaphorically.'

'Ah. Let's – what was this woman's schedule? She was in your house every day?'

'Nearly. And she'd tidy up, do up meals. Made an absolutely gorgeous carbonara, actually. Though it was a bit on the creamy side. But she'd add peas. You wouldn't be caught dead in Rome with peas!'

'I myself am not averse to peas.' He smiles. 'So the suspect was very kind, attentive, yes?'

Despite her exciting wave of self-determination, it feels briefly like a betrayal to label her friend this way. 'Suspect, yes.'

'What exactly did she steal from you?'

'What didn't she!' Millie cries. 'She's after withdrawing thousands from my current account in the Bank of Ireland, every last ha'penny.'

O'Connor whistles. 'How did she manage that? Did she have access to your bank card?'

'Well, yes, but not at first. Part of her job was to run errands with me, you see, and there came a day the two of us were in my Renault. I couldn't find a parking spot and, you know yourself, the parking situation here is atrocious. In fact, if I had more time, I'd have half a mind to lodge a formal complaint about it.'

'So you were looking for a parking spot?'

'And we were looping round and finally she said why didn't I stay with the car so as not to get a ticket? And I thought, that's grand, and so I handed over my card.'

'And told her your PIN?'

Millie winces and he says, 'You're not the first person to be conned, Mrs Gogarty. This is a very common crime. These are skilled professionals – they know exactly how to prey on all sorts of innocents.'

'She was nearly like a daughter.'

From a different hidden pocket, O'Connor retrieves a folded wad of tissues and hands one to Millie. What'll he come out with next, a rope of colourful handkerchiefs pulled endlessly from his gob? But he's a darling, especially for a copper – really, she couldn't ask for a nicer policeman.

'And on that particular day,' he says, 'do you remember if she gave you a receipt?'

'That's just it! Yes. Hadn't taken a penny more than I asked.'

'Hmm. And so you began to trust her after that?'

'Sergeant O'Connor, I don't believe I ever looked at another receipt from that moment on … I know, I know.'

'Not at all. OK and can you tell me about the home burglary? When did that happen?'

'I don't know. I just discovered it this morning. I've been in Rossdale Home due to the fire – did you know I'd a fire in my house?'

'I had heard that, yes.'

'You should see my kitchen. Black as your hat. And my arm caught alight.' She begins to unbutton her cuff.

'You're grand there,' he says, blocking her from the unveiling. 'Exactly what was taken? Laptops? Phones? That sort of thing?'

'Everything. Electronics. I can't even find my curling iron.'

'I see.' He clears his throat and begins to shift away from the table. 'And was there anything else? Credit cards? Cash in the house?'

Millie looks at a tiny speck of dirt on the ground and, with a hanging head, says, 'I did give her a loan,' and explains about Sean and the phoney surgery.

O'Connor listens intently, pulling an almost tender face – mouth sheepishly squared. 'It's a terrible crime, Mrs Gogarty,' he says gently. 'How much money did you loan her?'

'Thirty thousand euros.'

'Jaysus.' O'Connor looks with genuine pity on her. 'And you say she's left the country?'

'Yes. She phoned me from New York just after.'

'How do you know she wasn't still here, in Ireland?'

'I don't. But she said she was calling from America. And she often mentioned returning there but she didn't have enough saved.'

He drums his fingers on the table. 'Look, I'm very sorry this has happened, and we'll be looking into all of this. I'll need you to make an official statement, all that you've told me here. And we'll take down an inventory of what's missing. That's where we start.' He gets up. 'But to be honest, Mrs Gogarty, if she's left the country, I'm not sure there's an awful lot we can do.'

'Wait,' Millie scrambles to her feet. 'I do need to see that file, please.'

O'Connor, who's not far from the exit, looks with longing towards it.

'Please,' says Millie.

'Let me ask you something, Mrs Gogarty,' he says. 'What do you think you'd do with that information?'

She knows, at least vaguely, what she would do. She would make Sylvia look her in the eye. She would get back what's hers.

'Please, it's very important. She stole the only possession I give a fig about and it happens to be very valuable. It was a ring. From my husband.'

'Sit down a moment.' He joins her back at the table and pats her hand and says, 'I have to tell you something, Mrs Gogarty, and I'd like you to brace yourself – can you do that?'

She nods.

'There is no file.'

'What do you mean?'

O'Connor sighs. 'Look. I don't know whether you're misremembering or whether you've been misinformed. But there was no agreement made here with anyone. We just don't do that. That sort of thing – banning trips abroad and home-care aides

– we don't have that kind of authority. It's not something that could have happened.'

'There was no paperwork? With the courts?'

'No paperwork,' he replies. 'No deal.'

Millie gawks at him as the truth of the situation presents itself.

'I'm guessing it was your son who explained all that to you?'

Millie pedals in a light drizzle back to her ransacked home. She paces her shabby rooms with a restless energy. Tricked again, this time by her own bloody son. All of this is his fault. He'd unwittingly invited a criminal into Margate. And she can't even locate the woman since the whole set-up was bollocks to begin with. Millie'll be destitute. She'll have to start shoplifting for survival, stealing bottles of milk from the neighbours' steps (metaphorically speaking, though she still longs for the days of dairy delivery), pushing jars of jam up her sleeve. Come to think of it, she might as well march to the main road, stick out her thumb, and get a lift back to Rossdale and give up.

She pours a whiskey – her Peter's salve for stress – and slugs it down, but it does nothing to soothe her. Maybe a bath. And another nip. She strips out of her clothes, brings the glass decadently in with her, and within minutes is immersed and feeling slightly calmer, thinking *America*. Sylvia must be in America.

When the tub is near to full, Millie turns the water off and hears a creak, distant but real. She sits up and clutches the sides of the tub, for now footsteps sound from the back of the house *and they are coming towards her.* There's a squatter in Margate. A gypsy or a drug addict or maybe it's Sylvia, returning to pillage the rest of her worldly goods. The steps seem to halt and hover just outside her very door. Millie climbs out of the bath gingerly; this is no time for a fall. She snaps a stiff towel from the rack and wraps it round herself. There is no exit other than the door; a house cat could barely fit through the only window and, anyway, she's done enough window clambering for one old lady for one day. She grabs the ancient toilet brush in one hand and a can of hairspray in the other. She must look a fright – pink shower cap atop her head, scant green towel barely covering her.

Millie tiptoes to the door. She envisions a massive burly man in a black balaclava or a skinny junkie with acne. The door handle shifts down slowly and Millie screams.

'Gran?'

'Aideen?'

'It's me.'

Millie drops her weapons as the door swings open and, for some reason, her granddaughter is standing before her with a suitcase.

'What are you doing here? Why are you not in Millburn?'

'Why are you not in Rossdale?'

Millie squints at the girl and then the case in total befuddlement. A memory seizes her, a glorious memory.

Aideen says, 'Something terrible has happened.'

'Luggage tag!' Millie cries, pushing past her granddaughter and down the hall.

44.
Kevin

As a kid, Kevin had done a few runners, brief and banal, so his concern with Aideen's disappearance, initially, is low grade. From the storage cupboard, she would have had to either pass him (she didn't) or head directly outside. He walks the perimeter of Fair House under a doomsday sky at a calm enough pace, calling her name and scanning the great lawn and picnic tables and courtyard and hockey pitch, where two girls are very obviously smoking. At least, he thinks, Aideen's not thus inclined.

He rings her phone three times to no avail. He does a quick check of her dormitory – bereft of students at this hour – and a pass at each of the other rooms. First through sixth year. Then the dining hall. School foyer. Gym. Lockers. Toilets, where a small child with militarily precise plaits gives him the stink eye.

'Girls only!' she scolds.

Story of my life, thinks Kevin.

His anxiety begins to build, not because he's afraid he won't find her – he will – but because he needs to do so quickly. The last thing they need is for the school to learn of Aideen's little disappearing trick. She's fucked as it is and he won't be able to assuage the powers that be this time round.

Kevin's finishing up his sweep through the Millburn halls when 'Rossdale' flashes up on his phone. What *now*? Has Mum propositioned an elderly gent in a dark corner? Or trapped some ageing lady in a wheelchair in order to deliver a monologue on the inherent injustice of paying for parking in the village? Kevin does as he always does, which is to send the call to voicemail posthaste.

Now Ms Murphy is suddenly bustling towards him, but he doesn't panic since her bifocals are like two wedges of bullet-proof glass – she appears to see nothing until it's upon her. He slips easily through the school front doors. Aideen's little game of hide-and-seek is decidedly not fun, and getting less so with every search zone he clears. Kevin stops to block out all noise and distraction, but cannot think where his daughter has gone, and, with growing unease, retraces his steps, beginning with her dormitory.

His daughter's bed is predictably unruly, the only one of eight whose duvet is knotted up and dangling mid-cliff from its standard-issue mattress. Her sheet looks to have been yanked off each corner, as if Aideen wrestles rather than sleeps here. Kevin opens her cubby: spray deodorant, an enormous palette of metallic eye shadows, a sample size of Eternity Eau de Parfum. It's a curiously girly collection for a girl like Aideen. He stretches the sheet back onto the bed and then punches her flattened pillow in frustration, only to hit a hard shape, a rectangle, through the pillowcase.

It's a spiral-bound notebook, marked, redundantly, 'PRIVATE' and 'CONFIDENTIAL'. He is mildly comforted that at least his daughter has a place to deposit whatever it is that goes on inside her head. As he's replacing it in the pillowcase, a number of loose sheets flutter from it onto the bed. Which he takes to be a sign.

There once was a mother called Grace
With a warm and a beautiful face
I watch her leave
It's like I grieve
No wonder my life's a disgrace.

Kevin puzzles over her verse. In one sense, it reads like classic, histrionic schoolgirl angst, yet he can't help but feel upset at how mature and cynical it is, with its whiff of irreversible doom. And sad.

Aideen is sad?

He reaches for the second scrap.

If I had a dinghy
I'd put it in the sea
I'd want it plain, not blingy,
The boat would be for me.
My sister'd stay onshore
While I undid the ties
I'd push off with my oar
And then I'd scream GOODBYE!

Kevin feels almost giddy by what is so clear: his daughter, his kooky, clever, stubborn Aideen, is a writer, or trying to be, and a good one, too. She's gunning towards truth, as he himself once was. So enamoured of this realization is Kevin that he fails to sense the energy shift in the room. In it, now, is a girl in an unkempt school uniform, her brunette waves streaked through with stripy hot-pink chunks, which frame a bone-sharp face smattered in a surplus of freckles.

The girl does not acknowledge Kevin, though she approaches the bunk area he currently occupies, moving to the bed directly beside his daughter's. Kevin shoves his disturbing discoveries back into the notebook and puts the lot away.

He faux-coughs. 'I'm looking for Aideen Gogarty. You haven't seen her, have you?'

The girl shakes her dyed splotches and pulls open the drawer beneath her bed.

'Are you a friend of hers?'

A pause, and then she says, 'Kind of,' and begins gathering a pile of tops, one by one, with a sort of mournful torpor. 'Are you her dad?'

'Yes and I really need to find her. If I don't, she's going to be in an even worse pickle than she already is.'

The girl shrugs.

'Are you not supposed to be in class right now?'

She says nothing, and Kevin turns away. He needs to get back on the trail, but he is at a serious loss; at this point, he's swept every student-permissible nook of Millburn School.

Despite the young lady's frosty mien, manners compel him to say goodbye. She is intently regarding herself in a mirror affixed to the interior of her cupboard door, dabbing beneath her eyes with nude liquid goop from a tube. At the top of the mirror, he notices a sticker: 'BRIGID' is spelled out in rainbow bubble lettering.

'Brigid Crowe?'

She nods, unfazed, and darts a series of compacts and lip gloss sticks into a bag.

'Ah,' says Kevin, studying her more closely, the freckles taking on a more subversive air. 'You're in your own pickle.'

Brigid snorts.

A message flashes up on his phone, from Mick, and Kevin involuntarily reads it.

> Mum swears yr mum was cycling by the house this am??
> Gone daft.

Immediately a second message follows.

> My mum daft I mean. Beers tonight?

Kevin pockets his phone. 'Looks as if you're going somewhere?'

'Yeah, onto the next shithole.'

But her voice, for all its defiance, wavers and Kevin understands why his daughter is drawn to her. What was her story again? Aideen had thrown her name around quite a bit in those first weekends home, but he can't recall a single detail beyond her father having some sort of glamorous profession.

'Have you been expelled?'

'No.'

Which means, reasons Kevin, his daughter may also be in the clear. Just. 'But you're leaving?'

'They phoned my dad. He thinks this place is crap, not strict enough. Not that he would have a clue.'

'We're not all so clueless as you girls might think, you know. There is usually a reason for our madness.'

'He's never even been here.'

'To the school?'

'Never.'

'Not the first day?'

'And not the last one either.' She zips up her bag and walks to the door.

'Well,' he says, with a stab of empathy for Brigid Crowe despite her hideous and undue influence on his own child. 'Listen, best of luck then.'

She reaches the door and turns back. 'Try the river.'

'Sorry?'

'Across the road, under the bridge. We sometimes go there after school.'

45.

Aideen

Ripping down the M50 with Gran at the helm after a close call with the wing mirror of a passing taxi, Aideen is keenly reminded of Dad's growing belief that Millie Gogarty ought to be relieved of her car keys. With one hand, Aideen clutches the door handle; with the other, she swipes away the frequent evidence of her parents' rising panic as they try and fail to locate her. This just in, from Dad:

PHONE ME ASAP WHERE R U

The fact that his text messages are all in caps doesn't concern Aideen as much as their glaring absence of punctuation. Under no circumstances does Dad fuck with grammar. Meaning, these circumstances are off the charts.

Back at Margate, Aideen had finally succumbed to her grandmother's multiple rationales. Mum and Dad, began Gran, don't let Aideen make any of her own decisions, do they? Sure they don't. In fact, they treat her as if she's a child, do they not? And she's sixteen years of age. Gran herself knew girls practically married at that age. It's all unacceptably patronizing, and she would know since that's exactly how they treat Gran as well, lying to her about a fake deal with the police, checking her into that house of horrors where 'clients' are always croaking, and if they're not, they're spewing nonsense or collecting all sorts of rubbishy ornaments. Maybe it's time Aideen makes up her own mind about some things, and a more than capable mind has she, Gran might add.

None of this was persuasive. Gran proceeded to point out that there was an off chance they might even bump into Sean – though, she'd added, he might have been in on the scam.

'I don't think so,' Aideen had said. 'No way. But anyway, he doesn't want to see me.'

'You don't know that.'

Finally Gran had stared at her, wounded eyed, and, in a deliberately small voice, which had its effect, she'd said, 'I don't think I can do this alone.'

The room had grown quiet while Aideen, compelled by Gran's need, began to envision fleeing Dublin, temporarily, where trouble was closing in on every front, and boarding an aeroplane, going to America. She's never been to America.

'We'll hardly be gone a few days,' Gran went on, 'just enough to pay a visit to the police, ya see, and, look, I'll tell your mum and dad it was my idea.'

'But we don't even know where they are. It's ludicrous! For all we know, they *are* in New York.'

'Why would they be? That was just part of her lie, wasn't it, because all the big hospitals are there.' Gran had stood in the lounge waggling the brown luggage tag she'd filched from Sylvia all those weeks ago. 'She's gone home, Aideen, I'm certain of it. She's probably tucking into a three-Michelin-star meal in ...' She squints at the tag. 'What does it say?'

'Clearwater.'

'Clearwater this very moment, compliments of yours truly.'

'I don't know ...' Aideen had said. 'It's too crazy. It's insane. And I'm in so much trouble already.'

'Exactly.' Gran had patted her hands like the debate was over. 'It'll give everyone a little time to cool down. And, really, at the end of the day, what have you got to lose?'

Together, their first task had been to locate Gran's car keys, which Aideen found on the very hook designated for them. Already Aideen was proving her indispensability. There followed a scramble of packing and gathering of Gran's scraps of cash from cracked bowls and lint-lined trouser pockets and coin purses and two twenties stashed in the freezer. They counted up nearly €300 in total and a Visa card Gran had once used to buy a Hoover.

But now that she's airport-bound for an unauthorized international jaunt, Aideen has time to reflect. What she can't deny is the profound and unprecedented piles of shite she's going to be in, even given Gran's willingness to fall on her sword.

WHERE DID U GO

PHONE ME

A call from Mum pops up, third and counting. Aideen hesitates – she'd definitely score points for not going through with this. She glances over at her father's mother, hands fisted tightly round the steering wheel, eyes on the road ahead. Aideen is shitting herself, but Gran looks fearless.

They ditch the Renault in long-term parking. How long, worries Aideen, will they be? Gran tosses the parking-ticket stub in the bin as they sweep through the automatic doors. Aideen can't decide – and is too scared to ask – whether there's any meaning behind it.

'The fastest way round here is with a wheelchair,' Gran announces as if she does this sort of thing all the time. After they procure a chair, Aideen wheels Gran straight past epic lines to the Aer Lingus ticket counter. Gran tries to apply the unused credit from her cancelled trip towards their tickets, but it's too complicated to work out, and they haven't the time. She retrieves her Visa card from the depths of her décolletage, the ruddy skin at her chest bunched vertically like a bellows. They luck onto the next flight, the last flight, to Florida – astronomically priced – which is boarding shortly.

Aideen steers Gran past great hordes of loud, bickering families already in the throes of nightmare travel fatigue. Boarding passes in hand, they are beckoned through a VIP line at security, where an officer frisks Gran, who laps up the attention with non-stop commentary despite the obvious discomfort of her humourless molester. All of this, needless to say, is severely embarrassing.

Aideen forgot that Gran is totally embarrassing.

Yet it's almost ... fun – moving through the terminal, checking and rechecking the monitors to confirm their boarding time and gate number (despite her wheelchair bluster, Gran seems pretty clueless about air travel protocol), being in charge of their documents (Gran would surely have dropped them somewhere between customer service and the ladies' toilets) and their grubby money fold with its alarmingly meagre quantity of cash. Even a teenager knows €300 won't last long.

Still. Every turn they make, Gran waving to small children, every moving walkway they roll onto, people in their path part biblically. There's a way Gran interacts with the world, even as it plainly dismisses her, that Aideen's beginning to absorb. She thinks: *Fantastic.*

THE MINUTE YOU GET THIS CALL ME PLS AM WORRIED

Now they're at the immense, newly renovated duty-free shopping area, where their fellow travellers purchase, with unchecked frenzy, all manner of products to Gran's vociferous disapproval: scented body lotion, Waterford crystal vases, family packs of Ferrero Rocher, chevron-striped phone covers, sheep-patterned coin purses, Belleek china overrun with shamrocks. Gran sniffs at it all and points towards the refrigerated cases in Wrights of Howth.

'Can't get this in Florida,' she says, selecting a packet of vacuum-sealed smoked salmon.

'You can't get fish in Florida?' Positioned behind Gran's chair, Aideen freely eye-rolls.

'Not Irish fish, Duckie.'

'Gran,' says Aideen, 'where are we going to eat that? Is there a kitchen even?'

When Aideen sees Gran's face, she wants to take it back. She doesn't really mean to be mean; she just has no idea how to envision their near future. A motel? A high-rise? A tent pitched on the beach? To Aideen, Florida is a jumbled fantasy grounded in a steady diet of Hollywood and the internet. It could just as well be Los Angeles or San Diego or Atlanta. It's Kentucky Fried Chicken, stubble-faced surfers in wetsuits unzipped enough to expose just that bit of chest, Disney World, blubbery men in gold chains parked beside coolers of Budweiser, blubbery women in tennis visors and neon bum-bags. What exactly will Aideen and Gran do once they land? Get laughed out of a police station? Steal a wheelchair and play detective in Clearwater? Book a room and subsist on smoked fish until they deplete their woeful cash reserves?

'Go on then,' says Aideen. 'We can eat it in a hotel, right?'

'Ah, you're a petal.'

'What about sausages? Might as well get some of those as well.'

'Oh, no bother, I've already got some.'

'You packed a string of sausages in your carry-on?'

'No! You can't take sausages in your handbag, I don't think, love.'

'I know that, Gran. But you can't put them in your luggage either. I mean, first of all, that's just gross. You can't –'

'I'm more worried about the rashers, if I'm being honest.'

'Did you bring eggs as well? We can do a fry-up at the gate.'

Gran cranes her neck right round and grins. 'You're just like your dad there.' In the unflattering glare of the institutional overheads, her grandmother's eyes flash with feeling, but they're lost in the deep trenches that have always been, to Aideen, her most striking facial feature. The woman is ancient.

There once was a saucy old dame
Who her family tried hard to make tame ...

'Listen to me, Aideen, are you listening?'

'Our flight's boarding soon, Gran. We'd better hurry.'

'We will. But listen: you can't speak to Mum or Dad yet. We've got to stall them until we're settled, and then we'll let them know we're safe. Right? We can't tip them off now, you see, so no text messaging, no phoning. Your father will get his knickers in a twist and he'll be on the first aeroplane to Florida and that, as they say, will be that.'

'No, he won't.'

'Yes, he will, love. You know what he's like. He'll come and bring us right back home, you can believe that.'

'No, he won't,' says Aideen. 'He can't.'

'Of course he can.'

'I've done something really wicked.'

'You put fish eyeballs in his coffee?'

Aideen gawps at her grandmother. She could eat the head off her; she could poke out Gran's own eyeballs. 'That is *not* funny.'

'Sorry, love. You're right. I'm sorry. Lost the head.'

'That is the opposite of funny.'

Gran sheepishly casts her face towards the floor and Aideen takes up her position behind the wheelchair and they roll in silence to the till. But almost as fast as it arrives, Aideen finds, for some reason, that fury with Gran is difficult to sustain. It was a cheap shot, yes, but Aideen gets that Gran's off-colour joke is rooted in a truth and so maybe it's fair game. She put a woman in hospital for no good reason, after all; she's been the cause of great pain.

'She's going to be alright,' Gran says, counting out a mess of euro coins. 'She's in the clear, remember? Stable.' Back at Margate, Aideen would only agree to America after Gran had impersonated the headmistress of Millburn School over the phone and got word that Bleekland's condition was improving. 'Stable is good.'

'That's the word they used?'

'The very one.'

They pay for the fish and wheel their way to their gate. Just before boarding, though there's no one near them, and no one cares, Aideen drops her voice and leans forward and whispers in Gran's ear the whereabouts of Dad's passport.

46.

Kevin

The bit of river that trickles through Millburn is not visible from the road. Kevin walks down a bank of weeds, the odd condom wrapper and a crushed can of Smithwick's peeping through the ragged scrub. He follows a long, hidden walkway and soon enough discovers what is surely the girls' spot on the far side of an underpass. They've left a rude mound of evidence behind: cigarette butts, an empty box of matches, crushed Sprite cans. He calls Aideen's name half-heartedly but knows she's not there – the whole place feels forgotten. He plunks to the ground, his back against rock. Back at Fair House, Rose Byrd had threatened to ruin him – not only unkind, but also preposterous. He's literally lost his daughter. He's figuratively lost his wife. His profession is nearly obsolete. He is currently contributing zero income to his household. And what about the long-ago notion of himself as a writer? What was the last word he's written that didn't concern celebrity fitness regimes or a peek into some ingénue's couture handbag?

How much more ruined could he be?

Kevin's phone buzzes. For the countless time today, he rejects a call from Rossdale. A small, wishful part of him feels sure Aideen's grand; she's just gone off for a bit of a cry or turned up at home. But a more primal part, the one that reigns parents from infancy, is all terror and makes him vulnerable to the wildest of scenarios – she's wounded, unconscious, kidnapped, raped, dying, dead.

Opposite him is a thick bank of forest, a copse of silver birches and wild brush. Across the river, a man emerges. At first, Kevin assumes he's just a drunk stumbling along in his raincoat, dishevelled, weaving through the woods, poor bastard. But a stretch of pale skin between the hem of his trench and the top of his shoes – and then the fact of his belt – tells Kevin all he needs to know. Across the road from an all-girls school. He scrambles to his feet in a huff, chest out, breath heavy.

'Oy!' Kevin yells.

It's almost comical, the effect of this. The man recoils as if a blow has landed on him, and then he turns and takes off so quickly and expertly, Kevin is left with all this teeming energy and adrenaline and nowhere to channel it. The fear rears its head again, all the possibilities of evil in the world, and his own twin demons – regret and failure – and having no control over any of it, he lifts his face to the sky and, with great frustration, screams.

47.

Millie

Millie is studying the laminated emergency landing card with its disingenuous diagrams. A family in life jackets bounces its way, not unhappily, down a giant yellow inflatable mattress into the ocean. As in, *whee!* She tucks it back into the seatback pouch and listens to the deluge of announcements overhead, learns that federal law prohibits tampering with, disabling, or destroying smoke detectors on this aircraft. Which brings to mind the twenty Dunhills in her handbag, which she'd found in Margate still sealed in their swank maroon-and-gold packaging. She'd taken the discovery as a sign that the universe was cutting her some slack. Do as you like, it was telling her, you need no permission. Had that *really* been just a few hours ago? She marvels that one day can be so brimming, others so bereft.

Since blast-off, the ride's been particularly bumpy, and with each cough and swoop of turbulence, Millie suppresses a Tourettian urge to say 'shit shit shit shit shit'. She ought to hide this fear from her granddaughter, of course, but Aideen doesn't notice a bloody thing anyway. Blissfully impervious to mortality, she's sitting with her purple cushioned headphones watching some violent drivel that features incomprehensible numbers of explosions, bodies flying, guns drawn, planets and cities wiped out in milliseconds. Millie quietly takes up her handbag and is soon clicking the bendable bathroom door into its locked position and lighting up a Dunhill. *Ah.* She feels with pleasure the sharp intake of smoke to her lungs. She luxuriates in it. As she calms, the tiny cabin fills with smoke. Yet no alarm sounds; no undercover federal agent swoops in. Millie cannot even detect a detector. As she'd half-suspected, it's all a bit of bollocks. She's just a little old lady having a fag.

For all her airport bravado, she'd realized moments after regrettably glimpsing into the space station of a cockpit that, in the many years since she was aboard a plane, she's become a nervous flyer. Even if the statistical likelihood of a plane crash is roughly equivalent to having your limbs gnawed off by a great white on an innocent dawn swim, she can't help thinking how plausible it would be for this Boeing to just drop out of the sky – and seven hours is an impossibly wide window of opportunity for such a calamity, a yawning chasm of potential doom. Like most of her fellow travellers, Millie has no sense of the science behind what keeps a steel goliath airborne. She simply boarded the thing, wilfully ignorant, or just stupid, and hopeful. Wait now, she thinks, doesn't flight have something to do with how the wind glides under (or is it over) the wings?

When she first hears it, Millie ignores the knocking. As it becomes persistent, she calls out, 'Might be a bit. Upset stomach!'

Who would want to be rushing in after gleaning that particular tidbit? When she's finished with her Dunhill, Millie sizzles the butt into the disinfected puddle of toilet water and watches as it whirls and vanishes down the steel vortex. She scrubs her hands carefully, something she seldom does, finding the modern obsession with hygiene and bacteria, like most modern obsessions, absurd.

Upon exiting, an unsubtle cloud of smoke wafts out along with Millie Gogarty. Directly opposite her stands a dismayed-looking female flight attendant with a taut ombré bun, dark outer rim orbiting an unnatural orange nucleus. Millie nods and moves past the woman.

'Hey, wait a minute. What were you doing in there?' The attendant – her nametag reads KAREN – sniffs. *The face on her!* 'Did you just' – *incredulous!* – 'smoke a cigarette?'

Something in Karen's voice calls to mind Sylvia Phenning. It's not just that the woman's American; it's also a wonky, foreign emphasis on the wrong words, a conversational clanger to her Dublin ears. Millie freezes. What will she say? And then it comes to her: she'll say nothing. She'll play dumb, though she worries, immediately, how to transmit muteness. Deaf would be easier, if only she knew how to sign.

'Ma'am?' Karen reaches across to take hold of Millie's wrist. 'Were you just *smoking* in there?'

Across the way, another loo door pops open and out steps a young fella in stocking feet (on a public aeroplane!), an unsightly slab of translucent belly leaking from beneath his grubby grey T-shirt. He sniffs the air, registers a look of mild curiosity, and mutters, 'Right on,' before walking off.

Millie barricades her mouth with crossed fingers. Karen ignores this, steps into the bathroom, and is greeted with lingering licks of smoke.

'Holy shit,' says the flight attendant. 'Don't move.'

Karen's reaction now strikes real horror in Millie's heart and her mind is deluged with nasty possibilities: visions of being hauled off the aeroplane, dragged down the gangplank. Handcuffed, arrested, interrogated, frisked, fined, incarcerated, deported. She can't be stopped now – Millie's unlikely to be on many more trips like this. Another item on her ever-swelling never-again list: never go abroad, never join a team, never mind an infant, never share a bed. And then what about Aideen? Would they deport her as well? Millie can hardly bear the thought, not now that they're on their way.

Karen scans the galley kitchen behind them until her eyes seize upon a red telephone attached to the wall.

'Gran?'

From the aisle, Aideen steps forward and completes this little tableau, the headphones now clinging to her neck like twin baby mammals, some pop tune blaring from each.

'This is my gran,' says Aideen. 'Is everything OK?'

'This is your grandmother?'

Aideen looks quizzically at Millie. 'She's been gone a while, I got worried.'

'Can she speak?'

'Yes, of course she can speak! Gran?'

Millie tries to beam her a message along the lines of *Let's pretend I can't speak*, but Aideen just looks baffled.

'Well, I caught her smoking in that bathroom right there.

Which is basically like breaking three different laws.' Karen's face is reddening. 'Stay here,' she commands, stepping again towards the phone.

When Aideen first appeared, Millie was surprisingly relieved: she had back-up. But sure, look at her. The shoulders of a girl, not a woman (shoulders, Millie realizes with a pang, to which she herself is adding an even heavier burden); a thick cuff of rubber bands clamped onto a delicate wrist; a T-shirt – SAVE THE DRAMA FO YO LLAMA printed below a sketch of the animal – that screams youthful heedlessness.

'Wait, hang on,' cries Aideen. 'You don't understand. My gran is –' Aideen stares at Millie. 'Say something!'

Millie does the only thing she can think of, which is: she winks. It's the tiniest yet riskiest of gestures, and, luckily, Karen's gaze is still fixed on her granddaughter.

'My gran's, like …' says Aideen and makes a cuckoo face, rolling her eyes and circling a finger at her temple: the international gesture for loony tunes, 'demented.'

'You mean, like, she has Alzheimer's or something?'

'Yes.'

Impressive, thinks Millie, but Aideen's lying is wobbly. Her eye contact is shady to nil; her cheeks are ablaze – that flaming ruddy Irish tinting impossible to hide.

'She gets confused and, like, wanders off a lot and does stuff like this sometimes. She probably forgot where she was.' Aideen gently places her hands on Millie's shoulders. 'It's me, Gran. You know who I am, right? I'm Kevin's daughter, Aideen. You're on an aeroplane, but you can't smoke on an aeroplane, remember, we talked about that?'

Millie squints at Aideen.

'Oh my God,' says Karen. Millie is so tickled with Aideen's performance, she might as well be struck dumb. 'Are you the person responsible for her?'

Aideen nods. 'Sometimes she doesn't know who I am, and I'm the closest one to her.' Both statements, Millie realizes, contain truth.

'How old are you?'

'Eighteen.' Aideen blushes again. 'I'm really sorry about all this. Come on, Gran, let's go back to our seats.'

Millie hangs her head, a cowed dog, like one of the poor souls from Rossdale.

'Wait a sec,' Karen drops her voice. 'I'm gonna need all your information. I have to report this.'

'Oh no!' Aideen says. 'Please don't. It was a mistake. It was *my* mistake. I nodded off. It won't happen again. I promise you. I'm going to drink coffee the rest of the plane journey, I swear. I'll be with her every minute. We'll take away her cigarettes – Gran, hand over those smokes.'

'Oh, honey.' Karen shakes her head sadly, the bun a slick immobile boulder. 'I know it won't happen again. But I have no choice. I have to report this; there's a whole protocol. Don't look so worried. I'll let the captain know the circumstances. Captain Tyler is the best.'

'But what'll happen to us?'

'I'm not – to tell you the truth, this is a new one for me. But I can assure you he's a very cool guy and I'll explain the situation. They might have to talk to her when you deplane at Orlando.'

'What? No,' says Aideen. 'Oh my God. No, please.'

'But since she's elderly and, you know, not well ...'

'No! You can't! Everything will be ruined,' Aideen says. 'Please, it was a mistake. I beg you. This trip is – all her life my Gran's wanted to go to America. It was her dream but she waited too long and now she's in this state, this Alzheimer's, which has been horrible.' Millie is astonished to see something like real tears. 'And so the idea was, like, for her to finally have her trip, a last trip to America. It was her dream.'

With that, Millie takes her cue. 'We're going to America?'

Not twenty minutes later, Millie's choking down a whiskey and trying without success to get Aideen to look at her. Her granddaughter hasn't spoken since Karen let the Gogartys off after a moving speech that began with the revelation that her own father-in-law suffered from Alzheimer's and ended with 'This is probably against my better judgement'. She'd brought Aideen and Millie each to the brink of pain with a lengthy and fierce embrace, blocking two passengers and a fellow flight attendant from passing by. It was a *moment*. Millie had felt so touched and grateful, so appreciative of American compassion and openheartedness, she'd had to reject her immediate impulse to confess their chicanery to Karen.

Aideen had made a great show, ham acting nearly, of lending an arm to her poor old dotard of a granny and guiding her down the aisle back to their row. But when Millie clicked her seat belt and whispered, 'That was an absolute showstopper, Duckie,' Duckie had glowered.

'Don't,' she'd hissed, 'say a single word to me. Not a word.' With that, she'd shut her eyes and leaned away.

With no warning, the plane begins to jolt, sporadically at first and then it's full-on jackhammering. Through the window, it looks as if they're trapped in an infinite wispy white mess of clouds. The mini-bottle of Jameson and Millie's plastic tumbler and Aideen's can of Sprite and cup tremble and hop across their tray tables. Another wrenching drop of the plane, Millie's stomach dipping with it, is followed by a collective gasp. Somewhere a baby begins to wail. Millie feels a hot hand snatch her own and she meets her granddaughter's wide and terrified eyes. Millie's never seen her look so hyperalert. Have they boldly booked passage to America only to perish in the frigid Atlantic? Will they, too, end up bouncing down their own yellow rafts?

The turbulence worsens. A mobile phone tumbles into Millie's foot and someone's paperback drops into the aisle. The fleet of television screens throughout the massive cabin simultaneously glitch and freeze, so many frozen images: Tom Hanks is on one, a blur of garden flowers on another. A few unflappable passengers continue their reading, but most, like the Gogartys, appear to have stopped breathing. The pilot's deep voice crackles on and he sounds oddly intimate, as if he's everyone's lover, a husky mumble that reassures his close friends, the passengers.

Millie squeezes her granddaughter's fingers and places her free hand on top of their little hand pile. They're like athletes rallying before the first whistle, and neither lets go. Minutes pass and then the plane is sailing smoothly once more. The clouds vanish, the televisions resume.

48.

Aideen

Stepping onto American soil for the first time, Aideen quells visions of being interrogated in the bowels of Orlando International – Gran's little airborne smoke break, or Dad having discovered their whereabouts, or those smuggled sausages, any could be their downfall. But they move, unmolested, through a disorienting maze of heavily air-conditioned mega-rooms. Everything is supersized. The moving sidewalks, the labyrinthine corridors, the signs, the citizens. America, or the first few minutes of it, stupefies Aideen. Silently, sheep-like, they trail the masses, who seem to know where to go.

The pair is eventually funnelled into a daunting queue of dazed non-Americans. Customs personnel in tidy uniforms with dark guns at their hips loudly direct them into a cordoned-off maze. When it's their turn, a seated officer compares photos to faces and runs both passports through a machine, setting off a series of blips. For a moment, Aideen knows they're fucked; an alarm has been activated in a security room, Gran will get done for kidnapping, Aideen'll be in the shitter.

'You're here for business or pleasure?'

Gran smiles and rests an elbow onto the counter, chin flirtatiously nestled on fist. 'A tricky question.'

The officer stops and peers more closely at her. 'What?'

'Pleasure, with a soupçon of business.'

'Pardon me?'

'No business,' says Aideen quickly. 'My gran's just being …' She searches for the word Gran's being. Annoying. Thick. Deliberately provocative. 'Just, like, joking. What she means is, like, gambling and stuff.'

'At Disney?' asks the man. 'There's no casinos at Disney.'

'Clearwater,' says Aideen.

'You all are driving to Clearwater from here?'

'Aren't we nearby?' says Aideen.

'Well, sure. You woulda been better off flying into Tampa, though. Tampa's right next door to Clearwater. Take you an hour and a half.' He studies Gran and says, 'Maybe two and a half. You have a driver's licence?'

'We flew into the wrong city?' Aideen side-glares at Gran.

'Ah, well,' says Millie. 'We'll get it sorted.'

The officer nods. 'You staying at a hotel in Clearwater? Or a rental?'

'Sorry?' says Aideen.

'You didn't fill out the address on the landing form.' He taps a blank space at the bottom of a card, which Aideen had completed on the plane. 'We gotta have an address.'

'Sorry, we don't have an address,' says Aideen, panic leaking into her voice.

'I'm gonna need an address. If you want to step aside …'

'Don't be silly, petal, of course we do.' Gran's already digging into her bag of grotesques. As if she were by her fire in Margate, she begins to fish out items and place them on the counter to make room – a foul serviette streaked with blood or ketchup, who can say which, a golf ball, a bottle with the word 'diarrhoea' screaming from it.

'My God,' says Aideen, this last item being too much to bear.

'You can't do that here, ma'am.'

'Bingo,' says Gran. She brandishes Sylvia's luggage tag in triumph and hands it to Aideen to copy down: 2895 Victory Towers, Unit 208, Clearwater, FL.

'This is where we're headed,' says Gran, with a sly smile at Aideen. 'To see our old friend Sylvia Phenning.'

Legally admitted into the country and set free, temporarily, from all the aggro back home, which Aideen does her best, with mixed results, to not examine, the pair find themselves in motion once more. Ahead, massive opaque sliding doors yawn open to reveal a hopping arrivals hall. On the front line stand throngs of men bearing hand-scrawled and printed signs in languages Aideen's never seen.

Aideen and Gran appear to be the only people not wearing shorts. Just ahead, a large, loud family in bedazzled matching T-shirts that read WELCOME HOME TANYA! WE HEART YOU!!! are raucously beckoning to a delightedly embarrassed Tanya, a slight blonde girl (also in shorts) who's pointing and laughing at the youngest among them. It's a baby held in a woman's arms, wearing a vest that bears a tiny version of the same rhinestoned message. The group moves collectively to huddle round Tanya until she's swallowed up and only her purple Havaianas are visible.

Through a wall of windows and transparent revolving doors that lead to the street, the Orlando sun is ablaze. Aideen thinks of home, and for the first time in days she grins – the sheer otherworldliness, the madness of what they're doing. She is actually in another country without Mum and Dad's permission. Without Mum and Dad.

Gran stops walking. 'If you were a car hire, where would you be?'

'I don't think we should hire a car. It's too far a drive.'

'Does that say rentals?' Gran asks, squinting at a sign that reads 'Taxis'.

'We'll get lost. We'll end up in, like, Utah. We haven't a clue.' Considering their hellacious drive to the airport, the notion of riding shotgun with Gran on the wrong side of a ten-lane Floridian highway strikes real fear in Aideen's heart. 'And you've never driven over here, Gran.'

'But sure, isn't that the point?' Gran proceeds to rabbit on and on, laying out her case – she's been driving for six decades, she's an absolute whizz behind the wheel, her Peter always said what a wonderful parallel parker she was. Until Aideen says, 'Alright, fine, fine.'

Aideen makes Gran fork over her credit card at a vending machine that sells SIM cards – they'll definitely need a working phone – but when they reach the car rental desk, they quickly learn that even the cheapest vehicle will cost them most of their remaining cash.

'We need to be smart,' Aideen insists, and they head outside in search of a bus.

49.

Kevin

If this were his daughter's first vanishing act, Kevin would likely be giving into stirrings of real fear. But he's already been, as the Yanks say, to this particular rodeo. There was the time Aideen had felt hard done by during some domestic squabble so she'd jammed tangerines and a notebook and runners into a draw-string bag and hid out in the church confessional for the better part of an afternoon. On the panic scale, this drama scored high, being the premiere. Once, during an otherwise uneventful dinner, she'd been set off by some perceived injustice. One minute, Aideen was at the table eating gnocchi; the next, the Gogartys watched through the window as she slipped down the drive and out to the main road. She'd gone to sit along the rocks at Bulloch Harbour, she'd told them upon her return – she'd just wanted to be alone, have a think.

And fair enough.

Ringing the police just yet strikes him as histrionic. She must be here, in Dalkey, somewhere. He drives to Bulloch Harbour and then all around the village, passing his local, Finnegan's Pub, and the handful of little shops and cafés. Panic building, he guns it to the supermarket and darts from produce to dairy to frozen goods, dodging a particularly chatty neighbour. He cares nothing now about any past dust-ups – he would drive to any corner of the country, he would do whatever was necessary to see his daughter's beautiful mug right now, to get hold of her. He zooms along the cul-de-sacs and back lanes of Dalkey, coasts up and down the main road, and stops at Aideen's former school on a whim – unless she's cleverer than he thinks, it's the last place on earth she would go to seek refuge, though he does spot Nuala in the auditorium, quite literally standing centre stage.

Finally, the call he's been dreading, the one to his wife, is officially unavoidable. He feels that he will be blamed for this, that this one – that all of them, really, the awful, relentless burden of responsibility, of adulthood – is on him. He parks on a back road; as much as an accident due to mobile-phone distraction synchronizes poetically with this crappiest of days, he'd like to avoid it.

Grace picks up on the first ring and, despite his plan to deliver his news in neutral tones, he blurts out, 'Aideen's gone! I can't find her!'

'OK. OK. Let's see.'

Under pressure, Grace is invariably collected. If anything, stress calms her. Really, how could he not have chosen her, whose very foundation is a stubborn refusal to admit things will go terribly wrong, a woman with a stingy capacity for worry. Kevin's comfort zone – nay, his baseline, these days anyway – is pure stress.

'Where have you looked?' she says.

'Everywhere.'

'She's not in her dormitory?'

'She left the school. I'm in Dalkey.'

'What?'

'She ran off after locking herself in that bloody cupboard. Right after we hung up, I went back and the door was open.'

Following a taut and troubling silence, Kevin's wife says, with deliberate, vexing enunciation, 'You let her leave that room.'

His pits grow hot. 'I'm confused, Grace. Are you asking whether I physically barricaded myself against a door that had been shut for a good hour? Or perhaps you're saying I should not have updated you during a major crisis? Fuck's sake, I'm not Aideen. I can't control if she slips out of a room.'

'Clearly.'

'What is that supposed to mean?'

'Oh, nothing, Kevin, it means absolutely nothing.'

'This is my fault then.'

'I'm not saying that.'

'You're always saying that.'

'I'm saying that I'm at work and you're the parent – you're supposed to be the parent – in charge. Extract from that what you will.'

'Really, Grace? Is that right? I'm the one in charge? Because in case you forgot, you banished me from the house, remember? You specifically instructed me *not* to deal with the kids.'

'And why was that?'

'Fuck!' He manages to swallow the 'you'. 'That is *not* the point.' His face boils. 'You are conflating two vastly different things. We're not discussing my non-infidelity.'

'Oh right, we're discussing the fact that you lost our daughter.'

'You are so sanctimonious, you know that. Which is easy, isn't it? How can you be accountable if you're *never fucking home.*' He experiences a great sense of release stretching these last three words slowly into the phone.

'I'm not home,' she says darkly, 'because I'm supporting my family. I'm putting bread on the table, remember? You were laid off, remember? I'm the one keeping our heads above water, remember?'

'I'm afraid you've reached your cliché quota for the day.'

'I'm not the one off doing the dirt with some twenty-year-old tart who works at my daughter's school. Did you see your little friend at Millburn today? Is that why you let Aideen get away, you were too busy –'

'Nothing happened!'

'Not for want of trying.'

'Oh, look, just forget it, just ...' Will he? Yes, he will, he will. 'Just go and fuck off.'

He disconnects the call and throws his mobile onto the seat beside him. His arms and face, even his hands, feel taut. He is panting. He's never spoken to his wife with such rage; though he wants to call it up and examine it, he can't remember the sequence of their battle, only the fury, and beneath that the panic, at its core. His phone begins to ring and he feels an almost giddy relief when he sees that it's Grace.

'Ring the police,' she says.

'What?'

'Ring the police.'

'You ring the police.' He is shocked at how brutal his tone is. 'I'm going to find my daughter.'

Kevin hangs up on his wife for the second time today and turns on the engine and roars towards home. He barely slows at each turn, tyres shrieking. He pounds a fist on the steering wheel when he's stalled at a traffic light. Finally, finally, he pulls into his drive, seething still and shaking, only to see two figures, a man and woman, standing in the rain – it's bucketing down – on his front steps. For a moment, Kevin has a keen, primal urge to turn right round and drive off to some other life, maybe head to Connemara and grow root vegetables and read Yeats.

At the sound of his car, both turn in his direction. They don't wave or smile. They appear grim and sombre, the woman with a sort of urgent, impatient posture, the man in an overcoat, stooped almost comically over. What news is Kevin about to receive? What has happened to this life of his?

He parks in what can only be described as an unhinged manner – herky-jerky and lurching, like a learner on day one trying to shift from gear to gear. He starts to get out of the car before it's even turned off, then doubles back and removes the key.

'Hello?' He jogs towards the pair – he can't possibly rustle up his trusty old disarming grin. He stops short upon realizing this is not anyone he recognizes from Millburn School.

'Mr Gogarty,' says the woman. He is familiar with this face, the sensible, short, clipped hair, the sparse eyebrows. It's a person he associates dimly with authority.

And then he remembers.

'We're in a very serious situation. May we come in?'

Kevin's mind is short-circuiting; he's in a delayed cycle, stuck on Aideen.

'We've been trying to get you all day.'

'Sorry?'

'Your mum wasn't in her room this morning,' says the director of Rossdale Home. 'We believe she may have wandered off. Are you alright, Mr Gogarty?'

50.
Millie

Millie learns that they'll soon be in Clearwater from Geraldine Adams, her verbose seatmate, a great-grandmother with a face like a sultana and a fascinating drawl. Geraldine is coming to the end, Millie can only hope, of an incomprehensible tale about her neighbour's tomcat who does his business in her garden, which somehow endangers her great-grandson's heart condition. *Christ*, she thinks, *is this what I'm going to be like? Twenty minutes on feline faecal matter?*

There were no side-by-side seats available on the Florida Express Bus Service (which, incidentally, dispensed to her a most welcome senior citizen discount), and for the first time since the Gogartys commenced this mad scheme, they'd had to separate. Millie had tried haranguing two undergrads in hooded FSU sweatshirts to swap seats, claiming her granddaughter was too young to sit alone. Aideen had glared at her with that deadly brew of teenage self-consciousness and indignation, snapped that she'd be fine, and disappeared into the back of the coach before Millie, or the students, could get another word in.

Millie watches the foreign night-time landscape roll by – warehouses, billboards, strip malls, vacant lots, petrol stations, palm trees, roads for forever. Her thoughts pleasantly float, fleeting shards of narratives, until she realizes the woman, Geraldine, has started up again.

'... brings me beefsteak tomatoes, which are sublime. Damn shame about her husband, though.' Geraldine shakes her head gravely. 'He's probably on the davenport with a six-pack screaming at the TV right about now.'

'Davenport?'

'It's like this: Leonard is either asleep or drunk. Those are his two states of being. There is no fluctuation. I cannot fathom how she tolerates him. I have racked my brain. I have prayed on it.'

'He sounds like a –'

'He's stumbling in the door every night stuffing his face with Big Macs and large fries and don't think he's bringing any of that home to share with Brenda and me, because he isn't. Man does not share. Does not consider his fellow man. Or woman. You know he actually makes me pay rent?'

'He doesn't! He makes –'

'But let me tell you: I'm having the last laugh on that fool. He got it into his head that I'm sitting on a big pile of money and he's gonna get it when I pass. Makes little mumblings about it when he's under the influence. Like I would leave money to Leonard Lowler! How stupid does he think I am?'

'So you *don't* have a big pile of money?'

Geraldine giggles at what is clearly preposterous. 'Put it this way,' she says. 'I get my dry goods, all my dry goods, at the dollar store.'

Millie is uncertain as to what this specifically means, but she absorbs the gist. She herself is a big fan of euro shops.

'All I can think is a long time back I had some stock from Johnson & Johnson. That's where I worked. Wasn't that much but, anyway, I sold it way back when. Went on some beautiful cruises with that money. But Leonard doesn't know that. And there's no law says I have to correct him.'

'There certainly isn't,' says Millie. A tiny germ of a thought almost catches hold, something to do with a person's worth after they've died, but it's interrupted by Aideen slinking up the aisle, her hair a thatch of muddy yarn. Millie proudly introduces her granddaughter to her new friend just as the coach driver coughs one word into the speaker system: 'Clearwater.'

51.
Aideen

Aideen spends her first hour at the Castaways Motel flattening singles into the poolside vending machine, discovering, devouring, its glorious collection of junk food, each item more exotically named than the next. Whatchamacallit. $100,000 Bar. Ding Dong. America is variety, infinite choice. America is brilliant. She taps in F-2 and watches something called Nutter Butter jerk towards her and drop.

Where other guests might have found their fifty-three-dollar 'garden view' room to be wanting – a wheezing air conditioner, chipped tile underfoot, shiny curtains – Gran had beamed and said, 'This will do nicely.' Within half an hour, poor Gran was snoring away on the king-sized bed, which Aideen is displeased to have to share. Gran's so lively, Aideen forgets how many decades she's been knocking about.

Aideen had used the rare moment of quiet to count their diminishing funds, $200, give or take. Studying Gran, she tried to imagine the beauty she once purportedly was – long lashes, high cheekbones, gorgeous hair straight down to her arse. But

Aideen can't get past the withered terrain of Gran's face and the chopped hair long drained of colour.

Getting old is fucked.

Aideen had pulled the slimy blanket up around her granny's shoulders, tucked her up like a child, and let her be. She hadn't packed a swimsuit – most of her items are useless here – but still she prowls the desolate pool area and, finding no swimmers or bathers anywhere, pulls up a white plastic sun lounger and takes her phone from her pocket just in case Sean Gilmore has changed his mind about her (Yes, OK, she's obsessed, she is *aware*). But no, of course he hasn't. Still, the fact that she may be geographically close to him, within a mere few kilometres, has a physical effect on her. She feels restless and buzzed, as if she's downed multiple Red Bulls and is on the verge of doing something bold and public and terrifying.

In the taxi on the way from the bus depot, Gran and Aideen had whisper-bickered over the appropriate tip. Gran had presented a single euro coin ('No way,' Aideen had hissed, forking over two dollar bills). Aideen had confronted Gran, for the second time, about contacting Mum and Dad now that they'd landed, but Gran had waved her off, stalling again.

Easy for Gran. She's not the one watching her parents' names – and Gerard's now too – blast onto her screen incessantly, though they've given up leaving voicemails. Aideen can't listen to the earlier ones; nor can she delete them. She's a documenter by nature. It's not in her to destroy evidence.

The pool is encaged within a metal chain-link fence through which would-be sunbathers can view a largely empty car park flooded in garish high-wattage street lights that showcase an industrial-sized bin and a turquoise computer from another decade that looks as if someone might have pummelled it to death in a fit of anti-tech rage. To Aideen, the whole scene feels cool, right out of a hundred films she's watched, poems she's read, or written, or thought about writing. She half-expects a hot, misunderstood twenty-something in frayed jeans to jump out of a pickup truck with a smoke in his mouth and knock on one of the motel doors and be let casually in by a girl who looks indifferent but isn't, by a girl like her.

There once was a parking-lot town,
Where broken chairs and dreams did abound
In a roadside motel
Can't afford a hotel
Sean Gilmore, will you ever be found?

It's so alien – no, surreal – to think that her family's across an entire ocean and she's sitting by a kidney-shaped pool in the beautifully warm Florida evening. That's what her next limerick ought to be about: independence, snacks in a vending machine, adventure. Her phone starts blitzing again. Dad. Dad. Dad. With every ring, she sees him walking back and forth in the kitchen, agitated, hands raking through his hair. He deserves to know they're alive, doesn't he? And what harm could it do? She taps 'Accept'.

'Aideen!'

He sounds so pitiful she nearly speaks. But she holds her tongue – Dad can be as persuasive as Gran had been adamant. Aideen can only hope that her breathing will be reassurance enough. So she breathes. He repeats her name over and over, a blend of terror and sweet relief that, quite frankly, infects her.

'Is that you? Aideen? Where are you? Aideen?'

It's agony to say nothing, but she says nothing.

'Just tell me you're OK.'

When his voice cracks, she can no longer bear it. 'I'm OK.'

'Oh, thank God! Thank God! Where are you?'

She manages to suppress an imminent breakdown mostly by swallowing the thick bullet in her throat and steeling herself against the great feeling she can hear in his every word. Has he ever been so kind, so concerned, so thrilled and emotive just from hearing her voice?

She should run away more often.

'Darling? It's OK. We're not angry with you. We're just very worried. We can sort everything out, but you need to come home.'

Of its own accord, her mouth lets loose a minute but unmistakable sob. 'Is she alive?' Aideen cries.

'Who?'

She wipes her face.

'Gran?' says Kevin.

'Miss Bleekland.'

'Oh! She's fine, she's fine, she's out of hospital. She's back at Millburn. Is that – where are you? I'll come collect you.'

Aideen absorbs this news. She hasn't killed Bleekland. Bleekland is out of hospital. Bleekland is so alive, she's already back at work!

'I'll come collect you,' he repeats.

She summons the strength – which is not easy, it's very

difficult – to hang up, but not before adding, 'I'm grand, I'm grand, Dad. I'm just sleeping at a friend's tonight.'

'Which friend?'

'From school. One of the day students. I'll be home soon, I promise.'

She disconnects the call and, for good measure, turns off her phone. Out of nowhere, a bird – pelican? crane? – swoops through the sky and as her eyes follow the graceful dip of its swift progression, she spots a turd, or maybe a bit of palm frond, floating on the surface of the pool. Something about it and Bleekland's recovery and the astonishing moment in her life that she finds herself in makes her laugh. At some point this morphs into a cry – therapeutic, she's sure, but also mortifying, if anyone were to witness her sitting here weeping like a total eejit.

Ah well, as Gran would say.

52.

Kevin

It's been eight days since Kevin started shacking up with Mick and Maeve, and so eight days since he's laid eyes on his wife. When Grace enters the Gogarty home and dumps her bag on the carpet, a thing that would normally annoy the living shite out of him, signifying as it does her unwillingness to heed his mild rules, he sees it now for what it is. She's worked hard, she's tired; ergo, she dumps her bag on the carpet. How narrow Kevin's lens has become since he lost his job, filtered primarily to benefit himself, to beef up his own case, one he alone is laying out, and to whom, by the way, and to what end? Why this perverse need to keep score?

'I just spoke with Aideen,' he blurts. 'She's OK.'

'Oh, thank God. Thank God. Where is she?'

'Sleeping over at a friend's – one of the day students, she said ... from school.'

'You think she was lying?'

'No, and she sounded – I don't know how to describe it. Ashamed, worried, contrite.'

'Are the others in bed?' Grace says.

Kevin nods.

'What did the police say?'

'Not much. They asked a lot of questions about Aideen running off in the past and how long had she been gone. They said to ring her friends.'

'But can they not *do* anything?'

Kevin gets up and cautiously approaches her. 'Remember the last time? Hiding in the confessional with a bag of sweets? She needs to cool off. I just spoke with her and, really, she's fine, she's safe. She sounded OK.'

Grace contemplates this.

'As frustrating as it is,' he says, 'she'll be back tomorrow.'

Grace, the most resilient person he knows, begins to cry, and watching her succumb to her distress when she's usually so stalwart is difficult to bear. He badly wants to comfort her, but he knows he's lost the right.

She really is beautiful. Though her pallor is paler than it ought to be and in disturbing contrast to the delicate skin beneath her eyes, which is all dark shadows, there is no denying her beauty. It is a fact that does not require fact-checking. He goes over to her and boldly puts his arms around her. He doesn't give a shite. He pulls his wife closer towards him fearing she won't allow this meagre consolation, but she does. Kevin feels a powerful peace descend, a righting of the world. After a long moment, during which she stands slack, like a peaceful protester neutrally submitting to police arrest, she begins to reciprocate. She presses back into him with growing force until their hold on each other is mutual. Her nose is a pinprick of ice against his neck, but under her coat where his arms encircle her, Grace feels warm, divine.

His mind empties. For a neurotic, unemployed, recently turfed-out father of four prone to stress, this is calm and bliss, however fleeting.

'I fucked up,' Kevin says, her hair pressed into his neck. 'I really fucked up.'

Grace's body tightens. 'You did.'

'Was I out of my mind?'

She snorts bitterly. 'You tell me.'

'I was. I was out of my mind. I'm sorry,' he says. 'Forgive me.' He tells her he's been missing her, which is true, even before all of this started, though they live in the same house.

She lets go of him. 'I know work has been –'

'No,' he says. 'No, that's not what I mean.'

He puts his lips to each side of her face and finds, to his great fortune, that she is receptive, or at least not giving him a clap across the mug. Could it be that he hasn't totally lost her? They kiss. He feels her body loosen slightly. He lands small kisses across her face and then works his way down her neck. This is their tried-and-true road map, hackneyed perhaps and with frequent shortcuts taken, but reliable, familiar. Only not now. This particular drive feels spectacularly, mightily new. It's a powerful reboot of chemistry, as if twenty-odd years of touch never occurred between them. Kevin wants to lose himself right here on the family settee, but he stops. He must tell her about the other thing. He nearly laughs: here is a gift, an ember of dormant passion, and the kids, his mother – family – even when the bloody house is empty still manage to douse it.

'We've got another problem.'

She stiffens, releasing him. 'Oh God. Do I need to sit down?'

'Yes. And a drink might help.'

Grace heads directly to the side table where stands a bottle of red, half-emptied, and pours two glasses. 'OK, so what am I bracing myself for?'

He exhales loudly. 'Mum's gone missing.'

'Oh Jesus.' Grace shakes her head and takes a deep swallow. 'What do you mean? She left the home?'

'In a certain manner, yes.'

'In what manner?'

Kevin plonks onto the very sofa that was the backdrop to his erotic domestic reconciliation of a moment ago. Beckett is purring languorously, his long ginger strands having been pompously shed across all three cushions.

'I'm not really sure where to begin. Maybe with the bit about how she escaped Rossdale in the middle of the night?'

'Last night?'

He nods. 'And may or may not have hitchhiked.'

'What?'

'Or would you prefer the part about her slipping a mickey into the night guard's café au lait?'

'You're joking.'

'I'm embellishing. It was coffee.'

'What in God's name …?'

'Apparently she's been working on an elaborate plan that involved pilfering linens from the laundry – a number of towels were found to be missing – oh, and robbing her roommate of forty-five euros.' He pauses for dramatic effect. 'Her dead roommate.'

Grace screams in laughter. 'Stop! That's awful. Stop!'

'They think –'

'You talked to the –?'

'Sheila Slattery, you remember, the head of Rossdale? She and her sidekick Quasimodo popped by.'

She hoots again. 'Don't!'

Kevin's beaming, laughing. 'Mrs Slattery and that knuckle-dragger were on our very doorstep quietly freaking out, though trying desperately to appear otherwise. Probably worried about a lawsuit. Turns out Mum's been going around visiting with half the residents, bidding all a dramatic farewell and furtively showing them random items pulled from her rucksack. Which were to be used while she was, and I quote, "on the lam".'

Grace is hysterical. 'Like what?' She has trouble getting her words out. 'What was in the rucksack?'

'Let's see.' He's enjoying this, is Kevin. This is what it used to be like. Kevin ventured into the world, a little lab mouse, to extract crumbs of stories and pithy observations about the people and places he visited, and returned to their little nest to entertain Grace with them. 'A can of lager, some toilet roll.' He is breaking his shite laughing now. 'Oh, and a bottle of Imodium … because you never know when a fugitive might suffer a nasty bout of the shits.'

Grace is howling.

Kevin finally recovers. 'But, sure, no one paid her any notice. They assumed she was talking rubbish.'

'I honestly – I don't even …'

'I know.'

'Go on.'

'Sometime in the wee hours – I'm not even sure of the order

– she sweet-talked the guard at the front desk, then laced his coffee with sleeping tablets. Like a film. And she hid out in a room, terrorizing some old-age pensioner. It seems they'd had some history, the two of them, some row. Which I never knew. Mum had been banned at some point from the common room.'

'I can't –'

'That's on me, though.' He looks away. 'Because Rossdale has been ringing and I never bothered –'

'It's not on you.'

But it is.

'Anyway.' He waves off her show of kindness, though it does go a small way towards alleviating his nagging sense of having failed. 'Oh, and did I mention, the *pièce de résistance*? Don't ask, but she was hiding behind some sort of tree or plant when your man found her, and she started going on and on about her daddy's horse farm.'

'What horse farm?'

'Precisely.'

She is still wiping her eyes. 'Oh my God. I need more wine.' Grace tops up both their glasses.

'And after all these theatrics,' Kevin says, 'she somehow slipped out through the back door.'

Grace scoffs. 'There's no security?'

'There's some kind of coded door thing but it sounds shoddy. They're investigating.'

'Unbelievable. Where is she now? Is she home? You checked Margate?'

'Of course. No sign of her. Her car's gone, though, so she must be about somewhere.'

Kevin regards Grace who suddenly goes quiet, head in her hands.

Eventually, she says, 'But how is it possible? How can two of them be missing at the same time? It's too absurd.'

The room grows terribly still. Beckett awakes to stretch, lick, and reposition himself. Kevin becomes aware of the second hand on the wall clock, sweeping past three, six, nine.

'Kevin?'

'Hmmm?'

'You don't think they're ...'

He's had no such thought, not one second's fleeting whim, not a glimmer that his mother and Aideen are together, that the stories are in any way connected. It's too outlandish, too premeditated. Mum wouldn't dare abscond with his daughter when she knows Kevin and Grace would be utterly beside themselves. It's beyond the pale, even for her.

And yet the moment the suggestion is loosed from his wife's lips, Kevin knows like he knows primal truths – we are born, we age, we die – that Aideen was lying to him and that she and Millie are indeed in cahoots. Of course they are. He stares at Grace as this churns its way through his addled mind and changes every one of his hypotheses of this cursed day.

Then he has three thoughts. First: he will bloody well brain Millie Gogarty once and for all. He will lock her up in her attic cupboard and bring her crusts of stale bread and water and weak tea without sugar. The irresponsibility! The deceit! The selfishness! Second: at least Aideen's not alone, she's with her granny. Third: she's with her granny.

53.

Millie

It must be said – and so she's mentioned it three times in the space of forty minutes – that Millie suffered a fitful night's rest, due in part to the punishing motel mattress, ancient coils knifing her each time she shifted. To say nothing of her sleepmate, who battled her for the single blanket from dusk till dawn, the pair of them tugging and thieving it to and fro like a comedy act. But it's morning now – it's half past nine – and the Gogartys are walking in the surreal blazing sunshine en route to Sylvia Phenning's apartment. Millie feels gay, optimistic, the kind of cheer she supposes Floridians state-wide must experience every morning by the mere act of stepping out of doors. Could she ever live in such a place, she wonders, without the damp and grey and rain?

Things hadn't looked quite so sunny yesterday. They'd hit a major roadblock at the Clearwater Police Department. Millie had relayed, in extraordinary detail, a breakdown of all of Sylvia's wicked deeds to an unlikely policewoman – shapely and glam with excessively plucked eyebrows and a lush set of false lashes. Millie was just getting to the bit about her safe with the emerald ring in the diamond setting stowed in one of Jolly Jessica's homemade sacs when the policewoman interrupted.

'Hang on. This all went down in Ireland?'

Not five minutes later, the pair found themselves on the pavement, in some despair. The Clearwater PD, they were told, don't investigate crimes that occur outside their jurisdiction, or, for that matter, outside the country, except in the very rare case of extradition. Millie, feeling the doors of justice swiftly closing, had brandished the luggage tag in a sort of 'ta-da' moment. Here's her contact information! Couldn't they just do a check on Sylvia Phenning? Drive to her house, say? Surely she's been up to all sorts of dodginess in *this* jurisdiction. But the officer was already turning away.

Back at the Castaways, Aideen had fetched two Gatorades and a Baby Ruth and they had sat on the viscous bedcover brainstorming next moves. It was late; they were jet-lagged. Both conceded that the only remaining option was to track down and confront Sylvia themselves. Millie had fantasized plenty about this course of action, but now that the possibility was at hand, it felt far scarier. Sylvia was no longer *Sylvia*. She was a criminal, after all. Aideen, for her part, was in full support of Gran's quest, but had very mixed feelings about the possibility of seeing Sean Gilmore again. He had hurt her, yes, but Aideen was fairly certain that Sean was not privy to his guardian's crimes. She felt she knew his heart a little, she said, and that there wasn't cruelty in it. There just wasn't.

The Gogartys' belongings overwhelmed the cramped room – bulging suitcases, maps, and glossy brochures Aideen had collected from the lobby pitching dolphin excursions and chartered yachts. Maybe, Millie suggested, they should just enjoy a few days' vacation and then head home, or take a coach to Miami, the city her mythical Golden Girls made famous. Or try the miniature golf in St Pete?

Aideen stepped into the other room to brush her teeth. When she returned, she clicked off the bedside lamp, climbed under the blanket, and said, 'We didn't come here to play golf.'

The presence of a tricycle outside the door of Unit 208 of Victory Towers – a massive three-storey complex on a traffic-filled avenue – is an unhopeful sign. If the Phennings lived here, Millie suspects, they no longer do. Indeed, the current tenant swiftly refers them to the manager's apartment downstairs.

Gus Sparks, according to the nameplate beside his screen door, greets the Gogartys in conservative attire, as if he's about to tee off – beige pressed khakis, freshly laundered, glaringly white polo, two out of its three buttons primly closed. He's sporting a pair of leather sandals, which reveal tidy, trimmed toenails. At Rossdale, Millie'd nearly be sick at the sight of some of the old fellas' feet – gnarled with patches the colour and texture of steamed cauliflower, or, worse, a grotesque ombré of purple-black, the nails a dull yellow as if nicotine-stained.

'Well hi there,' Sparks says.

Millie clears her throat but is suddenly overtaken by a violent onslaught of sneezes.

'Goodness,' says Sparks, followed by a dutiful 'Bless you' and then three more.

'I beg your pardon,' says Millie, fishing in her bag for a long rip of wrinkled toilet paper, like a crepe-paper party streamer, and pressing it to her old watering eyes. 'Terrible! I blame the American air conditioning.'

'Well then,' he says, 'on behalf of America, I apologize.' Sparks smiles. His is a face of warmth, the shape of it narrow, no jowls, remarkably, and yet open as a plain, some lonely tenderness in it, as if he's suffered but blames no one. 'Where are you ladies from?'

Despite his years – at least three or four further down the road than she – Sparks's eyes are bright, clear, verdant. Millie dabs at her nose, hoping there's nothing extraneous dangling from it, and introduces herself and Aideen as tourists from Ireland. 'We thought you might be able to tell us about someone who used to live here.'

'I'm happy to be of assistance.' Then, as if worried he might fail them, Sparks adds, 'If I can, that is. Come in, why don't you? Come on in.' He holds the door open for the Gogartys and proceeds immediately to the wall-mounted air-conditioning unit and turns it off. As its hum peters out and dies, the three of them stand in awkward silence.

Gus Sparks's home is a neat and sparse open-style studio condominium kitted out with the basics of bachelorhood: two corporate wood-framed club chairs, a clunky colonial-style coffee table piled with little towers of books – military and presidential biographies, from a brief glance – a small TV at low volume, as if for the company more than the local news that's currently chattering out of it. Millie can relate, though she's reminded that Sylvia Phenning relieved her of this small pleasure as well.

On the far side of the room stands a twin-sized bed with no

frame or headboard, but already precisely made. She thinks of her Peter, who never did up a bed a day in his life. Gus, though, has tucked sheet and cover tightly round the mattress, barracks-like, as if prepping for morning inspection. From the open galley-style kitchen, Millie now hears the violent spitting of a coffee machine in brew.

'Here, have a seat. Please.' Gus swats away a folded newspaper from one of the chairs. 'I was just making some coffee. Can I get you a cup?'

'Oh no, we wouldn't want to be a bother, sure we wouldn't?' Millie looks at Aideen, whose expression betrays no feeling either way.

'It's definitely not a bother. Seeing as you're not a tenant with a clogged-up sink, this is a real treat.'

Millie feels herself blushing and wonders if it's obvious, like during one of her more hideous menopause flashes back in the day, when her body, from within, would, with no warning, spontaneously combust, the opening of windows and removal of cardigans frustratingly futile. She had learned, in time, that you had to just let the fire burn.

'I don't want to toot my own horn, but I do make a decent cup of coffee.'

'Well, that'd be absolutely lovely, then, wouldn't it, Duckie? It's high time you tried coffee.'

'I've tried coffee.' This is said with high-voltage animus. 'I'm not a child.'

Gus jumps in. 'How old are you?'

'Sixteen.'

'She's wonderful,' says Millie.

'She sure is,' he says. 'And lucky too.' He directs this, there is no mistaking it, at Millie Gogarty.

Over coffee, Gus tells them he's 'career military' and has led something of a transient life – Germany, central New Jersey, Okinawa, Camp Pendleton – before ending up here, more or less where he began. He does not mention a wife or kids, though one brother, a retired cop, lives 'next door, in St Pete'. This biography spans the time it takes Millie and Aideen to add milk and sugar to their mugs and stir, and it's relayed choppily, as if he's reading bullet points off a list, efficient if slightly embarrassed. Still, there is a charm in his delivery, a sense of modest withholding. When he's finished, he turns his gentle gaze on Millie Gogarty, who is, of course, constitutionally incapable of brevity, especially when it comes to a story, and specifically, her own.

Millie takes it far back, to the day she met her Peter in town when she was a young woman of thirty at a bus stop and how, once aboard, they were so engrossed in conversation that Peter missed his street entirely. Oh, they'd later laughed at that! She learned he was a widower and, on their second outing, he showed her a photo of his son, a deliciously plump, wide-eyed little boy, a motherless boy. After Peter and Millie married, they bought the house in Dún Laoghaire with the idea of having more children. Here she hesitates, the ghost of pain from her dead infant paying an inconvenient visit, and does something she never has before: she tells Gus Sparks, a perfect stranger, about Baby Maureen. She isn't exactly sure why, other than an intuition about his goodness.

'Those were very dark days,' says Millie. 'The darkest.'

'Ah, Gran, I never knew that,' Aideen says. 'That's awful.'

'It was.' To Gus, Millie says, 'Anyway, I must be boring the pants off you, gabbing away.'

'No,' says Gus. 'Never. Stay and talk all day.'

Millie brings the mug of coffee to her mouth to mask the colour she feels rising, for a second time, to her face.

'Well, we do have something to ask you,' says Aideen. 'Shouldn't we tell him why we're here, Gran?'

'Oh yes,' says Gus. 'You know someone in the building?'

'Used to be in the building. A woman called Sylvia Phenning,' says Millie, and watches his face closely for a sign of recognition.

'Huh.' Gus closes his eyes and then opens them. 'Nope. Name doesn't ring a bell. Do you have a photo?'

'We don't,' says Millie.

'But you think she lived here?'

'Yes, but we're not exactly sure when,' says Millie, realizing, not for the first time, how little she knows about the woman she spent so many hours with. She should have listened more; she is a woman who ought to pay more heed. 'She said she'd travelled for a bit, you know the way, before she arrived in Dublin. So six months ago? Ten? A year?'

'I do have our lease agreements pretty squared away.' He flashes an abashed smile, then stops. 'She's a friend of yours?'

'Not exactly,' says Aideen and, after getting the nod of consent from Millie, tells Gus an edited version of the saga, ending at their doomed trip to the police station.

Gus listens intently, shifting his still strong jaw now and then. When Aideen's finished, he sets his mug down on a dark coaster emblazoned with an anchor and a globe and the words 'United States Marine Corps'.

'Let me see if I can dig up those agreements. Would you ladies care for more coffee?'

Both shake their heads. In fact, Millie is shocked at the appalling size of the mug – madness! – though she wouldn't like to say. When Gus turns towards his desk, she and Aideen exchange a look of suppressed excitement. He reaches into his shirt pocket and unfolds a little metal square that turns out to be a pair of reading glasses. Slowly, he flicks through a great many hanging files.

'That's funny. No trace of any Phennings here.'

'Fuck,' says Aideen.

'Aideen!' says Gran.

'Sorry, Gran.' To Gus, she says, 'Sorry. It's a very Irish thing, to say that word.'

'Oh, well, I guess if it's cultural ...' He winks at Aideen. 'Maybe this woman was using her maiden name or an alias?'

'She would've been with her nephew,' says Aideen. 'He's a bit older than me. He's – oh, wait! I have a photo of him! Hang on, hang on.'

She scrolls through her phone and stops: there's Sean at the river, squinting up at her from the pavement like a total bang, a can of Fanta tipped over beside him.

Gus peers at the photo. 'Oh! I do know him, yes.'

'Do you?' says Millie, standing up.

'I'd forgotten about him. He *was* here, a good ways back though. Let me see ... quiet kid. Used to see him in the laundry room. That would've been ... over a year ago, maybe.'

Aideen says, 'Did Sean – the boy – ever say anything, like any clue, like where they're from or …?'

'Honestly, I can't remember. He was polite, I do remember that. Some tenants, they'll dump people's clothes on the ground if you haven't put them in the dryer fast enough. It's a real problem here. But he wasn't like that. He would just come back until the machine was free. Nice kid.'

'He is,' says Aideen.

Gus says, 'Mrs Gogarty?'

'Millie.'

'Millie,' Gus repeats, with a slight tremor. 'There is one other thing. Remember I told you my brother is a retired cop? They have access to all kinds of information, you know. Maybe he could help you.' Gus looks away shyly. 'Us.'

54.

Kevin

Kevin works his way through his mother's ancient address book, which all his life has sat more or less on the wobbly telephone table in her kitchen. Francesca O'Brien, Netty Jones, Gretel Sheehy. My God, he thinks, they're all dead. He hadn't quite absorbed the sheer volume of death in her orbit – how many funerals she's attended (she who famously dislikes mass), the melancholy hymns, the mournful finality of burials.

He flicks to the final page and sees Jessica Walsh's name. Jessica, bless her, is alive. He dials and hurries his way through asking after her family.

'You haven't heard from Mum at all recently?'

'I haven't, Kevin. Not in weeks now, I'd say. I was going to ring you because I'd heard – I've been thinking about her. We've had a bit of – I suppose you'd call it a falling out. After she had to postpone our trip, this is going back a ways now, she stopped returning my calls. It just went silent. I thought she was upset with me for some reason.'

'Did she tell you why she cancelled the trip?'

'She said it was related to her health and that –'

'You know that's not true, right? You heard about the –'

'I did. Donnelly's cousin's son lives just up the way, he does the odd job for me, and so I knew Millie had gotten into a spot of trouble in the shop. Sure, if you ask me, Kevin, she's just lonely and looking for a bit of attention – you know how your mum is. That's how I thought of it. I just wish she'd have told me.'

'I think she was probably a bit mortified.'

'Yes, but we've been friends since school.'

'I know you have, Jessica. It's – but look, you haven't seen or heard from her in a few days?'

'Not at all. I called in over the Christmas – I always bring her a fruit cake, you see – but she didn't answer. I left it at the door but never heard back. Then someone told me there'd been a fire in the kitchen and she was recovering in Rossdale Home.'

'That's right.'

'I sent a card there but, again, nothing. Is she alright, Kevin?'

'I don't know. I'm sure she is, but no one's seen or heard from her since Wednesday. She left Rossdale in the middle of the night.'

'She didn't!'

'And I think she's got Aideen with her as well.'

'Your Aideen? No, she wouldn't! Why would she?'

'I don't know. I don't know. Where do you think – do you have any idea where Mum would go if she were leaving town?'

There is a silence while Jessica presumably runs through the possibilities.

'I've got a text message buzzing in here,' Kevin says. 'Look, if you think of anything ...'

Kevin cannot remember how the call ends for the message that arrives on his phone is an alert notifying him that his data usage has reached epic proportions. His current bill is a breathtaking €753. This is hardly the time for bureaucratic fuck-ups and further debt accumulation, the type of nonsense that will surely test the sanity to which he is already struggling mightily to cling. Yet it's the sort of thing that must be cleared up at once. Cursing technology and longing for the simpler, less fraught predigital days of yore, Kevin rings the mobile company.

'Whoa,' says the young lad on the other end after incessant tapping of a keyboard. 'Looks like you've been using data like it's going out of fashion.'

'No, I haven't.'

'Let me just have a look … I'm showing seven hours of data at … let me scroll here … er … two oh seven this morning.'

'Not possible!' Kevin blurts. 'There's clearly been some kind of mistake. Or my account's been compromised. I must have been hacked.'

'Would you like to open an investigation?'

'Could you just check again?'

'Hang on. Are there other numbers linked to this account?'

Why, yes there are. There are four. Grace. Gerard. Nuala. Aideen.

'Holy fuck.'

'Sorry, sir?'

'My wife and son and daughters.'

'Have you checked with them? Because it looks like someone on … let's see, the number we're dealing with here with the excessive usage, it's comin' up now … ends in 098.'

Hallelujah! Kevin immediately rescinds his disavowal of technology. He *loves* technology! Technology will lead him to his missing daughter.

'Why is it so expensive?'

'Hang on. Need to put you on hold for that one.' A jazzy ragtime number clangs directly into Kevin's ear, but he's not listening – he barely registers it.

'Sir? You still there?'

'I'm going nowhere.'

'Those are actually international charges. Which would explain why they're so high.'

'She's ringing someone in another country?'

'The person with the 098 number?'

'Yes, the person with the 098 number.' Fuck's sake. Does no one under the age of twenty-five possess a critical mass of grey matter?

'No, the 098 number shows data use *in* another country.'

'In another country?' Kevin says. 'What are you saying? She's not in Ireland?'

'I don't even know who we're talking about.'

'My daughter.'

'Is it possible the phone was lost or stolen? I don't know – I'm just saying that this number, ending in 098, is using data not in Ireland.'

'Ah, for Christ's sake.' His spirits plummet. He's back on the familiar terrain of panic and stress. 'Where is the roaming data happening? Can you tell me that?'

'That, I can tell you ... let's see here ... The roaming data is happening in Clearwater.'

'What? Where is that? Is that in England?'

'No, it's in Florida. Clearwater, Florida. In America.'

55.

Aideen

There is a cooker at the Castaways. Well, more like a single burner, but Aideen can't figure out how to turn the thing on, which is a pity since soup at Dollar General is only a dollar, as was the small saucepan in which to warm it. Aideen is mystified by this country, how a saucepan can cost the same as a tin of soup.

Gran's a bit under the weather, which casts Aideen in the dubious role of nurse, fetching tissues and glasses of water from the bathroom tap. Her illness, which mightn't incapacitate someone of Aideen's age, seems to take a firm hold, and after a miserable night, Gran awakes shivering. What, Aideen worries, constitutes a fever and how even to measure it? They've no thermometer. Channelling her mum, she puts the back of her hand to Gran's small forehead. The heat burning off her grandmother's skin scares her. Zero experience in this and yet she is certain: fever.

Aideen hasn't a clue whether this is a code-red hospital-level crisis or just a cold or what. She picks up her phone to ring Dad because *what if Gran is dying*? She's old, she's sick. Old sick people die. What if Gran keels over right here in this room? Who would she call to report a dead body? How could she ring Dad and say, 'I'm in Florida with Gran but she's died.' Aideen could have done something but instead she sat, a clueless child in a motel, and did nothing.

'Gran?'

'Um hmm.'

Not dead. She puts the phone back down. Maybe she's overreacting. Maybe this is not an ambulance situation. If she rings home, their trip would have all been for naught and Gran would be gutted. She types the symptoms – sneezing, coughing, fever – into her phone and, after some poking around, feels fairly confident that she's dealing with something non-lethal, that she needs to cop on. Besides, Gran herself, who is an adult (however unconventional), is downplaying all of it, murmuring that she'll be grand and could Aideen just find two paracetamol from the bottom of her toilet bag?

Mum and Dad would act; they'd go out and buy, like, fluids of some sort, medicine. They would *take care*. Um, hello, but she does not recall signing up to deal with a sick/dying grandmother. Yet here she is, sliding two twenty-dollar bills into her sock, pulling on her runners and, loath to roam the streets of a city so alien to her, Aideen nevertheless heads to the chemist's.

Her solo trek takes her along a choked motorway, no pavement in sight, wading cautiously through scrubby, straw-like grass grown wildly and too high, no other pedestrian (do people *walk* here?) save the occasional drifter, a plaid shirt tied round his waist or no shirt on at all, chest baked an impossible brown.

One is currently headed in her path – soiled Marlins cap, leathered face, blue wasted eyes (at ten in the morning!). He carries a carton of beer on his right shoulder like a boom box from some old film. Bollocksed? Homeless? Psycho? Aideen, unnerved, takes pains to give the derelict wide berth, though not so wide that he senses her anxiety. As they pass each other, he looks directly at her and nods. She nods curtly back and, having survived, carries on.

There is a constant and loud stream of cars on this massive roadway, many driven glacially, a comical slow-motion stop-and-go, traffic signals on every block, so different from her fellow Dubliners back home bombing round the bendy roads, whisking through mini-roundabouts and crossroads, barely braking at the odd 'Yield' sign. She walks past a tan-hued warehouse called Shoot Straight Gun Range; a 'motor court', whatever that is; a clapboard Pentecostal church; Best Buy; and three personal injury billboards, one advertising a Harvard-trained attorney. 'Injury is personal,' it reads. 'Justice pays.'

Walgreens, though a pharmacy, is as large and gleaming as the supermarket back home. Aideen wanders its many aisles, disoriented beneath a vast fluorescent glare of bulbs. She discovers an entire section devoted to sex: condoms and lubricants, yes, but also vibrating bullets and vibrating eggs, something called a pleasure ring, male enhancement capsules, feminine cleansing cloths. So fascinated is she that an officious male employee approaches her without her noticing and asks does she need help. Aideen blushes wildly even though he is not remotely good looking. He stares blankly at her when she stammers a request for Lucozade.

'Is that a medication?'

'Sorry, no, a drink, it sort of has a gross taste. Like when you're sick you drink it.'

'Sick like a stomach bug? Or like a cold?'

Aideen lists off the symptoms and he guides her to Vicks and Theraflu.

She pops into Dollar General and then makes her way back to the Castaways without passing a single dodgy person, though she feels slightly more prepared. Aideen administers the medicine to Gran, who turns out to be a surprisingly compliant patient. The tablets Gran took earlier seem to have helped; her flesh is no longer scorching. Aideen slumps with relief onto the bed. Maybe she can handle this. She starts to tell Gran about the pharmacy, how it was filled with products and empty of shoppers, but Gran falls asleep as she says, 'I'm going to fall asleep ...'

People don't always get how funny Gran can be.

With a new hint of swagger in her gait, Aideen decides to leave again, this time in the other direction, to the Sunshine Diner. Here she lingers over a stack of pancakes served with an unseemly smear of butter and a supersized jug of sticky syrup. She accepts countless free coffee refills (adding this to her growing tally of brilliant quirky Americanisms) and records in her journal as many details of her adventure as she can recall, including the vibrating eggs. Gus Sparks (and his obvious crush on Gran) takes up half a page. Never has she considered that people their age would be, like, into each other. Gran with a chance! Naturally, she pictures Sean and pens a fictional passage about a boy and a girl who get locked into a storage cupboard all night at a boarding school. She tries to nudge away thoughts of what will happen when, or if, she returns to Millburn.

There once was a dumb girl at school
Who thought it would make her quite cool
To fuck with some mints
She's regretted it since
Will the world only know her as cruel?

By lunchtime, Aideen's body is flooded with coffee and her hand tired from writing and her brain drained from thinking. She beckons shyly to the waitress to place a takeaway order of chicken soup. Willow is a single mother from Fort Lauderdale (everyone here is the opposite of private) with black roots that contrast sharply with her choppy, platinum pixie cut. Aideen covets this sort of style – different without screaming different. Willow's been traversing the worn walkway between booths all morning, a glass pot of decaf in one hand, regular in the other, familiar with every customer, usually by name or even nickname. She brings the bill over along with the soup and smiles and says, 'Have a nice day.' Aideen has always loathed this expression so prevalent in Hollywood pop culture, dismissing it as the ultimate in Yank phony. But being on the receiving end when it's delivered in earnest is another thing. She surprises herself when she says, 'You too.'

Gus Sparks – same sandals, fresh, collared shirt – is seated in the motel room's only chair, lending the room an unprecedented dignity, when Aideen turns the key in the door. She greets him and nods to Gran, upright in bed. Aideen raises a single cheeky eyebrow, as if to say, *Hmmm, what's this now?*

'There you are,' says Gran, blowing her nose loudly. Aideen makes a mental note to advise Gran against future aggressive honking in Gus's presence. 'I thought you'd got lost.'

'Not at all,' says Aideen and goes about setting up the little meal at the bedside table: paper serviette, plastic spoon, steaming broth.

'You're taking good care of your grandmother,' says Gus.

'She's a good egg.'

Aideen, pleased though not letting on, says, 'Are you feeling any better?'

'Not one hundred per cent yet, Duckie, but I'll survive. Sure amn't I eighty-nine?'

'No. You're eighty-three.'

Gran pats the bed. 'Come here to me. Gus has an update for us, but I wouldn't let him utter a single word until you came back, sure I wouldn't, Gus?' She puffs up the two deflated pillows behind her back, resettles into them against the headboard, and gingerly takes up a spoonful of broth.

'Well, I'm not sure yet,' says Gus, 'but we may have something.'

'You're our hero,' says Gran.

'Oh no, I can't take any of the credit. It's Bob.'

'Bob's just a cog. We'd be back to square one if we hadn't met you.'

Gus hands Millie a file, a tremor in his fingers that Aideen hadn't noticed the day they met him. She studies both hands and realizes that, in fact, both are shaking. Has he got some horrible old person's disease like epilepsy or diabetes? Or could this be Gran's effect on him?

'We started by reviewing the lease agreements of every female renter in the past two years. Then Bob took the licence-plate numbers of each and looked those up on the computer. He whittled that group down to women between the ages of twenty-five and forty-five.' Gus waits, smiling at Gran. 'You want the good news?'

Gran puts the soup down. 'Is there bad news as well?'

'There isn't. I'm not really sure why I said it that way.'

'Maybe you're as excited as we are?' says Gran.

'This sure beats plunging a toilet for ornery tenants.' He grins. 'Well, the good news is there are only three women who fit that description.' Gus stands up. 'Would you like to see if any of these is the person you're looking for?'

Aideen holds her breath. Gran reaches for the folder and two balled-up tissues flutter loose from her sleeve.

'I need my specs.'

'Can I have a look?' says Aideen.

'Lovely to be so young!' Gran says.

Aideen snatches the file from her grandmother's hands and freezes at the first photograph of a cross, scowling woman in her mid-thirties. The few times Aideen met Sylvia, she was amiable, vivacious, pretty. And yet this is, without a doubt, Sylvia Phenning.

'Oh my God.'

'Is that her?' says Gus. 'According to this, her name – her married name – is Sylvia West,' says Gus. 'Phenning is her maiden name.'

'Aha,' says Gran. 'Aideen, would you ever find those glasses? I need to see.'

'Maybe mine would work?' says Gus, stepping forward. 'Try these.'

Gran looks cerebral and sombre in his tiny wire frames and she pulls an exaggerated straight face, hamming it up, before turning to squint at Sylvia Phenning. She stares for a long time at the picture. 'Wow,' she says, her nose leaking.

'It's her,' says Aideen.

'Definitely her,' says Gran.

'The cow,' says Aideen.

'If you're sure,' says Gus, 'Bob can look her up, find out if she's paid taxes or run a credit check or gotten a parking ticket. With any luck, we can locate her current address.'

'Funny,' says Gran. 'Those glasses did the trick. We have the same vision, haven't we, Gus?'

56.

Kevin

Kevin paces his kitchen, squinting as he mentally calculates a complicated bramble of arrival times and cities and prices. The first flight to Florida with an empty seat, the ticketing agent explains, is the day after tomorrow, lunchtime. It won't be a doddle, but his family, he's deeply pleased to note, has rallied. Grace goes off to the local cashpoint to collect euros, dollars being only available in certain banks in the city centre, and they haven't got time for that. He will just have to submit to extortion via the *bureau de change*. Gerard offered, of his own accord, to come home for a brief stint and help out with the younger ones. That was magic. Nuala's back any moment from debate practice and Ciaran's on passport detail. Lovely Ciaran, still young enough to get a kick out of being charged with a task.

Then a wrinkle. The flight in question lands in Miami, hours from Clearwater. This option would require a long night-time trek on the intimidating highways and byways of southern America. Under other circumstances, he would love a family jaunt to Miami. Bit of Latin música, bit of a buzz, poolside mojitos while the children splashed in the sun, a group tennis lesson with the pro, breakfast buffets and pontoon rentals. But this, of course, isn't *that*. The agent explains that if Kevin were able to wait yet an additional day – two days in total – he could fly to Atlanta and then board a second flight to Tampa, which is close to Clearwater. Googling it while on hold, he discovers that Clearwater is universally known as ground zero for Scientology, its opulent block-long Scientology 'super-building' headquarters located splat in the middle of town. Maybe Mum's been lured by the promise of personality tests and spiritual awakening. The idea of it – Scientology taking on Millie Gogarty. Good luck!

No matter how he tries, Kevin cannot fathom why his mother and daughter would go to Florida of all places. Mum despises nothing more than extreme heat and old people. Nevertheless, she's there, she must be, and so, despite the frustrating wait he must now endure, he tallies up the exorbitant costs of this last-minute booking and gives over his credit card number, thereby planting yet another seed of financial worry in his already overtaxed mind. He has tried to phone Aideen many times since discovering their whereabouts, but each time he is maddeningly greeted with the long American trill of an unanswered call. Never mind. He's through with powerlessness. He's coming for them.

Amidst all this tumult, Nuala arrives home in a dark mood. The debate teacher, it seems, has given her unflattering notes – she's overly emoting. When she learns from Ciaran that her father is going to America, she stamps one slender foot on the floorboards and hunts him down.

'But you'll miss my first debate!' Nuala is livid – indeed, over-emoting. '"Adversity introduces a man to himself." You *have* to be there!'

Kevin shushes her and jabs a finger at the phone on his ear.

She ignores this and deploys, from her arsenal of weaponry, a distinct high-pitched whine designed to do his bloody head in. 'This is so unfair!'

'Quiet!' Kevin hisses.

She stands glaring at him until he is thanking the agent and hanging up with some sense of relief: the plan is crystallizing.

'Dad!' Nuala demands. 'Can't you go next week?'

'I'm not having this discussion.'

'Aideen ruins everything!'

'Listen to me.' He gets right up in her face, close enough to glean a whiff of salt and vinegar off her breath, then tells himself to calm down. This isn't Nuala's fault; this is collateral damage. He lowers his voice. 'I'm sorry. And I'm sorry to miss it, but Mum'll be there. Aideen's your sister and she's in trouble. It's not about you. It's not about you today. Understand?'

Nuala, flushed and defiant, refuses to acknowledge his warning. They stand glaring and panting, like a pair of pugilists after a particularly dirty round late in the fight. They might do so for longer but Ciaran interrupts the moment with a breathy announcement from the doorway.

'I can't find your passport. I've looked everywhere.'

Crikey. The next twenty minutes are spent futilely ransacking the study. Every Gogarty passport is in a file marked 'passports', except for Aideen's and his own. Intellectually, he knows this, he sees this, and yet how many times does he open the file and look through the little pile of booklets? Five? Ten? Gerard checks the other rooms half-heartedly; really, they all know the passports are kept in the desk and that Aideen has struck again.

If he were not an evolving man, he might throw a mickey fit right about now, if for no other reason than to experience the potent release of his profound frustration and anxiety, to momentarily purge the feeling that he is constantly thwarted, whatever his objective. It seems to Kevin that, at the age of fifty-three, not only does he often not know what he wants, but in the rare moments, such as this, when he does, when his goal is perfectly lucid and ought to be within reach, he can't seem to fucking attain it anyway. He has no control.

But he refuses to capitulate to such bollocks today. Today, he must stick with evolution. He will channel his anxieties, his inclination towards doomsday thinking, into the practical art of problem-solving. Kevin sits in the living room, closes his eyes, and carefully considers his options. He could systematically dismantle the house. He could apply for an emergency passport replacement, which would take at least two, three days. There's some courier service he's heard of, some astounding rush fee. He pictures a helmet-clad messenger on a bike tearing out of the embassy doors, a package tucked up in his armpit. But this plan wouldn't get him to America until next week. He could keep phoning Aideen until she weakens and convince her to put her grandmother on the line and then demand, under threat of death, that they get their arses on the next plane home to Ireland.

'Kevin?' Grace is beside him, placing a cautious hand on his shoulder, as if a bomb is strapped to his torso and he needs to be dissuaded from detonating it. 'I'll go.'

He hadn't even considered this option, and what does that mean? It means he's been in the weeds. Or, more to the point, he needs to cop on because his co-parent, his wife, his bride, still loyal, still his somehow, is here offering to shoulder his burden. But even as he turns to Grace with relief, Kevin knows it's all moot. She has a big work do in the North in two days' time, a conference that's been in the pipeline for months, one that she's helming.

'What about Belfast?'

'I'll have to miss it.'

'They could sack you.'

'They won't,' she says. 'And you'll get something. Any day now.'

'I'm trying.'

'I know you are.'

'Will I?'

'Will you what?'

'Get hired.'

'Don't be daft.'

'Grace …'

'Yes?'

Kevin knows he must look cringey since what he's about to reveal slightly terrifies him, but he is reassured by his wife's frown of concern.

'I think I might make a go at writing again. Like real writing.'

He can see he has surprised her. 'Really?'

'Well, as Maeve might say, it's high time I pulled the finger out.'

Grace mulls this. 'Your wife tells you this for twenty years but one week with Maeve Rooney and you're sold?'

Kevin laughs. 'What can I say? She's a font of wisdom.'

'I think it's a brilliant idea.'

'Yeah?'

'Yeah. In fact, hurry up and get on it already!' She motions vaguely to the house, the children. 'And in the meantime, we keep doing this?'

'I'm shite at this.'

'You're not, actually. You just think you are.'

'But I should be the one to go to the States,' Kevin says. That Grace is willing is enough.

'But you can't and that's that.'

'It's *my* mother.'

'Oh, I'm not getting her. Her, I'm leaving in Florida.' She smiles wickedly. 'Ring the airline and change the ticket to my name.'

They hear Ciaran shouting from the study. 'Found it!' he's calling out. 'I found it!'

He dashes into the living room, stands heroically in the doorway waving an EU passport.

'What the fuck?' says Kevin.

'Dad!' The look on Ciaran's face – shocked delight – is priceless. 'You said fuck.'

'Terribly common of me.' He steps towards his son. 'Is that really mine?'

The photo was taken a few years back. Slightly more hair, fewer lines, a jauntier glint in the eye for sure. But it's him. He checks the expiration date – this had been worrying him – and finds he's still got years to go. He had worried for naught. He's always worrying for naught.

'Well done, Ciaran. Where was it?' says Grace.

'Between two books sticking out of the bookshelf.'

'You are an amazing human being,' Kevin says and kisses his son and then his wife and then tracks down Nuala and plants the biggest and most obnoxious one of all on her cheek.

57.

Millie

The Gulf Coast doesn't smell like the Irish Sea – no powerful, distinct whiff of seaweed. Less briny, more like a diluted salty waft. The beach itself is different too – expansive and decadent with its vast, flat plains of ridiculously perfect sand. Not like the rough, jagged cliffs and mossy rocks back home, the dramatic vertical drop-offs, the smaller strands, the sandy bits more often than not coarse and wet and unpeopled.

Earlier, Gus had found the Gogartys poolside, cooking their pale Irish skin on Castaways loungers. Basket in hand, he'd invited them for a sunset dinner, if Millie felt up to it? Now he helps her step onto the beach, Aideen following behind them. Die-hard, zealously tanned, oil-ridden sunbathers are milking the last of the day or going for a jog or taking in the sunset, many having brought along complicated and abundant accoutrements – umbrellas, coolers on wheels, beach recliners, fold-up chairs, prams, one giant inflatable red lobster sporting a pair of goofy black shades. Further down, by a concrete pier, Aideen wanders away from them, feigning interest in a huddle of men sitting on overturned pails, fishing. Gus guides Millie to a picnic table planted in the sand. When Millie removes her shoes, he gawks.

'Is it that they're mismatched or in need of darning?'

'Both,' he replies. 'You are something.'

'Not at all,' Millie says, thrilled.

To think, four thousand miles across this water is her beloved city. Anna and Mrs Colding and the others at Rossdale must be well asleep, and here she is sitting on the edge of Florida. She pictures Ciaran and Nuala and Gerard. When Kevin was around Gerard's age, she remembers how he'd lope up the drive, calling out, 'Home, Mum?' and clomping into the house to entertain her with local gossip or a funny adventure he'd had in town. That was a time.

But so is this.

Gus unscrews a Thermos of homemade beef stew and dishes it out into Styrofoam bowls he's brought along. The sky is aglow in colour, the sun just dipping into the sea. She wants to lock in every detail of this place; she must tell Kevin and Grace how extraordinary it is.

'Magnificent, isn't it?' Gus says. 'This is why I came back here. I used to surf. Learned when I was at Pendleton. In California.'

'Do you still?'

He laughs. 'Now I just watch.'

'Is that not a bit frustrating?'

'Not really. More a matter of adjustment.'

A curious man, unlike any she's come across. And not just the manners and the thoughtfulness. He seems to her simultaneously tough and not tough.

'Tell me what your home is like,' Gus says. 'Describe it.' He keeps his gaze on the horizon as if to give her licence to speak freely, without the pressure of eye contact.

'I'm right on the sea.'

'Lucky you.'

Without considering, she says, 'You must come visit.' So brazen! What would her Peter think of her now?

'I'd like that.'

She'll bake him a chocolate cake with flaked almonds and pour him tea and Gus will sit in the window seat beside her.

'Any chance you two could stay here longer, make a little vacation out of it? There's so much you haven't seen yet. We could rent a boat, go fishing.'

Unlike both her grandsons, Millie Gogarty does not care for worms or the sharp hooks or the sustained silence that seems to constitute fishing trips – a snore if ever there was one – but she's flattered by the invite. She wonders if she looks cracked; she certainly feels cracked. Did she ever consider, other than a blind date with the captain, a lifelong bachelor with a hook nose and halitosis, which her bridge crew put her up to years ago, that romance wasn't lost to her?

'You don't have to answer that yet. Just think on it a little while.' Gus coughs politely. 'Also, there's been a development in our case.' Millie beckons Aideen to come join them. The Gogartys watch Gus intently as he fights a smile and says, 'I don't want to get you too excited, because it could be a dead end, but my brother got Sylvia's address.'

Millie's thrilled, of course, absolutely chuffed, but also her thoughts pleasantly circle back to the moment ago with Gus. He'd like her to stay longer; he'd like to visit her in Ireland.

'How did he find her?' says Aideen.

'He just ran her name – well, her married name – through the system. She renewed her driver's licence in February of last year, and in order to do that, you have to list an address. Now whether she's still there ...'

'Let's go and pay her a visit,' says Millie.

'Well, hang on,' says Gus. 'We might want to just work this through. Say you go over there and knock on the door. She opens the door ...'

'And slams it shut,' says Aideen and they laugh.

The three of them sit quietly pondering, the waves ripping ever closer and darkening the strips of sand between the water's edge and the huddled humans. At the first hint of evening breeze, Gus moves to Millie's side of the table and wordlessly places a light blanket around her shoulders.

'What if we could get her to come to the Castaways somehow?' says Aideen.

Gus shakes his head. 'With all due respect, that's a little fishy.'

'Yeah, you're right,' Aideen says. 'And how would we get her there anyway?'

Millie's mind is snagging on some niggling thought from days ago. She holds up a hand to silence the two of them. She must focus. It was on the Florida Express Bus Service with your woman, Geraldine. The old lady had been talking about the tight-fisted ne'er-do-well who lived with her, some idea that her value was in her being dead. Millie says it aloud and, bit by bit, a plan begins to take shape among them – delicious, imperfect, risky – just the sort of plan, perhaps, that suits Millie Gogarty altogether.

58.

Aideen

The trio spends the next morning in Gus's squat brown Ford staking out Sylvia Phenning's apartment building – another generic Floridian behemoth. Aideen and Gran are smooshed together in the back bucket seat, Gran shiteing on the whole time and Gus loving every bloody story, every little phrase that sets sail chaotically from her lips. And then, in the middle of Gran waxing on about her tennis elbow in 1984, the door to Sylvia's unit opens and there she is.

She's just there.

To see the American again in the flesh! They watch, agog, hardly breathing, while their adversary, in a breezy white tunic and cute metallic gladiators snaking up her calves, steps into dazzling sunshine. With a quickening pulse, Aideen cranes for a glimpse of Sean, but that awful snake closes the door immediately behind her. Sylvia bends towards the FedEx envelope Gus had left, at dawn, peeping from beneath her welcome mat, and pops it into her bag and strides out, tapping at her phone the entire journey from her front door down two floors of an exterior staircase to a very expensive, very sleek silver Mercedes convertible (top up), compliments, no doubt, of Gran.

'Shit,' Aideen says. 'She didn't read it.'

'Not to worry,' says Gran. 'She will.'

The letter, composed by Aideen with much help from Gus and Google, was printed on thick stock at Staples late last night. There had been much debate over its particulars, especially which *nom de plume* Gus would use. In the end, he'd chosen the name of his deceased high school football coach who was admired by all during his lifetime for his sense of honour and fairness.

Ms Sylvia Phenning
9857 South Main Street, Apt. 509
Clearwater, FL 33764

Dear Ms Phenning:

My office has been retained by the Executor of the Estate of Amelia S. Gogarty of Margate, Sea Road, Dún Laoghaire, Dublin, Ireland. You have been named as a beneficiary of the late Mrs Gogarty in the amount of €350,000.

Please call me at your earliest convenience to discuss claiming your inheritance.

I look forward to hearing from you.

Sincerely,
John W. Howard
Trusts & Estates Attorney
Howard Group, LLC.
Tampa Bay, FL
727-850-3452

They watch as Sylvia's car reverses from its spot across the lot and glides towards the exit.

'Now what?' Aideen says.

'We have to wait,' says Gran, 'and see if she takes the bait.'

When Gus frowns, which isn't often, Aideen notices long, deep trenches appear on his brow. 'Now that we've found her,' he says, 'I'm almost afraid to let her out of our sight.'

Gran and Gus exchange a look – they are grossly cute – and Gus taps Gran's knee gently. 'Let's tail her.'

Sylvia puts on her indicator outside the Belvedere Estates, a high-end inland gated community on the outskirts of Clearwater. Beside a set of gates, a 'Luxury Homes for Sale' banner flutters in the mild breeze. They watch Sylvia wave to a stout guard who's manning an adobe kiosk and then steer through the gates and onward. Gus, who's proven to be such a cautious driver they nearly lost Sylvia at two yellow traffic lights, holds back. After a beat, when they can no longer see Sylvia's car, he drives up to the kiosk. The guard waddles over with a clipboard under one armpit and leans his bulbous face towards their window, tells them there's no one here to show them the model unit, but they're welcome to drive through and get a feel for the place.

Gus and Millie and Aideen creep down a web of lanes lined with beige McMansions of varying faux-Euro designs – Mediterranean, Versailles, English Manor. Some appear deserted, all with identical landscaping – sparse rows of cute baby palm trees have been planted between each mega-house. The air reeks of fertilizer and baking tar. They find Sylvia's Mercedes parked outside the biggest mega-house of all, 149 Ocean Lane, though there's no ocean anywhere.

The home is not only gargantuan but also breathtaking in its ugliness. The bottom floor is a mosaic of beige and white and black brick; the second story is painted the colour of a mushroom. The garage alone is the size of a disco. Aideen counts a whopping eighteen windows, six columns, and two oversized, elaborately carved wooden front doors, their brass knobs as big as grapefruits. Nouveau, Dad would call it.

Gus whistles. 'Whoever she's visiting, they're not hurting for cash.'

As they sit in the Ford with the house in view, a message from Dad pings on Aideen's phone.

Coming to US. Stay where you are.

With horror, she reads it aloud.

'Seems as though your father found his passport,' Gran says. 'Don't look so worried, lovie. I'll phone him the minute we're back at the Castaways. I will. It's time.'

Twenty minutes in, they're beginning to grow bored and hungry and Gus discloses some anxiety that if they remain here too long, Sylvia might spot them. A discussion regarding lunch options is underway when they hear a rumble: one of the house's six garage doors is automatically peeling upward and revealing a medium-sized U-Haul truck. From inside the garage, Sylvia Phenning emerges. She's carrying a very large, flat box, which by the strain of her posture, looks to be heavy.

Gus tells the Gogartys to duck and, slumping a bit lower himself, he narrates what he sees, which isn't much: Sylvia's unlatching a lock at the rear of the U-Haul and, with a pull-strap, raising the truck door all the way up.

'What's in the lorry?' Gran whispers.

'It looks like ... I'm not sure. Stacks of big flat boxes. Some of them are wrapped up in moving blankets ... Stay down, ladies, she's closing the door.'

On their way out, the guard starts to wave them through, but Gus stops at the kiosk.

'Nice, huh?' the man says. 'You can get a tour, you know. You just call up.'

'Good idea,' says Gus. 'Do you happen to know if the huge one's for sale? 149 Ocean Lane?'

The guard takes a moment and then shakes his head. 'Nope. But I'm pretty sure there's a few other Ocean Lane houses on the market. I can check for you?'

'Oh, that's too bad. I thought they might be moving, you know. Saw the U-Haul.'

'U-Haul?' The guard looks puzzled, moist jowls spreading into a grimace like wet folds of dough. 'Oh no, no, Mr Pale's not moving. Nah, I think he's just got someone helping him clean out some of his stuff. He's a big art collector. Or was.'

'Was?'

'I shouldn't say was. I just meant – he's not well. He's very elderly, you know, not one hundred per cent.'

This enlightening conversation – Sylvia, the wagon, has clearly found her next victim – is cut short by a sound from within the car. They thank the guard, and as soon as they're clear of the place, Gus pulls his Ford to the side of the road. The three of them are hooting and giggling and then shushing each other because it's Gus's new disposable flip-phone ringing, and only one person on earth has the number.

59.

Kevin

At the foot of his marital bed sits Kevin's carry-on, crammed with enough clothing for three days and zipped securely. As relieved as he is that Grace has consented to him being here once more, and as grateful as he feels to not be waking up into a cloud of Maeve's Benson & Hedges, he's too wired to sleep. He sometimes copes with these growing bouts of insomnia by searching his laptop for the most unlikely career callings: software engineer, lorry driver, detox nurse. He is mulling over the responsibilities of an accounts payable assistant when the phone beside him rings, his daughter's name flashing onscreen. Kevin reaches across to rouse his wife as he answers the call.

'Aideen?'

'Kevin, can you hear me?'

Silence.

'Kevin?'

He squawks a shocked 'Mum?' just as she, eclipsing him in the annoying way of mobile calls, says, 'Can you hear me?'

'Mum?'

'It's me.'

'Is Aideen with you?'

'Yes, she is and she's fine. Kevin, I wanted –'

'Put her on.'

'Well, she's not actually here at the minute.'

'Where is she,' he echoes with profound bitterness, 'at the minute?'

'She's just stepped out to buy a bar of chocolate. I know you're probably very –'

'A bar of chocolate?'

'There's a vending machine at the motel, you see.'

'What motel?'

'The Castaways.'

'Is that a joke?'

'Kevin, I need to tell –'

'Where *are* you?'

'That's why I'm ringing. Aideen and I are fine. We're safe so you don't –'

'In Clearwater? Are you and Aideen still in Clearwater, Florida?'

'How did you know? Well, we flew into Orlando, which is about a two-hour drive northeast –'

'Are you taking the piss? You're after *leaving the country* with my daughter, you're after kidnapping –'

'Oh now, that's –'

'You think I'm in the market for a geography lesson? I should have you arrested.'

Grace sits up. 'What's happening? Is it Aideen?'

Kevin mouths 'Mum' and grips his wife's arm. 'They're still in Clearwater.' Into the phone, he says, 'Put Aideen on.'

'I'll have her ring you tomorrow.'

'I don't even know where to start,' he starts. 'Just stay there. I'm coming to you. I'm landing tomorrow.'

'Now, you're not to come, Kevin. We're perfectly alright. We're having fun, actually. We'll be home the day after tomorrow, assuming all goes well.'

'Well with what? I mean, how about – can you just explain why you would take our daughter to Florida? I mean, are you just on a little random holiday? You just thought, oh, I'll bring my granddaughter for a lark in the sunshine?'

'That's not what this is.'

'Without any word? You didn't think we deserved a call?'

'Well, yes, I did and, listen, Aideen wanted to ring you every day but I wouldn't let her because you would only have stopped us.'

'You're fucking right I would have!'

Kevin's wife and mother gasp. His use of the F-word, with Mum anyway, is unprecedented.

'She's sixteen years of age!' he says. Grace squeezes his hand.

'Calm,' she whispers, 'calm.'

'She has school!' Kevin goes on. 'You can't just buy a ticket in the middle of the week … I don't … and – you know, the other stuff – the shoplifting and the lying and the drama and breaking out of the fucking care home …'

Another one! It's positively raining fucks.

He is poised to tell her how irresponsible she is, how selfish, and that she has no idea what it's like to worry that your child is dead, when he thinks of his sister, Maureen, who lived and died when he was too young himself to remember.

'I know you're upset,' says Mum, maddeningly chirpy, 'and I knew you were worried, but I also knew she was fine, Kevin, she's wonderful. It's just a few days of school she's missed. And if you want to know the truth, I've a bone to pick with you as well.'

'Put it on speaker,' says Grace.

His mum's voice streams into the dark bedroom: 'You told me the police had insisted I have a caretaker, but that wasn't true. That was you. You made it all up. The whole thing.'

'The American woman?' Grace whispers.

He nods.

'And I don't think you know that Sylvia Phenning, the woman you hired, was actually a con artist. Did you know that, Kevin?'

He did not.

'She's after stealing Dad's ring – the whole safe, in fact – she took the whole safe. And the telly and everything else as well.'

Kevin's fury abates, at least temporarily, as his mind slows to digest this strange new information.

'What do you mean, everything else?' he says.

'So my feeling is there's culpability enough to go round and I think in some ways we're even. And there's no need to worry, anyway, we're grand, we're safe, but we've got a very important project going and one more day's not going to make a bit of difference, so you're not to waste your money coming over.'

'Mum.'

'We're absolutely fine, Kev. Do give my love to Grace and the children, won't you? Pip-pip!'

60.

Millie

Sylvia Phenning, legs crossed demurely at the ankle, is prettily perched on a sofa in a furnished but unoccupied fourth-floor one-bedroom corporate unit of Gus's building. Gus and Sylvia have already covered the coincidence of Sylvia having once resided in Victory Towers. Now she's telling him about her favourite local spot for barbecue. As Sylvia hands over her IDs and signs his phony papers (a legal will kit they'd picked up at Staples), she recommends the sweet and spicy wings at Hot Jazzy Joe's. From the shadows of the back bedroom, Millie and Aideen watch as Sylvia slides the pages with a flourish across the coffee table, as if she's blessing a fan with her autograph. Then she seems to check herself and looks down into her lap, shaking her head wistfully, as if burdened by a sudden and terrific sorrow. 'It's so sad. Such an amazing woman.'

The duplicitous cow.

Sylvia pops the biro – Gus's biro, mind you – into her oversized slouchy leather tote and straightens a slight crease on her frock. 'So that's it?' she says.

'That's it.'

'Well, that was easy.' She laughs. 'And how do I get the cheque?' Millie can't see Gus's face, but she imagines he's masking strong distaste. 'Is it mailed to me?'

'Oh. I have an envelope here for you.'

This is Millie's cue, and though her moment is at hand, still she waits and watches. It's terribly compelling to see someone breezily accept your death and wangle yet more cash while small-talking about chicken parts.

'Oh, even better,' says Sylvia. 'Perfect.'

Gus, quite dashing in a dark suit and tie, is marvellously steady. He hands her the envelope. Once it's in her possession, she relaxes back into her seat with a sigh and says, 'Please give the family my condolences.'

'Of course.'

'I miss this neighbourhood,' she says. 'I've had my eye on that new development, Paradise Found, just down the street on Broadway – you know it?'

'I don't think so.'

'Oh, they're all new condos, really high-end. Steam shower, fitness room, Olympic pool. Like, amazing.' She clutches the envelope to her cleavage and looks up to the ceiling. 'Thank you, Millie Gogarty!'

'Well,' says Gus dryly, though Sylvia is oblivious, 'I'm glad it worked out.'

She gets up and thanks Gus, shaking his hand. Still Millie doesn't move.

'I'm not sure I'm even allowed to ask this,' Sylvia says haltingly, 'but, I mean, can I ask about other people, like, other beneficiaries, in the will?' She sits down again. 'Was there any mention of a Sean Gilmore? He's my nephew. Not that I'm expecting – just – well, I figured I might as well ask because you might not know that I'm his guardian, so any paperwork or whatever would go through me.'

This extra dollop of greed propels Millie into action. Honestly, can she stomach another second? She exchanges a nervous smile with Aideen, her face a bit peaked, beside her.

'Showtime, Duckie,' she whispers.

The Gogartys step boldly into the arctic chill of the living room, the AC fully blasting. It's a small room for four, probably too small for such a large moment. But it'll do.

Millie's eyes meet Sylvia's and hold. Are there any words in all of the English language to express the glee of witnessing – at long last – the exquisite bafflement that crosses her foe's normally sunny features? There aren't, of course, not a single one. Sylvia is also speechless. Millie sees quite plainly the gears of the woman's loathsome mind churning through the impossible logic that's been presented: Millie's not dead, she's standing in this Clearwater condominium, Gus Sparks is not a wills and estates attorney hired by an Irish bank, there is no money in the envelope, Paradise Found is lost.

'What the hell?' Sylvia starts up from her seat on her wedge sandals, upending her tote onto the floor. Her phone, a packet of baby-sized pills in a pink plastic horseshoe, and a set of keys on a glitzy Coach ring spill forth. Millie scans the lot for something incriminating – bogus credit cards, passports, another bit of proof they can nail her with.

'What is this?' Sylvia shrieks.

'This is the ghost of Millie Gogarty,' says Millie with a diabolical smirk that Aideen will later replicate every time she tells this tale.

'What are you *doing* here?' Sylvia is either incredulous or stalling.

'I would think it's fairly obvious. I came to watch you collect my inheritance,' Millie air quotes, 'though you've already stolen most of it.'

Sylvia looks from Millie to Aideen to the envelope, which contains, in fact, one folded sheet of blank paper. 'This is ridiculous.'

She begins raking her hands across the carpet, scrambling to collect her scattered items but, slightly frantic, she's making a general hash of it. Now she's on her knees, arse in the air, stretching her greedy fingers beneath the sofa to recover a rogue twenty-dollar bill. Millie glimpses a narrow swatch of turquoise knickers – thongs, she believes they're called, a strip of cloth wedged straight up Sylvia's bum – and feels a flash of pity for her.

But only a flash.

'You stole quite a bit from me,' Millie says.

'I have no idea what you're talking about,' says Sylvia, getting up from the floor, the bill safely in her grip. 'And I don't have to sit here and listen to this.'

Now her clever granddaughter – perpetually underestimated – snatches up the Coach key ring from the floor.

'Give me that!' Sylvia screeches.

Aideen shoves the keychain down the front of her new cut-offs, which she'd cleverly fashioned the night before from a pair of denims.

'What are you *doing*?'

'You do have to sit here and listen to this because my gran's not finished.'

'Give me those keys back right now, you crazy little bitch, or I'm calling the police.'

Gus takes a protective step in Aideen's direction. Though Millie should have expected it, Sylvia's transformation – her sweet, helpful Dublin demeanour peeling back to this hideous, vile lying creature – still shocks.

'That's a grand idea,' says Millie. 'Let's call the police.' She's already on her way to the beige push-button phone mounted on the kitchen wall, where she presses '0'.

'You need to dial 9-1-1,' Gus says.

'Oh, do I?'

Sylvia snorts. 'And you're gonna tell them what exactly?'

'I'm going to tell them that you're not who you say you are.'

'Oh, they'll be over here double quick. Officer, this lady is not who she says she is!'

'Then I'm going to tell them that you're a thief. That you siphoned thousands of euro from my bank account. That you swindled a cheque out of me with your horrible lie.'

'You really are batshit crazy, you know that?' says Sylvia and shakes her head at Gus as if they're in agreement.

'The charges would be … let's see … forgery, fraud, embezzlement,' says Millie. 'Am I leaving any out, Aideen?'

'Just, like, theft.'

'Grand theft auto,' says Gus. 'Didn't she steal your car?'

'I did not!' Sylvia says. 'I don't know what you're talking about. Now give me my keys right now. I'm not kidding.'

'What I really want is my ring.'

'Totally demented.'

'You know what it means to me. I deserve that at least, Sylvia. I was good to you.'

'*You* were good to *me*?' Sylvia scoffs. 'Get over yourself! I listened to you yammer on and on and on. *Oh, my house is draughty! Have you seen my glasses? I've run out of toilet paper. No one visits me! Waaah!* Never mind your son was over every other day. You have no idea how lucky you are that your family puts up with your shit. That they don't shove you down the basement and lock you away forever. Are you kidding me?' She's spitting in exasperation. 'I earned it.'

'Well,' says Millie, 'let's see if the police agree.'

'I hate to break it to you, but the Clearwater Police Department doesn't exactly give a shit about some alleged crime in another country.'

'Maybe not, maybe you're right,' says Millie and she lets the room grow still. 'But I wonder what they'll think about Mr Pale.'

Sylvia's eyes register not mild surprise.

'I wonder what the police might find if they did a little check on Mr Pale's recent bank statements?' Millie allows the moment to stretch, for the panic to wash over Sylvia's wild-eyed face, and then adds, as an afterthought, 'Or his art collection?'

Without warning, Sylvia lunges at Aideen, who screams so loudly that Millie can hardly believe the neighbours aren't galloping in (then again, a fair few are likely hearing impaired). Sylvia grabs hold of Aideen's arms roughly and, though Aideen struggles to block her, Sylvia is far stronger. Both grunt with effort. Gus pushes his way between the two women, tries to pry Sylvia from Aideen, but they all tussle and Sylvia shoves Gus hard. He falls back and the crack of his skull as it meets the wall behind him is chilling. Millie runs to him.

'Gus? Gus? Gus?'

'Give me those fucking keys!' Sylvia screams.

'I'm OK,' he squawks.

But he's not. He's slumped over, his breathing ragged, eyes shut. He looks positively ancient. Millie puts her hands to his face. 'Where are you hurt, Gus? Will I ring an ambulance?'

Sylvia, ignoring this, has Aideen's narrow wrists clamped tightly in both of her own fists. She releases one to slap Aideen hard across the face. Aideen howls in pain. It's all going to pot, and so fast.

'I'm OK,' Gus repeats and reaches to the back of his head to feel the wound. His fingers come away bloody. When Millie gasps, Sylvia and Aideen pause to glance at the drama and Aideen seizes her only shot: she elbows Sylvia sharply in the gut, momentarily incapacitating her. Aideen takes off, bounding to the bathroom, practically dives into it, and then slams the door and Millie hears the click of its lock. Sylvia tears after Aideen, banging away and screaming for her keys. She hits the door again and again until Aideen says, very calmly, 'If you don't leave this minute, I'm phoning the police.'

The apartment goes very quiet and then Millie hears a long ringtone. Aideen must be making a call on the speaker function.

'9-1-1, what's your emergency?'

'Motherfucking lunatics!' Sylvia says and she's charging through the living room, violently, blurring past Millie and

Gus, both still on the floor. She snatches up her tote and in three giant steps is at the front door.

Millie wants to pursue Sylvia, who by now must be racing down the corridor and getting into the lift. Surely they will never find her again. Even as Millie's poised to follow her, paralyzed by indecision, she finds that she can't. Gus is bleeding.

'Aideen!'

'Is she gone?'

'Get a towel quick,' she says.

'Is she gone?'

'Yes! And phone an ambulance.'

Aideen unlocks the bathroom door. 'Oh my God,' she whispers when she sees Gus.

'Hurry up!' Millie shouts.

Aideen's left cheek is stamped with Sylvia's handprint and her face is a sloppy wet mess.

'Sorry, love, I don't mean to snap, but do please hurry.'

61.
Aideen

Aideen studies the families all around her, trying to conjure up clinical words that might establish a medical setting for a possible poem. There is quite a lot of material, it turns out, to inspire Aideen Gogarty in Clearwater Urgent Care. Gus's injury, while not rising to slasher-level gore, is still bloody and therefore terrifying, not to mention the astonishing ascent of a colourful, cartoonish lump rising up like lava from the seascape of his head, as if he's just been smashed by a naughty mouse with a cast iron skillet.

Together, Gus and Gran had disappeared through the green door, a magical portal that very rarely opens – say, twice an hour – though when it does, every last head in the silent, packed waiting room swivels eagerly towards it. They wait. Some play on their phones; one lady fans herself absentmindedly with a pamphlet titled 'Rectal Itch: Causes & Treatments'.

Back at the apartment, Gus had brushed off the need for an ambulance and Millie had briefly considered driving Sylvia's Mercedes, but in the end, they'd rung a taxi. Aideen sat up front listening to Gran say over and over, 'You're going to be grand,

Gus. You're going to be just grand.' By the third round of this mantra, Aideen realized her grandmother was talking shite; she was actually very worried. Lies can be necessary – noble, even.

Though the wait is tedious and the smell clinical and the room overly chilled and the chairs institutional, there is something oddly intimate about the place. It's certainly the most personal setting she's yet to share with the citizens of this country, nothing akin to her solo trek down the highway or the pharmacy or the diner or her hanging about at the pool wondering about Sean. (Aideen never got a chance to ask Sylvia about him – that ship had sailed the moment things had turned ugly.)

The people all around Aideen are in some pain or, at least, discomfort, and in need, and this seems to strip them of airs and armour. Which fascinates Aideen, she who can never strip her armour in front of anyone beyond her family. Opposite her, in a vinyl seat the colour of watery urine, a tired-looking, top-heavy mother in denim leggings with a thin gold belt at the waist holds a baby. The little girl – tiny specks of lavender diamonds stud each earlobe – stares at Aideen with wide, wet eyes so sombrely that Aideen feels rude not responding. She mimes a shy peekaboo with her fingers three times, but the baby doesn't crack a smile, just continues to gaze professorially at her, cool and detached. Which makes Aideen want to laugh. Maybe her next poem will be written from a baby's point of view.

Now and then, the entrance door from the car park swings open, a gush of warm Florida evening washes in, and Aideen watches the injured and sick enter, usually flanked by family members, and be promptly told by a humourless woman at the admissions desk to check in at one of the self-check computer kiosks on the far wall. The elderly seem befuddled by this, but they're redirected to the terminals nonetheless. This begins to irk Aideen – to be in obvious need of basic human help and get none. A pale, wrinkly midget of a woman in a purple windbreaker stands confused before one of these screens, talking softly at it. It might as well be a cockpit or a time machine.

No longer able to bear it, Aideen, in a very un-Aideen moment, walks over and says, 'Can I help?'

Aideen finds herself fishing through an ancient wallet and plucking the woman's driver's licence from beneath its plastic sheath. Aideen guides her through each bureaucratic step: the licence blips under a red light; first one side, then the other. Next up is a request for a health insurance card.

'You mean Medicare?' asks the woman.

'I'm not sure ...' says Aideen and takes the woman's little bit of unlaminated cardboard – so flimsy for such an important thing – and runs it under the sensor. Now a series of questions and confirmations and verifications until a screen asks if she has fasted.

'Huh?' says the woman.

'It's asking whether you've, like, eaten or had a drink in the past twelve hours?'

'I had a bran muffin,' says the woman.

Aideen presses no and carries on until they arrive at the final screen. The woman thanks her and offers Aideen a dollar; Aideen pleased, politely refuses it. Then she hovers near the machine in case she might be needed (which she is, twice more) until, finally, the green door swings open and Gran's bustling through it.

'He's OK. He needs a few staples,' she says, 'so I'm just going to pop over to the office store now and pick up a box.' Gran's deadpan is so bang on that Aideen stares at her blankly until she spots the cheeky smile.

'Jesus!' Aideen says, and laughs, though she's not sure if this is the worst or best time for a joke.

Gran ushers her over to a less-populated corner of the grim room and tells Aideen to sit down.

'He's going to be grand, Duckie, thank God. Well, no thanks to God. He's lucid, anyway. He's chatty. But they'll need to transfer him to a hospital because they don't do the staples here.' She looks at Aideen. 'I'm going to go with him.'

'Then I will as well.'

'No,' says Gran. 'That's silly because –'

'I want to go with you.' There's a tiny smear of Gus's blood on Gran's blouse.

'I've decided to stay on for a few more days, maybe a week or two. With Gus. He has a concussion and he needs someone to stand guard and make sure he doesn't nod off forever.'

'Can't his brother do it?'

'I suppose so,' Gran says, 'but Gus asked me. And in any case, you've got to go home, Aideen. I promised your dad. If you don't get on that plane tomorrow, he'll really have my head.'

'Not alone!' Aideen says, loud enough to stir curiosity amongst her waiting-room comrades.

'Why not? Didn't you go round here on your own, not a bother on you?'

'I can't.'

'You can.'

'But, I mean, that's it? That's it? We're, like, done? Like, what was the point? Sylvia's got away scot-free, you didn't get your money back. I never saw Sean.'

Gran appears to be smirking. 'Well, in actual fact, we didn't get nothing.'

'That's a double negative.'

'You're a great one for the ol' grammar, Aideen.'

Aideen, growing narkier by the second, is done with this conversation, this clinic, this lark, this country.

'Come here to me and I'll tell you,' says Gran. 'They could put a warrant out for Sylvia's arrest. Bob said what happened to Gus is considered assault, if he were to press charges. But even if he doesn't, it's a jolly good thing we followed Sylvia to Mr Pale's house. Apparently he's a bigwig here, or was, something to do with investing in a laser hair-removal system. Would you know what that was? Anyway, the police are on the case. They don't take elder fraud lightly here. They've a whole unit devoted to it.'

'If she goes to jail, what would happen to Sean?' Aideen has visions of her love being shunted to another rando in the family or, worse, amongst strangers, in a state-designated foster home. Or a facility. Or on the streets.

'Well, he's nearly eighteen, isn't he?'

'In May.'

'There you go,' says Gran. 'He'll be grand.'

Aideen contemplates what is too unthinkable, too dangerous, which is to go straight over to Sylvia's apartment and demand entry. She sees herself climbing the stairs; she can hear the primal thump of his music even before she's at the door. Maybe his guitar's strapped to his torso because he's just been playing it.

'You know what shocked me the most, if I'm honest?' Gran's saying. 'Sylvia was scared. For a minute there, she was really scared.'

'She was.'

'That's very satisfying to me – not that I want to go round scaring people. But the fact that –'

'Yeah, I get it.'

'I might be old,' says Gran, 'but I'm not feckin' dead.'

'You're gas, Gran.'

'And you with the keys down your knickers!'

Aideen smiles. 'I got the feeling she didn't like that very much,' she says quietly, for comic effect, and the two of them, remembering the absurd trauma of their afternoon, are in stitches.

'Whatever happened to the keys? Did you leave them there?' Gran asks.

Aideen takes them from her pocket. 'I didn't know what to do with them.'

'A souvenir?' Gran stands up. 'You ought to go now and get your things together. I'll meet you back at the Castaways.'

'Oh, Gran, but your ring.'

Gran sighs and folds her hands together. 'Well now, that's a loss. I'll give you that one. I was thirty-one when your granddad proposed to me, did you know that? I'll never forget his face. He looked absolutely terrified, like he was about to wet himself. I don't think I believed he loved me until that moment. And the ring – that was his grandmother's ring. And I've had it in my possession every day since, except for that first day. Did I never tell you that story?'

Of course she has. Aideen Gogarty herself could bloody well tell it.

'I don't think so.'

The mother with the baby is watching them carefully; half the room is probably eavesdropping out of sheer boredom. Gran straightens herself up and then she's off – it's a gorgeous day in Dublin, the ring, too loose, slips from her finger, but they don't know when or where, her betrothed's on his knees in the weeds (Aideen thinking, *What the fuck does 'betrothed' mean?*), he spots the sign the next day, and then Gran and the lady who found the ring have tea in the Shelbourne Hotel – sandwiches and scones with clotted cream.

'Clotted cream?' says Aideen, noting the addition of this new detail and wondering is it fact or fiction and does it matter.

'And strawberries, too, now that I think of it.'

62.

Millie

Even if the number of useful roles Millie Gogarty can play diminishes as time unfolds, was there ever a more suitable one than to simply keep Gus Sparks company, to chatter merrily away as he rests, depleted but grateful, in his hospital bed? She brings great gusto to her task, sharing with the possibly concussed building manager various colourful observations gleaned (à la Aideen) from her time spent in the Urgent Care waiting room before his transfer here – this gentleman had a poxy eyeball, that nurse with the hideous shoes was twice seen leaving her station to smoke fags beneath the clinic's awning, and so on.

It's evening but not yet night-time, and Gus's fairly generous sixth-floor window lays bare a vast rose sky. Though she isn't one to frequently take her own emotional pulse, Millie would have to admit, at this point in this room in this country with this particular person, she is experiencing a sort of lightness. Despite the day's terrible upset and injury, she feels she's where she ought to be.

But Gus voices concern about where she isn't – namely, with Aideen – so Millie borrows his mobile and soon learns that her granddaughter, suitcase at the door, is safely ensconced in the Castaways, devouring something called XXtra Flamin' Hot Cheetos while lying abed watching *19 Kids and Counting.*

It's official: Aideen's gone American.

Millie fusses around Gus like an old married lady, pours him water from a carafe on his bed tray, and places the straw carefully to his mouth, holding the cup steady as he drinks. She remembers nursing Peter after his strokes, though that was far worse – she'd had to teach him how to sit and stand and eat and speak again. *I am Millie. I am your wife.* Peter would have found Gus to be obscenely literal, but a decent enough fellow.

After a while, Gus nods off and Millie steels herself for her next, less pleasant task. She steps into the quiet hallway with a scribble of digits to ring her son again. Years ago, Kevin had been the one to find his father slumped on the garden chair, his cap covering his face so that precious minutes were wasted, Kevin not wanting to wake him, not realizing he'd suffered a heart attack. At the hospital, Kevin had said, 'I thought he was asleep' to anyone who would listen – the staff and nurses and doctor. And to Millie who, in her own mute terror, failed, perhaps, to assuage him.

A nurse in pale-pink Winnie-the-Pooh scrubs clicks officiously by, rolling complicated machinery that looks like an aeroplane drinks cart run amok with tubes and wires. Millie hears her son's 'hello'. She tries to remember the last time she told him that she loved him or, even, thank you. And when had she last owned up to Kevin for anything, held herself accountable?

Millie glances back into Gus's room: he's trussed up under the bedclothes, his wonderful, handsome old face turned in her direction. She may regret this when Kevin refuses to hand over her car keys or speaks to her like she's a dozy granny, and, painfully, she senses she's relinquishing power. But nevertheless she does; she tells him she's sorry.

63.

Aideen

At Dublin Airport arrivals hall, Aideen beelines towards Dad and he picks her up, her untied scuffed-up high-tops swaying inches over the floor, and smothers her with possibly the most mortifying public display of affection Aideen's suffered in her wobbly adolescence to date. She is briefly visited by the old scorn. It's so annoying that he assumes she wants to be hugged, that she gets no say in the matter.

At the same time – she's not going to lie – a part of her secretly glows under this flood of paternal attention and she dips into it and basks, even as she furiously blinks away tears. She's home. Aideen doesn't discount that Dad can be irritating and overbearing and all *up in her grill*, as her American counterparts might say. But it's Dad, for fuck's sake. At some point that she can hardly remember, the fact of her parents' love seemed in question. Which strikes her now as quite daft. She thinks this moment could contain the makings of a decent limerick, but now's not the time.

'You do realize,' he says as they make their way to the car park, 'that you're on lockdown for the next quarter century?'

Indeed, what punishment will be exacted? Nine hours in the sky proved to be an extended purgatory of worry. Yet there is surprisingly no discussion of any of the school malarkey. She may be expelled, she may have to change schools, she may be forced to face Bleekland back at Millburn.

They pull up the drive to the house in Dalkey, which looks like a grand thing of regal beauty to her traveller's eyes compared to the newer pastel architectural backdrop of her recent adventures. Nuala and Ciaran and Gerard – her brother has come – all file out the door, a scrum of bony beauties, and make their way down the stone steps. They look strangely indecisive, as if no one knows what to say or do. Gerard reaches her first and shakes his head wistfully. 'You alright?' he says and then he hugs her and calls her a numb-nut. Her twin, too, pulls her into an embrace and blathers away excitedly. She's never been to America, what are the boys like, do all the girls wear bikinis? Little Ciaran quietly takes Aideen's hand. This, Aideen knows, is how Clean-Cut must feel when the fans descend. Fucking rock star.

Aideen grabs her bag from the car and turns back to the house. Mum is standing in the doorway, arms crossed, bearing an inscrutable expression. Is she happy? Sad? Relieved? All of the above? Her lips tug downward into a grimace. She's wearing Dad's 'You People Must Be Exhausted From Watching Me Do Everything' apron. She lifts a bottom corner of it to dab at her eye. *Maybe*, thinks Aideen, *all of the above?* Aideen is totally capable of keeping her shit together, she really is, until Mum says her name and opens her arms.

*

Banned from signing out, Aideen spends her pre-prep afternoons in the Fair House common room playing table tennis and making toast with Fiona Fallon. Fiona's not a wild whirlwind like Brigid, but neither is she dog-eat-dog. Aideen admires that her new friend can't resist smashing balls that are obviously unsmashable, and she's grown to appreciate Fiona's (albeit winding) stories about the slew of hens (each named) on her family's farm and how she pines away after William Rush, the bushy-browed twenty-year-old country boy who sells her father tractors.

Aideen's up by six points when Bleekland, from her glassed-in headquarters, calls out her name. The two girls exchange a look. Per the terms of her re-entry, Aideen had delivered Bleekland a handwritten letter of apology, but she's managed to avoid all dialogue and eye contact with the woman since she slipped quietly back into dormitory life. Which is the plan. Continue at Millburn for the next two years without interaction.

Fiona mouths, 'What?' as Aideen, with a shrug that belies the wash of nausea grinding in her belly, puts down her wooden paddle.

Bleekland stands in the central foyer organizing the day's post into little piles for the mostly young, terminally homesick foreign girls who depend on them for an outsized portion of their mental equilibrium. She silently hands Aideen an envelope, and though Aideen doesn't recognize the blocky writing, the return address reads 'Clearwater, Florida'.

Gus.

She's on her heels to flee when Bleekland says, in her maddening no-affect voice, 'Did I see knickers hanging on the radiator beside your bed?'

As if. Aideen Gogarty wouldn't dream of displaying her knickers in public, even amongst a bunch of girls.

'Clothing on the radiators is a fire hazard.'

'I'll go and move them now,' Aideen says and wonders if this isn't a sort of détente, Bleekland telling her off for such a humdrum offence, the normalcy of it.

The old spinster trains her impenetrable stare on Aideen. It pains her, but Aideen manages to meet Bleekland's eyes. She hopes the woman gets the message she's trying to telegraph: *forgive me*. Then she heads straight for the second-floor toilets.

Hey Aideen,

Can you believe this is the first letter I've ever written in my life? Lost my phone (with your number) so I'm reduced to this caveman communication. We're back in Florida but you probably guessed that? I'm going to school again and getting my old band together, but we need a bass player. I'm working on this new song – there's a funny part in it about that flasher guy we saw, remember that? How you doing? How is that jailhouse treating you? How is that fascist gimp? I'm really sorry about not meeting you at the coffee shop. Feel really shitty about that. Long story, too much to write. Call me? Hey, did something sketchy go down between your 'grandma' and Sylvia? Heard a wild tale. Are you listening to my playlist?

I miss Dublin, and you.

Call me?

Sean 727 873 0980

When she arrives at his name, Aideen realizes she's stopped breathing. She reads the note through three more times. Then she allows herself to experience the thrill, the demented free-fall joy of those two words. Since all the others are signed out or at hockey or wherever they go, and the place is empty, Aideen lets loose a raucous 'Yes!' and does a kind of dorky victory dance, banging her elbow against the bog-roll holder in the process. *Call me!*

64.

Millie

In America, Millie never could locate floury enough potatoes to make proper roasties. She'd tried new potatoes (too waxy), Yukon Gold (wrong consistency), and so on, tried every bloody type of spud in Publix, which had struck her as a scandalous name, especially for a grocery shop, but she couldn't manage to magic up the beautiful dish for Gus which she'd had in mind. Normally, the fact that she'd boasted and then been unable to produce might have left her a bit scarlet. But not so with Gus. The man is grateful for all and sundry – a cup of lukewarm coffee, a note she left on his table one afternoon that said, 'Back in a few,' a glimpse of a whale on an excursion designed to spot such a beast (or no glimpse of a whale), even an imperfectly roasted potato. Gus Sparks would probably express gratitude for a hot meal of roasted cow dung. She marvels at this, especially considering how little he has – no wife, no children. Her own string of heartaches, on balance, strikes her as scant and humbling. Maybe she has plenty, or enough.

Kevin and Aideen are officially late, which suits her, since she's still trying to navigate the new cooker whose newness she nearly resents. Millie Gogarty doesn't need all these fancy appliances! But the insurance cheque had come in, a whopper, and Kevin had ordered all sleek, chrome, top-of-the-line gear, despite her loquacious protestations. He was adamant: if she was going to be back at Margate, about which *she* was adamant (with a new, thoroughly vetted part-time companion called Tara Whalen, about whom the jury's still out), then she needed, and deserved, a kitchen that isn't burnt or broken or frigid or filthy. The day the cabinets were fitted, which Jolly Jessica helped her choose, Kevin had brought her a box wrapped in silver paper so lustrous it pained her to open it. Inside was a fire extinguisher.

Some high-tech beep sounds from the cooker and 'READY' appears in alarming red on an otherwise invisible black screen. Millie, who's ready herself, bungs in her peeled spuds along with the beef and carrots and turnips. On the quartz countertop – as slick and flawless as a freshly paved road – she's placed a bottle of pink champagne and three crystal flutes instead of two because, sure, why shouldn't Aideen have a swallow?

Millie's set a fire in the living room and it's roaring. Later, when they've gone, she'll ring Gus at the usual time on the Skype, an innovation that she's come to rely heavily upon, the most brilliant invention since the electric kettle. They've his itinerary to confirm. First of the month, the eagle will land.

On yesterday's call, Millie had learned that the Pale family was so grateful for Millie and Gus's tip-off that there was now talk of a financial reward. The Americans are a fascinating people – and kind, especially *her* American and her granddaughter's as well. Aideen and Sean, happily reunited, have apparently spent long hours on their phones comparing notes on the Sylvia saga. Indeed, so appalled was Sean to hear the entirety of his aunt's crimes that, following a big row, he's moved in with a friend, at least for now. Sylvia had really done a number on him. To justify their abrupt departure from Ireland all those weeks ago, she'd told him of a bogus job opportunity she'd been offered in Florida and then nicked his phone. Once back home, Sean asked Sylvia for Millie's contact information – he was only desperate to reach Aideen – but his aunt refused. She told him that Millie was deranged (would you believe?) and that she'd accused Sylvia in Dublin of horrible abuse; she warned him the Gogartys were rotten to the core and forbade him all contact. But Sean, good man, was having none of it. He tried ringing Aideen at Millburn School, but no one there would pass along a message. So he'd taken out pen and paper and done what few in his generation seem to these days: he'd written Aideen a letter. Sylvia had tried to thwart his and Aideen's communication. But they would not be thwarted; *love* would not be thwarted!

In time, Millie hears her family coming through the door – the stamping of their feet, a draft of briny air blasting rudely in from the sea along with them.

'Come in, come in,' she says, bustling them into the hallway.

Kevin does a stage sniff. 'Heavenly,' he says.

'Worth returning my car keys for?'

He rolls his eyes and bends to kiss her. 'I believe you've shrunk since Monday. Bit dark in here, isn't it?'

'That bulb needs replacing,' Millie says, 'but I can't reach it.'

'There's a joke here somewhere.'

'Would you ever find the step stool? I think it's in the garage.'

Millie hasn't considered that step stool since the day she sat on it to smoke her fag, setting in motion all that came after.

As soon as Kevin's out the door, Aideen grabs her grandmother and pulls her into the gleaming new kitchen.

'Close your eyes.'

'What?' says Millie.

'It's a surprise. Just close your eyes.'

Millie stands dumbly peering at her granddaughter. 'You look gorgeous. Is that mascara?'

'Gran! Close!'

She finally does as she's ordered, but only because it's Aideen doing the ordering. She feels something small and soft, like velvet, in her hands – one of JJ's handcrafted pouches, and there's some object, something with heft, inside it.

'OK, now open.'

'Very bossy today, Duckie.'

'Go on.'

So Millie does. She opens her eyes.

The End.

Acknowledgments

I am indebted to Lisa Erbach Vance, a true partner, as kind and steady as she is funny and brilliant.

And to Daniella Wexler, who guided this story with immense care and wisdom, improving it immeasurably.

I am very grateful to the hardworking team at Atria, especially Loan Le, Felice Javit, Carla Benton, Kayley Hoffman, Kyoko Watanabe, Jim Thiel, Isabel DaSilva, Gena Lanzi, and Paige Lytle.

Thank you to Kate Ballard for her championing of this book, as well as Ed Faulkner and the whole gang at Allen & Unwin: Carmen Balit, Jamie Forrest, Emma Heyworth-Dunn, Alan Craig, Clive Kintoff, Gemma Davis, Patrick Hunter, Alice Latham, Jamie Forrest, and Kate Straker.

Deep gratitude to Deborah Goldstein and C.J. Prince, the original loafers, for their encouragement, insights, and laughs. Your turn.

Thank you to early readers Tina Dall, Mark Hardiman, Shala Anastasio, Dorri Ramati, Roger Rosen, Alix Clyburn, and Ben Strouse. And, for their help and encouragement, Tara Jerman, Robin Hardiman, Ben Hardiman, Bonnie West, Peter Ahern, Rob Dall, Laura Smyth, Joanne Serling, Jami and Marc Kurschner, Victoria Rowan, Diane Spechler, and Wendy Bihuniak.

Special gratitude goes to MaryAnne Briggs and Jeanne Sterling for tolerating my nonsense, and to Michael Slezak, Mitch Rustad, Alexis Auleta, and all the crazy Queens for their years of abuse. Allevia!

I am profoundly appreciative of the heroic force of nature that is my mother, Patience Humphrey, and my brother, Ben Jerman. Bulls buy.

And thanks most of all to the GOATs: Declan, Zac, and Simon, and my husband, Alex, fiercely intelligent, wickedly funny, patient, and kind – a good egg through and through.

About the Author

Rebecca Hardiman is a former magazine editor who lives in New Jersey with her husband and three children. *Good Eggs* is her first novel.